W0038433

AN ENDURING VOICE

A Musical Journey from Italy's "Singing Woods"
to the Great Valley of Virginia

PETER GIVENS

©2024 Peter Givens. All rights reserved. No part of this publication may be reproduced, distributed, or transmitted in any form or by any means, including photocopying, recording, or other electronic or mechanical methods, without the prior written permission of the author, except in the case of brief quotations embodied in critical reviews and certain other noncommercial uses permitted by copyright law.
ISBN: 979-8-35096-177-5 (paperback)

INTRODUCTION

It may seem unusual for a book to be written about an object, but this one is. An Enduring Voice, in essence, is a story about an 18th century violin, lovingly and expertly crafted from trees harvested in the "singing woods" of the Italian Alps in an era that gave birth to the world's greatest violins and greatest violin makers. Beginning in a small workshop in a village outside of Cremona, Italy, this story follows the journey of an instrument through the hands of its creator and a variety of owners, in a myriad of cultures, and across two continents. Although never playing the kind of classical music it was intended to play, its voice is a lasting one and its impact on the lives of those who owned it, played it, or listened to it stretches across the globe to America's first frontier in Virginia's Blue Ridge Mountains.

The idea for this book comes from a simple notion that objects help us tell stories where words alone often are inadequate. They help us to imagine things or visualize the past, perhaps seeing complex events in a way we can better relate to. We may be drawn initially to a good story because our attention is captured first by an object from which the story then springboards and continues to develop. Any touchable, physical item can be the beginning of the process of expanding and unraveling an interesting, meaningful, or compelling narrative.

This is what archeologists do as they practice their skill. The trowel unearths a fragment of fine porcelain china, an eyeglass frame, or a hand-wrought nail, none of which are vastly important in and of themselves. But when the object becomes a tool leading us to bigger stories or discoveries, there is something rich and wonderful about them. We hold the artifact in our hand and begin to ask the who, what, when, where, why, and how that are all parts of good history and a good story.

Similarly, a quilt may be thought of as simply a bedcover until it reveals a narrative of family or community connections or how it protected children during a raging blizzard. The Liberty Bell is two thousand pounds of cast metal, similar to many other such bells crafted by foundries around the world. But when the historian unveils it as a symbol of liberty, freedom, struggle, and independence, we see its greater meaning. We see its real story.

So, it is the narrative that then takes over and leads us from the tangible object, into the story where survival, risk, patience, perseverance, or love define the story line and the characters. The more interesting the item, the more likely it is to draw the listener or reader into the story. And a particularly rare, or beautiful, or unusual object works best because it draws and commands our attention immediately. We can't help but begin to imagine the story it can tell us.

In An Enduring Voice, Luigi Caruso's beautiful violin is the object that begins the story and from which the narrative continues to develop. The spruce trees carefully harvested from the "Singing Woods" in the Italian Alps already had a sweetness and a rich tone that radiated up the massive trunk as some-one with Luigi's skill could hear by thumping on the tree with a mallet while it was still standing in the forest. But the pinnacle of the luteria's craft was to uncover the instrument hidden within and create a work of art that would carry those rich tones, improving over time.

The characters in this story who eventually owned and cherished Luigi's masterpiece called it a "fiddle" and they felt an almost haunting responsibility to care for it and play it well. The mysterious label inside, containing only the barest of details about its origin and its maker, brought constant speculation *about the master luteria whose instrument they were so fortunate to hold in their possession.*

The great trees from the "singing woods" and Luigi Caruso's instrument with its enduring voice have all of the elements of a good story. Enjoy!

CONTENTS

PART 1

From the "Singing Woods" to the craftsman's bench, c.1720

Their names stand at the pinnacle of any discussion of the Cremona, Italy tradition of fine violins. Andrea Amati is credited, in 1564, with the first of the instruments in the form we have today. His sons followed in their father's footsteps and his grandson, Nicole, taught and mentored the most famous of the Italian instrument makers, Antonio Stradivari. These and scores of other Italian luterias across the centuries have trudged the steep and often snowy slopes of the Italian Alps near Cremona, in search of the perfect tree, hoping to create the perfect violin. The abundant number, age, and size of the spruce trees here have supplied the raw material for the instruments from the hands of the masters. The legacy of these men survives in the creations that emanated from their workshops scattered throughout the region.

Luigi Caruso is a fictional character whose life story begins An Enduring Voice, but realistically, he represents any one of the luthiers (or, in Italian, luterias) over the centuries who has worked his magic with treasures from Italy's "Singing Woods." As a child, Luigi had dreamed of playing the violin expertly, but discovered that his talent lay, not in playing beautiful music, but in building beautiful instruments. And in a pre-industrial age without the machines and technology necessary for mass production, Luigi worked with his hands, slowly and meticulously, as any artist, carpenter, or stonemason had to do in his era.

His best instrument came near the end of a long life. He and other luterias like him never knew how long their instruments would last, what type of music would radiate from them, or how far or to what continents their creations would travel - where they would find their final home. Had his original dream come true, his music would be heard only in his lifetime and never again. But his instrument and its enduring voice live on, full of sweet and powerful sound.

CHAPTER 1

Luigi Caruso began his climb up the steep Italian mountainside on this brisk December morning with the same feeling of excitement and anticipation he had experienced scores of times before during his nearly eighty years of life. But he acknowledged more often in recent years that he was, indeed, an old man standing in this old forest. That thought came with more clarity and the feeling was more evident each passing year. As time took its toll and his health declined, he found his stride growing shorter, his breathing more labored, and his path more carefully selected in his attempts to avoid the steepest of terrain.

"Watch your steps," he warned himself time and again. As a younger man, he had bruised himself stumbling on rocks and roots, or had twisted ankles only to recover quickly. He could not recall ever missing a planned trip to the mountain. But now, such recovery would not be so certain… perhaps not even possible. As that reality swept over him, he repeated the warning. "Luigi, watch your steps."

Steadily and expertly, one foot in front of the other, Luigi began to find the rhythm he loved in climbing the mountain. He could now begin to enjoy the surroundings, letting his mind and heart go where they tugged. There was always the music swirling throughout him. Sometimes there were simple melodies, but at times the complicated arrangements written by the great composers as well. Whether he was singing, humming, or whistling, music seemed his constant companion. Especially here on the mountain, the tunes were not just in his own head. Oddly, he could hear music in the wind, in the rustling leaves, and even in the rain as droplets fell through the canopy to the forest floor. Everywhere, Luigi heard music and it was as much a part of him as breathing itself.

Before he trekked too far up the mountain, he stopped at a favorite spot – a massive log, falling perhaps before Luigi was born. It was covered in thick moss, and he sat down for a much-needed rest and a drink of spring water. Examining the log, and thinking about its age and its demise at some time in the past, once again he thought… "Yes, Luigi, you may be an old man, but this is a far older forest." Despite knowing the truth of that, he smiled and gathered himself to continue upward.

Part of his ritual was to stop here to examine his boots before the most difficult portion of the climb. These were the same boots that had supported his hikes here for most of his adult life. No others he had considered among the cobbler shops he knew fit as well. So, he had them resoled many times. At this spot, he always cinched the laces once more. Not too tight, but tight enough to protect his ankles and support his body. Likewise, he examined his favorite trekking pole, nearly as old as the footgear. This was an essential item, especially now at his age, as he ventured up the steep and rugged terrain. More out of admiration than any need for adjustment, he ran his hand over the length of the stick, examining the many carvings he'd added over the years. He found himself thinking of it more as an old companion than a tool.

As was often the case, his thoughts turned to Isabella. She did not approve of these solo trips, but she knew their importance to her husband. Many of her friends, as well as Luigi's friends, talked sternly to her about the hikes he continued to take on a regular basis, but she thanked them for their words of advice, spending little time discussing their concerns with her husband. Isabella's words as he left their cottage outside of Cremona before daybreak were simply words of caution. Luigi remembered them now and made one last inspection of his boots and trekking pole.

"Yes," he said, in his mind to himself, but also out loud to Isabella, "I will take care."

Pulling his scarf higher, the collar of his tattered woolen coat tighter around his neck, and adjusting his cap to fight the winter chill, he took another drink from his container of spring water. Then, forward and upward, one step at a time, and ever nearer his destination.

Luigi's gaze moved upward once again to the surrounding peaks. He spoke to himself as if he were introducing some new friend to their majesty. These were the Italian Alps – the Dolomites - where his Caruso ancestors had lived for over a century. Hiking up the slopes out of the Fiemme Valley, it was always with a singular focus – the trees. The site of them never grew old for Luigi and for others who ventured here. These were the largest, straightest, and most prolific and beautiful Norway Spruce anywhere in the world and Luigi never tired of his trips here. On this day, once again, they did not disappoint.

These trees had been growing here for hundreds of years above the Valley floor. His grandfather had told him of coming here as a child with his father. Perfect specimens they were, and because of them, some would call this an almost sacred space. If so, then its temple pillars were the massive, straight specimens standing tall in front of Luigi, treasured by many others on journeys like his.

Luigi's trek had a purpose, however, beyond simply gazing at and admiring stately trees. There was always an excitement and an expectant mood here. Thanks to an opportune combination of climate and altitude, these had come to be what the locals called *"Il Bosco Che Suona"* — The Musical Woods. It was here that Andrea Amati – the greatest of the master stringed instrument makers had traveled from Cremona for the finest of woods. Other *luterias* that Luigi knew of, but had not met, also sought out the purest of woods from these forests. One of them, Antonio Stradivari, was already gaining a great reputation for his creations. Like those masters, Luigi stopped and listened closely. Within the breeze, among the rustling leaves, cocking his head just right, perhaps he could hear the sweet notes echoing through the wind from these groves. At least this was the story on the streets of Cremona where these fine men practiced their craft. The trees as they stood in the forest already had a sweet voice, but the *luteria's* craft was to give energy and to amplify that voice through the instrument, creating magic by shaving away one sliver of maple or spruce at a time.

This was Luigi's craft as well and the process of building a fine violin or viola began here in *Paneveggio – the forest of the violins*. Luigi had the gift and the hands and, some would say, even the spirit of a master *luteria* and the first step in the creative process began here. He had learned through the decades the importance of observation, looking for the perfectly straight, cylindrical trunk with no lower branches. He had learned how to find the flawed specimens and cross them off his list. He had learned the skill of patience. Most of all, however, Luigi had learned to listen. A sharp wrapping on the trunk with his hammer or sometimes even with his bare knuckles would reveal to his trained ear the resonance provided by these majestic trees. The light and elastic wood, after being properly dried, would project the pure notes of an instrument flawlessly. Look, touch and feel, but most of all… listen. This is what the masters had learned, and what Luigi had learned as well. But acquiring such skills was not simple or quick. The process was, in fact, never finished. It lasted a lifetime… a lifetime of patience and passion.

He believed deeply that the trees here in the "Singing Woods" longed to tell their full life story to those who knew the right questions to ask and the right signs to look for. So, Luigi, on this day and too many other days to count, hoped and even prayed that he would ask the right questions and discover the spruce with the sweetest of instruments trapped inside, aching to get out and begin creating the magical and enduring voice whose life would last longer than his own.

Luigi was now in a more familiar area of the forest. Not that he didn't know each step up the mountain to this spot, but here, he felt as though he knew each tree - individually and more intimately. They seemed to be the best specimens, perhaps because of the elevation. Or was it the angle of the sun, or perhaps the minerals deposited here? All of the *luterias* he had known had strong opinions on why the Paneveggio produced such exquisite trees. He had examined a number of them on earlier trips, waiting for the right year and the right time of year to mark them for cutting. Would this be the day of finding the perfect tree, cutting it on the new moon in December, applying his craft, and praying for the right results?

These thoughts about great trees and great instruments - about the masters of his craft - were thoughts about the future and about possibilities and dreams. For now, the day was moving on and the hour would soon approach when his long trip home should begin. Luigi's friend, Angelo Cantelli would be coming by with his wagon at the bottom of the mountain on his way home, and Luigi must not keep him waiting. He recalled his earlier days when he could pack the necessary supplies to camp on the mountain, increasing his coverage on the slopes and the number of trees to examine. Those days were long gone, however, and he felt blessed at his advanced age to simply be here, if only for a few hours on a single day. This place held such memories and was so much a part of him.

Now, for *pranza* – his lunch that Isabella had prepared lovingly and artfully for his sustenance this day. It was always a delightful surprise, her creation for Luigi's lunch on the mountain, but he enjoyed that part of the adventure. As he shed his small backpack and pulled out the food, he was thankful for the care she had taken, and thankful to God, even for this simple meal. After all, he surmised, this was the Italian way. Pasta and ragu left from the day before, a small loaf of Isabella's bread, fresh-baked early in the morning, a few pieces of fruit, and jam all carefully folded into waxed brown paper along with the necessary utensils wrapped in a checkered napkin. A small container of wine and he was set.

Lunch seemed especially fulfilling on this cold day and Luigi fought the desire to find a sunny, warm spot to nap. But there was too much left to do and, in order to get back home before Isabella began to worry, he needed to focus on the task at hand. In his workshop outside of the city of Cremona, Luigi had a supply of wood, much of it ready to be worked and shaped, but the process here today was meant for a decade or more in the future. He understood that if he found a perfect tree today, it would probably be crafted by another *luteria* in another shop, sometime in the future. But those loving the craft as Luigi did would not think in such terms. Somehow, he knew that selecting a tree today, even if he was not the one to use it, was part of the skill and the care necessary simply for creating an instrument in his shop. It was all part of the magic.

For the moment, however, only a sharp eye was essential. Any evidence of a lightning strike... any disfigurement... any knots? The sharp eye then was followed by a sharp thump with a special mallet and listening with an even sharper ear for the first hint of sound radiating perfectly up through the massive trunk. Luigi carefully took a core sample to examine the tightness of the rings, critical for the best of instruments.

One specimen in particular captured his attention. It did not stand out for its size, or even for its straightness, but for what it did not have. No knots or imperfections observable to Luigi all the way up to the first main fork. Surely, he thought, this tree had not escaped his notice on his many trips to the mountain before. Perhaps he had not approached it from this exact angle, or the early afternoon sunlight allowed him to observe it in a new way. Whatever the reason, Luigi saw, in this spruce tree, what he could only describe right now as "possibility."

At moments like this, Luigi often began acting and thinking as only someone who knew his craft would understand. "Look carefully," his mentors had told him when he was much younger, "observe them, touch them, perhaps even hug them. They will tell you everything - their joys derived from ample rain, perfect temperatures, and warm sun... or the trauma caused by storms and winds stronger than the tree could stand." One old *luteria* had ingrained in Luigi's mind... "they will tell you their life story."

So, with a sharp rap from his mallet, he spoke out loud the words he had spoken to many trees here on the mountain. "Tell me your story, old friend." The crack of his mallet was sharp and crisp and clear, echoing throughout the singing woods. The sweetness of the sound convinced Luigi that he had found a special tree. More special than any other in his long life? As special as any tree the masters before him had found? The answers to these questions, Luigi could not know today. But there was the possibility, he knew, as he rapped the trunk over and over, listening with delight to the magic... the mellow notes drifting up the trunk and off into the winter wind. Removing his core-sampling tool from his pack, Luigi pulled a sample from the tree and confirmed what he had seen and heard – the growth rings were as close and consistent as any he had ever collected. This was another sure sign of the quality of the tree for producing powerful and sweet music. After marking the tree for cutting on another day when he had helpers, Luigi moved upward.

Suddenly, an even more chilly blast of winter wind began to rustle the treetops and Luigi knew from experience that a storm was likely approaching. Any time the wind blew like this, he was reminded of how thin and inadequate his overcoat was against the elements. Again, he recalled his earlier days when weathering a storm may not have been so risky. But now he knew without question that this day on the mountain must come to an end.

Going down was in many ways more difficult than climbing up. His knees and ankles were not as strong as before, but moving safely as well as quickly was now his focus. At one particular place he could climb up on a boulder and catch a glimpse of the country lane adjacent to the field at the bottom of the mountain. This was where Angelo would be stopping for Luigi and together, they would take the long ride back toward Cremona. Angelo's cart was not yet at their arranged meeting place... good news that allowed Luigi to breathe more easily and perhaps focus more on a careful descent. Isabella would approve.

Within an hour, he broke out of the forest and saw Angelo's cart topping the hill … perfect timing! Angelo was one of Luigi's closest companions and one of those who did not approve of his old friend's solo hikes in this rugged terrain. He had expressed his concerns to Isabella and, only occasionally to Luigi himself. But like Isabella, Angelo could not bear to take from his friend the joy and excitement that these ventures brought. Without them, how much longer would Luigi be with them? So, at every opportunity, Angelo planned his trips to neighboring villages for supplies when Luigi had a strong desire to be on the mountain. Angelo would drop Luigi off at the base of the mountain and pick him up on the return trip. The two friends enjoyed the long wagon rides together in conversation. Isabella felt much more secure with this arrangement, knowing that Angelo would offer one last warning to exercise caution as Luigi began his ascent.

Angelo had seen the incoming storm as well and knew that snow would be falling soon. If not here, then surely on the mountains where, thankfully, his friend had found safe passage once again. Now it was on to Boschetto, their village on the outskirts of Cremona.

"How did the forest of violins treat my old friend today?" Angelo asked as the rhythm of creaking wheels and horses' hoofs became the backdrop of their conversation.

"The forest always treats me well and Isabella's *pranza* was delicious. I was blessed to find perhaps the perfect tree that will one day deliver to another *luteria*, the finest of violins. Will Angelo go to the mountain with me soon to fell that tree and to retrieve the best parts?" Luigi's words, half statement and half question, were met with only a smile and a single word from his friend. "Perhaps…"

Insistent upon getting in the last good-natured plea, Luigi, staring off into the twilight, replied, "That tree has within it a fine violin… an enduring voice. One day if I live long enough, I will play beautiful music for you from that tree, Angelo."

The village fires of Boschetto shown in the distance and the snow was falling faster. In a short time, he would be at home, eating his evening meal and telling Isabella once again, of his venture up the mountain into the forest of violins… the musical woods.

CHAPTER 2

Along the streets of Boschetto, there was little activity. The village seemed virtually deserted with only an occasional cottage lighted up and alive with laughing and loud voices within. Luigi and Angelo's conversation was in quiet tones, almost whispers and the creaking of the cartwheels on cobblestone echoed through the village.

"Thank you, Angelo. Without your help, my trips to the forest would not be nearly so frequent."

"I enjoy the time with you as well," Angelo answered. "I love to hear of your discoveries and your dreams in the forest of the violins. "Do not be a stranger, Luigi. Come and visit with my family whenever you can."

Isabella Caruso had heard the wagon and the conversation, so, as always, she met her husband at the door, relieved at his safe return. In the dim light, she could still see the glisten in his eyes, and she knew from the years of life with Luigi, that such a glisten – the sparkle – revealed something to her of the stories and his adventures that he would soon be sharing between now and bedtime. She looked forward as always to those stories from her husband.

Their cottage was warmer than usual, or so it seemed to Luigi. Perhaps it was just because of the wind and snow on the long ride with Angelo. As he moved toward the hearth, Luigi could see that Isabella had just recently added wood to the fire. She knew that the cold weather settled deeply within their bones at their age and that Luigi would need the extra warmth to ward off the chill from his day on the mountain. He smiled at her thoughtfulness as he warmed by the fire, and he began removing the layers of outer clothing. He was only now beginning to realize how hungry he was. The pranza was wonderful and sufficient earlier in the day, but that was hours ago. The smell of Isabella's fresh bread permeated every room of their cottage and, along with her creamy and rich risotto, the table was hearkening.

"So, tell me of your day," she began. Isabella knew what the answer would include. She knew how long the stories would last, for she had asked this same question many times before, and, with little variation, Luigi's answers were the same. She never tired, however, of hearing them once again.

"It was, as you know…" he paused before adding with a twinkle "because many times before I have told you. It was a magical day… it is a magical place. I could hear the music … in the trees and in the wind … as always, but not as clearly as is often the case." Luigi thought back to his younger days on the mountain when everything seemed more alive with the music from the forest.

Then he began to describe what made this day perhaps better than others. "There was one beautiful specimen that I had never before noticed." In his mind's eye, he was back on the mountain standing at the base of the Spruce and hearing the echo of his mallet through the trunk. "I think this may be the one," he dreamed out loud. "The sound was so pure and so sweet when I struck it with the mallet. Whether there is a great violin trapped inside is not for me to know."

Luigi paused and decided not to suggest going back to the mountain soon with helpers to claim this tree as his own. If he lived to another new moon in another December when the time for cutting was right, possibly then he could harvest the tree with help from his younger friends. Cut into the right lengths, split into the right portions, and hauled to his shop in Boschetto, the years-long process of drying out could begin.

For now, this was only part of his dream and one that he would not share with Isabella or, at least, not until the time was right.

"You look tired, and I am as well" Isabella said as she reached across the table to stroke her husband's callused hands. "We need our rest. I know you will be awake and in your shop early… that is always your habit after you have been to the mountain.

Luigi smiled in agreement, blew out the lamp, and banked the fire. Hand in hand, he and Isabella headed to their room and settled into bed. "An extra quilt?" she asked. "Of course, dear… always after a cold day on the mountain." Isabella was asleep soon, but Luigi's mind raced with thoughts that kept him awake for the next hour or more.

The past six months had been spent on a cello and a viola, both of which were now in the hands of young musicians in Cremona who would hopefully share their music with their generation. Tomorrow, however, would be a day of beginning the work on his next violin, his favorite of instruments. The first important step was the selection of wood. Bundles of rough-cut spruce, maple, and ebony were matched, stored on shelves, and waiting for Luigi's hand. Some of these had been collected decades earlier, and tomorrow, Luigi must look carefully for the bundle of material from which he would craft his next violin.

In Luigi's mind, it was difficult for him to separate the craft - his building of an instrument - from the music that radiated from it. And when he reflected on the music, he reflected as well on his childhood.

From his earliest memory, Luigi's dream had been, not as a builder of instruments, but as a musician, a player of instruments. Large audiences and concert halls were the visions of which his dreams were made, so he had sat under teachers from his earliest days. Without doubt, they had profound impact on his life, not only teaching, but sharing their love for the instrument and the music. They encouraged Luigi and taught him the disciplines of practice and perseverance. But his hands did not cooperate with his heart for music and his teachers recognized this.

"You do not have what the great ones have. The proficiency and the expertise do not come easily, nor do they always come to those who strive for them." His secondary dream – building instruments – thus became his life's goal. He had determined long ago that he would not be bitter that his dreams had taken another course. He loved being a *luteria*, the craft that kept food on the table and a simple, yet comfortable life for he and Isabella. He loved being part of a skill that was so much a part of his Italian heritage. And some day, Luigi prayed, his hands would produce an instrument that was more than just adequate, more than suitable or respectable. He would produce an instrument that was in a class by itself, unlike any he had produced in his lifetime. An instrument with a voice that would last longer than his own life or anyone's memory of his life. Could that be the violin he would begin in his shop tomorrow?

As Luigi finally quieted his mind and fell into a deep sleep, the echo of rich tones from the spruce tree on the mountain alternately haunted and then enhanced his dreams. In and out of sleep, his mind played with reality… were the tones in his dreams those of the spruce waiting for him on the mountain or did they come from the violin he would begin working on at daylight?

CHAPTER 3

As he opened his eyes in the morning darkness, Luigi remembered Isabella's words from the previous night. "You will be awake and in your shop early." She knew him well and he took comfort in that. He was dressed and had his morning breakfast quickly, but before heading out onto the streets of Boschetto, Luigi stirred the coals to life with some added twigs and two nice logs. Isabella would welcome the warmth when she awakened later. Toolbox in hand, he walked out into the cold.

The snow had fallen ankle-deep overnight. Luigi enjoyed walking down the street, the powder squeaking under every step, to the edge of the village where his tiny shop stood. Upon entering, he lit lamps and built a fire in the stove, then stopped to gaze around this place where he had worked for the last half century. There were scores of shops similar to his throughout Cremona and, in each one, there was a craftsman with a dream that matched Luigi's... the perfect piece of work coming together on the bench. An instrument that was, at the same time, both powerful and sweet... breathtaking when played expertly.

His workbench under the single window was a piece he had built when he first began his work as a builder of instruments. It was plain and sturdy, but just right for the size of the shop and a perfect fit for Luigi. Many violins had come to life on the top of this bench. Countless curls of maple and spruce, along with slivers of ebony had covered the floor over the years, swept up at each day's end and becoming fuel for the stove, at least during the cold months. Various kinds of saws, clamps of every size and shape, and pieces of emery cloth were in place on the hooks and cubbyholes along the back of the bench. But in Luigi's toolbox that he carried from home each day were his most important and valuable tools. He carefully took them out and lined them up in admiration. Each block plane, gouge, scraper, his collection of knives, and rulers with precise measures… these were implements of his trade, each fit his skilled hands perfectly, and each one had a story. Some he had found in shops in Cremona and were perhaps older than Luigi himself, used by liuterias before him. From these tools, the rough slabs would become beautiful instruments that produced similarly beautiful music.

But the beginning of each violin or viola was the wood itself. Lining two walls of Luigi's shop, bundled together in matching pieces, was that raw material, without which none of this would be possible. He walked among the stacked piles and, in the dim light, read the attached tags he had written on each one. These identified the location and date when he had collected each. There was more wood here than he could possibly use in his remaining life, but today was the day to begin his next violin, so the most important task of choosing the material was his priority.

The process involved a routine that Luigi had executed more times than he could recall. It was a slow, thoughtful, tedious routine and Luigi took his time. Half of the wood before him could be eliminated simply because it had not yet had adequate time to cure and dry properly. But among the remaining bundles, there were still many factors to consider. The matching grains and their tightness were visible even in this rough stage, but only with the luteria's trained eye could one tell how the planed and smooth surfaces of the bottom and top of the instrument would enhance the beautiful patterns of spruce and maple, how the surface would take the stains and varnishes, and, most of all, which patterns and which woods had the potential for producing the best sound. The same skill he brought into play as he tapped the trees on the mountain yesterday were also necessary here… listening to the wood as he thumped one piece after another. Even at this stage, there was a sound that gave some hint as to the tone of his finished product. In some pieces he held in his hand, Luigi could tell that the base notes would be full and rich and powerful. At the same time, he was uncertain that the brightness of the E string, so important to the musician, would ring as clearly or as purely as necessary on the finest of violins. So, he moved on throughout the morning, carefully from stack to stack… looking, feeling, and, most of all, listening.

Somewhere along the way, Luigi realized that he had perhaps passed up some pieces that, in his earlier days, he would have simply chosen and begun to plane and glue matching sides together. Today seemed different. In some ways, he was more determined than ever – even driven or possessed – to find the magic that a bundle of splintered and rough wood held. He could not find satisfaction in any pieces he had seen thus far, and Luigi was lost in finding an explanation for his unwavering quest.

Early in the afternoon, he sat down and enjoyed Isabella's soup that had been simmering on the top of the wood stove all morning. As he enjoyed the bread, slices of mozzarella, and a glass of wine, he still pondered his odd sense of urgency throughout the morning as he searched for the perfect bundle of wood.

At his age, it was not unusual for Luigi to find himself wondering how many more times he could begin - and finish - such an instrument. One slip of a knife or one careless stumble on the mountain would be all it would take for his work as a *luteria* to come to an end. He held his hands out at arm's length. They were not as steady as they had been as a young man, but they were still stable enough to do the work. But how long would that last? Such ponderings were not common to Luigi, and they did not keep him awake at night. But as with anyone of his age, those thoughts did come his way occasionally. Finishing his meal and preparing to search once again, a thought suddenly struck him. Was his strange determination to find the perfect bundle of wood perhaps a reminder, even a sign, that this could possibly be his last instrument? Would this violin be his legacy - an enduring instrument passed eventually to someone unknown to him in future generations? If so, Luigi thought, then the search is necessary. To himself and to anyone who may be listening from outside, he said, "the tree on the mountain is for someone else - the wood for me and for this instrument is here and I will find it."

Stack by stack, Luigi rummaged through – looking, tapping, listening - until late in the afternoon. Trying not to get ahead of himself or settling for something less than he desired, he found himself saying over and over, "Patience, Luigi, have patience." The day grew late, and shadows fell across the streets of Boschetto. Then, under a stack of wood in the corner of his shop, Luigi discovered a small, wooden trunk that he did not even remember being in his shop. Was it left by the previous owner decades ago? Had he put it there himself?

Luigi had to move and climb over bundles of wood and remove numerous bundles from the lid of the trunk in order to open it. He could not see in the bottom of the trunk back in the dark corner and, fearing some insect or rodent that had taken up residence, he did not dare to reach down to see what the trunk held. So, he climbed back out of the corner and retrieved his lantern. In the light, Luigi could see a single bundle of wood, looking no different from the scores of bundles he had inspected carefully during the day. He pulled out the wood and, to his surprise, there was no tag… no identifying marks or writing that would tell him where or when this wood was placed here and who had harvested it.

A half hour earlier, Luigi had been weary and ready to close his shop and head home. But now, as he laid his new discovery on his workbench, his heart raced with anticipation. Untying the bundle of wood and running his hand over each piece, he admired the grain and the obvious absence of any knots or flaws. The spruce and maple both seemed perfect. The true test, however, was in the sound. First with his knuckle and then with a small hammer, Luigi tapped at multiple places on each piece and listened for tone and resonance. Without doubt, these were the finest pieces of all the wood in his shop.

Although Luigi knew that the ultimate test was in the finished product – the instrument itself – he made a vow to himself as he continued to admire the raw, rough wood on his bench. "This fine material is a gift I have been given and it will not be wasted. I will do the work that is required – with precision and with patience. I will make every effort to produce the violin that is concealed here." Tears welled up in Luigi's eyes. "Tomorrow will be a special day!"

CHAPTER 4

Once again, the lamps burned in Luigi's shop before daylight in spite of a restless night of sleep. The dreams and visions of his new violin kept his mind racing with excitement. Oddly, there was also a sense of worry as well. Material of the kind he had discovered yesterday may come only once in a lifetime and he could not afford to make any mistakes. He had never felt such responsibility in his years as a *luteria*.

For the better part of the morning, the only sounds in the shop came from Luigi's gouges and the block plane. Two matching pieces of beautiful spruce must be joined together, and for that to happen, the edges must be perfectly flat. Carefully, Luigi guided the plane across the edge of each half, taking away ever so small bits and curls of shavings until the two halves lined up and matched perfectly. A small container of glue that he had mixed and set on the stove in the morning was ready and the pieces of spruce were joined. Clamped together, they would be ready for cutting into the proper shape and, with a variety of gouges, Luigi would begin peeling away the excess wood, measuring the thickness at various spots, and watching his violin take shape.

Day after day Luigi focused on the task before him. As the instrument took shape and as he tapped, listened and examined, he became more and more confident in the quality of this violin over other fine instruments that had come from his bench. "The vibrations and the resonance are exquisite," he whispered to himself. The excitement was almost unbearable as he dreamed of the day when he would put the proper stain and varnish to the violin, string it up, and draw the first notes from it.

Two months into his devotion to this piece, the long hours and intensity of the work had begun to wear on the old man. He was accustomed to hours of work over his bench, but this was different. His days began earlier and lasted later than before. He sometimes worked through lunch. He gave himself no breaks, no stepping out into the streets of Boschetto to speak to friends. As he had realized when he began working on this violin, he felt driven in a manner that he had never known. Isabella recognized this and fretted over it, gently trying at every opportunity to get her husband to slow down. Most of her pleading, however, was to no avail.

"Your hands hurt, do they not?" she questioned over dinner one evening. Knowing that he could not hide the truth from someone who knew him so well, he nodded quietly but without comment. She pried further. "And your legs? Your back?" Luigi acknowledged this but insisted that he must continue the pace and finish the violin. He had not shared with Isabella his thoughts from months ago, pondering his mortality and whether this could be his last instrument. He didn't know whether his silence was simply because he did not want to voice his fears, or whether he simply suspected that she already had the same thoughts. Either way, he remained quiet on the subject.

Hunched over his workbench once again the following morning, Luigi was now entering the final stages of his work on the instrument, although several weeks of the task still lay ahead. Smaller planes for the finest of detail, a variety of scrapers for the final smoothing of the front and back of the instrument, and Luigi's own collection of special knives that allowed him to smooth edges and add decorative details. These were the instruments for this phase of his craft and Luigi, even more than usual, took his time, exercising patience.

A knock on the shop door startled Luigi. He could not recall the last time he had friends drop by his shop. Isabella visited slightly more often these days, but he recognized her slight tap on the door and the way she opened it just a crack, peering in before calling his name. This was someone other than her.

"Luigi, my friend" came a voice that the old *luteria* instantly recognized. "Angelo, welcome, welcome. Come into my place of business." Luigi cleared away his toolbox and overcoat from the one extra chair in the shop. "How long has it been since you have come by? It is so good to see you – the one who always gives me a ride to the mountain and back," he said with a smile. "What brings you here?"

"I saw Isabella in the market this morning. She is preparing a special dinner for you, but I will keep silent and let it be a surprise. She hinted that I should pay you a visit." Luigi saw the concern in Angelo's face. There was a long pause before Luigi realized that Angelo, although not posing a question, was nevertheless expecting a reply.

"Isabella - I love her and she cares for me, but she worries too much about me. So, tell me…what did she say? No," he added with a smile. "I will tell you what she said – 'Luigi is working too hard … Luigi's hands hurt… Luigi goes to his shop early and stays late… he will not rest from this latest project.'"

"She is a good wife, Luigi, and she cares for you." Angelo said softly.

"I know this better than you," Luigi replied.

"Of course you do, Luigi." Angelo acknowledged, "Of course you do."

Taking a deep breath, Luigi began. "What I have not told Isabella, I will tell you, Angelo. I have a feeling, or a sense, or a knowing - call it what you wish - that this may be my last violin. I have lived a long life and crafted many instruments. Mine have been good, but not great… until now. Here in my shop, I found an unmarked bundle of wood, perhaps left here by the previous owner or perhaps by me… I'm not certain." Picking up the unfinished violin and holding it out toward Angelo, Luigi continued, "This is remarkable wood. Look at the exquisite, beautifully tight grain, no flaws in the wood, and the richest of tones, at least to my ear." He thumped it and listened again. "I am sure that the sweetness and depth of music from this instrument will make it my finest creation."

Angelo thought he detected tears in the eyes of the old man. Luigi continued, looking deeply into his friend's face. "You are a much younger man than I am, Angelo. I have received a gift near the end of my life that I must not waste. I am responsible for putting my best efforts toward this instrument even if it makes my hands ache or makes me weary. If this is my last instrument, so be it. I'm an old man whom God has blessed, and I will finish my life well."

Angelo had no response, or, at least, no response that seemed appropriate in this tender moment. He had made no promises to Isabella except that he would pay her husband a visit. That he had done, but it did not seem right after Luigi's comments, to take the conversation any further. At some point, he would explain this to Isabella, or preferably, Luigi would explain it to her himself.

The two friends talked for over an hour until dusk began to settle on the village. "I need to be heading for home, Luigi," Angelo said after a pause in their conversation. "I will visit again… soon."

Luigi answered, "I will expect that, and I look forward to your next visit."

One more comment, Luigi could not resist. "The tree on the mountain, Angelo – the one I told you about and promised to make music for you from the violin trapped inside of it – I know that tree is not for me, but for another *luteria*." Then, turning again to the instrument on the workbench and running his callused and wrinkled hands across it, he promised his friend, "This is now the instrument that I will make music from – sweet music for you, my friend."

Luigi Caruso gave Angelo a long hug in the doorway of his *luteria* shop in Boschetto. As he watched his friend's cart slowly wobble away, the lights in the cottage windows of the village were beginning to brighten the streets, signaling the end of another day for farmers, craftsmen, and merchants in town. "My day will end now as well," Luigi thought to himself. "This will be the earliest I have left the workshop in many weeks. Isabella will be pleased." Extinguishing the lamps, packing his tools, and donning his coat, he rubbed his hand once more over his new creation on the workbench. "I will see you tomorrow," he whispered. Locking the door, Luigi began the stroll toward his house, and for the first time in weeks, he forgot about his work. He wondered, instead, about the surprise Isabella had prepared for dinner.

CHAPTER 5

His pace was brisk as Luigi walked down the street toward home. He thought about his conversation with Angelo, and somehow, he found comfort in having shared with his friend his determination, as he had said it, to "finish life well." Soon, he would share these deep feelings with Isabella – soon, but not tonight. He would enjoy the meal she had prepared, the warmth of their cottage, and a good night's rest.

He had not even reached the front door when the aroma of dinner hit him. So many of the smells throughout Boschetto, especially at dinner time, were similar and not at all unusual to a thousand villages in this part of Italy. Any number of tomato-based dishes along with a combination of herbs and spices grown in their tiny yard and dried on their back porch carried much of the same sweet smell. But Isabella's sauce - her *ragu* - was, in his opinion, the best.

As he stepped inside, Luigi instantly recognized the dish as chicken parmesan. Isabella's was known as the finest throughout Boschetto. Without even looking inside the oven, he also picked up the aroma of focaccia, always rubbed with garlic and with liberal amounts of Rosemary. He smiled and gave his wife a long hug.

"What is the special occasion?" he asked. Her response was good natured, but somewhat out of irritation. "Do I need a special occasion to surprise you with your favorite meal?"

"Not at all," Luigi responded with a smile.

As he washed up for dinner, he called to Isabella. "The dinner is not a complete surprise to me, you know. Angelo stopped by my workshop today... apparently at your insistence?"

Isabella did not try to hide her conversation with Angelo at the market. "It was a suggestion – only a request. I hoped he would go to see you, but no, I did not insist as you say." There was a long, awkward pause before Isabella continued. "Did your good friend talk any sense into you? About your long hours?" Isabella wasn't sure that she wanted an honest answer to her query. There was a longing within her for a quiet evening of good food and conversation that did not involve his work or her recent concerns about his health.

"For now, let's enjoy dinner," Luigi offered. "This conversation can wait."

As they began dinner, Luigi smiled. "As fine as your chicken parmesan is each time you serve it, this has a hint of something different – and even better." Isabella kept silent, playing along with his guessing game. "It must have been something from the market instead of from your pantry," he surmised. One more mouthful and Luigi exclaimed, "Marzanos… it is Marzano tomatoes!"

"Your discerning Italian palate is, as always, remarkable!" said Isabella with a hearty laugh.

"They do make for even better dinners, do they not?" Luigi agreed, adding "their sweetness and intensity sets them apart – and with just the right acidity. Delicious! How did you come about finding Marzanos," he asked.

"A farmer at the market this morning had a few small baskets from his travels along the southwest coast. I knew how much we would enjoy them in this dish. They did not disappoint, did they?"

"No, they did not disappoint at all," Luigi answered.

"There is great benefit to being an early arrival at the market. I'm sure the Marzanos that the farmer had were gone quickly. I arrived at the market almost as early as you have been arriving in your workshop these last months."

Luigi looked at his wife intensely. He could not tell if there was sternness in her voice or a pleading about his long hours that were taking their toll on him. "Perhaps," Luigi sighed, "the conversation about my long hours over my workbench should not wait after all."

So, for the next two hours, first at the dinner table and then in front of the crackling fire, Luigi and Isabella Caruso talked. Their conversation included many things about their long life together, the good times and the bad times. Mostly, however, as Luigi opened up about his premonition – whether his life as a *luteria* was coming to an end and whether he had, on his workbench, his last violin – they talked about the future.

Isabella's eyes filled with tears and, as much as she still wanted to tell her husband to rest and not push himself so hard, she resisted. She understood and wanted him to know that. So, she voiced the only thing that seemed appropriate as she looked deeply into Luigi's face.

"How can I help?" she asked. Then, leaning forward and taking his hands in her own, she asked, "How can we be part of each other's lives in this venture as we have been in all of the other times together?" Isabella asked this question knowing that she had no skills or talent that would help Luigi finish the violin on his bench. Still, she wanted to be present with him and support him in any way she could.

Luigi looked into the fire thoughtfully, searching for an answer to her offer. He turned to Isabella. "How can you help? You have already… by listening and understanding this old man's dreams. Keep doing this and I will be happy." After more thought, Luigi added, "Isabella, why don't you visit my shop more often as I work. I have only my own self to talk to, and, occasionally, I talk to the violin on my bench." He laughed out loud as he finished, "Talking to you would be much more pleasant. Perhaps you can surprise me with a special *pranza* on occasion.

"I can do that… and I will," Isabella answered. "I love you, and I love your dreams, Luigi Caruso."

"And I love you as well, Isabella," he replied. As the clock in the village chimed eleven, Luigi smiled and said, "I have not been awake at this hour in a long time. Perhaps keeping me up this late is your way of making sure that my day in the workshop will not start so early tomorrow!"

The old couple banked the fire together and headed for the bedroom. Luigi enjoyed a peaceful, uninterrupted sleep, with no dreams of trees on the mountain or the violin waiting for him on his workshop bench.

CHAPTER 6

As the sun rose bright on a frosty morning, Luigi's walk to his shop was especially brisk. He could hardly wait for the next step of his work, carving the channel for the decorative purfling around the top and bottom of the body of the instrument. Luigi particularly enjoyed this tedious step, because, to cut the channel, he used a small knife that had belonged to his grandfather. No other tool was so perfect for the task, and he delighted in taking this family heirloom in his hand for the task.

It took Luigi a full day over his workbench to carve out the channels and glue the purfling into place. With his smallest and sharpest plane, he carefully trimmed the decorative pieces perfectly flat. They looked flawless, but the real test came as he closed his eyes and ran his fingers across the purfling, over and over around the edges of both the top and the bottom of the violin. "Perfectly smooth… perfectly in place," Luigi said quietly. Then, opening his eyes and holding the instrument to catch the late afternoon sunlight streaming through the window, he concluded, "and perfectly beautiful!"

As much as he wanted to continue, Luigi knew that this day in the shop was at an end. Only when he stood up did he realize how stiff and tired he was from the long day hunched over the workbench. His back, his hands, his eyes all ached, but the results were, without a doubt, worth the effort.

Each day in his shop brought joy to the old *luteria* as he watched the instrument take its final shape. After each step, even the smallest of detail, he would hold the violin lightly by the scroll and tap various places on the top and bottom, listening for the sound. Each time, a smile of satisfaction would spread across Luigi's face, knowing the quality of instrument he held in his hands and anticipating the music and the joy that it would bring. For the next few days, once again with his grandfather's knife, he carefully finished the decorative carvings on the scroll until they were up to his lofty standards and to his satisfaction.

A week before Christmas, as a blanket of fluffy snow covered everything in the village and masked most outside sounds, Luigi spent an entire day on one of the most essential elements of the violin and, ironically, a piece that would be almost invisible to anyone other than a *luteria*. Called by some "the soul of the violin," this piece was the sound post, carefully carved from the same spruce used for the top plate of the instrument. This was a seemingly simple, pencil-shaped piece of spruce, inserted through the treble f-hole and wedged between the top and bottom of the instrument. It was essential in supporting the pressure from the strings, but even more critical in carrying the sound through the top and bottom plates.

Luigi worked slowly and carefully, but expertly, trimming the soundpost to the correct dimensions to ensure a perfect fit. As was his habit as he hunched over the workbench, Luigi talked in whispered tones through the process to himself, inserting, then assessing the tone, and then removing the sound post to make miniscule adjustments. Slivers of spruce curled up on his knife blade and fell on the floor, adding to the accumulated bits and pieces of excess. Finally, Luigi had the post perfectly carved and ready. The time would come soon when the "soul" of his violin would be inserted in its place permanently.

Luigi had promised Isabella that he would take a holiday break from his work for a few days, so he was determined to put at least one coat of varnish on the violin so that it could dry while he was gone. Each *luteria* that he knew had his own recipe for the varnish and each knew that this was another critical stage in the creation of a fine instrument.

As the day ended, Luigi carefully mixed the proper amounts of resin gum, alcohol, and linseed oil in a small pot on the stove until the mixture was bubbling. Mostly because of the beautiful color it added,

Luigi liked to mix in a small amount of amber, yielding a beautiful reddish tint to the finished instrument. But the varnish was more than just a matter of appearance. An instrument "in the white" sounded sharp and unrefined. The cooked varnish, especially with the added amber, gave a protective coating and a warmth of tone that enhanced the sound provided by the wood.

The pot of varnish gradually cooled as the fire died down throughout the night. The following day, Luigi reheated it and began applying the initial coat. He had a picture in his mind of how the instrument would look with his red stain, but he was stunned at the beautiful color. Never had he seen such a tint – such beauty on an instrument from his work-bench. Hanging the violin up, Luigi locked his shop door and headed down the street through the crunching snow. In his pocket he carried a rough-cut violin bridge that he had purchased from another crafts-man. With his grandfather's pocketknife and relaxing in front of his own cottage fireplace, Luigi would whittle and trim it to his own speci-fications. Tomorrow was Christmas Eve and he looked forward to time with Isabella and friends. Within a week, he anticipated being able to string the instrument and listen to his dreams come true.

CHAPTER 7

For Luigi and Isabella Caruso, Christmas in recent years had, more than anything else, been beautifully quiet. Their children and families were scattered in distant places and other than the evening services at church and visits from a few friends, they were more than satisfied with the simple things, good food, the warmth of a blazing fire, and reflections on the life they had enjoyed together. Some townsfolk in Boschetto with more material blessings may see this aged couple and have pity on them, but Luigi and Isabella felt truly contented with their long life and shared experiences. For them, Christmas was a time to be grateful and happy together.

At the evening church service, their friends gathered for a time of remembrance and reflection on the significance of the season. The candlelight and voices lifting in traditional song touched their hearts once again. These also brought back Luigi's recent premonitions about his own mortality. But the message of Christmas and his own personal faith brought peace and contentment, allowing him to put those concerns aside. He also found himself having to clear his mind of the work that awaited him after the short holiday break. "The day after tomorrow will be soon enough to begin the final steps," he reminded himself. "Be patient, Luigi. Be patient. It is Christmas Eve."

Isabella had made arrangements for their best friends to bring holiday dishes and join them for the evening. The Accardi and Bonetti families had been friends for decades and enjoying Christmas Eve together would be grand. Long into the evening, the three couples ate heartily of fine Italian dishes, enjoyed the best wine that any one of them could afford, and shared story after story of Christmases past and adventures that naturally flowed from their long lives and deep friendships.

As midnight approached, along with the new Christmas day, the jolly and light-hearted mood among the old friends turned more subdued and reflective. The traditional carols rang throughout the Caruso cottage. Despite the obvious fact that none of their voices were as sweet or power-ful as when they were young, the music was still lovely and the message of the songs spilled onto the streets of Boschetto, warming the hearts of late-night street walkers. Long hugs, more laughter, and a few tears in the doorway brought the evening to a close.

Isabella looked around the cottage and, despite the late hour, she began her usual habit of cleaning up everything before going to bed. Luigi took her arm, "This can all wait until morning, can it not?" She smiled and nodded in agreement. After extinguishing the candles and lanterns and banking the fire, Luigi and Isabella Caruso fell into bed, exhausted, but rejoicing in the memories of this unforgettable Christmas Eve. Luigi could hear the faint sounds of friends in some other cottage, also singing in the day with their favorite carols. "We are not the last ones awake in Boschetto… listen!"

Isabella replied, "They are much younger than we are, dear." Luigi did not answer… he was in a deep sleep already. Isabella chuckled to herself, slid closer to her husband, and was soon asleep as well.

Luigi awoke on Christmas morning later than his usual time, partly because of the late night with the Accardi and Bonetti families and partly, he knew, because of too much wine. Isabella was still asleep, so Luigi rolled gently out of bed, retrieved his slippers, and closed the bedroom door carefully to allow her a bit more rest. As he added wood to the fire, he looked out the window and, with a childlike disappointment, saw no fresh snow to dust the village streets for Christmas.

He retrieved Isabella's gift from where he had been hiding it for months. Luigi's skills as a *luteria* easily transferred over to other woodworking projects. He could look around the cottage and find many items, some useful and others merely for decoration, that had come from his workbench over the decades. He ran his hand along the arm of the rocking chair he was sitting in and could remember precisely where the wood had come from, how each piece was crafted, and every joint that was required. Bowls and spoons that Isabella had used all their married lives lined the cupboards as well.

The gift he would give her today was both functional and, in Luigi's prejudiced opinion, beautiful as well. He certainly hoped that Isabella would feel the same. He would find out soon as he added a bow to the rather plain box and placed it at her seat at the table. He then added spices to the cider they reserved for such special mornings, set it on the stove, and put their loaf of sweet Italian bread in the warming drawer.

There was no stirring from the bedroom, yet, so, with his cup of Christmas morning cider, he scooted the rocking chair closer to the fire, took out his pocketknife and began trimming the rough-cut bridge into the proper proportions and shape for his instrument. Thin enough to carry the notes from the strings to the body, but strong enough to support the pressure – these were his primary objectives as he whittled away. "A few decorative curls would be nice," Luigi thought to himself, "but not necessary. The sound and tone... and clarity are of more importance."

Luigi was lost in the process for close to an hour before he became aware of the morning sun and the sounds of Christmas morning on the streets of the village. Joyous voices blended with the laughter of children enjoying their simple gifts from loving parents. Luigi knew that in a small village such as his, most of these parents had sacrificed the entire year for just this moment. The bells of the church rang in the day, and in more than one nearby cottage, families were singing carols. The old *luteria* whispered a prayer of thanks for the ultimate gift – the Christ child – and His blessings and presence in their lives.

The bedroom door creaked open and Isabella, somewhat embarrassed for what she considered her laziness, greeted Luigi with a "Merry Christmas" and a rather large gift bag which she set on the table as well. The couple walked to the door, stepped out into the crisp air with cider in hand, and enjoyed the village celebrations in progress.

A loud, cheery, and familiar voice called their names. "Luigi… Isabella… how is my favorite Italian couple this fine Christmas morning?" It was Angelo, hustling down the street, obviously in a hurry. He crossed over to give them a hug. Luigi insisted that he come inside and out of the cold. "For only a minute," Angelo replied. "I must get home to my family." Their friend took them up on the offer of a bit of hot cider, and then Angelo smelled the sweet bread and spied the two gifts on the table. "You have not even opened your presents or had your morning meal, have you? I am so sorry to be intruding."

Turning to Isabella and, in a half whisper so that Luigi could hear, he joked, "Did you convince your husband to sleep in this morning? I expected that he would be in his workshop even on Christmas day!" Isabella confessed to Angelo that she was the late sleeper this morning, and that Luigi had prepared the cider he was enjoying while she was still in bed.

"We had the Accardi and Bonetti families here for dinner and we were awake longer than many of our much younger neighbors. I guess we also indulged in perhaps a bit more wine than is our custom," she confessed. "The result? A leisurely Christmas morning!" All three of them laughed heartily.

On a more serious note, Angelo turned to Luigi and asked about the status of his latest instrument. "It has been several weeks since I was in your workshop, even though I promised you that I would stop by more often. The violin from the special wood you discovered in your shop – how is it coming along?" Before Luigi could answer, Angelo spoke again. "Perhaps I should ask in another way." Then, bowing in dramatic fashion, "When shall I have the pleasure, kind sir, of hearing with my own ears, the sweet music that you promised me from your new creation?"

"Soon, my friend… it will be soon." Come by my shop later in the week and see the most beautiful of violins!"

"I will do that, Luigi… I will do that." Once again with warm hugs, he wished Luigi and Isabella a Merry Christmas and walked briskly down the street toward his cottage.

"Such a good friend I have in Angelo" Luigi sighed. "And now for breakfast and gifts… which will be first?"

"Breakfast!" Isabella responded. They sat at the table and savored the sweet bread and a newly opened jar of her Italian plum jam that Isabella had been saving for this morning. After lingering at the table and enjoying the sounds from the village, Luigi announced that it was time for them to open presents.

Isabella unwrapped her gift, gasping in delight at the most beautiful walnut sewing box she had ever seen. It was polished and hand-rubbed to a glistening shine with double hinged doors and a delicate, spindle handle across the top. Opening the doors with the small, brass knobs, she pulled out the tray inside, revealing a red felt lining. "It is beautiful, Luigi. Something I will treasure… always."

"A beautiful gift for my beautiful wife." Luigi replied with a hug. "A much more useful gift than the violins I spend my time on?" Isabella laughed and began to wipe tears from her eyes. Then she noticed that the spindle handle matched the spindles on the backs of the rocking chairs. Calling Luigi's attention to the similarity, he replied with a smile, "Leftover pieces are never wasted! Now, look on the end of the box."

Isabella saw her initials intricately carved into both ends, along with the Caruso family crest. "How did you manage such delicate work," she marveled. Her husband smiled and pulled his grandfather's knife from his jacket pocket. "A special tool for special work."

"Your gift… open it now," Isabella urged excitedly. Reaching into the bag, Luigi pulled out a new, heavy wool overcoat. Without asking, he knew that this had come from Isabella's skill as a seamstress. Throughout the village, she was known for her accomplished work at repairing or altering old clothes, or, less frequently, creating new pieces.

"This will keep an old man much warmer on the mountain," he said as he pulled the coat up to his face.

Isabella responded, half in jest, "Yes, this coat will be a perfect companion for you…if I ever let you go back on the mountain again."

Examining her handiwork and the fine Italian wool, he could not help himself by asking, "Where did you come across such superb material… how could we afford this?"

Isabella smiled and replied, "sometimes my skills and my work for others can be bartered for things we need." She hesitated before adding, "or for things we just want our loved ones to have." The old couple embraced and, looking into Luigi's face, Isabella asked playfully, "Did you feel inside the pockets? There may be something else."

Reaching deep, Luigi gleefully pulled out a pair of woolen mittens, obviously from Isabella's hand as well. "Ah, what good is a warm body without warm hands?" Sliding his hands into the mittens, he briskly rubbed his wife's face. They laughed and embraced again, thankful for their precious gifts on this Christmas.

The couple enjoyed their Christmas lunch and spent the afternoon walking the streets of Boschetto, stopping to talk to friends on the street and visiting others around the village. Luigi was bundled up in his new coat and mittens, not hesitating to show off Isabella's handiwork to anyone they met, always pointing out her precise, even stitches and the fine material.

As the temperature dropped toward the end of the day, they were back in their cottage enjoying more cider before the fire. Isabella had gathered all her sewing thread, needles, scissors, buttons and various assorted implements and spent most of the evening filling up her new sewing box. Running her hands along the sides, she continued to marvel at the beautiful work her husband produced for her. Once again, Luigi was lost in the work of making final and intricate adjustments to the bridge for his violin. In the morning, he would be back at his workbench and closer to completion of his instrument.

Within an hour, Luigi's knife fell from his hand and bounced across the stone floor through the splinters and curls from the bridge he was carving, waking them both from sleep in their rocking chairs. They chuckled at each other and agreed that the late Christmas Eve, along with their busy day, was taking its toll and retiring for the evening was a good idea. Hand in hand, the old couple headed to bed. Blessed with another peaceful night of sleep, Luigi dreamed again of being on the mountain and listening to the forest of violins. The only difference between this dream and other similar ones, was that this time he was much warmer in his new woolen coat.

CHAPTER 8

Luigi's tasks for this first week back in the shop after his short holiday break was finishing the bridge, adding more coats of varnish to the violin, and choosing and rehairing one of several old, but fine bows he had in the shop. Without a fire in the stove for several days, the workshop was unusually cold. The practical first step of this first day back would be a nice fire, partly for his own comfort, but also important for the drying of the varnish.

As the workshop warmed and his pot of varnish slowly re-heated on the stove, Luigi rubbed the instrument's first coat of varnish with a slightly abrasive cloth, polishing it to a beautiful luster. Day after day over the next two weeks, he repeated the process of applying the varnish, letting it dry overnight, then buffing the finish smooth. Each application of varnish only enhanced the beauty of the instrument. At his workbench, he took a small decorative piece of paper and carefully inscribed "Luigi Caruso… Boschetto, Italy… 1720." He paused for a moment and then added… "for Isabella." He applied glue to the back of the label and carefully lowered it into the body of the instrument, pressing it securely in place. Finally, the morning arrived when Luigi could set the soundpost in place, install the tuning pegs, and string up what he hoped would be his life's master work.

The night before, he had excitedly shared the news with Isabella. As she promised, his wife had visited the shop more frequently, brought Luigi his lunch occasionally, and, most of all, watched him work and now shared something of his passion for the instrument sitting on his bench. Anyone who saw the violin would take note of its beauty as did

Isabella, but only another craftsman would understand the significance of such a high-quality violin.

Stringing up the instrument that morning, Luigi could hardly contain his excitement. His hands shook as he tightened each string and began with the simplest of scales, progressing to more difficult tunes, and complicated pieces. He had not played music since beginning work on the violin a few months ago, so his fingers did not move in a fashion that would allow for a true and full test. Nevertheless, Luigi attempted up-bow staccatos, arpeggios, and single string scales up to the very top of the fingerboard, the best his eighty-year-old hands would allow. The feel of the violin's neck as he played was superb, the high notes were sweet and pure, and beautifully married with the depth and power of the lower ranges. After an hour, his hands, arms, and neck were too tired to continue, and Luigi sat the instrument on a quilt that now covered his workbench and provided protection from scratches.

As he leaned back and simply gazed at the finished work, a flood of emotions suddenly overwhelmed the old *luteria*. He dropped his face down into his open hands and simply wept. The many thousands of hours at this workbench, scores of violins he had built, the few cellos and violas he had crafted, and the countless trips into the singing woods – all these bits and pieces of his rich life as a *luteria* in Boschetto flashed before his eyes and filled his heart with gratitude. Luigi fought the temptation of pride – of thinking, even if only to himself, "look what I have done!" Instead, he felt only humility and gratitude. He recalled the vow he had made to himself months ago upon discovery of the treasure of spruce and maple in his shop. "This is a gift I have been given," he had told himself that day. "It will not be wasted, and I will make every effort to produce the violin that is concealed here."

Luigi heard steps on the street that were coming closer to his shop door. He gathered his emotions, wiped the still-flowing tears from his eyes, and headed toward the door to greet his caller. Before he had taken more than a few steps, the door opened, and he saw Isabella's silhouette profiled against the morning sun. His emotions overflowed once more. Isabella knew the importance of the morning and that Luigi's test of his violin was probably finished. What she could not discern, however, was whether the tears streaming down her husband's face were from joy or disappointment. "Tell me," she begged as she held his face to hers. "The violin… is it good?"

Luigi smiled amid the continuing tears. "It is the most wonderful I have ever heard. It has the sweetest voice… a voice that will surely endure as long as it is played." The avalanche of emotions now swept over Isabella as well and the old couple cried and embraced in the doorway on the streets of their village.

CHAPTER 9

At home, Luigi played more music than any evening he could recall in recent years. He pulled out his small but precious collection of written scores, some that he had purchased and some gifted to him by friends in the past. A few of these were original compositions of his own. Certainly, he was out of practice, but his passion for the music and for the instrument soared within him and hopefully, translated to the results coming forth. Isabella sat close by and, knowing many of the tunes herself, hummed along. She could not recall a greater shared joy between them, and gratitude soared in her heart. When Luigi's weary hands would not allow him to continue, he set the instrument down and, from a wardrobe in their bedroom, returned with a violin case. He retrieved the instrument inside, the one he had built when he was much younger. It was a good violin, fitting his hands well, and he had played it most of his life. He now replaced it with his new one.

"You have been my friend for many years, and this case has been your home," he said. "But now, another has to take your place until I can secure a second case." Isabella was not unaccustomed to hearing Luigi speak this way to his instruments as if they were children that he had given birth to. She stifled a laugh, but also loved to hear such tender talk from her husband. Luigi polished the old instrument and wrapped it carefully in a small quilt, tucking it away in the wardrobe again. "Tomorrow," he said, "I will clean this case, make a few repairs, and replace the worn felt. Then it will be a more suitable home for the new violin."

He closed the case and latched it carefully, sliding it under their bed. As he returned to the fireplace where Isabella had resumed her sewing, he announced, "I will go to Cremona soon to hear what others think of my instrument and to hear much better violinists play it. I would like for you to go with me… we can borrow Angelo's cart, perhaps." Then he continued, "if you do not want to go, Angelo may be willing to take me himself."

"I have not been to Cremona since last summer. I would love to go with you and maybe browse the shops or markets." With a twinkle, Isabella added, "Most of all, I would like to hear others brag about my Luigi's beautiful violin!"

"I will talk to Angelo tomorrow," Luigi concluded." "But now, it is bedtime." As Isabella extinguished the lanterns and her husband banked the fire, she pondered, "The music from your violin will certainly provide the background tonight for my dreams." Luigi smiled at the thought as he fell into a deep sleep.

CHAPTER 10

Angelo Costa heard the knock on his door that faced an alley two blocks off Bocshetto's main street, but he could not imagine the reason for such an early visit from anyone. He opened the door to find Luigi and greeted him warmly. "The coffee is fresh! Please come in." As the old man stepped into the cottage, Angelo saw the instrument case and questioned, "Is that what I think it is, Luigi? Have you completed the violin?" Without responding, Luigi sat the case on a table and opened it. Angelo was astounded at the beauty and when Luigi played a few simple tunes, despite having no musical inclination at all, he was amazed. "This is indeed a beautiful piece of work, my friend. You are to be commended for your dedication and patience." Then, he added, "I recall you telling me that the material for this violin was a gift that you would not waste. You have been faithful to that pledge as I knew you would be."

"Thank you, Angelo. And now I have a favor to ask."

"Anything for you, Luigi," he replied.

"I have a few friends in Cremona who are fine *luterias*. Other friends there are much finer violinists than I am. I would like to go into Cremona and show them my instrument… hear it played as it should be played. Could I persuade you to loan me your cart? Isabella tells me she would like to go as well."

"Yes, of course… but I would love to accompany you. All three of us can fit in my cart. We will have a grand time together!" Then Angelo added, "But it will be next week before I am able to go. Can you wait that long?" Luigi was grateful for Angelo's help, but disappointed at the same time. He was anxious for the opportunity to show his instrument, but he also recalled that, throughout the process for the past few months, he had often reminded himself of the need for patience. "Next week will be fine," he told Angelo, hoping that he did not convey his disappointment.

"Then, next week it will be, my friend! I will stop by your shop and let you know what day we will go. "I look forward to seeing the look on the faces of your friends when they see and when they hear your creation!" Angelo then exclaimed, "I was so intrigued by your violin that I did not notice the beautiful new coat you are wearing. Isabella has been busy with her sewing skills, has she not?"

Luigi smiled and nodded in agreement. "It is beautiful… and warm!"

Angelo refilled Luigi's coffee mug and the old man headed down the street toward his workshop. Today he would be working on repairs to the case that now carried his treasured possession.

The weather was sunny and bright as Luigi walked toward his workshop. He saw a number of friends on the street that he stopped to chat with, and, as he walked by one of the corner bakeries, he could not resist the smell of fresh-baked *gubana*, one of his favorite Italian sweet breakfast breads. The owner offered him a sample, and the dates, walnuts, and honey blended perfectly with the warm bread. "Two slices, please," he smiled. "One as I walk to my shop and one for lunch!" Wrapping one in paper and dropping it in the pocket of his coat, he enjoyed the other as he hurried on down the street.

Rummaging through drawers and storage bins in the cluttered shop, Luigi found a fine piece of red velvet cloth he had stored away for such an occasion. He removed the tattered cloth from the instrument case, and carefully marked the new piece to the exact size and shape. Cutting out two identical pieces, one each for the inside top and bottom of the case, he applied glue and pushed the cloth to the edges with a scraper, removing every wrinkle. With a leather conditioner that was Luigi's own blend of oils and wax, he carefully rubbed the entire outside of the case and buffed the brass latches until they glistened. He would now leave the case by the wood stove overnight to allow the glue and conditioner to dry thoroughly. Luigi looked in satisfaction at the refurbished case which was now more than suitable for protecting and displaying his new violin.

The weather, although quite cold early in the morning, was now sunny and pleasant, so Luigi opened the door and the window above his workbench to allow some fresh air to flow through. He relaxed and ate his remaining slice of *gubana*, accompanied by some cheese and bread left over from the holiday meals.

At home the previous evening, Luigi had found a few more pages of sheet music, a favorite composition of his own from his youth when he still cherished the dream of performance. He played the score for several hours late into the evening and every muscle in his hands and wrists ached this morning. He was, however, pleased with the results and he had mastered the most difficult parts, at least by his own standards. His new violin made the experience exhilarating.

As he finished eating, Luigi picked up the violin and began to play the same piece he had worked on the night before. With the door opened, his music filled the street in front of his shop. Before long, friends, neighbors, and other shopkeepers began to take notice. It had been a long time since anyone had heard Luigi play music, and with his hours of practice, plus the new violin, a small gathering took place. Luigi was unaware of them since they hid from view of the open doorway and only in the quietest of whispers did they voice their amazement to each other. When Luigi had finished playing and was wrapping up his violin, the small crowd began to clap and laugh with delight, spilling from the street into his shop. Luigi was somewhat embarrassed but laughed along with his friends at their spontaneous applause.

It was only then that Luigi noticed Angelo in the group. Like the others, he was clapping and laughing, but, in addition, Luigi saw tears in the eyes of his friend. "Remarkable..." was all Angelo could manage to say. After a pause, he added, "Your friends in Cremona must see and hear your instrument, and next week is not soon enough for our trip, my friend. Shall we go tomorrow?" "Yes," Luigi answered. "We will go tomorrow… early tomorrow!"

Reveling in the attention and thanking his friends once again for their kindness, Luigi turned his attention to the instrument case he had worked on that morning. One more buffing of the outside of the case and he would head home. For some reason, he felt the need to sweep up the workshop, put a quick sharpened edge on his two best planes, and straighten the tools on his bench. He looked around the shop with its supply of wood and variety of tools hanging on the wall, suddenly realizing that he had no plan for his next instrument. The awareness of this disturbed him. Luigi could not recall a time in his decades as a *luteria* when he did not have a "next project" – perhaps even several – already in his mind. "Perhaps in Cremona, someone will ask me to build them an instrument," he said to himself. Putting the thought out of his mind, Luigi pulled on his new coat, bringing a smile to his face. As he checked the fire in the stove and extinguished the lanterns, he closed and locked his workshop door. This was a routine end to the thousands of days Luigi Caruso had spent as a *luteria* on the streets of Boschetto, Italy.

CHAPTER 11

As Angelo Cantelli guided his cart through the streets in the pre-dawn darkness the next morning, he sensed a commotion and a level of activity in the village that was unusual for so early in the day. He turned onto the main street, and he could see the Caruso cottage. There were lights in the windows which did not surprise him. They were, after all, expecting him. But there were also people standing around in the street and walking in and out of the front door. Angelo stopped his cart and a sickening feeling rose from deep within him. Slowly making his way closer to Luigi's home, he heard crying from within the cottage. He stopped his cart and ran for the door of the cottage. He found himself immediately face-to-face with Isabella.

"Luigi…" was the only word he could manage.

"He is gone, Angelo," sighed Isabella. "No trip to Cremona, no more beautiful music, and no more creations from his hands." They embraced for several minutes without words, but only tears. Finally, Angelo spoke, "Luigi did what he said he would do… he finished life well."

Then taking her face in his hands, Angelo spoke what he hoped would be words of assurance for Luigi's wife. "When I say he finished life well, it is more than his fine violin I am thinking of. Luigi loved you, he loved the people of this village, he loved me, and he loved the life he had been given. You said there will be no more beautiful music, but you are wrong, Isabella. Not from Luigi's hand, but from the instruments he has passed along to others during his life. Especially his last creation… the beautiful voice of that instrument will endure as long as his violin is played."

Two weeks later, Isabella still had not been to Luigi's workshop, nor had she given thought to disposing of his possessions, the remnants of his long life spent in the workshop. She could not bear doing this alone, so she welcomed Angelo's offer of assistance when it came. Together, on a blustery day with light snow falling, they strolled the few blocks that Luigi had walked so many times, unlocked the door, and stepped in. Isabella took a long look as she walked through the tiny space, her hands touching every item.

Stacks of carefully selected and dried wood, each bundle tagged in Luigi's careful handwriting. More tools than she could imagine. She could not resist picking a few of them up and remembering his callused hands wrapped around them. The vestiges of her husband's work and craft were, in some ways, easier to dispose of than the personal items in their home. She turned to Angelo, saying "Surely someone... some other *luteria*, perhaps in Cremona, would want all of this, and would pay a fair price?"

Angelo agreed, saying "I hoped you would feel that way. I have already been in touch with someone who was a good friend of Luigi. He was at the funeral, and I spoke with him there. He is an honest and good man, Isabella – would Luigi have any other kind of good friend? He will buy any or all of it." Then, looking around the shop again, he told Isabella "Is there anything that you want to keep? Anything that maybe Luigi would want you to have?"

Without hesitation, Isabella responded. "The small knife that his grandfather gave him. I would like to keep that. And, of course, his most treasured creation, his violin. I will find an appropriate way to ensure that it is in good hands and played lovingly." Isabella took Angelo's hands in hers. "You were such a good friend to my husband. Is there anything here that you would like to have?"

Angelo smiled and confessed, "I am not an artist with wood as was Luigi. Nothing here would be useful to me. But I do thank you, Isabella."

Strolling back to the cottage and arriving at the door, a thought occurred to Isabella. "I have something of his that may be useful. Wait just a moment." Returning from the back bedroom, Isabella held out her husband's new coat. "It is yours... please take it, Angelo. That way, I will see Luigi when I see you in his coat on the streets of Boschetto."

Angelo was visibly moved. "I will pay you for it, Isabella." "No, no, no," she replied. "It is my gift to you. It is Luigi's gift to you." Angelo promised to have the items from the workshop removed as soon as he could contact Luigi's friend again." He left the Caruso cottage in his new coat, trusting that he had made a difference that morning, and that he had guided Isabella to good decisions.

At the market early one morning, Isabella saw her good friend, Greta Bonetti. They had not seen each other since Luigi's funeral and neither of them had adequate time this morning for anything other than a short conversation. After arranging to get together for lunch the following week, they embraced and turned to go their separate ways. Then, Greta called out, "Isabella, what do you plan to do with Luigi's violin. I was one of those at the doorway his last day in the shop. The music was wonderful... all who were there are still talking about it!"

Isabella's response was the same as it had been in Luigi's workshop with Angelo. "I will ensure that it is in good hands and played lovingly... how and when that will happen, I do not know."

Greta responded, "I will pray, Isabella, that you will know the right time and the right person."

Later, as she approached the cottage door, Isabella saw a cart on the street with a driver that she did not recognize. He approached her and spoke. "Mrs. Caruso? I was at the market this morning and overheard your conversation regarding a violin... one that you may want to sell?"

Isabella responded, "Yes, you heard correctly. Excuse me, but have we met?"

"No," he replied. "I am Mario Denalo. This is all quite by accident… or by fate, perhaps. I am passing through on my way to Cremona and stopped at your market where I heard you speak of your husband's instrument. I would love to see it, Mrs. Caruso."

Remembering Greta's promise to pray for the right time and the right person, Isabella welcomed a stranger, Mr. Mario Denalo, into her cottage and handed the instrument case to him. She had not opened it since Luigi's death, and seeing it brought tears once again. Mario tuned the violin, tightened the bow, and began to play beautiful music. He had not played more than a minute when he looked at Isabella. "Your husband was a fine craftsman and has left the world a fine instrument. I would be honored to be its next owner, Mrs. Caruso. I am in a very fortunate position to be able to say to you that I will pay whatever price you ask."

So, within an hour of their meeting, Mario Denalo was riding his cart down the cobblestone streets of Boschetto with Luigi's violin. Isabella slept well that night, confident that her husband's creation was, as she had hoped, "in good hands and being played lovingly."

For the rest of her life, Isabella had frequent dreams of the sweet voice coming from Luigi's violin. In her dreams, it was always her husband playing one of his own compositions. She would awake, not sad, but content that wherever it was being played, it was bringing joy, as Luigi would want. The sweet voice of his last instrument would endure, perhaps for many generations, in cultures and lands that the Caruso's could never have imagined in their Italian village of Boschetto.

PART 2

From Donegal to the Great Migration c. 1760

Luigi Caruso's violin was in the hands of its new owner for less than a decade before several unfortunate events led to it being sold, first to a French soldier and, then to the family of a German merchant living along the Lower Rhine River near Dusseldorf. In each case, the instrument was appreciated, but never with the passion that Luigi had envisioned. Across borders of countries and through a variety of cultures and musical traditions, his violin traveled from one owner to another.

Each time it changed hands, there was a sense of wonder about its origin. Each new owner or prospective buyer peered inside the instrument at the hand-written label "Luigi Caruso, Boschetto, Italy, 1720… for Isabella." Each one asked the same questions, "Who is Luigi…and who is Isabella? What role did she play in the life story of this beautiful work of art?" At times, the violin sat silent for months in dark corners or musty attics. Perhaps it had not reached the hands it was destined for or it was unappreciated by the surrounding cultural traditions. There was always curiosity, always intrigue, and always fascination, but never the emotion or determination to bring Luigi's creation to the fulness of its potential. It was never "in good hands or played lovingly" as Luigi… and Isabella… had hoped.

Finally, decades after Isabella watched Mario Denalo ride down the cobblestone streets of Boschetto, whether by fate or fortuitous circumstances, her husband's violin fell into the right culture, the right country, and, most of all, into the right hands.

The rise in popularity of violins… or fiddles… was common in most European countries in the 18th century, but nowhere were they as perfectly blended with the cultural traditions as in Scotland and Ireland. Fast-paced jigs and reels or slow ballads, all told the stories of heritage and history among these people of the British Isles.

Luigi's violin would now find a new voice in a new culture, playing melodies that were unknown to him. Tuned in a minor key, his fiddle invoked sounds eerily similar to the bagpipes from these ancient islands. It had finally found its way into "good hands" and would be "played lovingly" as he had desired.

CHAPTER 12

Molly McCourtney sat as still and quiet as any fourteen-year-old could be expected to sit. She could not imagine being in a better place. Molly treasured moments such as this, and they came far too infrequently to suit her. She was an audience of one, sitting cross-legged on the floor at the feet of her grandmother, Grace Campbell, known to everyone in the family – even the grandchildren – as simply "Gracie." The ballads, the melodies, and the stories of Gracie's life in Scotland and her migration to this place, County Donegal in the region of Ulster in Northern Ireland never ceased to excite Molly. Even as her aging grandmother repeated details or sometimes entire stories during their times together, Molly never corrected her. She saw this as just an opportunity to work on her own memorization, especially of the long ballads with their seemingly endless lyrics.

Molly's Irish heritage and ancestry were obvious simply in her looks. The long deep red hair, penetrating blue eyes, and freckled skin were typically Irish, and characteristic of many of her friends at church and school. Her thick hair was always brushed back into a long, simple braid as it was today. In the proper season, she would insert her favorite flowers, Irish Eyebrights, or the more common Shamrock among the weaves. Anyone who had known Gracie as a young girl would have looked at Molly and marveled at the resemblance. Gracie's hair had long ago turned white, but the piercing blue eyes and pale skin spoke clearly of her Scottish and Irish lineage.

It was an unusually bright and sunny day for this region of Donegal and the rest of Molly's family was taking full advantage of the opportunity to enjoy the out of doors. Her younger brother Patrick had no patience for Gracie's stories and songs, so Molly was grateful that the family was occupied elsewhere. Darren and Kate McCourtney seldom made the trip from their home in Letterkenny to pay a visit with Kate's mother and for a visit to coincide with sunny and mild weather was rare, indeed. Everyone knew that the fog and rain could come quickly, rolling in along the desolate, wind-swept shoreline of the Atlantic - what Gracie and others of her generation called "the Sea of Green Darkness." So, when the sun was shining and the wind was not so fierce, those who could do so rambled out of doors, climbing the grassy hills where, on clear days, the view of the Derryveagh Mountains was beautiful.

Molly's grandmother was pouring a cup of tea and still humming the tune of the last ballad she had sung. So, while Gracie provided this accompaniment, Molly took the opportunity to sing the lyrics, as best as she could remember them…

In Scarlet town, where I was born, there was a fair maid dwelling
Whom I had chosen for my own, and her name was Barbry' Allen
All in the merry month of May, when green leaves they were springing
This young man on his death bed lay, for the love of Barbry' Allen

Breaking from the song, Molly turned to her grandmother. "Gracie, why are so many of your songs sad? Were the Scotts sad people?"

Chuckling at Molly's curiosity but taking a deep breath and thinking carefully about how to answer such a question in a way that a fourteen-year-old could understand, she began. "My grandfather, your great, great grandfather, was one of the Covenanters, those in Scotland who signed the National Covenant in the 1630s. By doing this, they confirmed their opposition to the interference by the kings to the affairs of our Presbyterian Church."

"Life for the Scotts has been hard, child. Not all the time, or in every situation, mind you, but our long history has a tremendous amount of sadness about it."

After a long pause, she continued. "We sing to remember who we are, sometimes as individuals, and sometimes as a whole community or nation of people. Scots like to sing of these things such as broken hearts, songs of having to leave those people or places that are dear to us, songs of lost loves, and songs of death. These are chapters in all our lives. And these chapters, put together, form a book. To us, that book is the record of our lives."

So slowly, slowly she got up, and so slowly she came to him,
And all she said when she came there, young man I think you are a dying.
He turned his face unto her then, if you be Barbry' Allen,
My dear, said he, come pity me, as on my deathbed I am lying.
If on your deathbed you be lying, what is that to Barbry' Allen?
I cannot keep you from [your] death, so farewell,' said Barbry' Allen.

Gracie stopped singing and seemed lost in another time or another place. Then, looking at Molly, she continued. "Lord Randal" ... "The Bonnie Banks of Fordie" ... and others... these are often songs of lost loves and of death. In the Scotland where I grew up, Molly, there were clear distinctions of order... classes of people, both high and low. More so than we see here in Ulster."

Gracie sighed deeply as if these were personal experiences that she was recalling. "Even something as powerful as the love between a man and a woman could rarely be allowed to cross those lines of class." Then, without any other explanation, the old woman began to sing once again...

My love she won't have me, so I understand
She wants a free holder who owns house and land
I cannot maintain her with silver and gold
Nor buy all the fine things that a big house can hold
If I were a merchant and could write a fine hand,
I'd write her a letter that she'd understand
I'd write it by the river where the waters o'er-flow,

I'll dream of pretty Saro wherever I go

Molly paused before speaking and let the tune and the lyrics sink into her mind and heart. "Gracie, I love these songs exactly as you sing them, with no accompaniment at all. But in Letterkenny, on the public green, I hear many of the same songs played on an accordion and a bodhran. But what I especially love to hear is these tunes played on the fiddle. If there are enough people and the tunes are lively, there is always dancing. It is so delightful with the fiddle." Then Molly added, "If you could only come to visit us on my birthday, I'd take you there to hear for yourself. What I'm really hoping for…"

But before Molly could finish what she wanted to say, there was the sound of voices from outside and her six-year-old brother burst into the room with his father, Darren, chasing him and laughing heartily. Molly's mother was not far behind. Kate McCourtney had the same red hair, although with a bit of premature gray running through it. She was tall and thin, and Molly often looked at her mother, hoping she would inherit her looks. "What a delightful day," Kate declared. "I do believe we could see the mountains more clearly than ever before."

"And the ocean," cried Patrick. "I could see the ocean!"

Knowing that the young boy's imagination was playing tricks on him, his father questioned, "Are you sure about that Patrick?"

Always defending the youngest child, even in a friendly family spat, Gracie interjected, "Let it be, Darren. If the boy saw the Sea of Green Darkness, even in his mind's eye… let it be." Then, with a playful wink at Patrick, Gracie announced, "the shortbread is ready, and still warm!"

No one in the family, or in the local village, for that matter, had ever turned down Gracie's Scottish shortbread. And today was no different for this small gathering of the McCourtney clan. With the freshly brewed tea, the buttery shortbread was a perfect mid-day snack. Kate McCourtney had enjoyed the treat for as long as she could remember but had never been able to match the texture or the taste, no matter how closely she followed her mother's recipe. Her own shortbread was delicious by her family's opinion, but Gracie's perfected version was, to Kate, simply a "wondrous mystery."

Darren McCourtney's earlier playfulness had now turned more serious as he began readying his family for the half-day trip back to Letterkenny. "Pack up," he called. "You all know your jobs. Molly, help me get the team hitched to the wagon. Patrick, help your mother get our things together. We'll be home soon after nightfall if we hurry and all do our part." Darren did not have to repeat himself as everyone was soon busy and preparing for the journey.

Grace Campbell had Irish stew on the stovetop and boxty cakes, fried earlier in the morning, now staying warm in the oven. These were common dishes… staples… throughout Ireland and heated on a camp- fire, they would be more than adequate for the family along the road. Molly and Patrick were so fond of boxty that, to them, the potato cakes were good even cold.

In less than an hour, the McCourtney's were giving goodbye hugs to Gracie and promising to return, if possible, once before winter weather set in. As Molly hugged her grandmother a final time, she finished a thought from earlier in the morning. Whispering in Gracie's ear, she begged, "Please try and find a way to be in Letterkenny for my birthday. I'm hoping for a special gift… a fiddle. Then I can hear your ballads and accompany you as well!"

"That is quite a hopeful wish, child… I would be careful not to set my heart on it." Molly didn't respond, but the tears in her eyes made it clear that she also knew her dream had little chance of happening." "Come anyway… if you can," she whispered. Molly and the others gave final hugs and their wagon lumbered down the boreen green from Gracie's cottage toward the gravel road at the bottom of the hill.

CHAPTER 13

As the sun was dipping below the hills and the first of the evening's stars shone brightly, both Molly and Patrick were asleep in the back of the wagon. They had learned during many journeys how to make a pallet in the wagon with the clothes they had packed, plus a quilt or two. It was not as comfortable as their own beds at home, but with the rhythmic swaying and padding arranged just right, they never had trouble sleeping along the way.

When the wagon pulled off the road and jolted to a stop, Molly woke immediately. The clear night sky was ablaze with stars and the sliver of a crescent moon hung low in the western sky. They were less than an hour from home, but on such a beautiful night and with relatively mild temperatures, Darren and Kate decided to build a fire, warm the stew and boxty cakes for a memorable dinner under the stars. Molly and Patrick were famished and thrilled with the prospect of a wonderful meal under these conditions.

Kate McCourtney had much of her mother's tendency as a "keeper of traditions," both in song and in story. But she realized even when Molly was just a small child that her daughter's inclination toward these things far exceeded her own. Kate was thrilled that Molly gravitated toward Gracie and toward the music of the region and she was determined to support Molly's interests in whatever way she could. After finishing dinner, Kate asked Molly, "So, did you learn any new ballads or hear any new stories during your time with your grandmother today?"

"Nothing that I would call 'new'," replied Molly after giving the question much thought. "But every time I'm able to sit with her, there are slight variations in lyrics and in the tune. So, in some ways, it is always new, I guess." Reaching back to her own childhood memories and the hundreds of times she had heard her mother sing these songs, Kate smiled and nodded in agreement. "This is part of the way it has been for centuries in our part of the world… first in Scotland and now in this region of Ireland. Everyone who sings or tells a story has their own slight variation, depending upon where they first heard it or who it came to them from."

"These stories and songs you are catching from Gracie at this young age will become yours," her father interjected in the conversation. "And one day in God's proper time and place, you may have children of your own to whom you can pass along your heritage. At that time, I have no doubt that there will be even more variations… probably some combination of what you are learning now from Gracie and what you have yet to learn from others in the future." Patrick was asleep, curled up in his mother's lap near the dying fire, but Darren, Kate and Molly sang until Molly was also drifting in and out of sleep. The last thing she could remember before her father guided her into the wagon and covered her up… was a line from one of the oldest ballads. But somehow that line was woven into her dream, and she was singing over and over…

> See, I will get a bonnie, bonnie boat, and I will sail the sea
> And I will go to Lord Gregory, since he came home to me

Molly was only half awake as Darren coaxed her into her own bed in their cottage. Her mother leaned down and brushing Molly's thick red hair from her face, giving her a kiss on the cheek. "Good night, dear" whispered Kate.

As she reached the doorway, Molly called out. "Mama… was I singing 'Lord Gregory' out loud or was that just in my dream?"

Kate replied with a laugh, "it was out loud… sort of. But you left out the best lines…" And together they sang…

> Who will shoe my babe's little feet and who will glove your hand?

Who will kiss your ruby red cheeks when I'm in a far off land?

They both laughed and Kate came back to the bed for one more goodnight hug. "Mama, guess what?" Molly said excitedly. "In my dream, I was playing a fiddle!"

CHAPTER 14

The McCourtney family's adventures to visit Gracie along the north-west coast were always the subject of stories and laughter for weeks to come. Molly spent many hours out in the rocky and grassy fields among her family's small flock of Galway sheep after each such outing, journal in hand, recording each story in detail, both the true stories from Gracie's long life and the traditional folk tales from Scotland and Ireland. Most of all, she added new verses to ballads, or edited lyrics she had captured from her grandmother on previous visits. As she worked on the lines of ballads, she would always sing them to herself. Molly could hardly wait to share these with her friends in catechism class and at school.

She often thought that, even without journaling, she would still come to these fields to be alone and to contemplate the world as it unfolded in her fourteen-year-old mind and imagination. Letterkenny lay along the River Swilly, and, in the distance, Molly could see the Lough Swilly, a narrow sea inlet created in the glacial past and with majestic, steep cliffs on both sides. The opening led out to the Atlantic, Gracie's Sea of Green Darkness. Letterkenny was a busy place, except during the dead of winter, with all manner of goods leaving and arriving constantly by boat. What kinds of places and what kinds of adventures were part of a life at sea, Molly wondered. What kinds of songs and ballads do these workers catch along the way?

Bringing her wandering mind closer to home, Molly gazed across the fields where her father's sheep were basking in the sun. Everything in this part of Ireland, especially now, was a vibrant green, the grasses long and flowing in the breeze. This year, there had been ample rain, so the grass was even longer and the green more vivid. Dundee, the McCourtney's Border Collie, was keeping a sharp eye on the flock. He was, to Molly and Patrick, as much a part of the family as they were. Everywhere that Molly had ever traveled in Ulster seemed to be filled with sheep… they simply went hand in hand with the country, at least in her mind. She had seen them alone on unimaginably steep and craggy cliffs, crossing roads, and in flocks, large and small, almost everywhere. "Our landscape and climate here suits them perfectly," Molly thought to herself and then added, "as it suits me!" The Galways, from a distance, all looked the same, but for someone like her father, each individual sheep was distinct in markings, in personality, and in temperament.

As the sun rose high over the grassy meadow and the slightly cool morning warmed nicely, Molly stretched her lanky frame out in a patch of the thickest grass she could find. Her bright red hair stood in stark contrast to the lush green around her. Molly adored the fresh, earthy scent of heather intermingled in among the grass. She had often heard Gracie speak of the hillsides of heather in the Scotland of her childhood. "Heather be quite bonnie if someone hands you a bunch," she would say in her strongest Scottish brogue, laughing heartily. So many of the ballads, poems, and folklore that soared within Molly almost deified this plant that was so much a part of her culture. And now, at this time of year, the heather was beginning to show its colorful side, pink and purple blooms that would last well into the autumn… and beyond her late summer birthday.

The thought of her birthday brought Molly back to her dream on the evening journey returning from her grandmother's home on the north-west coast. But playing the fiddle was so much more than just a dream for her. It was hope, desire, and ambition all wrapped up together. The dream in the back of the wagon was just a picture of the end result … if she could only secure such a treasure!

Other, more serious thoughts had also been swirling around in Molly's heart since the visit with Gracie. Her grandmother had spoken to her about the sovereignty of God in her life and her parents had reminded her of His time and place in Molly's life for a family of her own and passing along her heritage to them. For certain, Molly had passing thoughts about these things, what young girl didn't, but she had mostly kept them to herself or shared them only with her best friends. Hearing such things spoken to her by the adults in her life compelled her to contemplate them more deeply. Molly always spoke important thoughts aloud to herself. It only made sense that speaking and hearing these things would help her make sense of them. Her journal added a third level to the comprehension of such things, helping even more.

From catechism class, she was being drilled in the faith by questions and answers to the major doctrines of her family's Presbyterian ways. Molly knew and believed without question that *"There is but only one living and true God… who works all things according to the counsel of His immutable and righteous will."* But her inquisitive nature and her human nature wanted more details. Did "all things" really mean all things… including a husband, children, or perhaps even a fiddle?

CHAPTER 15

Throughout the latter part of the summer, Molly was busier than usual helping Darren McCourtney with some of the repairs on their small farm, repairs that were necessary before winter set in. Snow and ice were not unheard of in their region of Ulster, but neither were they common occurrences. Nevertheless, Darren made certain that any mending of the barn and fences was done long before any chance of freezing precipitation. At her age, Molly was expected to help as needed. She never failed to tell any classmates that would listen about the accomplished work and her part in getting it done.

A week before Molly's birthday, Kate McCourtney came running up the grassy lane that connected their house to the nearest market on the outskirts of town She was breathless with excitement. "I saw Alex Gallagher at the market and he says Gracie is going to make the trip here for your birthday next week."

Molly could hardly contain herself. Grace McCourtney's home in Gweedore was about a half day's travel by wagon, a rough ride for anyone. But at her advanced age, Gracie was not inclined to make the trip. It would be so special to have her staying for what the family expected would be a nice, long visit. Alex Gallagher traveled to Gweedore on a regular basis for business and he would usually stop in to see Gracie and let the McCourtney family know how she was doing. She told him of her desire to pay the family a visit, so Alex had made arrangements to bring Gracie back to Letterkenny with him next week.

On the day before her birthday when her grandmother was to arrive in Letterkenny, Molly found herself at the main market early in the morning along the docks at the River Swilly purchasing some food items and running errands for her mother. "It is a good day to be here," she thought. The summer sun made for a warm morning, and the bustling of activity around the ships was, as always, exciting. Most of all, there were several groups of musicians and storytellers gathered at street corner cafés and on the public green. Molly wished that her time was her own this morning, but she knew that she needed to get her mother's things back to the cottage. She did manage to wander among the musicians in the green and hear a single lovely ballad. There was fiddle accompaniment, and this only fostered more excitement within Molly as her birthday arrived tomorrow. Her grandmother's words of warning – "that is quite a hopeful wish, child and I would be careful not to set your heart on it" - pressed hard against her excitement.

Molly ran up the grassy lane toward the cottage, knowing that her mother would likely give her a scolding for not being back sooner. She could hardly believe her eyes when she saw Alex Gallagher's wagon at the doorway. Alex's wagon was easy to spot because it was always overloaded with a wide variety of boxes and sacks of miscellaneous goods that he delivered to and from villages in Ulster. Molly's heart skipped a beat. She'd been told that Gracie wouldn't arrive until evening. Could she be here already?

Molly ran in the doorway, dropped the sacks of market goods on the dining table, and squealing with glee, skipped across the floor to hug Gracie. "I certainly couldn't keep my entire visit a secret from the family, could I?" declared her grandmother. "So, arriving early was the only surprise I had left in my bag of tricks."

"Oh, I'm so glad you came. I know I begged you to when we visited earlier in the summer, but I…. I just didn't think you'd be able to make the long wagon ride." Molly hugged her again.

Gracie responded, "You didn't think I'd miss my granddaughter's fifteenth birthday, now did you?"

"Tomorrow, we can go to the public green where the musicians and storytellers gather. It is my favorite place and I know you will love it as well." Molly continued almost without taking a breath, "Then we can go up to the meadow and sing around the big rocks…. And you can watch Dundee work the sheep… and in the evening…"

"Slow down, slow down," laughed Darren and Kate together. "First, let's allow Gracie to get some rest from her trip. Perhaps we should also consider asking her what she would like to do while in Letterkenny!"

Then Kate added, "Molly, it is your birthday, so we need to save time for celebration." "And cake," added a gleeful Patrick.

Molly could not recall a better time with her family than that first evening of Gracie's visit. Kate and her mother had prepared a special meal of Molly's favorites. Shepherd's Pie, bubbling hot and hearty, was more popular in the deep winter months, but Molly loved the meat and vegetables topped with crusty brown mashed potatoes any time of the year. Gracie's soda bread with chopped apples, raisins, and cranberries was her all-round favorite dessert.

With a twinkle in her eye, she handed a gift to Molly after dinner. "Just a little something that a fifteen-year-old lassie should have." Molly unwrapped a new dress that Gracie had secretly been working on during her visit.

"Green and blue floral… it looks like my special place in the meadow on a clear, sunny, Irish day" Molly giggled. "I love it, Gracie."

A night of dancing, singing, and storytelling could not have provided a more delightful pre-birthday celebration. The Clarke family, close neighbors and good friends, came after dinner and joined in the festivities. Liam Clarke was a few years older than Molly, and they had become good friends at church and in school. Not only did their neighbors add to the singing and dancing, but Liam's father, Finn, was quite the fiddler, so Molly couldn't take her eyes from watching and listening to the beautiful instrument.

Long after her normal bedtime and with Patrick sound asleep in the other bed across the room, Molly tossed and turned with both excitement about her birthday tomorrow, and with the sounds of fiddle music still lingering in her head. "Could fifteen be that much different than fourteen?" she asked herself over and over. "Mother, Daddy, and even Gracie seem to think so, but I just don't see it. Perhaps when I wake up in the morning, I will know for sure? We'll see."

Then, as was often the case with Molly McCourtney, the entrancing phrases of an ancient ballad began swirling about in her head as she drifted toward sleep. Some people counted sheep, an easy thing to imagine in Molly's world, but poetic lyrics brought the same effect, rocking her to sleep with dreams of oceans, and home, and love …

> *See, I will get a bonnie, bonnie boat, and I will sail the sea*
> *And I will go to Lord Gregory, since he came home to me*

Molly was the first to wake up the next morning, and today, even earlier than usual, no doubt because of the occasion. She didn't feel any different than the evening before and, using the small mirror on her bedside table, she examined herself as best she could in the early dawn light that was just beginning to creep across the meadow and toward the cottage. Nothing to see, either. "All of this fuss about being fifteen must be just something that grown-ups say!" Quickly, she got up and brushed the tangles from her hair, braided it as she did every day, and slipped on her favorite dress.

"If I don't spend a few minutes on my catechism questions, I know mother and father will make me do that before any celebrations or presents." So, she retrieved her journal from the top drawer of her dresser and, finding the shortest question with the easiest answer to memorize, read it carefully, closed her eyes, and repeated to herself: *"What is the work of creation? God's making all things of nothing, by the word of His power, in the space of six days, and all was very good."* This was a favorite question for Molly, and not because it was so short. All her time along the river, in the rocky meadow with the sheep, gazing at the starry skies, the times she was able to glimpse the mighty ocean, or the Derryveagh Mountains near Gracie's home… all of these spoke to Molly of the wonders of creation and the words she had just recited. A quick prayer of thanks, and she was out into the house where she could now hear others stirring.

As Molly burst into the kitchen, her mother was the only one there, busily preparing breakfast. "There is a bit of soda bread left from last night. The honey you bought for me at the market yesterday will be delightful with it." Then Kate reached out her arms and welcomed her daughter in a tight embrace. "Happy birthday, dear… happy fifteenth birthday! I can't believe I'm even saying that!" After kissing each other on the cheek, Molly glanced at the dining table to see a large box wrapped in plain white paper and decorated with ribbons and a few fresh flowers from the meadow.

She gasped, but before she could say anything, her mother warned her, "No presents until everyone is awake!"

"Oh, I remember you as a girl, Kate Campbell McCourtney," called her mother as she walked into the kitchen. "You were no different when it came to a gift at Christmas or your birthday!" Gracie could sound stern and serious in the tone of her voice, but the slight smile and sparkle in her blue eyes let everyone know she was speaking at least partly in jest. "But I agree with your mother, Miss Molly. No gifts until the whole family can enjoy."

Then Kate added, "And no gifts without at least some work on your catechism lessons, young lady!" Molly quickly recited the question and answer from this morning to both ladies' satisfaction. "Since it is your birthday, I suppose that will be adequate," her mother acknowledged.

After pouring a cup of tea, Gracie took Molly by the hand and headed toward the doorway where the sun was just beginning to shine in. "Take me to that rocky meadow that you are always telling me about, young lady." So, Molly and her grandmother went through the pasture gate and trekked up the hill. It was not a steep climb nor was it far from the cottage, so, taking her time and watching her step, Gracie made her way, taking pride in her accomplishment. Molly spread out a blanket since the grass was still damp from the morning dew. She shared with her grandmother new versions or lyrics to ballads that she had heard since they were together earlier in the summer. From their vantage point, the River Swilly and the docks along the banks were visible, and Molly pointed out her favorite places, including the village green.

A short time later they heard the familiar clanging of the dinner bell at the back cottage door. Looking down the hill, Molly could see her mother waving them home. "Breakfast must be ready," Molly exclaimed, and, as quickly as she could go without losing Gracie behind her, she headed for the cottage. Molly's mind swirled with excitement as she burst into the kitchen. The aroma of biscuits, fried sausage, and eggs filled the house. Even Patrick was awake and came running across the room to give his sister a birthday hug.

"Come to the table… breakfast is served," Darren called out and everyone scurried to their places. "Patrick, help your grandmother to her seat, please. Let's all join in giving thanks for this day." Looking at his fifteen-year-old daughter, Darren added, "and for the one whose birthday we celebrate." Squeezing Molly's hand, he chuckled, "Don't worry, children. My prayers, as you know, are never very long!"

As he began praying, Molly could hear an emotion in her father's voice that did not come often. She didn't dare open her eyes and look at him, but she was certain, if she had, that there would be at least a few tears falling from his cheeks.

"Our sovereign and loving God. Every day we have is a gift from you, only possible because of your kindness toward those you have called to be your children. So, this day, like all other days, we give you thanks. But in our home, this is a uniquely special day because of our Molly's fifteenth birthday. She is such a blessing to our family. And as we celebrate, keep us mindful of your

mercy and your sovereign guidance in her life and in the lives of each of us gathered here. Amen"

Breakfast was delicious, and after several of Kate's biscuits covered in honey to finish her meal, Molly pushed away from the table, exclaiming "that should last me until dinner!" Patrick was the first to speak up about the package which was now sitting on the mantle above the open fireplace. "Now for gifts?" he called, aiming his question at no one in particular.

Darren, Kate, and Gracie exchanged mischievous looks. "Yes, now is as good a time as any!" announced Gracie.

Molly walked to the fireplace and took the decorated box from the mantle. As she looked more carefully at the ribbons and flowers decorating the gift, she spoke quietly, "Irish eyebrights... and shamrock... my favorites!"

Kate added, "Adornments for your hair when you finally get your present opened!"

Patrick couldn't resist his own input, "If you ever get it opened... Now hurry!"

So, Molly, surrounded by her family, unwrapped her birthday gift, and opened the box. Her heart skipped a beat as she gazed at a polished leather fiddle case. Tears filled her eyes, and she looked around the dining table at the members of her family, each with glistening eyes as well. Her hands shook as she popped the latches and slowly opened the case.

Before her lay Luigi Caruso's master work. This was the most beautiful fiddle Molly McCourtney had ever rested her eyes on. For a moment, she was unable to move, only staring at the instrument. Surely, this was the most remarkable moment of her short life and Molly knew, without question, that she had before her a gift that would be a part of the rest of her life. Almost fifty years since coming off of the bench in his Boschetto, Italy workshop, the fiddle now had a new home. It showed some slight wear and a few scratches, but the deep, red luster was as rich and warm as ever. It was, in some ways, even more beautiful than the first morning when Luigi had drawn a bow across its strings. His instrument would no doubt be "in good hands and lovingly played" just as he and Isabella desired decades before.

CHAPTER 16

Molly hugged her fiddle, stroked it with her hands, shed tears of joy, and, more than once, wondered out loud if this could even be real. As promised, Kate put Shamrock and Irish Eyebrights in her daughter's braid and the mother and grandmother commented more than once on the color of the fiddle and its similarity to the sheen of Molly's red hair.

Within an hour, she was skipping across the meadow toward Liam Clarke's family cottage to show them her instrument and to get it tuned. Perhaps, she hoped, Mr. Clarke would take the opportunity to demonstrate a few scales or simple tunes. "Anything," Molly thought, "to get me started!"

Liam was in the barnyard when he heard Molly squealing and running toward him with case in hand, her long red braid trailing behind her and her favorite, but faded, flowered dress gleaming in the late morning sun. As she approached Liam, she was still running at breakneck speed, and babbling incessantly about fiddles… and dreams… and gifts. Then, she lost her balance, slid uncontrollably in the wet grass, and would have run right into the fence had Liam not reached out to stop her fall. Molly found herself with her arms around her friend's neck, both of them laughing hysterically. She had never had her arms around any boy's neck, even her good friend Liam, and felt somewhat embarrassed. She quickly took a step back, drew a deep breath, and opened the fiddle case to show him.

"Oh, my goodness," was all Liam could manage, over and over, for a full minute. Then he collected himself and continued. "Aren't you going to be the belle of every gathering of musicians in Letterkenny? Yes, every young man will have his eye on you and asking 'Who's the red-haired fiddler?'" Again, the two friends laughed together. "And I almost forgot... Happy fifteenth birthday, Molly!"

"Thank you, Liam. But no one will pay any attention to me at all... in fact, they may actually run from me... if I don't learn how to play it! That's why I'm here. I'm hoping your father will tune it and perhaps show me a thing or two that I can practice. We all know that Finn Clarke plays a fine fiddle!"

"Did I hear my name?" came a voice from the barn. Liam's father came out into the sunlight, tall, tanned, and smiling as always. "What in this world do you have there, Miss Molly?"

Molly raised the case lid again and Finn Clarke's reaction to the beautiful instrument caused both Liam and Molly to chuckle. "Let me go wash up a bit and we'll get a better look at that fine fiddle... and see how it sounds in this Irishman's hands!"

With the first draw of the bow and the first notes of a traditional ballad, Molly once again teared up. Wiping her eyes on the sleeve of her dress, she turned to Liam. "How long will this last? Surely I won't cry every time it is played!" Liam and Finn both laughed at her concern.

"Now, watch and listen carefully..." said Finn Clarke. "This second string is the D note and here is the major scale starting there. If the finger position is not precise, neither will your notes be precise, so take it slow, getting the finger position exact. You can do exactly the same thing, beginning on this A string. Now, your first song with only four fretted notes and that open D and A. Listen carefully... tell me what song you are hearing." Within a few notes, Molly picked up the familiar refrains of Barbry' Allen, closed her eyes, and began to sing along...

In Scarlet town, where I was born, there was a fair maid dwelling
Whom I had chosen for my own, and her name was Barbry' Allen
As she continued, she was suddenly aware of Liam singing along. She had never heard him except in a larger group, but his voice along with

hers was wonderfully smooth and in perfect harmony. Molly thought to herself, "This is surely how Barbry' Allen was meant to sound."

All in the merry month of May, when green leaves they were springing
This young man on his death bed lay, for the love of Barbry' Allen

Finn Clarke grinned. "Beautiful music... from two fine voices and a fine fiddle. Treasure it, Molly. And that, my dear, is your first lesson. Learn it well!"

"I will, Mr. Clarke. Thanks so much!" And Molly was skipping across the meadow toward home, stopping only briefly to wave over her shoulder to Liam. She and Gracie had places to go!

Molly wore her new dress as she and her grandmother strolled along the River Swilly docks during the afternoon. They went to the village green and to all her favorite places where the ballads and storytelling routinely occurred. Molly imagined the day when she could contribute to such gatherings with her new fiddle. In her mind's eye, she was already there, singing, dancing, and fiddling. In her journal, she excitedly jotted down lines or stanzas of ballads and lyrics that were slightly different from what she had heard before from Gracie and others.

As they munched on biscuits and cheese brought from home, the two of them wandered through the market and watched the ships coming and going with all manner of cargo.

One ship, in particular, captured Molly's attention. The cargo it was loading was not boxes, livestock, or pallets of goods. It was filling with people, what looked to be entire families and groups of friends. All of them had trunks and baggage. The ship was larger than most, with multiple masts and larger sails. Molly noticed covered shelter throughout the ship, as if the passengers intended on a long voyage.

Molly wondered out loud "Where do you suppose those ships and those families are headed?"

"These seem to be part of the large number of people headed to the new world, people leaving the islands for a new home… America. No doubt they hope for a life with better opportunities and perhaps more freedom. I know a number of families in and around Gweedore who are venturing there."

"Venturing?" asked Molly.

"Yes," replied Gracie. "By venturing, I mean daring to do something… daring to go somewhere… even if it involves dangerous or unpleasant risk. Of course, they don't plan on that… they trust that all will turn out well."

Rapidly, Molly fired off a list of questions. "How long does such a trip take, Gracie? Why do they want to go? And what is America like?"

"My, aren't we inquisitive?" Gracie mused. "Such deep questions for a young lady of fifteen," she chuckled.

"Well…from what I've been told, if things go well, the weather is good, and if the captain charts the proper course, it could take as little as a month. But that is not always the case… the weather is often bad out on the open ocean… on that Sea of Green Darkness, as I call it. Double that time may be a more realistic guess for such a venture."

"Why do they go?" Gracie repeated thoughtfully.

"As I've said before, child, the people of Scotland and those of us who are now here in our region of Ireland have not had an easy life. Sometimes it has been persecution for our faith, and at other times it has been economic difficulties. The Irish have never been the most favored people among the various heads of state. So, our natural inclination has always been to wander, always hoping and trusting for a place to lead our own lives and worship God in our own way. Perhaps that history is what has led to our hardness and durability, and what some would call our dourness as a people. We've learned to fight back when threatened and we have learned to endure hardships."

"So, what is America like? Well, Molly, I haven't been as you know, but I have heard the stories from some who have been and returned. And this much, I believe I can say for certain. America is a vast land, in terms of size, compared to what any of the European countries know. For those taking the risk, there is also vastness of opportunity, both in the large cities along the coast, and in the less inhabited lands, fertile lands that extend far, far beyond the coast. Some have told me that they see a similarity between the Scottish and Irish landscape and that of the new world. They feel comfortable there... it reminds them of home. Economic troubles here seem to be the primary reason for many to immigrate. But for me, Molly, America seems to be a wonderful opportunity where freedom of conscience is allowed, and where communities can be established free of repressive religious regulations that have plagued people here. I understand that entire congregations of Presbyterians are making the move to America."

Molly pondered all these answers to her questions, and, although she had more of them swirling around through her mind, she refrained from asking. She was itching to get her hands on her birthday fiddle and practice as Finn Clarke had demonstrated to her that morning.

"Are you ready to head home, Gracie?" Molly asked.

With a gleam in her eye, the old woman replied, "I'm ready if you are, my dear. Is it for my Irish stew and boxty cakes that you are looking forward to, or is it to hold your fiddle?"

"Both, I suppose," Molly answered.

Darren McCourtney had given them a ride into town in their wagon earlier in the afternoon, but they would have to walk back home. It was an uphill climb, so Molly started out, steadily, but slowly, stopping periodically for Gracie to rest a bit. On one of these stops, Molly asked her grandmother a question that had been troubling her since opening her present after breakfast.

"How could they afford such a gift, Gracie? Yes, I had dreamed of it, but didn't expect it. And it is not just a fiddle… it is as beautiful as any I have ever seen! You had told me yourself not to set my heart on such a gift, didn't you? How could I be so fortunate?"

Molly's grandmother knew the answer but was not sure how to go about telling her granddaughter. As Molly waited for a response, she looked deeply into Gracie's eyes, knowing that there was an explanation coming. Gracie began slowly, searching for the right words. "The gift is from all of us, Molly. Everyone contributed something, even little Patrick. But the truth is, I am the one who came across the instrument, and I am the one who insisted on it being yours. I'm reluctant to tell you this, because I do not want to demonstrate any pride or take away from the contributions of the rest of the family. It is from us all."

Gracie continued, "That day early in the summer when you shared your dream with me, I knew the fiddle was available. The pastor of my church had bought it at a shop in Galway over a year ago. It sat unused most of that time when he decided he did not have the time or inclination to learn it."

"Now, he did not tell me this, but I know that many in the church foolishly think of the fiddle as 'the devil's instrument.' Perhaps he didn't want to stir up a controversy among his parishioners… I really don't know. At dinner one evening with his family, he showed me the fiddle. I immediately thought of you and told him of your love for our ballads and music."

Gracie continued with feelings that Molly could tell, came from deep within. "Pastor Kevin asked a fair price, I'm sure, but it was still beyond my means. However, when you shared your dream with me, I knew I had to talk to your mother and father and go back and talk to Pastor Kevin. So, I gathered some savings, sold an item or two, and… let's just say, we worked out a deal!"

"Molly, your love for our musical heritage is a gift that must not be wasted. Whatever your family can do to foster that gift is worth it." Molly was overwhelmed as she pondered the sacrifice from her family that allowed her dreams to become reality. Gracie interrupted her thoughts, "Now, let's get back home and see if that stew is ready!"

Entering the cottage, Molly headed immediately for her room and pulled the fiddle from under the bed. The excitement she experienced as she slowly opened the case and gazed on the instrument was almost as strong as when she first opened it that morning. She worked her way through the scales and the melody of Barbry' Allen, as Liam's father had demonstrated. Somewhat scratchy and slightly off pitch, she had to admit, but after several times through, Molly could hear the improvement. In her head were the words of Finn Clarke from that morning. "Take it slow… get the finger position precise… treasure your fiddle." Molly was convinced that these words would guide her efforts for quite some time.

The birthday dinner was delicious, and the conversation was delightful. Gracie's stew and boxty cakes were much better fresh from the oven than reheated along the road as during their return from Gweedore in the early summer. Gracie had sewed a new dress for Molly. Her stories, especially about Kate's mischievous ways as a young girl, were always amusing to Molly and Patrick.

After several such stories, Kate insisted, "Enough, mother, enough. You are putting ideas into your grandchildren's minds that their father and I may not want!"

Darren McCourtney responded, "Actually, I like them. A side of young Kate Campbell that I never knew. Continue, please!" The whole family laughed heartily, and Gracie agreed to one more tale.

"Your mother sang quite well as a wee child and does to this day. I have a vivid picture in my mind of the first time she did so in public.

We had a yearly Irish Heritage Festival and your mother insisted that she would sing a verse or two of Lord Gregory."

Kate interjected, "We called it The Lass of Loch Royal, if I'm not mistaken."

"Yes, it is known by that name as well," acknowledged her mother. "So, young Kate Campbell stepped up on that platform and sang a verse or two, simply astonishing the crowd. And delighting them as well, I must say!" Gracie took Kate's hand and added, "Your father and I were so proud… until you tripped and stumbled off of the stage. I had never heard such screaming and squalling. I'm not certain, but you could not have been more than about four years old. It was a bit scary at the time, but after we were certain that there were no real injuries, it became quite the amusing story in our family over the years."

"Sing it now," begged Molly and Patrick. After several minutes of pleading, and only because Gracie agreed to join her, Kate and her mother began what turned into an evening of balladry.

Who will shoe my babe's little feet and who will glove your hand?
See, I will get a bonnie, bonnie boat, and I will sail the sea
And I will go to Lord Gregory, since he came home to me

Molly held her fiddle in her lap the entire evening, but only when they sang Barbry' Allen did she even attempt to play along. "The day will come, and sooner than you think," she promised, "when I will be able to play them all!"

Darren adjusted the two oil lamps as darkness fell and Molly laid her fiddle on the top of the table, still rubbing her hands across the smooth varnished surface and delighting in every detail. She tilted it at an angle so that the lamplight illuminated the inside of the instrument. Toward the base of the fiddle, and partially covered by decades of dust and grime, Molly could see what appeared to be a label of some kind with writing.

"Look," she called out. "There is a label inside… mother, do you have a small brush that I could use to clean it and see what is written?" Everyone in the house stopped what they were doing and gathered around the fiddle on the table, turning it one way and then the other, trying to cast more light on the writing.

"Try these," Kate said as she handed Molly a small wooden scraper and a long-stemmed brush.

Carefully, Molly scraped away and then gently brushed the label until the writing became more visible. "Luigi Caruso…" Molly whispered. "He must be the one who made my fiddle!" She handed the brush and scraper to her father because her hands were shaking so.

Darren began working carefully to expose more. "Boschetto Italy, 1720…" he read. "Almost fifty years ago, somewhere in Italy, an instrument maker crafted this fine piece… and now it is yours, Molly."

"Is there anything more?" Molly asked. Darren continued to gently brush away dust and dirt.

"Yes, but it is hard to read. It appears to just say "for Isabella."

So, for the remainder of the evening, the family pondered the origin of Molly's fiddle. But all they could do was speculate. There was no more information and no way to verify what they had discovered. Molly went to bed that night thinking not only about the wonderful gift tucked away in its case under her bed, but about its maker, its origins, it's very beginnings in another culture and another country. Her mind swirled with questions that she would never know the answers to. What were the first notes that came from her fiddle in 1720? Did Luigi Caruso know the ballads of the British Isles that so enamored her? Was her fiddle even meant to play the jigs and reels of Scottish and Irish dances? Or was his instrument made for another kind of music entirely? Most of all, Molly could not help but wonder if Luigi had loved this instrument as much as she surely did on this special day. In some strange way, Molly felt that she was now carrying on a legacy and had inherited not just a beautiful instrument, but a responsibility to its mysterious creator.

Before falling asleep, Molly recalled the events of the day in her mind, as she often did. But this had not been a normal day. Opening her present, the way she felt singing with Liam while his father brought music from her fiddle, the time alone with Gracie, watching families depart for America, and now, thoughts of an unknown Italian man in an Italian village who gave birth to her fiddle. "Certainly, this has been one of the most extraordinary days of my life," she thought as she drifted off to sleep. "Maybe there is something special about turning fifteen!"

CHAPTER 17

It was a cool and foggy Sunday morning in Letterkenny near the end of Gracie's first week with the McCourtney's. The family was finishing breakfast and preparing to head into town for church at their Presbyterian meeting house. It had been more than two years since Gracie last visited them here and she was anxious to see if their place of fellowship held to her high standards. Since her grandfather's time, when the impact of the Reformation had swept over Scotland, the family had held tightly to both Presbyterian polity and the Calvinist teachings of John Knox.

Molly's father had other, church-related, but less doctrinal matters, on his mind this particular morning as he dressed. Darren understood from conversations with several church leaders that their pastor, Thomas Durkin, would be addressing the question of members of their congregation immigrating to America. Darren was aware of such movements being taken by entire congregations in the past few years. Although his family's situation had been relatively stable raising sheep and selling small amounts of crops, Darren and others in similar situations saw small villages throughout Ulster gradually falling into decay with trade restrictions imposed by the crown. As farming declined in many rural areas, there was less need for laborers. These factors were leading many to respond to the stories of opportunity and prosperity in the new world. To make such a move as a group of like-minded believers and close neighbors was certainly preferable to traveling with strangers. Darren would listen closely this morning and have many discussions with his family and other church members about the matter.

As everyone was about ready to leave, Molly's mother called out, "Enough fiddling for now... it's time for church, Molly." Packing up her instrument, Molly slid the case under the bed and ran outside to join her family. The rain had stopped, but the fog still hung heavily along the river and through the town below them. Passing the Clarke cottage, Molly saw no activity and assumed they had already headed to church. She looked forward to seeing Liam and letting Mr. Clarke know of her progress on the fiddle. Molly had heard some of the discussion in the house about Pastor Durkin's announcement this morning, so she was anxious to hear more details about such a venture, if it were to become reality.

Pastor Durkin's sermon that morning was perhaps not as fiery or as lengthy as usual, but just as thoughtful and as stimulating as ever. He kept his focus on the text of the message, and, as she had been taught, Molly leaned over to look at her mother's Bible to see the passage for herself. The Presbyterian denomination as a whole, as well as each individual congregation, believed that each person could search for truth themselves through the reading and meditation on the message of the Bible. The church had a history of desiring to wipe out illiteracy so that an educated clergy would be guaranteed. In many ways, as Molly understood it, this separated their denomination from many others growing out of the Reformation and helped foster an independence that enhanced their Calvinist beliefs.

As Thomas Durkin concluded his sermon, he made a very short announcement about the question he would be addressing in a few minutes. He invited everyone to stay and hear the discussion, but he also made it clear that anyone who was not interested was welcome to leave. At that invitation, a few people, mostly the older congregants, chose to leave, many of the children went outside to play, and those remaining moved to the front, anxiously awaiting Pastor Durkin's remarks. The Clarke family moved over next to the McCourtney's, and Liam slid across the bench next to Molly. They exchanged a brief glance and smiles, causing Molly to hope that whatever came of today's meeting and discussion, their families would be in agreement.

"What I have to say today will not take long," Pastor Durkin began. "And I want all of you to know that I am only proposing an idea. This is, in no way, a directive on my part. It is simply a suggestion that the Elders of this congregation are in discussion about. But rather than having rumors swirling throughout Letterkenny, we want to address this openly now and to foster discussion as a body of believers. Every individual family must decide for themselves what is right – what is best – for them."

"During the past decade or two, tens of thousands of residents of Donegal and other counties of Ulster – some of them our own friends and family - have decided to make the challenging voyage across the Atlantic to America. You have heard some of the stories of those travels, and, like me, you are left to wonder about how much truth is contained in what you have heard. Some of what we have heard is about successes and accomplishment, while some is about failures and disaster. I don't stand here today before you to verify any of these stories. I have heard them as you have. I have seen the broadsides distributed near the docks, and seen the occasional letters that have come to families of those still here."

"Most of you are caretakers of small farms scattered throughout the countryside. My understanding is that there is great availability of fertile land beyond the coastal settlements in America. Many of our Presbyterian friends who have made the voyage have been able to establish their own settlements and their own places of worship. America seems to be a place where you can forge a livelihood from the land, and a place of opportunity for exercising our faith in freedom."

As she listened, Molly recalled the words Gracie had spoken to her a few days before, almost exactly the same as Pastor Durkin was speaking now. She also remembered her grandmother saying "our natural inclination" for centuries was to wander, hoping for the best place to lead our lives and worship our God as we see fit. What she was hearing from Pastor Durkin seemed so consistent with the words Gracie had said to her. Was this such an opportunity facing them now, being revealed before her?

Thomas Durkin continued. "I would ask all of you to consider this possibility and, of course, to pray that our Sovereign God would lead and guide us as individual families and as a congregation. I have asked a few of you and our congregation Elders to look into some of the logistics of such a venture if, in fact, we decide to do this. Things like the cost of the passage, finding an adequate boat with captain and crew, the proper time of year to depart… these are things that we are looking into and will be updating the congregation on. In addition, I would ask each of you to find as much reliable information as possible as you hear conversations in our town about such a move."

Molly heard a deep sigh from Liam, and, for the first time since their Pastor had begun talking, she turned to her friend to see if she could sense his thoughts about what was being proposed. There was an overall seriousness to his face, but also a slight grin as he looked at Molly. Was that fear or excitement in Liam's face? She couldn't tell for sure, but she suddenly realized that she felt both of those emotions churning within her. She could hardly wait for an opportunity to have a conversation with her parents, and with Liam about this possible life-changing adventure!

Pastor Durkin's next words abruptly brought Molly's mind back to the meeting. "I have one more thing to say before we open this up to your thoughts or questions. I am willing, as the leader of this congregation, to make the journey myself, ahead of any of you. There is value in this as you can probably see for yourselves. I could scout out the opportunities, the availability of land, and perhaps jobs to be had in the city of Philadelphia, where most Ulster Scots have arrived in America. I think there is a possibility that we would need to locate there temporarily before heading inland to our final destination. Once there, I would write back to you regularly and give counsel and advice about the voyage. This is a pattern that other congregations have followed since the migration to America began decades ago."

As Thomas Durkin finished and opened the opportunity for questions, Molly looked around, first at her own family, then at the friends, neighbors, and acquaintances that were all absorbing this proposal, each in their own way. Molly teared up as she looked down the pew and saw, in her grandmother's eyes, both sadness and fear, emotions that many of the older members were undoubtedly feeling. A long voyage on a crowded ship was fraught with potential danger. Anyone Gracie's age would have serious reservations about such a move.

The questions that were asked were ones that, at this point, no one had real answers for. There was lots of speculation given, stories about what people had heard, but facts were hard to come by. Pastor Durkin was patient, but firm, as time and again, he answered questions the same way, "We will find out more as we delve into the details."

There was a pause in the questions that led Molly to believe the meeting was ending. Then, much to her surprise, Liam rose and addressed Pastor Durkin and the congregation in general.

"I believe I am perhaps the youngest man remaining here for our meeting today, but I am trusting that this means I have a longer future ahead of me and, therefore, have more at stake regarding this proposal. If I could be certain of safe passage, a nice piece of farmland, freedom of worship, there would be very little choice for me. I would gladly go to America. But none of us can be certain, can we? The dangers are real, and the possibility of economic failure does exist. But then, I find myself asking, 'Do those risks not also apply here in Ulster?'"

Looking around at the members, at his own family, and one time directly at Molly, she was sure, Liam continued, more impassioned than before. "Friends, we take risks every day. We face dangers that could disrupt our lives in an instant, every one of us. We have only to review even our recent history to see what could await us here, in our home country. Crop failures on a regular basis, harsh winters that have taken a toll on your cattle, hundreds of thousands have died due to famine, land is becoming more and more scarce with rents rising beyond what many of you can afford, and the collapse of the linen industry in many places. Any of these could be our lot if we stay here and make what appears to be the "safe" choice."

"Pastor Durkin reminds us regularly to maintain our faith in the God of the Bible who, above all, loves us and will guide us into a future, either here in Ulster or in a new world across the Atlantic. Whatever choice we make, I believe it should be a quick one, and I for one would like to see our pastor go ahead of us, guided by our trust in him… and a deeper trust in God."

As he sat down, Molly was captivated. She could not take her eyes from Liam. Never had she seen her friend the way she saw him now. No one else in the congregation had been as thoughtful or mature, on either side of this question, as had Liam Clark. She glanced around the meeting house and saw that almost everyone seemed as captivated as she was, not only by his bold words, but by the maturity that they were seeing in him for the first time.

She found herself trying to remember, "Did Liam call himself one of the men?"

Pastor Durkin spoke directly to Liam. "Thank you for reminding us of the importance of placing our trust in Him as we think and pray through this decision, Liam." Molly noticed the pleased expression on Finn Clarke's face at the words his son had spoken. It was all Molly could do to keep from reaching over and squeezing Liam's hand as he sat down. How proud she was to have him, at that moment, as her friend!

Outside, Molly was anxious to talk to Liam, but several men of the congregation were gathered around him. Again, seeing him in conversation with the leaders of their church gave her a completely different perspective of Liam, and Molly admitted to herself that she was pleased! Darren and Kate were elsewhere on the church grounds, and Molly knew that they would soon be calling her to head home. She desperately wanted to speak to Liam before having to leave. A long conversation wasn't possible, but she did take the opportunity to step up behind him and touch his arm to get his attention.

"Excuse me for interrupting," Molly spoke to all of the men. Then, turning to Liam, "I just wanted to say I was never prouder to call you my friend, Liam Clarke. There is so much I want to talk to you about, so I will come over early this week if that is alright. Tell your father that while I'm there, I will gladly take another fiddle lesson."

"I believe tomorrow afternoon would be fine," Liam responded. He gave Molly a friendly hug, saying "Until tomorrow." Molly bounded across the church yard and around the building where Darren had left the wagon. "Until tomorrow," she called out to Liam over her shoulder.

CHAPTER 18

Molly had only two thoughts on her mind between leaving church and going to bed that evening. First, listening and joining in all of the family conversation regarding Pastor Durkin's comments at church and secondly, of course, practicing her fiddling. Nothing else seemed important on this day.

Darren McCourtney was generally a thoughtful and quiet man, and when there were serious matters to think about, these qualities were even more pronounced. Molly noticed those things in her father at the dinner table, perhaps more than she ever had before. When he finally began to talk openly, she knew that he had carefully considered his words.

"I believe that there are enough positive reasons for considering a move, and that having Pastor Durkin go ahead of any of the families is a wise thing to do. Perhaps a provisional count of those considering immigration would help the congregation decide whether or not to send him ahead. If, perhaps, half of the families were considering such a thing, that would be enough to collect some funds and send him off."

Gracie listened intently but Molly had not heard a word from her since breakfast that morning. Gracie's thoughts about ensuring that their church was up to her standards had long ago faded as this important question of immigration now was the central topic at hand. Darren's comments offered the opportunity for Gracie to join in.

"If such a provisional count were taken now…?" She did not have to finish the question, but all the family knew what the question was and wanted to hear the answer from Darren.

"I liked Liam's words in the meeting," Darren continued. "Of course, I would want to hear from each one here at the table, but I'm inclined to think this would be a good opportunity for our family. I suppose that means I would side in favor of such a move, depending, of course, on the reports and information we received back from Pastor Durkin."

Kate saw the tears welling up in her mother's eyes. Gracie simply could not withstand the weeks, perhaps the months, on the seas in a crowded ship. The thought of watching her family sail off and, in all likelihood, never to see them again, was disheartening. Kate did not want to contradict what her husband had said without having a chance to discuss it with him, so she simply gave a reassuring hug to her mother without saying a word.

Darren was sensitive to the impact of his initial thoughts, especially on Kate and Gracie, so he suggested that this was enough for tonight. "Think and pray as we move forward," he said, looking at each member of the family. "We need to share our thoughts on this matter with each other, so that we're together on this decision."

Then he added, "I will suggest to the church leadership that we have a provisional count after the service next Sunday. If Pastor Durkin is to go, it is best that he go before winter sets in. He has no family to prepare for, so he should be able to leave soon."

Then, in an effort to lighten the mood, Darren suggested, "One short ballad and everyone off to bed! Would our red-haired fiddler provide some music?" Molly skipped to the bedroom and within minutes the notes of Lord Gregory echoed through the cottage, and Kate and Darren waltzed while Patrick took his grandmother's hand and attempted to follow their steps. Some of their favorite lines seemed more significant on this night than ever before...

See, I will get a bonnie, bonnie boat, and I will sail the sea
And I will go to Lord Gregory, since he came home to me

Gracie Campbell could not withhold her emotions as she picked up Patrick and echoed the last line to her grandson…

Who will shoe my babe's little feet and who will glove your hand?
Who will kiss your ruby red cheeks when I'm in a far away land?

Molly slid under the covers in her bed that night thinking to herself, "I was part of an important family conversation this afternoon and I played my fiddle – the two things I was determined to do."

Her mother came in to say goodnight and sat on the bed. Looking across the room, she observed, "Your brother is already asleep, it seems. So, what are my Molly's thoughts on this proposed immigration?"

Molly had certainly not yet processed all she had heard today and told her mother so. "One thing I do hope and pray for, mother, is that the Clarke's will make the same decision. I would miss them terribly."

"All of them… or just one of them?" Kate questioned with a smile.

"All of them, somewhat," Molly responded, "but Liam most of all. He was so grown up with what he said at the meeting, wasn't he, mother?"

"Yes, he was," Kate agreed. "He is quite the special young man."

With those words and a good night kiss from Kate, Molly pulled the quilt over her head and dozed off to sleep. Fiddle music and ballads ran through her head and heart, but also thoughts of Liam Clarke.

CHAPTER 19

Molly was up early the next morning completing her list of chores out in the barnyard, opening the gate leading out into pasture for the sheep, and feeding Dundee. Then, she swept the kitchen as Kate had asked. Wrapping a sausage biscuit in a cloth and tucking it in the pocket of her dress, she grabbed her fiddle case from under the bed and skipped out the door, headed up to the rocky meadow. From this vantage point, Molly could see all the fence surrounding the pasture and make sure that there was no overnight damage to repair. She also looked over the herd to see that all the sheep were accounted for. Having taken care of these things, she knew that she could lie in the morning sun, watch the fog dissipate from along the river below her, journal a bit, and, most of all, play her music.

She was excited thinking about her visit to the Clarke farm in the afternoon and getting a few more fiddle instructions from Finn Clarke. Most of all, she wanted to have some time to talk to Liam about the possibility of immigration and the things he had said to the congregation yesterday. She hoped that he was not too busy with farm chores to be able to spend some time with her.

Lost in her thoughts, Molly wasn't aware of Gracie coming up the hill toward her. "Hello there, my child. I couldn't resist coming to your special place to watch the day begin. I thought I would find you here." Gracie sat down on a rock, looking out over Letterkenny and toward the Lough Swilly.

"I can see why you come here. If this were my home, I would no doubt do the same. Tell me, does your music sound any different in the out of doors than it does in the house?"

"I'll let you decide," Molly replied as she pulled out her fiddle. It was still a thrill for her just to open the case and see her instrument. Shining in the morning sunlight, it was even more beautiful. Molly turned to her grandmother and said, as she had dozens of times since her birthday, "Thank you, Gracie... I will treasure it always." She played a tune or two, ran through her two scales that Finn Clarke had showed her, and set it back in the case.

"Better every day, I do believe," Gracie complimented.

Molly could think of no way to avoid the question she had for her grandmother, or any indirect way to bring it up. She pondered the question and wondered in how many families throughout Ulster was the same thing being asked. How many of her friends in Letterkenny were looking at their parents, asking "Will we be one of those on the boats to the new world?" Taking a deep breath, she looked at Gracie, already guessing what the answer would be. "You won't go with us if we choose to leave for America, will you?"

"I would love to go with you, dear. I suppose you would want that as well?"

"Of course," Molly replied quickly. "Nothing would please me more. Nothing would please the family more... you know that don't you?"

"I know that, Molly, but look at me, child. I'm old and tired... set in my ways. As much as I love being here with you and your family for even a short visit, I miss my own home, my garden plot, my neighbors, and my church. I can't imagine months on a crowded ship, perhaps living in the city for a time, long wagon ride to a new home never to return to Donegal. I hope you understand that."

Molly hugged her grandmother's neck. "I don't think of you that way, Gracie... old, tired, or set in your ways. I don't ever want to think of you that way. I suppose that is why it is so hard for me to think about us being separated by an ocean."

"Listen to me, Miss Molly. I have friends who will look after me. I have a comfortable little cottage your grandfather left me. I have my church. But most of all, I have our Lord's protection. He will sustain me according to His mercy. And I don't want you or your family to forget that. Do you understand?"

Molly managed a "Yes ma'am," but she was not very convincing to herself, and probably not to Gracie.

"Letters travel across the Sea of Green Darkness, you know, Molly. And you can tell me in letters about all that is going on, and the progress on your fiddle, and the words to any ballads you hear." Gracie added, "And I will do the same… often."

Again, the two of them embraced and Molly realized that much of the morning had slipped away. Right after lunch, she would head across the meadow toward Liam Clarke's house. "Let's go back home," she said to Gracie as she began skipping down the hill. "I've got things planned for the afternoon!"

"My, what excitement," Gracie teased. "It must have something to do with that Liam Clarke!"

Blushing, Molly thought to herself, "Surely it isn't that obvious, is it?"

After eating, Molly headed to her bedroom, brushing her hair and putting a few flowers in her long braid. With her fiddle in hand, she headed out the door and up across the meadow. Darren McCourtney stood in the doorway watching Molly bounding up the hillside until she was out of sight. He continued his gaze until Kate's voice brought him out of his trance.

"What are you thinking," she asked her husband.

"Whether our daughter will ever again run toward me with that same excitement," he sighed.

"Yes, some day," Kate assured him. "Just not now."

Molly could see the Clarke barn as soon as she topped the hill out of sight of their own cottage. It was still too far away, however, to tell whether Liam was outside. Within a few minutes, she could see the empty barnyard and also notice that their wagon was not in its usual place. She gave her shrill whistle, which was the envy of every boy in school, but no one appeared. Molly walked around to the front door of the cottage and knocked. In a few minutes, the door opened, and Liam's mother appeared in the doorway. Shannon Clarke was, in Molly's eyes, one of the most beautiful ladies she knew, second only to her own mother. They looked a lot alike, Molly thought, except that Shannon's black hair revealed something other than a full Irish heritage.

"Why, Molly McCourtney and her fiddle! We hardly see one without the other these days." She gave Molly a hug, saying "Please come in. Liam and his father are in town but should be back soon. He told me to expect you and to not let you leave before they returned. I need an extra hand or two getting my dough ready for baking. I'll bet you can handle that?"

Molly was delighted knowing that Liam had mentioned her arrival to his mother. Equally delightful was helping Shannon in the kitchen. Just the two of them baking together was enjoyable... and special.

As they kneaded dough and made loaves, Shannon remarked, "I'm thinking that you have done this before with your mother. You're a great help, and I'll have to let Kate know that! Liam told me you were coming over, but he didn't tell me why. I assume, since you brought your fiddle, that you're wanting another short lesson from Mr. Clarke?"

"That's one reason I came by for certain," Molly replied. "I don't want to interfere with any work he has to do, but ten minutes of suggestions, at this point in my learning, can last for a long time!" Shannon Clarke let out a hearty laugh and Molly, without thinking, commented, "That sounds like Liam's laugh!" They looked at each other for a few seconds and then laughed together over what she had said.

"Please don't tell Liam what I said," Molly begged. Mrs. Clarke promised to keep it a secret, "just between the girls," as she called it. Molly was surprised but delighted to have a secret... "just between the girls."

"I want to talk to Liam about what he said in the meeting at church yesterday. It was so thoughtful and wise... I need to hear more from him, so that's why I asked if I could come over today. I hope he has some time to talk."

"I'm sure he will make the time," Shannon assured her. "All of our families faced with this decision need to talk it through with each other. Weighing both sides of the question is the only way to make the best choice. Along with prayer, of course. Liam is certainly correct when he says that it is the younger people who have the most to gain or lose... more at stake, I believe he said."

Shannon paused, and looking directly at Molly, she concluded, "The opinions of people like you and Liam need to be considered as our families wrestle with this decision. I'm glad you are here, Molly, and that the two of you will have a chance to talk."

Then, giving Molly a hug, Shannon said, "You know you are welcome here any time, Molly. We'll have to have your family over for dinner soon, so we can all talk about this. Now, let's get this bread in the oven before our men get home!"

Shannon's choice of words stopped Molly in her tracks. "Did she really say 'our' men?"

All of the loaves were made and in the oven when Molly heard the wagon outside. Liam and his father came in, in deep conversation about something they had seen or heard in town, but at the site of Molly in the house, along with the smell of baking bread, the mood shifted quickly.

The first greeting came from Finn Clarke. "Well, there's our red-haired fiddler. To what do we owe this visit?" he kidded.

"Molly has an open invitation from me," his wife chimed in. "And the bread you smell comes from both of our hands, so you can thank Molly for her assistance."

"I see that you brought your fiddle, so I'm assuming that you also came to show off your skills… or to get another quick bit of instruction. Am I right?"

"Yes, sir, you are right on the second part at least. I'll be glad to 'demonstrate' what I've learned, although I wouldn't call it 'showing off' in any way at all. A few more tips or bits of instruction would be wonderful. I promise I won't take much of your time." Molly responded gently.

"Can you stay for a bit of tea and this bread we made? I know, without asking, that the men are hungry. We'd love to have you stay."

Liam finally joined the conversation. "All of this talk about music and bread, when I thought, all along, that you were coming to see me!"

Although she could tell that Liam was joking with her, Molly did find herself a bit embarrassed. It must have shown, because before she had a chance to respond, Liam laughed and said, "I believe there is time for food, music, and banter," he grinned.

The bread, cheese, and tea were wonderful, along with the conversation among the four of them. Finn Clarke brought his fiddle out and he and Molly began. She played her scales he had taught her on her birthday and the simple ballads she had picked up on her own.

"Molly, you are a natural at this. Many young people would spend months trying to just get to where you are in a week."

She was thrilled at his compliments and Finn spent the next few minutes talking about and demonstrating the knack of two strings played together in harmony, sometimes sounding like the bagpipes that were so much a part of the music in the region. Then, examining her fiddle, Liam's father made an astute observation.

"Some previous owner of this instrument has 'flattened' the bridge from its original high curved arch so that catching two strings in harmony is easier."

Molly had not showed Liam or his family the label inside until now. Finn was excited to see this bit of the history of the instrument. "Certainly, Luigi Caruso had more classical music in mind when he created this in his shop in Italy. And here we are playing Irish jigs, reels, and ballads, music that perhaps he had never thought about or imagined in his life."

Molly pondered out loud. "Luigi Caruso... and Isabella, whoever she is... are probably no longer living, but his music and the sound - some call it the 'voice'-of his fiddle will endure through whoever plays it and wherever it is played. I feel almost as if he is watching over my shoulder, that I owe him something. It is as though I have a responsibility to play it well."

Looking at the others, Molly asked "Is that a foolish thought?"

"I think it is a lovely and mature thought," Shannon Clarke responded quickly, then added "from a lovely and mature young lady."

"I couldn't agree more, mother," Liam answered. Hearing these words from him touched Molly.

She carefully returned her fiddle to its case and then said, "Let's see, we had tea... played music... now wasn't there some other reason for my being here?"

Liam played along with Molly. "Well, you said you wanted to talk to me, remember?"

So, the two friends headed outside in the warm sun and sat on a bench in the edge of the pasture. Molly knew that her favorite spot in the high meadow was a perfect place for such discussions. It was about halfway between the McCourtney and Clarke cottages and she longed to show it to Liam someday. For today's conversation, however, this spot would be just fine.

Molly began, "What you said in the meeting yesterday has been rolling around in my mind and I need to hear more. I believe you have given this a great deal more thought than just the things you said in church. I'd like to hear some of those thoughts… anything, that is, you are willing to share with me. Is that fair to ask?"

"Of course, it is fair," Liam responded. "But there may be less than you think other than what I said." He took a deep breath and, as he spoke, he looked off in the distance and then deeply into Molly's face. "As I tried to say yesterday, I'm just aware that, at our age, there are decisions to be made that will affect the rest of our lives. Some of those are risky – like moving across the ocean to a new land and new life - but staying could be risky as well."

"Our age…!" he had said, just like his mother a while ago! From that point on, Molly found herself unnecessarily focused on the fact that Liam was including her in his thought process.

He continued, "I know it has only been a day, but I have been aware of this great migration for quite a while. I've heard men in town talking about it, so I've been contemplating the idea. I'm willing to take the risk, Molly. I believe our family is willing. I know that each family must decide for themselves, so I don't want to influence anyone else's choice."

"That being said, Molly, I would be so disappointed if your family decided otherwise."

"Yes, so would I, Liam. We have had one discussion – at dinner last night – involving the whole family and I can tell you that my father is going to suggest a provisional count next Sunday to see how many families are leaning in the direction of immigration. If perhaps half of the families are, then he will suggest that we send Pastor Durkin before winter sets in."

"I'm encouraged that Darren McCourtney and I see this the same way."

"Your words yesterday made sense, Liam. They were thoughtful and mature. My parents said so... 'He is quite the special young man' is, I believe the way my mother put it!"

"And you agreed with her, I hope?" "Yes, I agreed," Molly answered, then added "We'll talk again about this?"

"Yes, any time. You are welcomed to come any time."

"I know," Molly responded with a grin, "Your mother already made that clear!"

Across the field, Molly skipped, red hair flying behind her and fiddle case in hand. She didn't stop running until she reached home. Running around the corner of the cottage, she met Gracie in the yard.

"How was your fiddle lesson, or perhaps I should ask first, how was Liam," she questioned.

"Both were wonderful," Molly responded gleefully.

"Before you go inside, let me tell you that I had the same conversation with your mother that you and I had in the meadow this morning. I don't think I should attempt such a trip. Kate understands, Molly, but it would still not be an easy thing to separate." Then Gracie added, "As I think about this more and more, I do believe it is the right thing for your family to do."

Walking inside, Molly could tell that her mother had been crying. Without a word, she walked across the kitchen and the two enjoyed a long embrace. Tears flowed in the McCourtney cottage and in other cottages throughout Letterkenny during those days as scores of families wrestled with this crucial, life-changing question.

After drying her tears, Molly strolled back out in the warm sun. To anyone who happened to be listening, she called out, "I need to learn some happy fiddle tunes!"

CHAPTER 20

The McCourtney's had a few other discussions as a family through-out the rest of the week, and Molly visited Liam after each one to share any new thoughts that she had. Darren had managed to talk to Thomas Durkin and the other Elders and convince them to support his idea of a provisional count after church to determine how many families may be contemplating a move.

Gracie had been with the family over two weeks and was a bit anxious to get back to "her own life" as she called it, in Gweedore. Alex Gallagher had another trip that way in a few days and he could accom-modate getting her home. Kate and Darren assured her that they would keep her advised of any plans and that they would spend as much time as possible with her.

On her last morning in Letterkenny, before Alex Gallagher came by to pick her up, Gracie and Molly were among the rocks in the high meadow, talking and, of course, singing. Suddenly, Gracie exclaimed "I forgot to tell you of a new tune I heard yesterday when I was at the market with Kate. I walked over to the village green and heard this. Appropriate for these times, I believe you will agree."

> I am a rambling Irishman, it's Ulster I was born in
> And many's the happy hour I spent on the banks of Lough Erne
> Ah, but to live poor I could not endure like others of my station
> To America I sailed away and left this Irish nation

Molly wrote down the verses in her journal as her grandmother sang "The Rambling Irishman," although Gracie was unsure of some of the words. "You'll have to go to the village green and find the one who sang it to be sure of the lyrics." Molly was anxious to share this new song of America with Liam and his family.

Darren had to be in town this morning and miss Gracie's departure, but Kate and the children helped her in the wagon where Alex had put some extra quilts for cushioning. They said their goodbyes, promising once again to keep Gracie updated and to arrange for another visit soon.

The following Sunday, Molly donned her new birthday dress, brushed her hair, and hurried ahead of the rest of the family to church. Word had spread through Letterkenny about the question of immigration that would be asked, so the meeting house was close to full before the service began. Scanning the congregation, she spotted Liam and slid across the bench next to him.

"What do you think the count will be?" she asked anxiously.

"What count?" Liam joked. "I'm just here for the sermon!" Molly gave him a playful thump on the shoulder, saying "You know very well what count I'm referring to, Liam Clarke! Now what do you think?"

"From what I've heard, and looking around at the size of the crowd, between one third and one half, I believe."

"And don't you look grand in your new dress! Somehow, it makes you look older. Gracie chose just the right material." Molly shook her head in agreement. Shannon Clarke leaned out from her seat and whispered, "I love the way your new dress matches your beautiful red hair, Molly!"

Molly could hardly keep her mind focused on Pastor Durkin's message. She spotted her family and caught Kate's glance in her direction. Molly knew that only because of the packed meeting house and the fact that she had arrived early was she sitting anywhere other than next to Patrick and her parents. Her mother smiled, so Molly knew that she was not displeased with their seating arrangements. Of course, it all suited Molly fine.

When the last hymn was sung and the benediction given, Pastor Durkin, as he had last week, invited anyone who wished to leave to do so. Molly did not turn around to observe, but she sensed that very few people left. Immigrating or not, everyone in their congregation had a stake in what was about to happen!

Thomas Durkin made few remarks and emphasized again that he would respect each family's decision on this matter and reminded everyone that this was simply a provisional count that would help determine what steps to take.

"How many families are considering such a move and would support sending a small group – perhaps only me – ahead to scout out the travel, land, location? One hand per family." The Elders walked among the benches and determined that about twenty families had made this provisional commitment. This was well over half of those in attendance. Those twenty families totaled about ninety individuals.

Darren McCourtney stood and made a motion instructing Pastor Durkin to leave as soon as feasible to avoid the oncoming winter weather. He also suggested that an offering be taken each of the weeks before Pastor Durkin's departure to help defray his costs. After overwhelming agreement was determined, the meeting was adjourned.

"One step closer to our travels to America," Liam said. Molly nodded in agreement, but to herself, she said… there's that word again… 'our.'" Out in the church yard, when she had Liam's attention, Molly started singing her new ballad to him without any introduction.

> *I am a rambling Irishman, it's Ulster I was born in*
> *And many's the happy hour I spent on the banks of Lough Erne*
> *Ah, but to live poor I could not endure like others of my station*
> *To America I sailed away and left this Irish nation*

Liam stopped and looked at her. "What's that? A new song about America? Aren't you getting ahead of yourself?" Liam exclaimed. Molly laughed and promised to teach him the rest of the ballad when she saw him next.

"I have an idea," Liam proposed. "Why don't I come to your house the next time."

"Even better, meet me in the rocky meadow I've told you about, Molly suggested.

"We have some work to do around the barn for a couple of days. Could I come on Wednesday?"

"That would be lovely. Meet me at noon and I'll bring a picnic... you bring dessert!"

"Agreed... I'll see you on Wednesday, Molly... and I do love your new dress!"

Molly blushed and headed through the lingering crowd to catch a ride home with her family.

Throughout the afternoon, Molly practiced the "double stops" as Finn Clarke had shown her. He was correct that, when this technique was applied to the lower notes, there was a sound strangely reminiscent of bagpipes. Molly had heard the pipes only a few times during celebrations or holiday festivities. She was particularly fond of the harmonies she could create on the middle or high notes, and she worked tirelessly to incorporate these into some of the slower pieces she was learning.

Shortly after breakfast the next morning, Molly asked her mother, "Can you teach me to make potato scones?"

Kate was curious at such a request. "Now why would my girl suddenly show such an interest? And, by the way, the proper name is 'tattie scones.' That is what my mother calls them. I haven't made or eaten them in quite a few years."

"Well... Liam and I are meeting at my spot up in the high meadow on Wednesday, and I agreed to bring a picnic. He's providing dessert, although I'm pretty sure that Mrs. Clarke will be the one preparing it!

This is, of course, if it is alright with you and father." Molly quickly added, "Any chores that need to be done I will take care of beforehand."

"I wouldn't put it past that young man to make the dessert himself… under Shannon Clarke's watchful eye! I see no problem with that but check with your father. I believe I can remember how to make them. Can you wait until this afternoon?"

"Yes… I'll go find father and make sure it is alright with him."

The tattie scones Molly and her mother made that afternoon were the highlight of the evening meal, so Molly was excited to make a batch of her own Wednesday morning to take on the picnic up in the meadow.

"Suppose Liam doesn't take a fancy to potato scones?" her father asked after finishing his second helping.

"I've heard him say they were his favorites… at least the one's his grandmother used to make," Molly replied. "So, I hope these are just as good as hers!"

"I'll bet they will be," Kate chimed in.

Wednesday morning could not come fast enough for Molly. She was out in the barnyard early, gathering eggs and letting the sheep out into the meadow. Kate asked her to sweep out all the rooms in the cottage and fill the oil lanterns. That being done, Molly began carefully following the directions for making the tattie scones and, although the first batch were not quite as golden brown as she'd hoped, she perfected the process, and the remainder came out beautifully brown and crisp.

"These will be wonderful with a block of Irish cheddar and a jar of jam just in case Liam forgets his part of the bargain… the dessert," Molly chuckled out loud.

She brushed her hair one last time, put on her favorite dress, and packed the food in a wicker basket. Grabbing her fiddle, she said goodbye to her mother and headed up the hill. She was somewhat early but wanted to have everything ready when Liam arrived. She had brought her mother's favorite quilt, a classic Celtic design of chains and crosses in shades of blue. Many of the ladies called it simply an Irish chain quilt. As she reached the rocks and began spreading out the covering, she was startled by a voice from the other side of the rocks.

"You're late," laughed Liam.

Molly quickly replied, "No, you are early,"

"I've been looking forward to seeing this place I've heard you talk about, so I just couldn't wait any longer. Besides, the shortbread I baked is still warm… much better that way!"

Molly could not restrain herself and flashed a wide grin. Smelling the short bread, she questioned Liam. "Did you really bake this? Now tell the truth, Liam."

"Under my mother's watchful eye," he admitted.

"Just as mother predicted," Molly laughed. Then she pulled out the plate of scones. "They're not still warm, but I believe I heard you say they were among your favorites?"

"Oh, yes… But I think you should try just a bite of shortbread while it is still warm."

"Oh, Liam… this is wonderful. It tastes just like my grandmother's!" Liam's reaction startled Molly. He laughed and laughed, again reminding her of Shannon Clarke's laugh. "What is so funny about that?" she demanded.

"It tastes like hers because I used her recipe!" Liam laughed again. "I had a chance encounter with Gracie down along the docks a week ago, and we saw someone selling shortbread at the market. One thing led to another, and I found out how much you liked her version, and so she gave me the recipe."

"Enough of just sampling and nibbling. Help me spread out this quilt and let's have a picnic!" Liam noted the beauty of the quilt and the two friends began enjoying their food. The weather could not have been more perfect.

"Potato scones and cheese! A great combination on this beautiful day. Thanks for inviting me here, Molly." Then, looking across Letterkenny and somewhat lost in thought, Liam asked "Can you imagine what our lives will be like outside of this town we've grown up in?"

Molly wasn't sure if that was just a thought that he had expressed, or whether Liam really expected an answer from her. "So, do you want my opinion or my dreams? Some of both, I presume?" Liam nodded in agreement.

"I guess that many of my thoughts and dreams will be based on the letters the congregation receives from Pastor Durkin. If he has a good voyage, finds adequate land for a settlement, and encounters no particular difficulties, then that will become, in my mind, what we can expect or dream to be our own experience. I understand that things could be very different, but the descriptions he sends back to us will form the pictures of America in my mind."

Molly continued, "In my dreams, America will be, a least in some ways, like this region of Ireland. More forests, as I understand it, but lots of hills and even mountains inland from the coast. When I close my eyes, I see green… I can't imagine a countryside that is anything other than green." Then, closing her eyes, and cupping her hand to her ear, Molly laughed out loud, "Oh, and I hear fiddle music! There will be fiddle music, I'm certain! If only what I bring myself!" In a more serious tone, she continued, "Having never been in a large city, I can't imagine what Philadelphia will be like. Most people seem to think that is the best place of arrival, and perhaps we'll have to stay there at least long enough to secure the necessities for traveling to our new home place."

"And your visions and thoughts about it all?" she asked as she turned to Liam.

"As far as my vision of the rural countryside, it is much like yours, Molly. Surely America is a wonderful place of opportunity and freedom. So many of our Ulster neighbors would not have gone otherwise, do you think?"

Liam continued, "I am most worried about the voyage itself. In a vessel filled with people, there is such danger of sickness. If we're a month or more on the ocean, we will surely have our share of bad weather. These things do concern me somewhat and that is why we're being told by church members and our own families, to be constant in our prayers, and to seek God's protection."

There was a pause in the conversation, Molly leaning against the largest rock, and Liam lying on the quilt. As they enjoyed the warm afternoon sun and the last bit of shortbread, Molly began to think about the last stanza of "The Rambling Irishman" that Gracie had taught her before she left. She had not shared that part of the song with Liam. She picked up her fiddle and worked out the melody, then began to sing...

Ah, but when we reach the other side, we'll both be stout and healthy
We'll drop our anchor in the bay going down to Philadelphy
Let every lass link with her lad, blue jacket and white trousers
Let every lad link with his lass, blue petticoats and white flouncers

Liam sat up abruptly and turned toward Molly. "I can't believe how those words and those you shared with me on Sunday from that ballad fit all that is going on in this season of life that we find ourselves in!"

"Quite remarkable, isn't it?" Molly smiled.

As the two friends cleaned up the remains of their meal and prepared to go their separate ways, Liam could not resist asking Molly one more time to sing the last stanza so that he could get the words and tune clearly in his mind."

"What a beautiful song, Molly." Liam paused before his next words poured out from deep within him. "Who are they?"

"What do you mean?" Molly asked.

"The lad and the lassie in those last lines. Linked together... If this song fits our current season of life, as we just said, Molly, then who are they... the lad and lassie in their fine clothes?"

Molly was uncertain how to respond. She found herself stammering and searching for a response. "I... I don't know for sure... Could it be the two of us? You and me... someday? I guess it could be, couldn't it ... Would that be alright with you?"

Liam reached out and took Molly's hands in his, "It would be fine with me, Molly. It would be absolutely fine... someday."

The two friends parted ways, each running toward their own homes and their own families. Both of them realized that their lives were changing, not just because of the possibility of joining the great migration to America but changing as their friendship was growing deeper than either of them had ever dreamed.

CHAPTER 21

Within two weeks, Thomas Durkin boarded *The America*, a sailing vessel that had successfully completed over a dozen voyages to the new world in the past decade. As was usually the case, the ship left Londonderry with close to one hundred passengers, bound for Philadelphia and returned with just a few passengers, but carrying a wide variety of cargo, including flax seed for the Irish linen industry.

In Letterkenny, the congregation of the Presbyterian meeting house marked the days and waited anxiously for some news about Pastor Durkin's travels. Each family that had raised their hands at the meeting the previous month was making provisional plans for this most important decision. What necessities did they have to take with them? What items could they not part with? If fortunate enough to own their house and property, how would they best dispose of it? New questions seemed to arise every day and, at the end of the day, it seemed there were always more questions than answers.

The Clarke and McCourtney families wrestled with the same matters as everyone else. Molly and Patrick each had a large trunk and were told that everything they would take must fit in that trunk and would be stored in the ship's cargo hold for the duration of the voyage. One satchel or item in each hand would hold everything they needed on a day-to-day basis. Molly had no doubt what one of those items in her hands would be. She had already heard stories about music and dancing on these ships to pass the time on the tedious and monotonous trip. Kate thought mostly about cookware and kitchen items, while Darren's concern was related to tools.

Throughout the autumn months, Molly felt as though she was living in two worlds. School lessons, church, and her chores around the farm went on as usual, as if nothing was changing. The other world, of course, was all about change and leaving behind everything she had ever known, going to a new life in a new, and unknown place. Her head swirled with the thoughts of these things, keeping her tossing and turning many nights.

One of the things that most pleased Molly and Liam was that their families were planning this possible migration together. Regularly, the Clarke's and McCourtney's were getting together and discussing how to combine or share the items they may take on the voyage, offering suggestions, and sharing any bit of information they had heard along the docks of Letterkenny. Finn and Darren would spend their time in the barns looking at common tools, while Shannon and Kate did the same in the kitchen. Without a doubt, the families were in this together. Molly and Liam could not be more delighted.

One Sunday morning in mid-autumn, Molly was working on a few fiddle tunes that she had added to her repertoire recently, along with a hymn or two which her father insisted on since it was, after all, the Lord's Day. The first wintery weather had arrived early in this part of Ulster. Darren was out in the pasture making a quick repair to a section of fence that had fallen during the night. He came in the cottage with a dusting of snow on his hat, stomped his boots, and hurried across the room to the warmth of the fireplace.

"I saw Finn Clarke out in the pasture mending the same section of fence, so we got it repaired together quickly. He tells me that a letter from Pastor Durkin came yesterday. We'll get the details at church, I'm certain."

Molly came bounding from the bedroom at the news, "Let's go," she cried out.

The family bundled up for the wagon ride down the hill and into town to the meeting house. The snow continued blowing across the grassy meadows, but the sun came out occasionally as well. It was, for certain, the most blustery and wintery day this autumn. Arriving at church, Molly could sense the excitement and anticipation. It was obvious that word had traveled throughout town about the letter from Thomas Durkin.

She scanned the crowd, spotting the Clarke family, and motioned for the rest of her family to hurry along. Molly moved across the bench, saving room for the rest of the McCourtney's, and sitting directly behind Liam. She leaned up close to him and began to quietly hum the tune to "the Rambling Irishman." Liam turned around and grinned, giving her a stern, but friendly "shhhhhh."

The church elders knew that there was little hope in keeping the congregation's attention for a sermon of normal length. A few hymns were followed by prayers for Pastor Durkin and a short message, appropriately focused on the wise and holy providence of God and his direction in all actions and all things in the lives of his children. The elders took seats at the front of the congregation and began...

"Pastor Durkin has arrived safely in America. And for that alone, we can thank God. As expected, he landed in Philadelphia, the largest city in the new world, with a population in excess of 30,000. He spent several weeks getting as much information and answering as many of our questions as possible before sending this letter, dated six weeks ago. We will summarize the news that seems the most relevant, although anyone who desires to read the letter in its entirety is certainly welcome to do so."

This was exactly what Molly wanted to hear. She was much more interested in the answers to questions than the formality of the letter. Of course, the primary thing to her, and to most of those considering the move, was whether or not Pastor Durkin supported their immigration. If so, there was little doubt about what her future held.

"Pastor Durkin's voyage to America was slightly over a month in duration, with only one significant storm. There was a fair amount of sickness and, unfortunately, one death, but no serious outbreaks of disease. The crowded conditions were obviously challenging and any who make the voyage must be prepared to endure this. He tells us that music helped pass the days."

"He did not spend too much time in the city before venturing out to the vast rural areas further inland, assuming that would be the area most appealing to our group of people. If we need to stay in the city for an extended length of time, there seem to be ample opportunities for temporary employment."

"Let me read one section of his letter that is perhaps the most enlightening for most of us. Pastor Thomas writes…"

> As I traveled beyond Philadelphia, I followed the wagon road out to the great valley beyond the Blue Ridge. You cannot imagine the vastness of this land. The valley is the widest and most fertile of any that I have ever seen. There is a diversity of kinds of landscapes and extensive tracts of rich land. Part of the beauty is found in the trees that remain standing on many hillsides. These contrast to the lush green meadows and fields below. The wagon road takes travelers and settlers southward into areas where Virginia is encouraging new settlement. Land can be purchased, rivers are abundant, and many of our Ulster neighbors have begun establishing themselves into communities that we could certainly join. The number of Presbyterian churches being established in the valley is increasing as more Ulster Scotts arrive. I suggest a spring departure.

Whatever else was read that day from Thomas Durkin's first letter from America, Molly wasn't listening. She had heard the things she needed to hear. The land was vast and rich and fertile. There were rivers and others from Ulster… and it was lush and green! She closed her eyes and saw America the way she dreamed. She would be part of those bringing music to the new world. Most of all, she was certain that Liam would be there. Surely their families would take the vision that had been cast today in Thomas Durkin's letter and make it their own. After a closing prayer, church adjourned, and Molly leaned forward toward Liam, whispering *"when we reach the other side, we'll both be stout and healthy."* Liam finished, *"We'll drop our anchor in the bay going down to Philadelphy."*

That afternoon and evening, there were gatherings of families all over Letterkenny agreeing that the report from Pastor Durkin was the confirmation they needed to take this leap of faith. At the Clarke household, the McCourtney's and several other families came together and arrived at the same conclusion. The winter months would be spent taking care of all of the necessary preparations for a spring departure.

Kate McCourtney agreed with the decision, but knew that a visit with her mother was at the top of her priorities before leaving. Though she had discussed this all with Gracie and had come to terms with leaving her behind, she was still dismayed at the prospect. Darren agreed that they could make one quick overnight visit before winter set in just to tell her in person of their final decision. Hopefully, in the spring they could spend a longer time with her before their voyage.

CHAPTER 22

A warm spell set in two weeks later, and, with no apparent prospect of worsening weather, the McCourtney's decided to make the trek to Gweedore. They departed after breakfast and arrived at Gracie's cottage in the early afternoon. They were not able to get word of their trip to her, so Gracie was surprised and delighted when she saw Molly and Patrick running through the yard toward her front door. Darren was unhitching the horses from the wagon, but Kate hurried to the cottage behind the children. Long embraces followed.

Finally collecting herself, Gracie exclaimed, "What a delightful surprise… and I assume there must be a special reason for your visit?"

Kate began tearing up, as she expected, at her mother's question. "We have made the decision to travel to America with twenty or so families from our congregation… I had to tell you in person, mother. We will leave in the spring."

"I expected as much," Gracie replied.

Molly did not see sadness or disappointment in her grandmother's face, but resolve and serenity. She knew that this would not be an easy time, but she remembered their earlier conversation… Gracie had friends, her church, her home and garden. Molly could tell that her grandmother was not happy but settled with the idea.

Over a pot of Irish stew that Kate had brought with them, along with fresh bread from Gracie's oven, the family talked until late in the evening about their plans. Darren and Kate shared what they had learned from Pastor Durkin's letter and their sense that this was all being orchestrated in some Divine way. "Moving with our congregation and having

Pastor Durkin there ahead of us makes the whole experience much more comforting" Kate confessed. "There are entire communities in the inland parts of the new world where the people of Ulster have been settling and establishing Presbyterian congregations. The land is rich and fertile."

"Lush and green, Pastor Durkin called it," Molly interjected into the conversation. Then, tapping her hand on her fiddle case, she added, "And there is music… on the ship, and what others, like me, are bringing with them!"

"Speaking of music, do you think we would wake up Patrick with a ballad or two? I believe he's been asleep since he curled up an hour ago in the quilt on the bedroom floor.

"He'll sleep right through it," Kate responded.

As Molly pulled out her fiddle, tuned it, and rosined the bow, Gracie asked with twinkling eyes, "And your friend, Liam? What are the Clarke family's plans for this venture?"

"Oh, yes, the Clarke's will be going as well!" Molly replied.

"Remember 'The Rambling Irishman' that you heard along the docks when you were in Letterkenny? That seems to be our favorite right now. It's a part of who we are!"

"Who is this 'Our' and 'we' you are talking about?" Gracie asked.

"I've just been teaching it to Liam and we sometimes sing it together." Gracie replied with a smile "I wondered if that was what you would say…" Together, they all sang…

I am a rambling Irishman, it's Ulster I was born in
And many's the happy hour I spent on the banks of Lough Erne
Ah, but to live poor I could not endure like others of my station
To America I sailed away and left this Irish nation
Ah, but when we reach the other side, we'll both be stout and healthy
We'll drop our anchor in the bay going down to Philadelphy
Let every lass link with her lad, blue jacket and white trousers

Let every lad link with his lass, blue petticoats and white flouncers

As was usually the case when they visited Gracie, the family made pallets of quilts near the fireplace. Although the stone floor of the cottage did not provide the same comfort as her own bed, Molly always slept well at Gracie's house. There was a different kind of comfort here, built around family and the heritage of her Irish roots that she did not feel as strongly anywhere else.

Darren helped Gracie with a few things around the house and took the opportunity to tell her that they expected her for a longer visit in the spring and would like her to be there to see them off on their voyage. Kate packed some bread and cheese for the trip back home and kissed her mother goodbye. Patrick and Molly did the same as Darren called out that the team was hitched up and ready to go. Gracie stood at the cottage door, watching her family ride down the lane and over the hills toward home.

"Only once more," she thought, "Will I get to say goodbye."

CHAPTER 23

Winter was relatively mild around Letterkenny, with only one significant snow that slowed down the family's activities and their preparations for the voyage. Friends and neighbors throughout the surrounding area, as well as other church members who were not leaving bought surplus items, helping them with the cost of the voyage. The McCourtney and Clarke families were more fortunate than many in that they owned their homes and properties. Darren and Finn had come up with the idea of trying to sell their adjacent farms as one, hoping to find a buyer more easily. Soon after announcing their parcels for sale, a church member made them an offer that would cover the cost of immigration, with hopefully enough remaining to buy supplies once they arrived in America.

A ship and crew had been secured. *The Allegheny* had carried several loads of passengers to America and would arrive in the harbor around the middle of March, leaving a week later, so as to give the passengers ample time to finish up packing before setting sail. Every ship that came up the River Swilly from the ocean and anchored at Letterkenny's docks gained the full attention of those in town. "Will our ship be larger or smaller? Will its sails look the same?" These were topics of conversation to all those who were bound for the new world.

Liam was bundled up along the docks one blustery day in early March when he spotted a ship coming along the river. As it dropped anchor and the crew began to depart, stacking goods and supplies along the dock, the word quickly spread that this was, in fact, *The Allegheny.* Liam finished his tasks, jumped into the wagon, and headed toward his house. Finn Clarke was working in the barn and Liam ran in to tell him the news.

"It's our ship… *The Allegheny,* he cried!" Can I take the wagon over to the McCourtney's to let them know?" Finn Clarke agreed but warned his son to hurry back. "There is work we need to finish here!"

Molly was out in the field helping her father when Liam arrived. He ran to the front door where Kate reacted by giving Liam a big hug. "I guess it is real after all, isn't it? I will pass the word along to the rest of the family."

Both homes, and many others in Letterkenny were filled with activity and excitement that evening and throughout the week. Molly and Patrick could hardly get to sleep and talked until long after the time they were normally sound asleep. Molly had a number of questions of her own, although most of the answers had come over the winter months. Patrick, however, was filled with questions that neither Molly, or anyone else had answers for. So much was still speculation. "How deep is the ocean? Will we encounter pirates? Will I get seasick? What if the boat springs a leak?" These questions and dozens more gushed forth until Molly was sound asleep and stopped answering them.

Kate's mother had arrived just a few days before, thanks to Alex Gallagher. It seemed that everyone in Letterkenny with any connection to the immigrating families was doing their best to help. Alex was certainly no exception to this as he had already promised the McCourtney's that he would take Gracie back to Gweedore as soon as the ship departed.

Molly and Patrick spent as much time as possible with their grandmother the last days before the voyage. Tears flowed freely before, during, and after songs and stories shared among the family. No one dared say the words on their last evening together, but everyone, even Patrick, was keenly aware that the likelihood of ever seeing each other again in this life was slim. Before retiring for the evening, they circled around the table, Darren leading in a prayer for protection and, as always, for the sovereign will of God to prevail in their lives. As Darren ended, but before they unlocked their hands, Gracie offered, in her thickest Scottish accent, the lyrics of a Robert Burns poem in song...

Should auld acquaintance be forgot, and never brought to mind?
Should auld acquaintance be forgot, and auld lang syne
For auld lang syne, my jo, For auld lang syne,
We'll take a cup o' kindness yet for auld lang syne.

The McCourtney's slept in their cottage for the last time that night. As always, Molly had music, lyrics, and ballads swirling in her head. But her last thoughts as she dozed off for the night were of Liam. Their adventure to America would begin in the morning!

It seemed that more than half the town came out on the March morning to say goodbye, offer prayers, and watch *The Allegheny* leave the port of Letterkenny, bound for America. The large trunks were packed and re-packed until nothing more could possibly fit. The ship's crew and many of the men making the voyage carried the trunks up the gangplank and down into the ship's cargo hold where they would remain until arriving in Philadelphia.

Long embraces and farewells ended as the passengers walked up onto the ship. Unexpectedly, merchants in stores along the docks emerged onto the streets cheering and applauding loudly for their friends who would be taking their Irish heritage to a new land. The McCourtney's gave Gracie one final collective hug and turned to head up onto *The Allegheny*.

"Where is my satchel to carry on board?" Molly cried out frantically.

"Don't worry, I've got it here." Liam answered, his hand outstretched to hers. "*Shall we board our bonnie, bonnie boat and shall we sail the sea?*"

"Yes, we shall," Molly answered. And with one hand firmly grasping Luigi Caruso's fiddle, and the other in Liam Clarke's hand, the two young people and their families joined the great Irish migration to America.

PART 3

Crossing the Sea of Green Darkness c. 1761

Beginning in 1717 and about every decade until the American Revolution, wave after wave of Ulster Scotts, a quarter million in all, took a risk and made the voyage to America. In 1729, one Pennsylvania official wrote of six ships of Irish immigrants arriving in one week, with two or three more every day the following week. Both looming peril and exciting possibilities faced all these Irish immigrants who confronted the new American frontier, hoping to escape either economic hardships, or facing religious persecution.

Those who made the voyage later in the period, such as the passengers leaving Letterkenny, were traveling at the height of the age of the sailing vessel. They were prone to be better off financially and better educated than earlier immigrants. This also made it more likely that they would not find themselves sailing as indentured servants, with years of work awaiting them as payment for the voyage.

Thomas Durkin's second letter from America to his parishioners arrived after The Allegheny had set sail. This time, their Pastor's letter contained more descriptions of the landscape, rich soil, and religious tolerance, but also many more details about the hardships of the 3000-mile voyage itself. He had no way of knowing whether his friends had sailed yet or not, but he offered guidance about the trip, nonetheless.

Search and pray, he advised, for the most reliable vessel and crew available, as that could make all the difference in safe passage. The good character of the ship's captain, if that could be ascertained, would mean a much more pleasant experience. Disease could be widespread with devastating results, so any ship with an official "clean bill of health" was much preferred. Finally, the number of Ulster Scotts who were arriving in Philadelphia was incredibly high and they often found themselves the targets of intolerance and prejudice among the city's elite populous. Be prepared for all these challenges, he warned.

Pastor Durkin's counsel and warnings were accurate but came too late for the McCourtney's, Clarke's, and their families and friends on The Allegheny.

The risk was taken… both peril and possibility lay ahead. Having already set sail on their square rigger vessel, they would discover those difficulties, and perhaps more, on their own over the weeks and months ahead.

CHAPTER 24

Kate and Darren McCourtney stood arm in arm with their children at the rear of *The Allegheny* as it slowly made its way toward the Lough Swilly in the distance. The sails would not be fully hoisted until the ship was through the narrow inlet and out in the open seas. Behind them lay the countryside and the town – the only home that Molly and Patrick had ever known. No matter how tightly she closed her eyes and tried to bring up her vision of America that she had painted in her mind for months, all Molly could picture now was their small cottage, the rocky high meadow, and Gracie.

The docks along the river and the town itself grew smaller as the ship headed out, but Molly could still see some of the lingering group that had bid them farewell. She was almost certain that she could still see Gracie's brightly colored dress next to Alex Gallagher who promised to see her safely home to Gweedore whenever she was ready. Kate wept openly as the distance between she and her mother grew. The same emotions overcame many other passengers as they waved good-bye to Letterkenny. Above the rows of businesses, shops, and steep-roofed white cottages, Molly could see the high meadow and knew that their Galway sheep were being cared for by new owners and still under Dundee's constant guard.

Molly turned her attention to the frantic activity of the ship's crew, and watched them pulling ropes, securing the anchor, checking the wind, and shouting instructions, none of which she understood. There was a moment of panic as she thought to herself about how completely dependent the passengers were on these activities, trusting these men they had not even met to handle chores that they did not understand. "If

I have anxiety now," she worried, "how many times in the next month will I have these feelings when we're on the open ocean, out of sight of land, and perhaps in stormy weather?"

"Here I am again," she thought, "Living in two worlds... sad to be leaving one but looking forward to another." She wondered if the excitement of America and all the promise it held would gradually replace the memories of her childhood that she was watching drift farther away. "Surely I'll never forget this place," she pondered. At the thought of this, Molly vowed that she would keep her face turned toward Ireland and remember this moment until there was not even a hint of the familiar rugged coastline, grassy green countryside, and the hills covered with sheep. Only then would she turn to the bow of the boat and look toward America, her new home.

All of these thoughts must have shown on her face as she felt a hand on her shoulder. "Not having doubts already, are we?" Liam asked.

Molly turned quickly and responded with a smile, "No... no doubts at all. I might call it confusing or conflicted emotions, perhaps! I feel like I have one foot in Ireland and one in America, Liam. Maybe I just need to work these things out somewhere along this 3,000-mile voyage!"

"I believe we all have some of that turmoil going on within us, Molly. We have to each work it out for ourselves... or, at some point, maybe you and I need to work it out together... for both of us." Molly knew that his remark was both a statement and a question, revealing his own emotions.

"Yes," she replied. "Let's work it out together. But for now, I hope you understand, I want to capture the moment for myself and soak in all of Ireland that I can. This place will always be a part of me, Liam. Someday, in God's providence and His timing, I will want to tell my children about my life here."

Then she added, "Writing all of these emotions and feelings in my journal, along with singing all of the ballads I've learned and will continue to learn… this is part of how I understand things… how I cope, I guess."

"I'm here, Molly, if talking through these things helps. It does for me, at least, and you're here for me as well, I hope?"

"Of course," Molly responded.

The Allegheny was close to the Lough Swilly opening out to the ocean. Molly had only seen the narrow passageway from a distance. Passing through the imposing, sheer cliffs and trying to imagine the glacial action from eons ago, she craned her neck to see the tops of the crags, overwhelmed with their imposing grandeur. Negotiating the passage took only a minute, then the ship was out into the open ocean.

As the crew hoisted the sails fully and the wind filled them with a snap, the sudden increase in speed caused passengers to grasp railings and steady themselves until the vessel's velocity stabilized. From Molly's understanding of the geography of Ireland, she felt certain that they would negotiate the northwestern coast and along the western coast for a short distance. She hoped that they would still be in view of land as their first day ended. Sunset illuminating the coast of her homeland would be a perfect farewell and she did not want to miss it! Lyrics once again swirled in her head…

I'm bidding farewell to the land of my youth, And the home I love so well,
The mountains stand 'round my own native land, I'm bidding them
all farewell

Kate was below deck, locating bunks for the family during the voyage. They claimed a corner space near a porthole in the upper-level passenger hold. This would perhaps provide some measure of ventilation and light. Kate covered each straw-filled mattress with a favorite quilt from home and placed her well-worn Bible on a wooden crate, their only "furniture." With the family all in one corner of the room, this would be the only semblance of togetherness and privacy they could expect for the next month. The Clarke family had chosen a place for their three bunks on the same level in an opposite corner. Shannon Clarke was making similar arrangements for her family.

Kate had thought during the months of preparation how fortunate they were to be traveling with friends from their Letterkenny meeting house. There were a few other families and individuals on board with them as well, but the vast majority of the one hundred or so passengers were people they knew and loved. As the reality set in of at least a month on the ocean in tight quarters and unsanitary conditions, Kate and Darren were even more thankful to be with friends.

One of the greatest concerns was the food which came with the cost of the voyage. It would be strictly for their nourishment and survival, not for flavor or satisfaction. Salted pork or mutton, potatoes, and hard tack, what sailors called sea biscuits… these would be rationed out at each meal through the entirety of the voyage. There was a supply of fresh water on board, held in barrels, but much of it would be undrinkable toward the end of their voyage, especially if their trip turned out to be of longer duration than expected. Weak beer was a better option for the adults, and possibly for the children if the situation became desperate.

All the passengers on *The Allegheny* knew of these details before setting sail. Kate McCourtney had packed as much fresh bread as possible, along with a shortbread and soda bread that Gracie had prepared the morning of their departure. The bread would give them perhaps a week of familiar foods, making these first days at sea a bit more tolerable. They also had a supply of some of their own dried beef and dried dates and raisins which should last them weeks into the trip.

Satisfied that they had done everything possible in terms of making arrangements, Kate and Shannon climbed the steep steps up onto the ship's deck to find their families and see if any of their friends needed assistance. They found Darren and Finn with a group of men, having just finished hauling the last of the trunks down into the cargo hold. Kate could see Molly and Patrick, along with Liam, at the back of the boat, all three pointing excitedly toward the rugged shoreline, spellbound by everything in sight.

Putting her arm around her friend, Kate sighed, "Look at our children, Shannon. Would we have ever thought when they were younger, that this would be a part of God's plan for them?"

"No," Shannon replied. "But how often do His plans surprise us… come upon us when we are preparing otherwise?" Kate nodded her head in agreement and wiped away a tear. "I'm trusting that their optimistic view… their energetic enthusiasm, I guess I would call it… will have a positive effect on all of us, keeping us focused on the promises, rather than the perils that may be ahead."

Both ladies turned their attention to their husbands. With an exaggerated bow, Kate teased, "Your room is ready, sir. You will find your accommodations on the top level of the passenger hold, just one set of steps below deck." All four laughed heartily, and Shannon curtsied to Finn Clarke with an equally dramatic "and yours as well, kind sir. I trust that you will find these quarters to your satisfaction."

It was late afternoon when the ship's crew adjusted the linen sails, the wind whipped through the riggings, and *The Allegheny* took a noticeable turn, pulling away from the coast out into the open seas. Liam had joined Molly after helping the men take the trunks below deck, and the two young people watched Ireland pass from view. As Molly had hoped, the sun was setting, giving an orange glow to the entire coast and the green hills rising in the background. The radiant view of their homeland would be embedded in their minds for the rest of their lives, and each of them realized the significance of the moment, staring without words.

Molly finally broke the silence. "It's true," she remarked.

"What's true?" Liam questioned.

As was becoming more and more common in the way she answered such questions, Molly responded in song. *"To America I sailed away and left this Irish nation…'* I really am a rambling Irishman, Liam!"

"Yes, we both are, Molly," he responded.

Just as expected, the evening rations for the passengers were filling and nourishing, but little more than that. Darren and Kate had prepared their children for what to expect, but Patrick needed a stern reminder about the importance of keeping nourished whether or not the meal fit his wishes. The bread and dried fruit, along with Gracie's shortbread, were a welcome addition. With their plates of rations, the passengers each found a spot on the deck to eat.

While the sun dipped lower beyond the western horizon, and the sky grew darker, Molly began gazing at the familiar constellations and planets coming into view, an activity that would occupy much of her time during the voyage. The vastness of what she could see overwhelmed her just as it did when she sat in her rocky meadow at home. But with no land in sight in any direction, the immensity was even greater. She was somewhat familiar with the use of stars as navigation aids, even in ancient times, but now she was dependent on the captain of this vessel who was relying on these same methods. The thought was hard for her to fathom.

Molly settled into her bunk later that evening, too tired from the activities and excitement of the day to be disturbed by the crowded conditions or unfamiliar sounds. Though some passengers complained, she found the gentle swaying of the ship restful and soothing. It suddenly occurred to her that, for the first time since her birthday last summer, she had not played her fiddle all day. She reached under her bunk and ran her hand along the leather case thinking about the days ahead when music and dancing up on the ship's top deck would hopefully be a regular occurrence. She raised up slightly and looked across the rows of bunks to the other corner of the passenger deck where the Clarke's were bedding down. She was certain that, even in the dim light, she could see Liam looking her direction. She mouthed "good night," gave a slight wave, and fell back on her bed. Her first day at sea was over.

CHAPTER 25

Early the next morning, Molly carried two pieces of Gracie's short-bread and some dried fruit along with two cups of hot tea from the ship's galley to the top deck where she found Liam out enjoying the warm sunshine. She walked quietly up behind him and quipped "Are we there, yet?"

Startled, Liam turned around and laughed, "Not quite." Molly handed him one of the shortbreads and a cup of tea. "Were you up early enough to see the sunrise?" she asked.

"No, not that early, but when the weather cooperates, I'll try to make that a habit. Would you join me occasionally?"

"As long as I wake up early enough," Molly replied.

The two of them leaned back shoulder-to-shoulder against some sacks of grain and closed their eyes, absorbing the sounds and smells that encircled them. The salty aroma of the sea was in every breath they took. The creaking of the ship, the steady roar of the waves, and the wind whipping away at the sails were the dominant sounds, along with the voices of crew and passengers. But the sounds most pleasing to Molly were those of the ship cutting through the water and the cacophony of birds circling in the skies above *The Allegheny* looking for a resting place or a morsel of food. She realized that she would grow weary of these as the days went by, but for now, everything was new… everything was enjoyable… everything an adventure.

"Mother insists that studies be part of each day…" Molly spoke with a touch of displeasure. "Except, of course, for the Sabbath."

"Your lessons are important, and your mother is right to make certain that you continue them," Liam chided. "Before I finished school last year, there were many times my parents had to compel me to study. Besides, having a routine will help pass the time as the days go by... you can't fiddle the whole time, Molly!"

"You're right, I guess," she agreed, jumping to her feet. "I'll do it for you," she grinned.

"Come find me when you're through with your studies," Liam shouted after her.

Like most Ulster parents, Darren and Kate McCourtney were insistent on keeping their children's education as a priority... even during their voyage to America. It was their responsibility and the church's teaching to help train up the next generation. Literacy, practical mathematics, geography, and a limited amount of Latin were standard studies. It was difficult to separate education from their Presbyterian faith, so training future congregations and possibly future ministers meant interweaving the Bible and *The Confessions of Faith* and *Catechisms* into lessons wherever possible. The goal of an education for these Presbyterian immigrants was to be able to read the Bible and think through its truths critically for themselves.

Molly knew these things, believed them, and was diligent in her studies, but so often she would rather be outside, or, of course, fiddling. On *The Allegheny*, she wasn't sure what Kate would require of her, but she knew there would be tasks assigned and excellent work expected. She also knew that Liam was right... the daily assignments would help pass the time. For this first morning, Kate gave writing assignments to both children. Molly was to take the observations she had kept in her journal the week prior to their departure and make a more formal composition of several pages.

"This will be something that you can keep and reflect on the rest of your life," Kate encouraged, "Perhaps sharing it with your children someday. Give it your best effort."

She was also to produce a map of Ireland as she understood its geography, and to determine the area of the upper deck of the ship, calculating the amount of space for each passenger. As always, her assignment included memorization of one catechism question and answer, one of Kate's choosing.

Finding a quiet place on the ship to study, journal, or practice her fiddling was difficult, but Molly was determined and began searching as soon as she had her instructions in hand from her mother. She opened doors and peeked in windows to no avail. Every place was too dark, too musty, or seemed to have some use for the ship's operation. Finally, near the stern of the ship, she discovered a number of large wooden crates with a space behind them where she could sit unobserved from any other passengers. She thought the sun would shine into the space by late morning. A small, discarded box was there and would serve well as a seat or a writing desk.

"Nothing like my grassy meadow," she whispered to herself, "but it will have to do for now." With that thought, Molly began thumbing through the pages of her journal and gathering her thoughts. She kept repeating her mother's guiding words… "Something to keep and reflect on the rest of my life… something to share with my children…" Molly could not imagine writing anything without including lyrics of songs. She reflected again how the ballads, those from Gracie and others, formed the framework of her deepest feelings and emotions about her home and her heritage. So, pencil in hand, she began pouring out her heart…

> *Everyone, including me, called her Gracie although my grand-mother's name was Grace Campbell. I will forever cherish my last week living in the town of Letterkenny in County Donegal,*

*Ireland. It was the only home I had ever known. Gracie had come
that week to be with us before our departure for America and I
absorbed all that I could of her wisdom, her heritage, her faith,
and always, her ballads. Gracie once told me that as Ulster Scotts,
our inclination has always been to wander, always hoping and
trusting for a place to lead our own lives and worship God in our
own way. This gave me great comfort and trust that our immigration was the natural and the right thing for our family. One
of her ballads was especially powerful to me that last week and I
hummed the tune and sang the words often as I sat in my special
place in the rocky high meadow on our small farm…*

> *'I'm bidding farewell to the land of my youth,
> and the home thatI love so well.
> The mountains grand in m'own native land,
> I'm bidding them all farewell.
> With an aching heart, I'll bid them adieu,
> for tomorrow I'll sail far away.
> O're the raging foam I'll seek a new home,
> on the shores of Amerikay.'*

Molly knew that her mother had given her a week to work on her
story, although Kate insisted that she see progress daily. Pleased with
these opening lines and not sure what should come next, Molly started
working on her map of Ireland. She now had a completely different
perspective of her homeland, having seen at least the north and west
coast from out at sea for the first time. The ruggedness and the countless
number of small islands, peninsulas, and coves dominated the view as
she had watched Ireland pass by and eventually out of sight. The size
of Donegal Bay was mesmerizing, and the Connemara Mountains in
County Galway rose majestically over the coastline. From Gracie's home
in Gweedore, Molly had seen some of this terrain, but never had she realized it's immensity. As her map took shape, she realized that any details
she included would be focused on the few areas where she had lived,

traveled, or had now seen from sea. As she sketched in those details, she was suddenly overwhelmed with sorrow that she didn't know as much about Ireland as she wished. She vowed again that what she did know she would write about, sing about, and fiddle about as long as she lived.

She spent the next two hours completing her map, shading in some of the landscape features and trying desperately to get the scale somewhat correct and the spatial relationships of things close to accurate. Molly paced off the width and breadth of *The Allegheny's* upper deck and completed the calculations of space for each passenger and ran to find her mother with her assignments.

"I love the opening of your composition, Molly. Spend as much time as you need to get it right. We'll look at it every day to see how it is developing. I'm proud of you."

"I don't know enough about Ireland's geography to get the map any better than it already is," she confessed. "I wish I did, but I can only recall seeing a map of it a couple of times in my life. Perhaps someday I will come across an accurate map that will allow me to fill in the unfamiliar places… Enough school for today?" Molly questioned.

"Yes, I think this is adequate, but keep thinking about your writing piece. Remember, something to keep… reflect on… to share someday with your children."

Molly headed down to the family quarters and pulled her fiddle out from under the bunk. Then she headed off to find Liam as she wanted his critique of her version of *The Irish Lad,* a dance tune she had recently picked up and was attempting to master. She also wanted to talk to Liam's father about spending some regular time with her, teaching her as much as possible. She was concerned that once they landed in Philadelphia, there may not be time for such things. This month of ocean voyage would be her best chance to learn.

She found Finn Clarke sitting alone, studying an account book so intensely that he wasn't aware of her approach. Molly called his name and Finn laughed that she had startled him.

"Well, Molly. What's our red-haired fiddler been up to this morning?"

"I've been doing some lessons that mother had assigned to me. But right now, I was actually looking for you… hoping to discuss a regular time for fiddling while we're out here confined to the ship."

"Well now, that would be a reasonable thing for us to do. Perhaps an evening activity as the sun in setting?" Finn suggested. "I know that there are dancers among our friends and I'm sure they would find this an enjoyable way to pass the time… Let's do it, and we can begin tonight after our evening meal!"

Molly was thrilled with the prospect and would begin circulating the news to their friends later in the day. She played *The Irish Lad* for Finn and he suggested a few slight variations in how he understood the melody as well as an added transition between the verses and chorus.

Finn did not have his instrument with him at the moment, so he cherished the chance to spend a few minutes with Molly's fiddle under his chin. "What did I tell you the first time I saw this instrument," he questioned as he handed it back to her.

"Treasure it," Molly said emphatically.

"Yes," Finn replied. "Treasure it… always! You are improving as they say, by leaps and bounds, Molly! Keep up the practice… you are becoming an excellent fiddler and our time here will help us both to improve our skills."

Molly thanked Liam's father with a hug, packed up her fiddle in its case, and hurried off, excited as always when she had even a short opportunity to bond with Liam's parents. Around the corner she skipped and found herself crashing into an older gentleman headed toward her.

"I'm so sorry, sir… I wasn't paying attention. I'm Molly McCourtney from Letterkenny." From his ruddy, weathered face and his long beard, Molly knew without a doubt this was a man who had spent much of his life on the ocean.

"I'm Captain O'Kelly," he laughed. "An Irish name that suggests I could be a warrior, or a fighter, or one who frequents churches! I've done all of those things in my long life, but for now, I'm at the helm of *The Allegheny* with my sole purpose being to transport you and the other passengers safely to Philadelphia! May God be with us! I'm pleased to make your acquaintance, Molly McCourtney."

Molly was mesmerized by the gregarious personality of her new friend. His hearty laugh, thick white hair, and piercing blue eyes in some way brought to her mind images of Gracie. She had heard that, for immigrants, the character of the ship's captain was vital, and she felt certain that they had such a man in Captain O'Kelly. Everything she could observe about him from his worn jacket to his sturdy boots spoke of exploring the oceans and the harshness of a life at sea.

When he noticed her fiddle case, the Captain spoke up again. "Ah, we will have music aboard our ship, I see. You know, Molly, I have been known on some of these voyages to pay a bit of money for such activity as it keeps the passengers' spirits up, especially if the trip gets …" He searched for the right words, "let's say 'tedious' at any point."

Molly was delighted at the prospect. Captain O'Kelly continued, "I'll be listening for the passengers' compliments on your entertainment. I have even danced a few Irish jigs myself, so perhaps I'll join in the festivities. I must go now, as this is the day that I try to meet as many passengers as possible. It has been a delight to meet you, Molly McCourtney."

"And you as well," Molly answered.

She continued toward the front of the boat and noticed a small gathering of young people, mostly girls, friends from church and school. They were obviously having a good time, with lots of laughter and conversation. Then Molly noticed something that churned up a wealth of emotions from within her. These friends... these girls... were gathered around Liam. He was the focus of their attention, and, to Molly's dismay, he seemed to be enjoying it.

The moment was flooded with so many feelings that she simply stopped in her tracks and looked, both at her friends, and at Liam. The intense heartache was unlike anything she had ever known. All of the bits of conversations they had exchanged about the two of them raced through her mind at the same time, adding to her confusion. The images that were sharply focused and that she thought about so often - their picnic in the rocky meadow, watching him address their meeting house congregation, walking hand-in-hand up onto *The Allegheny* - these images that usually brought joy, now were unclear and part of the confusion racking her mind. Not knowing how to react or which way to turn, she found herself running. "Anywhere," she thought, "where I can think, write, pray, or sing about what just happened and what it all means."

CHAPTER 26

Tears filled Molly's eyes and the heartache lingered as she hurried along the deck with her head down to hide her face from any of the other passengers. Just a few days earlier, she would have run up the hill to her high, rocky meadow, but now, her new quiet place on the ship would have to do. As she approached it, she looked up and found herself face-to-face with Shannon Clarke. Not having the right words to express herself, Molly hesitated for a moment and then fell into her arms, sobbing.

Shannon walked them over to the ship's railing to shield themselves from others passing by. Molly collected herself, took a deep breath, and stared out across the ocean. "Now, tell me what brought this on," Shannon began, "if it's any of my business, that is."

So, Molly poured out her heart to Liam's mother, so fast and so out of control that, afterwards, she wasn't even sure of all she had said. She only knew that somewhere in the flood of words, she had confessed that she realized the depths of her feelings for Liam, the jealousy had come upon her unexpectedly – out of nowhere, and she knew that the jealously was wrong and she needed to control it.

"Yes, you do need to gain control of your emotions, Molly," Shannon counseled with both firmness and compassion. Then she continued, "I'm glad to hear of your growing feelings for Liam – so will his father – but anything more than this is something you and Liam need to work out yourselves. No one else can do that for you."

"You're right," Molly responded. "Just hearing you say these things helps."

Shannon continued, "I would also strongly suggest that you share your feelings with your own parents. Your mother is such a dear friend and filled with wisdom. Her counsel is important for you in situations like these."

Kate McCourtney spent a good bit of the afternoon talking with her daughter and helping her work her way through and understand her emotions that triggered such a turbulent day. "None of this surprises me, Molly. I've watched the two of you and listened to the things you share about your time with Liam. I guess I expected something of this sort for a while. Keep in mind that you are still not quite sixteen years old. There is time, although that may not be much consolation at this point. I agree with Shannon, dear… control your emotions, especially the jealousy, and talk to Liam. Pray that God will work out His will in both of your lives, separately or together."

"I should have come to you first," Molly confessed.

"Don't scold yourself. If I had been the one you bumped into, you would have fallen into my arms, crying. Shannon just happened to be there. Now, go find Liam, and whether he is alone or surrounded by your friends, continue to be friends in the same way you have been these past few years."

Molly was off to find Liam. "We will talk and figure this out… together," she said to herself.

Liam was just where she had seen him last and continuing to enjoy conversation with their group of friends. As she approached them, Molly paused and reflected on the gathering.

"These are my friends," she thought. "They have been my playmates, schoolmates, and friends from church, some for as long as I can remember. Liam has known them in the same way. My jealousy of them isn't right and I can't expect to be the only friend that he has!"

She eased her way into the group, giving smiles and friendly hugs to each one in the circle. Embracing Liam in the same fashion, she quickly whispered "We need to find a time to talk… alone!" He acknowledged with a nod and a smile.

Molly turned to the group and announced, "Music and dancing tonight after dinner. Captain O'Kelly encourages it and may even join in the frolicking! We'll have two fiddles, a flute, and perhaps a tin whistle. Anything more will be a surprise that I'm not aware of right now. Pass the word to everyone you see."

"When did you meet our Captain and how do you know these things about him?" one of the group questioned.

"I bumped into him… literally… and we introduced ourselves to each other, with a short conversation. He is a seasoned veteran of voyages such as ours and seems to be a wonderful man!"

"And you'll sing Barbry Allen with me tonight?" Liam inquired. Molly's thoughts immediately returned to her birthday when she first showed her fiddle to Liam and his father. As Finn Clarke played Barbry Allen, she and Liam sang this ancient ballad, and Mr. Clarke praised them for the beautiful blending of their voices.

"Surely this is the way that song should be sung," Molly thought on that day almost a year ago. So, with a teasing bow in his direction, Molly responded, "I would be honored to join with you, Mr. Clarke." This gesture brought giggles from all of her friends and a laugh from Liam.

Stories of Letterkenny, recollections of their times together, and lots of laughter followed. Later, as the group dispersed, Liam approached Molly. "What is this about finding a time to talk?" he asked. "What's going on in that head of yours, Miss Molly?"

"Before Letterkenny even left our sight, I told you that talking helped me work out my thoughts and emotions, along with writing and singing. I believe you said the same was true for you?"

"Yes," Liam responded. "And, as I recall, we agreed to be available for each other when those times arose. This is such a time, I'm guessing?"

"Yes, but not here… and not now. It seems as though we're in for a beautiful evening. After the music and song tonight, could we find a place to be somewhat alone? There are some things I want to share with you."

"I'll look forward to it," Liam promised.

CHAPTER 27

Molly spent the next hour or so at her quiet place near the back of the ship, working on her writing assignment and pondering her planned conversation with Liam this evening. She was leaning on the ship railing, enjoying the breeze, when her mother approached.

"I'm going to the galley to get our evening rations. We'll have some shortbread for a day or so more and dried fruit. I suggest that we eat together at our quarters below. I think we've all had enough sun for one day." Molly promised to meet the rest of the family shortly.

"Pork, potatoes, and hard tack," Patrick grumbled, and then noticed the stern look from his father.

"And it will be the same until we arrive in Philadelphia, son. Get used to it and let's all be grateful for what we have. Complaining does us no good!"

Molly had arranged with Finn Clarke to start playing music early as a way to call passengers to the gathering. She quickly finished eating and, behind one of their hanging quilts, she slipped into the dress Gracie had made. Kate helped her brush and braid her thick hair, both of them commenting about the lack of the usual wildflowers in her braid.

"I'll find another favorite wildflower when we get to America," she promised, clutching her fiddle case under her arm and heading up on the top deck.

Molly had her fiddle tuned and was working through some scales when Finn Clarke arrived. *The Irish Lad,* " she said, "that's what we'll start with to gather everyone and get this started."

As they began playing their music passengers slowly gathered. One of their church friends had a bodhran to keep up the beat and soon a few individuals began clapping to the music and adding some informal dance steps. Everyone who knew Molly was amazed at the level of skill in the short time she had been playing. Finn Clarke was more accomplished, both faster and smoother, but playing with him simply drove her toward dedication and devotion to her music.

After playing through *the Irish Lad* several times, and increasing the tempo each round, scores of passengers had gathered, and the musicians brought the tune to a close. The group gave them a rousing applause. Molly had never fiddled in front of this many people and she delighted in the enthusiastic response from friends and family. She had given a great deal of thought to making these gatherings fun and exciting, but also meaningful as well.

"It is so good to have friends to share this adventure with," she began as she addressed the crowd. "Whatever the days, or months, or years bring us, we'll be in this together and that makes all the difference to me and my family. I trust that it does to you. I've chosen a ballad that many of you may know, as a way to begin each of these gatherings. In case it is unfamiliar to you, I'll go through the lyrics once and then we'll all join in and sing it together."

Molly scanned the crowd and caught Liam's eyes focused on her and his smile warmed her heart. She felt that there was no one else there except the two of them. She then took a chance that she had not planned on or thought about until this very moment.

"I'd like to invite my dear friend Liam Clarke up here to help me sing." And without any hesitation, Liam found his way through the crowd and came up to the makeshift stage. Molly and Liam's father played through the melody once, and together, she and Liam captivated their friends with the blending of their voices.

'I'm bidding farewell to the land of my youth, and the home that I love
so well…
O're the raging foam I'll seek a new home, on the shores of Amerikay.'

By the time they had ended the last verse, the chorus of voices swelling from the deck of *The Allegheny* was remarkable. Liam knew how sound carried across still water and he turned to Molly, "How far do you think these songs can be heard? I wonder if passengers on other ships can hear us?"

"I have no idea," Molly replied, "but I know how much I enjoy singing with you and hearing our voices together."

"So do I, Molly." Liam began another song and Molly soon joined in.

I am a rambling Irishman, it's Ulster I was born in…
To America I sailed away and left this Irish nation…

Then, along with the crowd in front of them, they raised the volume of their voices and, as joyously as they could sing, turned directly into each other's faces…

When we reach the other side, we'll both be stout and healthy
We'll drop our anchor in the bay going down to Philadelphy
Let every lass link with her lad, blue jacket and white trousers
Let every lad link with his lass, blue petticoats and white flouncers

Everyone laughed and cheered until someone called out "How about a dance tune?"

So, for the next hour, Finn Clarke and Molly McCourtney played every Irish jig and reel they knew as the revelry continued until the first sliver of moon rose on the horizon and a few stars came into view. As they had agreed earlier, Molly and Liam sang *Barbry Allen* and the group of passengers began to disperse. Molly didn't think her fingers had ever been so sore or her arms so tired as that night, but the gathering was a rousing success and she knew that, as the weeks went by, these times together would be incredibly important for keeping up the passengers' spirits. She then noticed Captain O'Kelly working his way through the scattering crowd and coming up toward them.

With an outstretched hand to both of the fiddlers, Captain O'Kelly offered words of thanks and praise. "Never, in my years of taking immigrants to America have I seen such delight and pleasure among my passengers! I know it is early in our voyage, but if we can have this on a regular basis, I can't tell you how much it will do for creating a more pleasant atmosphere onboard *The Allegheny*."

He mingled among the remaining passengers while Finn and Molly packed up their fiddles and shared in the excitement of what they had just witnessed over the past couple of hours. "I'm so proud to have you as a partner, Molly. You're incredibly accomplished in such a short time. No doubt you'll be passing me soon! I'll be on my way, now, but we'll talk tomorrow about when our next gathering should be. From the response tonight, I'm guessing it will be sooner rather than later!"

As Finn walked away, Molly turned and saw Liam sitting on some packing crates at the bow of the boat and looking in her direction. There was space next to him and he motioned to her to come join him.

"My goodness, what a grand time tonight. I'm already anxious for our next musical gathering." After a pause, Liam added, "You were wonderful, Molly and I've never been so proud to call you my dear friend."

"Thank you, Liam… and thank you for joining me on a few of those songs. That made it less nerve racking for certain!"

The two of them gazed for a few moments toward the gradually darkening western sky and the growing number of stars coming into view. Then Liam broke the silence. "So, what is going on that brings us here to talk?" he questioned.

Molly had decided earlier that, above all, she would be as honest with Liam as she dared. She did not expect to resolve all of her questions or express all of her feelings and emotions in a single conversation with him. Hopefully, this would be the first of many serious talks about the two of them. She took a deep breath and reached out, taking Liam's hands in hers.

"I'm confused," she began. "Confused about what is going on inside of me, what is going on inside of you, and, most importantly, between us together. I've been thinking about these things since the day of our picnic up in the rocky meadow."

"I remember," Liam interrupted. "When I asked you who the lad and lassie were in *The Rambling Irishman*. I believe we admitted that someday it could be us. So what happened today to bring this to your mind… and why the confusion?"

"I saw you this afternoon simply enjoying the time with our friends. I saw the other girls looking at you and enjoying your company and perhaps for the first time, I realized how much I care for you. All of the special moments we've enjoyed together simply rose to the surface. It was wrong and I owe you an apology… please forgive me, but I couldn't stop the jealousy that swept over me. I didn't expect it and I didn't know how to handle it. I just burst into tears, turned around, and ran… right into your mother!"

Fortunately, Molly could look back on the incident and laugh through her tears. Liam couldn't help but chuckle at the thought himself.

"I was embarrassed, Liam. But as she held me and asked what was wrong, I couldn't resist pouring out my thoughts and feelings to her. At her suggestion, I did the same with my own mother afterwards."

Flashing a smile that put Molly at ease, Liam asked, "So, what kind of sage advice did you get from our wise mothers?"

"That's why I'm here now," Molly replied. "Both of them said that we needed to be honest and talk through this… together. Neither of them seemed surprised at what happened and, of course, they both advised seeking God's will for our lives… whether it is individually or together."

"Is that all they said?" Liam questioned.

Molly grinned and replied, "The rest was what you might call ladies talk. Someday, if you're good, I'll tell you the rest." Both of them laughed and were relieved that their conversation, although serious, had taken this kind of lighthearted turn.

"My turn to talk?" Liam asked.

Molly shook her head and chuckled, "Please do!"

"I've never had a friend or been as close to anyone as I have to you, Molly. None of our friends, boys or girls, hold the same place. We have a special bond and I believe we've both known that for quite some time. Am I right?"

"Absolutely," Molly thought, wondering where Liam was going with his words and thoughts.

"I want you to know," he continued, and Molly thought she detected a glistening tear in his eye. "None of our short conversations or even jesting remarks when we have talked about 'us' have been careless or frivolous on my part and I think that you would say the same."

Molly was now tearing up as well but shook her head in agreement.

"But you are not quite sixteen, Molly, and I'll soon be eighteen. It is true that our lives are following a similar course, one that we're both excited about. We have visions of what life in America will be like, but we don't know. As the future unfolds for our families and our friends in our new home, I think we must, as our mothers said, pray that God will guide us to His place for us and do so in His timing." Liam reached over to wipe tears from Molly's cheek, and she did the same for him, both of them laughing at the other.

Liam continued, "In a couple of years, we'll have a clearer picture of the future and we'll both be more prepared for such important decisions. In the meantime, Molly McCourtney, we'll sing, and we'll dance, and we'll continue to be the best friends possible."

"And don't forget… we will talk and figure this out… together," Molly interjected.

"Yes, together," Liam agreed. He surprised her by leaning over and giving her a kiss on the cheek. He then took her hands and voiced a short but sincere prayer for God's will, His wisdom, and His perfect timing in their lives. "Sweet dreams tonight, Molly."

"And to you, Liam."

As Kate McCourtney helped her children get settled in their bunks that night, she commented on the grin radiating from Molly's face. "My goodness aren't we happy tonight?" she exclaimed.

"Yes, happy and content. Remind me to tell you about it later," Molly promised.

"Oh, believe me, I won't let you forget!" her mother replied.

So, with the quilt pulled up tight around her neck, her fiddle tucked under the bunk, and the memories of the day swirling in her head, Molly fell asleep to the gentle swaying of *The Allegheny* and, as always, with ballads in her heart.

CHAPTER 28

It was the beginning of the third week of their journey and the passengers on *The Allegheny* began to grow increasingly weary of the difficulties of their life at sea. Any sickness that arose soon spread due to the close quarters, especially in the passenger hold. This, accompanied by the unsanitary conditions brought fatigue and disillusionment that only increased as the days continued. Fortunately, the sicknesses that came upon this group of immigrants were not serious thus far.

On more than one occasion, and when the weather cooperated, families would take their quilts and find a place on the upper deck to sleep at night, hoping to reduce contamination and the spreading of sickness. Molly and Patrick enjoyed these nights, the ocean air, watching the stars, and listening to *The Allegheny* cut through the water. Molly reminded herself that each moment she heard that sound meant a moment closer to America and their new home.

All of the passengers were well aware before leaving home of the food rations on the voyage, but most everyone was frustrated with sameness day in and day out. Mothers reminded their children and themselves as well that the food was nourishing and this was what mattered more than anything. It was, after all, a temporary condition. The fresh bread and Gracie's sweets had disappeared by the end of the first week at sea, but Kate's ample supply of dried fruit and some remaining dried beef continued to add some sense of home to their daily rations from the ship's galley.

Severe weather on the open seas was always a threat and thus far, *The Allegheny* had managed to avoid any storms that would pose a risk. Nevertheless, even moderately strong winds and waves rocked the ship enough to cause uneasy stomachs and difficulty in just moving around the deck.

All of these things, the food, weather, and sickness made the voyage, as Captain O'Kelly had told Molly, somewhat 'tedious,' to say the least. She understood the value of the regular gatherings for music and entertainment, something that the captain had also told her the first time they met. Each time the passengers gathered and began singing of seeking a new home in "Amerikay" or of dropping anchor in Philadelphia, Molly could sense, in the rising volume of voices, the renewed excitement throughout the crowd.

Early one morning, Molly, with fiddle in hand, headed for her quiet place that had become an increasingly important refuge as the days went by. She was still working on the composition that her mother had assigned weeks before and, as always, mathematical calculations and catechism questions and answers. She spent an hour or more on these things and then spent some time working on her latest fiddle tunes.

She had rearranged the crates to give herself a bit more room and now she could stand up and lean on the ship's railing, the wind whipping her long hair and gazing across the vast ocean. As soon as she looked out, she caught sight of a magnificent school of porpoises rising high from the still waters. Molly had heard Gracie often speak of these creatures in abundance off Scotland's western coast, in the Firth of Clyde. Following behind these creatures, Molly thought she spotted a whale rising near the surface. She had read about both of these great sea dwellers, but never seen either for herself.

She was excited to think of the many new discoveries awaiting her in America… plants, animals, foods, and culture. She was reminded of her discussion with Gracie about "venturing" to America and the risk they were taking in hopes of new and exciting opportunities. Discoveries of this sort would certainly be part of this new life that awaited them. She quickly packed up her satchel of books, pencils, and papers. She gave her fiddle a quick shine making sure that no salt water had splashed on it and then headed toward the bow of the ship, looking for Liam. She found Captain O'Kelly and Liam together at the bow looking over an instrument that was completely unfamiliar to her.

As she walked up to them, she exclaimed, "Whatever that is you two are studying, it makes you look very intelligent compared to the rest of us."

Both men laughed and Captain O'Kelly answered in his usual outgoing fashion. "Why, Miss McCourtney, how are you this afternoon. Actually, you have guessed our sole purpose… simply trying to impress you and the other passengers with our nautical skills." All three shared a good laugh.

"This, my dear, is a sextant, a relatively new instrument for seafarers, but is becoming more common all the time. It measures the angular distance between two visible objects. For our purposes, that measurement is between an astronomical object such as the stars and the horizon. This angle can be used to calculate a line on our nautical charts of the ocean."

The confused look on Molly's face brought a chuckle from the captain and from Liam who quickly interjected, "I don't understand it completely, either, but quite simply, it tells us our location."

"And does it tell us the direction to Philadelphia? More importantly, does it tell us how long until we arrive?"

"You're not the first one to ask me that question," Captain O'Kelly smiled. "As I've told others, it is hard to ascertain. I'm sure we are more than halfway and, if we do not encounter rough weather or headwinds, I speculate that we'll drop anchor in that city in about seven to ten days. Thus far, we have made excellent time."

Molly was excited at this news, even if it was little more than an educated speculation. She had the utmost confidence in Captain O'Kelly and his knowledge of Gracie's "Sea of Green Darkness." She could now focus her prayers and wishes on good weather and calm seas.

Molly changed the subject and questioned, "Did you see the porpoises?"

"Many times along this route, but not yet on this voyage."

Molly pointed to the location where she had observed them earlier, but none were visible now. "Is it possible that I also saw a whale barely breaking the surface near them?"

"Yes, quite possible," Captain O'Kelly replied. "This is about where we begin to see them and this means that we may be able to drop our nets and catch some of the fish they are feeding on. This, I believe you would agree, would be a delightful change to our routine rations... if only for one meal."

All of the men were gathering this morning near the rear of the ship to discuss plans upon arriving in Philadelphia. Each family would, of course, make the decision on their own, but it only seemed logical that the group from the Letterkenny church would stay together in the city as long as was necessary and then travel inland where other Ulster families were already established and settled. Most families, in the course of preparing for the trip, had sold enough household items, tools, and perhaps even houses and land to have some funds available for the necessary supplies to move to the backcountry. Everyone understood, however, that they would have to pool much of their money to purchase wagons, teams of horses, and other items that may not be readily available once they left the more populated area. Now was the time to begin making those decisions and prioritizing purchases.

Darren McCourtney and Finn Clarke had already agreed to combine the profit from their farm sale and then share in purchasing many of the larger items. The group of men shared ideas and offered suggestions until mid-day but the same conversations in small groups were taking place constantly throughout the days for the remainder of the voyage. There was some confidence based on discussions with Thomas Durkin before he departed Letterkenny that he would be in Philadelphia and watching the docks regularly for the arrival of *The Allegheny*.

Molly listened to some of these discussions and her mind was filled with images of life, although temporary, in a city of 30,000 inhabitants. It was something she simply could not fathom. She could transfer her mental pictures of a rural life on the outskirts of a small town in Ireland to a similarly rural life with a community of friends in America, but she had no reference for living in a city and what that would look like. She had never even known anyone who had lived in such a place and shared their experiences with her. She would just have to wait for that day they arrived in Philadelphia and see it for herself.

The gathering of men dispersed, and Molly got some dried beef and fruit that would last her until their evening rations. Another music gathering was scheduled for this evening and she wanted to work on a few tunes on her own and perhaps get together with Liam's father if time allowed. She had convinced her mother to allow her second composition to be more focused than the first one, writing about the various ways people could keep their Irish heritage intact as they moved away, likely never to return.

She knew her own answer to this question… for her, it was all about music, ballads, and stories. But she acknowledged that for others, it could be about other arts, crafts, or maybe the keeping of family recipes. An idea suddenly came to her. Why not have discussions with some of their friends on the ship on how they envisioned keeping their Irish heritage, combining these into the paper? She would let people know at the evening's musical gathering and see what kind of response she received. After an hour or so of practice and spending a few minutes with Finn Clarke talking about the music for tonight, she sat at the bow of *The Allegheny*, journal in hand, and jotted down some thoughts about her composition.

After dinner, she grabbed her fiddle, and headed for the gathering. By this time, all of those in attendance both knew what to expect and needed no coaxing to sing along with the ballads or to join in with some dance steps. A few of the best dancers, including Molly's parents, had been teaching others since the first gathering weeks ago. When she arrived, Molly was delighted to see Captain O'Kelly demonstrating some dance steps to other early arrivals.

As had become their usual way to begin, Molly got everyone's attention and signaled for Liam to come up front with her. She noticed her mother arriving and waved toward her. "Kate McCourtney," she called out. "Would you make your way up and help Liam and me get this started tonight?" Somewhat embarrassed, Kate joined them. Molly drew one note on her fiddle and the voices rang out in beautiful chorus…

'I'm bidding farewell to the land of my youth, and the home that I love so well.
The mountains grand in m'own native land, I'm bidding them all farewell.
With an aching heart, I'll bid them adieu, for tomorrow I'll sail far away.
O're the raging foam I'll seek a new home, on the shores of Amerikay.'

As the cheering began after raising the volume on the final phrase, Finn and Molly began a rapid succession of three Irish jigs, Captain O'Kelly leading the dancing. With the final notes of the last jig ringing out and everyone needing a rest, Molly took the opportunity to speak about preserving their Irish heritage.

"Thanks again to all of you for making these gatherings of singing and dancing so much fun… and so meaningful. Thank you, Captain O'Kelly for joining us this evening. The captain told me earlier today that he feels certain we are over halfway through our trip. We're all trusting and praying for good weather and safe passage. If so, we could be within sight of America in another week or so."

A cheer went up from the passengers and Molly quickly added, "But safe passage is far more important than quick passage, I think we'd all agree, so we'll keep that foremost in our thoughts and prayers… along with wisdom for our captain!"

"My mother reminded me in the last day or so - in the form of an assignment for my studies - I am to complete an essay that may involve many of us. She has prompted both my brother and me to find ways to hold fast to our Irish heritage as we begin a new life in America. We all need to do that, perhaps by keeping a journal, or preserving some family traditions that remind us of Letterkenny or other parts of our homeland."

"I think you would all guess that this is what these songs and these dances do for me... they are my way of recalling the heritage that I have been blessed with. Many of these came to me from my grandmother, Grace Campbell, whom some of you know. She was unable to make this trip with us, but for as far back as my memory goes, it was 'Gracie' who sang the songs and told me the stories of her life in Scotland and then in Ireland. I will remember her and our home in Letterkenny as I sing and play these songs and hopefully, pass them on to my own children someday."

Then Molly held out her fiddle. "We need something in our hands... an object... that will help us recall those memories and that heritage. It may be a quilt handed down to you, or a painting of some scene that is meaningful, or a tool that conjures up a special memory. This is that object for me." Molly was now heading down a path that she had not planned, and found herself speaking simply from her deepest feelings to those in front of her.

"All of my family joined together to allow me to possess this treasured instrument, but the idea came from Gracie... she made it happen and she did it because of my love for our heritage, our homeland, and how that is brought to life in our music."

Molly looked down at her fiddle and noticed the label inside. Her unplanned but heartfelt words continued. "Over a half century ago, a craftsman named Luigi, living and working in a small Italian village, produced this instrument. It became part of his heritage and the heritage of his country and his culture. He may not have even known about the place called America and certainly never fathomed that his instrument would one day be in the hands of this Irish girl and making this journey across the Atlantic. Playing these songs on this instrument is the way I will remember and pay tribute to my heritage. I may want to engage some of you in conversation and thoughts about how you and your families plan to keep your heritage alive."

As the music started up again and the western sky turned orange in the setting sun, Molly and Finn Clarke played livelier than ever and Captain O'Kelly continued showing off various Irish dance steps. His outgoing personality showed up in his footwork, and, even at a distance, Molly could hear his laughter above the music. His blue eyes sparkled as always. At one point, he took Kate by the hand and brought her to the center of a circle formed by the other passengers to demonstrate a simple reel. Molly found it difficult to keep up with the pace of the music as she delighted in this and watched her father and brother clapping and laughing at her mother.

"This is a moment that I want in my memory forever!" Molly spoke, leaning over to Finn as the dancing ended.

"Yes, forever," Finn agreed.

These gatherings were, without question, a welcome and enjoyable reprieve for everyone onboard *The Allegheny* but this particular gathering surpassed them all in Molly's mind. Whether it was Captain O'Kelly's presence or the renewed focus on connecting the music with her heritage, she really couldn't determine. Perhaps it was simply knowing that, as their time on the sea grew more tiring and monotonous, the gatherings took on increased importance. She took pride in knowing that she was doing her part in "keeping up the spirits" of the passengers as the captain had said when they first met.

They finished the gathering as always with a refrain from the chorus of *The Rambling Irishman*…

To America I sailed away and left this Irish nation…

When we reach the other side, we'll both be stout and healthy
We'll drop our anchor in the bay going down to Philadelphy

Molly and Liam spent a short time together at the bow of the ship watching the night sky and talking, mostly about their dreams of Philadelphia and the "Great Valley" that Thomas Durkin had spoken of in his letter. The "lush green meadows and abundant rivers" he had referenced fueled Molly's imagination while Liam pondered aloud about the wagon road that traversed "the widest and most fertile landscape" their pastor said he had ever seen. Having a community of Ulster neighbors and established Presbyterian meeting houses gave them both hope that there would be many reminders of their Irish home and heritage.

It was late in the evening, the night was cool, and the sky was brilliant with stars when Molly and Liam headed down into the passenger hold. Except for the two of them, the deck of *The Allegheny* was empty of passengers. At the bottom of the steps, they whispered good night, and each headed for their own families, carefully stepping around and sometimes over sleeping passengers. As she slid under her quilt, Molly realized how exhausted she was, not from physical exertion, but from the excitement of the music and dancing, and her late night on the deck with Liam. She propped up on her elbow and squinted across the dark room but couldn't see to the far corner. Just in case Liam was looking her way, she smiled and waved, then fell back on her bunk and was soon asleep.

Molly's dreams that night arose from the things she had talked about at the gathering earlier. In her dream, she was wandering the streets of the small Italian village of Boschetto and peeking in the windows of Luigi Carusso's workshop, where he patiently crafted wood of spruce and maple to create a piece of his heritage that was now a bit of her own. She woke suddenly from the dream and reached under her bunk to stroke the case of her fiddle. "How could I be so fortunate?" she whispered to herself as she closed her eyes again and drifted off to sleep.

CHAPTER 29

Molly awakened the following morning with the sun streaking across the room through the porthole nearest their bunks. It was the latest she had gotten up since leaving on their voyage. Her mother was standing over her, calling her name.

My goodness, we are sluggish this morning!" Then, with a grin, she added, "Perhaps you were up a bit too late last night?"

"Perhaps," Molly agreed as she rubbed her eyes and stretched.

"Remember that we're having a short church service this morning. You had better get ready."

Molly jumped up and, after she brushed and braided her hair, she put on her dress and headed up the stairs to the main deck. Although it was a bright and sunny morning, all the passengers noted the strong winds blowing across the deck. *The Allegheny's* sails were full, the riggings were taught, and it took little knowledge of ships or sailing to know that they were moving at a much more rapid clip than most days.

Two of the elders led the service which consisted of continued prayers for safety and for Captain O'Kelly and the ship's crew, lots of singing, and a short message. These services occurred weekly during their time at sea and became a great source of support and encouragement for everyone. On this particular day as everyone was keenly aware of the approach of their fourth week of travel, there were special prayers for Pastor Durkin who was waiting for them in Philadelphia and the one who would take a leadership role for the group upon their arrival.

The service was dismissed, and Liam and Molly strolled toward the bow of the boat just in time to see Captain O'Kelly and a few passengers pointing excitedly in the distance. The captain had his spyglass extended and aimed at the western horizon.

"Another ship!" one member of the group called out, but Molly could see nothing across the water that resembled a vessel. Captain O'Kelly confirmed the sighting, and with his directions and orientation, they were soon able to spot the small silhouette of a ship.

Molly fired a stream of questions at the captain. "What does this mean? What kind of ship is it? Are those more immigrants heading to America? Does this mean we're close?" Everyone in the group laughed at her excitement, but the same questions were on each person's mind.

"First of all," began the captain in response to her questions, "that vessel is far too distant for me to give you answers with any certainty. However, there are many vessels of immigrants crossing the Atlantic and a number of them are bound for Philadelphia. It is not uncommon to encounter more ships as we get closer to the American shoreline. It is for certain, a good sign."

"What other signs can we look for in the days ahead... letting us know that we're getting closer to America?"

Captain O'Kelly responded thoughtfully and carefully, so as not to create overly zealous expectations among the passengers. He understood after numerous trips that, depending on their precise location, the ship may have to navigate along the dangerous coastline of the Carolinas or Virginia before entering the bay and navigating up the river to Philadelphia. If they were north of their destination, he would be looking for Cape May, the northern entrance point of the bay.

"The large Bay and River – called the De-la-war – is our entry point to Philadelphia," he explained in detail. "It is a tidal inlet of the sea... where fresh water and saltwater meet with marshes and muddy sediments forming along the banks. These areas are what we Irish sometimes call 'slobs.' This large bay is rich with horseshoe crabs and their eggs are devoured by many kinds of shorebirds this time of year. So, to answer your question, as we begin to approach land, we typically see a change in the kinds of birds circling overhead."

The word quickly spread to other passengers and the rest of the day was a buzz of conversation and gatherings of families and friends craning their necks for a glimpse of other ships, unfamiliar birds, or land. Molly found the time to work on some of her school lessons, but the conversation with Captain O'Kelly and spotting the other ship made concentration on anything else difficult.

Most passengers were up later than usual that evening, not wanting to miss the first sighting of land, whenever it should be. As Molly and Patrick climbed into their bunks, they talked about the day and the possibilities that lay ahead for well over an hour. Kate and Darren had been out on the deck with the Clarke family and other friends as well. It was close to midnight when they descended into the passenger hold.

"You children should have been asleep long ago," Kate scolded. Neither of them needed another reminder as they quieted down and quickly fell asleep.

As they awoke the next morning, Molly was aware of a stirring of excited voices both in the passenger hold and up on the top deck. Quickly dressing and heading for the galley to get some hot tea to go with her dried fruit and sea biscuits, she headed for the bow of the boat where most of the people were gathered. As her eyes focused and adjusted to the bright sun reflected across the water, Molly realized that the western horizon she was looking at this morning was more than just the line marking where water and sky seemed to meet… what they had grown accustomed to each day over the past month. There was something else there this morning… a thin line of sand and trees, still too far in the distance to make out any detail, but within sight, nonetheless.

Molly stopped and took a deep breath, trying to take in the moment. Day after day as The Allegheny had sailed west, the ocean had been their world, truly one of the most magical wonders she had ever experienced.

The deep blue-green abyss, Gracie's "Sea of Green Darkness," had brought with it a fascinating combination of both fear and calm. So many passengers had made this voyage only to have their dreams destroyed by devastating storms or disease. As she continued to fix her eyes on the coastline that represented her entire future, she whispered a prayer of gratitude for a safe passage. Molly's solemn reflection was interrupted by Liam's voice behind her.

"A prayer of thanks, I trust?"

"Yes," Molly cried. "Eternally grateful."

In an enthusiastic stretching out of both arms in the direction of the land, Molly squealed, "It's America, Liam… In just a matter of days, we'll drop our anchor in Philadelphia."

Liam wrapped his arms around Molly's neck and whispered, "stout and healthy!"

"Yes," Molly agreed. "Stout and healthy!"

CHAPTER 30

The crew of The Allegheny shifted its riggings and linen sails early in the afternoon to chart a more northerly course as Captain O'Kelly recognized the Cedar Islands and Chincoteague south of False Cape, Maryland. They should enter the Delawar Bay around twilight and would shelter there overnight before heading the hundred miles upstream to the port of Philadelphia very early in the morning.

Molly watched the thin, green and white line on the horizon grow larger and come into clearer focus throughout the afternoon. At one point she imagined that she could hear waves crashing on the beaches, but then realized that land was still too far away for the sounds to carry out to *The Allegheny*. Her imagination, once again, had gotten the best of her and she smiled at the thought. "I feel like I have one foot in Ireland and one foot in America" she had said to Liam as her homeland faded from view a month ago. "Now," she thought to herself, "the one in Ireland is cut loose. It is two feet in America from now on!"

Captain O'Kelly spent most of the day at the bow of his ship, spyglass steady, and leveled toward the west. As she had observed him during their voyage, Molly was amazed at how much he knew... about the ocean, the currents, the weather, the constellations... and now, about the coastline they were approaching. Then she noticed that he had what appeared to be a tattered map lying out before him. He was making careful notations or changes based, it seemed, on what he was observing through his spyglass.

"A map that you drew yourself?" she questioned him as she approached.

"Well, Molly, let's just say that I'm making adjustments to someone else's map… someone who knew the coast better than I and had made many more trips than I have made. Each detail of the coast that helps me navigate goes on my version of this map." He then pointed on the map to a large opening in the shoreline and identified for Molly the Delawar Bay. "This is what we're looking for… that opening, my dear, is our doorway to Philadelphia. In this Bay, we will drop anchor for the night."

"Our doorway to Philadelphia," Molly repeated to herself over and over. "Our doorway to America… a new adventure and a new life!"

A short while later in the afternoon, she heard Captain O'Kelly exclaim loudly, followed by shouts from the passengers around him. She knew even without asking what all the excitement was about… the Delawar Bay and their entrance to Philadelphia was on the horizon! Negotiating the ship into the bay took the captain and his crew's full attention for the next hour. As they got closer, Molly could now hear, not just imagine, the relentless sound of waves upon the smooth, sandy shore.

"So different," she spoke out loud to anyone who happened to be nearby. "So different from our rocky, craggy Irish coast. How many other images of this new world that I've stored in my mind will be turned upside down in the days, weeks, or months ahead?"

As *The Allegheny* slipped quietly into the still waters of the bay, there were immediate changes none of the passengers had anticipated or even thought about. Most noticeable was the sound. The constant wind, the creaking of their ship, the cutting of the bow through the water… all of these had been exchanged for the quietness of the bay, the sounds of innumerable kinds of birds in the adjacent woods and marsh lands, and, as *The Allegheny* came to a stop, even the sounds of the ship on the ocean were now behind them.

The evening sun was setting, and for the first time in over a month, the sunset was not on the horizon, but behind trees, casting shadows across the deck. Molly and Finn Clarke had passed word among the passengers that there would be one more gathering this evening for music. Captain O'Kelly surprised everyone, making it known that his crew had caught enough fish out on the ocean to supplement the standard rations this evening.

"It will not be a feast," he laughed, "but a welcome addition to our regular diet."

That evening carried with it a sense of uncertainty, but the food was a treat, and it was an exciting time for everyone. Many prayers of thanks were offered wherever passengers gathered that evening. The music and dancing were as fine as ever, but with a greater depth of emotion than before. Molly began by getting everyone as quiet as possible to hear the night sounds in the marsh and the still waters of the bay.

"Listen," she coaxed. "This is the sound of our new home... this is the sound of America!" Then, in her loudest voice, she called out, "What will we do tomorrow?" Finn Clarke, standing beside her, loudly answered, *"We'll drop our anchor in the bay!"* He then paused for everyone to chime in together, *"Going down to Philadelphy!"* The crowd laughed and cheered, then Molly once again quieted them down to begin their gathering in what had now become a familiar refrain for everyone. Emotions overflowed as the chorus of voices echoed across the marshland and the still waters of the bay...

'I'm bidding farewell to the land of my youth, and the home
that I love so well.
The mountains grand in m'own native land, I'm bidding them all farewell.
With an aching heart, I'll bid them adieu, for tomorrow I'll sail far away.
O're the raging foam I'll seek a new home, on the shores of Amerikay.'

Molly didn't think she had ever heard the music any better than this last night on *The Allegheny*. The friends with bodhran and a tin whistle joined in and the passengers danced until exhausted. Molly watched her mother and father delighting in the festivities and Patrick even joined in with several of his friends. When the evening came to a close, one of the elders from their meeting house offered one more prayer of thanks for safe passage and for wisdom in making many decisions individually and as a group when they stepped on the docks in Philadelphia. A rousing "Amen" followed, and everyone gradually headed toward the passenger decks.

Molly and her entire family took their quilts and slept on the upper deck that night. They talked for a good while about what tomorrow may bring. Always the pragmatist, it was Darren who brought them a wise word before everyone fell asleep. "Hold on to your expectations lightly," he warned, "because the reality may be quite different."

Everyone on board seemed to be up early, packing their bags and rolling up quilts, even though it would take most of the day to reach the city. Molly and Liam met in the front of the boat early in order to see the landscape and watch their new world go by. Neither of them wanted to miss anything along the river this final day.

The Delawar Bay gradually narrowed into the river channel. Along the banks, the passengers began to see evidence of settlement that had been taking place in America for over a century. Fertile fields were cultivated and a few homes or barns could be seen. Small communities seem to have been established in some locations. All of these scenes filled Molly and Liam's minds with youthful optimism of what their own lives could look like here.

Late in the afternoon, the scenery began to change as a more settled landscape dominated the view. Roads, activity along the riverbanks, ferries across the river, and larger buildings all pointed to the approaching city. "Certainly," Molly thought, "Philadelphia will come into view just around the next bend." She wouldn't dare leave the bow of the ship for fear she would miss the first glimpse of the city.

When they finally reached the edge of the city, Molly was overwhelmed, along with all of the other passengers on the ship. No one that she knew of from their small Irish port had ever seen the number of ships or the number of people crowded into one place. Molly counted at least two dozen vessels of various sizes, many smaller than *The Allegheny* but some larger. Mostly they were loaded with cargo, but at least two others she saw had passengers, probably immigrants with the same hopes and aspirations as hers… as well as the same uncertainties.

"Quite a sight, isn't it?" Kate commented as she walked up behind her daughter. "We need to gather our bags to be ready to disembark when we're told, so come get your things. I've already told Patrick not to leave my sight and I guess I need to say the same thing goes for you."

"Can I just stay close to Liam? We'll be safe together and watch closely for our families."

"I suppose that would be fine," Kate replied. "Everyone has been told that the dock where we arrive is the place to go if we get separated from each other. Remember that!"

It didn't take long for Molly to gather her satchel of clothes, her quilt, and her fiddle before meeting Liam again near the side of the ship where they would depart. Within the hour, *The Allegheny* had been tied up to the dock and the gangplank put in place for their departure. Molly found Captain O'Kelly and the two embraced in tears. "I'll never forget you or be able to adequately thank you for your guidance," Molly said. "You will be part of the story of my coming to America everywhere I am able to tell it."

"And I will never forget you, the red-haired fiddler who made this voyage of *The Allegheny* so special. Perhaps someday on these busy streets, we will see each other again. Now, as promised…" With those words, the captain dropped a small leather pouch with more coins in it than Molly could ever remember having in her hand. "God speed, Molly McCourtney… God speed!"

Liam was now calling her name and the group was beginning to head down the gangplank into a new world and the next step in their adventure. She ran to him and took him by the hand. "I promised my mother I'd stay close to you and that we would be safe together, so don't let me go!"

"Never," Liam replied. "Lad and lassie, linked together!"

PART 4

Preparations in Philadelphia c. 1762-1763

The city where the colonists from Letterkenny found themselves for a year after stepping off of The Allegheny – strangers in a strange land some would call them – was, without doubt, one of the grandest in America in the mid-18th century. Other ports on the American coast were closer to Irish departure points - New York being 200 miles nearer – but it was this "City of Brotherly Love" with a population of around 30,000 that attracted most of the Irish who came to America in the colonial period.

The supply of natural resources and its location along the river made Philadelphia a commercial hub for the region. William Penn had seen to it that the city was laid out in an organized pattern that facilitated commerce, trade, and culture. Mid-century maps identified 65 separate docks that lined the Delaware River. Market Street, with its shops, taverns, and inns, was one of the most significant avenues in all the colonies. In addition to commerce, the city provided hospitals, libraries, and colleges.

As important as these things were to the residents of Philadelphia, it was the connection to the Great Wagon Road at the western end of the city that attracted the attention of the Ulster Scots. Virginia was opening its backcountry to settlers and this colonial thoroughfare was their gateway across the low, blue hills into the fertile Shenandoah Valley.

Large boarding houses provided accommodations for many immigrants in the city and the men were able to find work on the docks, in factories, or in agricultural areas outside of the city. Ulster Scots had long been known for their adaptability in difficult times, and this was being played out once again. Molly was now an eyewitness of that special character trait, claiming it as part of her own story. The steady stream of wagons rolled out of the western end of the city, loaded with each families' life possessions. Heading out across hills and rivers into the fertile valley of promise, groups with similar dreams provided constant encouragement and challenge, a challenge that she would meet with all the determination she could muster.

The multi-cultural stream of settlers into America's first frontier – the back of beyond – began here, and these colonists from Letterkenny in Ulster would gather their provisions, pledge their lives to one another, and somehow, meet the challenge.

CHAPTER 31

Liam Clarke strolled the streets of Philadelphia, grateful for the brick sidewalks as the steady rain pelted the city, creating a sloppy mess along the side streets. He had stepped off *The Allegheny* more than two months ago, but the sights he laid his eyes on today were as new as they were then. He was still barely able to fathom the scenes unfolding before him in such a city. So many people, stores, and brick homes, the finer ones appearing to hide behind brick walls.

His work at the docks loading and unloading ships had ended early today due to storms on the ocean, keeping many ships offshore until the seas calmed. Liam was glad that he had the afternoon free since he had a special purpose in mind this day as he wandered in and out of shops and gazed in windows along Market Street. Shopping was not something he was accustomed to, even with a modest income. Liam understood, along with all the other Letterkenny men, that embarking on this journey and pledging their lives to one another meant pooling their resources for the day when they would head west and down the Great Wagon Road to their new home. Pastor Durkin had met the group within a few days of their arrival and was living in one of the boarding houses near them, also in the western part of the city. He spoke of the probability of buying a large tract of land in Augusta County, Virginia, a tract that could then be divided into smaller farms, along with areas for a church and a school. Liam would contribute to any such purpose of land, along with the needed supplies and tools. He was determined to carry out his role as one of the men since he had, after all, been one of the early strong proponents of taking the risk of immigrating.

Finding employment in Philadelphia had not been too difficult for the Letterkenny immigrants as long as they weren't particular. Wages for most jobs were meager, but anyone willing to work hard at an available job could find steady employment. A number of the men worked on the loading docks along with Liam. The whole purpose for these immigrants was to pool their resources in a wise way and get the equipment and supplies necessary to begin life in a new community on the frontier. Kate and Molly served food to guests in a local tavern and, when needed, cooked and cleaned rooms as well. Patrick was in a school run by several of their friends and, if Molly started early enough in the morning at the tavern, she could be home by the time his school was finished. Shannon Clarke had steady work as a seamstress in a nearby dress shop.

With some extra money in his pocket that he had been saving, Liam was focused this day on Molly's approaching sixteenth birthday. He had never bought a gift for someone as special to him as Molly, so shopping was a challenge, especially with the options available in such a city, even in his small price range. Shannon Clarke had offered to help her son in choosing the gift, but he made it clear that he wanted to do this himself. The gift needed to be something a young woman of sixteen would appreciate. Liam admitted to himself that more and more, he was beginning to see Molly in that way – as a young woman.

In a small shop on a side street, Liam found a few displays of ladies' pendants that caught his eye. Obviously second hand and thus more affordable, he asked the shopkeeper for a closer look at several of them. He could not ever recall seeing Molly wear any kind of jewelry in the years he had known her. "Just what she deserves on this birthday," he thought. A small, oval-shaped garnet stone on a silver chain was his choice, imagining the rose-colored luster as a perfect match to her red hair. After settling with the shopkeeper for a reasonable price, Liam walked out onto the streets feeling satisfied and excited with his purchase. He could hardly wait to see it around Molly's neck.

Picking up his pace and heading down Market Street, Liam noticed a shop with a sign indicating musical instruments. Out of curiosity, he stepped inside where a display of several violins hung on the wall. "Molly would love this," he thought. "I will bring her back here one day soon." He engaged the proprietor in conversation and told him about Molly's fiddle. Liam's accent and perhaps his clothing gave him away as one of the thousands of Irish immigrants flooding into Philadelphia. As was becoming more apparent, many of the more settled residents and merchants such as this gentleman did not think very highly of these Ulster Scots who were becoming more and more a part of the city landscape. Liam tried to ignore the surly attitude, asking about the price of a set of new strings since he knew that Molly had mentioned needing them. He made the purchase and headed back out on the street where the rain had stopped, and the sun was beginning to emerge from behind the remaining clouds.

He took a short detour in order to walk around the majestic Pennsylvania State House, always a hub of activity in the city. He walked past a library and again thought of that as a place he and Molly would enjoy exploring together. As he crossed the bridge over the Schuylkill River and headed out to the western edge of the city toward the boarding houses, his mind was filled again with the wonder of such a city and the diverse opportunities available, not only here, but throughout America. He knew of other large cities along the coast and wondered how they compared to this one.

He reached the edge of the city where there were small factories and workshops and observed the hum of activity associated with the production of a variety of goods. Finn and Darren had found work here that would perhaps bring the most benefit in the long run. They had steady work in a factory that specialized in building and repairing the most commonly used wagons that were seen heading west out toward the Great Valley. These Conestoga wagons, as they were known, were specifically designed for heavy loads, each capable of carrying several tons of cargo. The canvas coverings, stretched over hoops and soaked in linseed oil, did an adequate job of keeping the contents dry. Darren and Finn were learning every aspect of the building and repair of these important vehicles necessary for the next big step in their travels.

As he approached the small patch of oak trees behind the row of boarding houses, Liam heard the gentle sounds of fiddle music and knew exactly where they came from and who was playing them. He smiled to himself as he recalled that it had only taken a day or so in their new living quarters for Molly to seek out, as she had done on *The Allegheny*, her quiet place to study, to write in her journal, and, of course, play her music. The sounds of the city were distant enough not to disturb her and the large oak trees provided cool shade. This was the best she could do for now.

Liam approached the grove of trees quietly and took a seat in the grass while he watched and listened. Molly had been playing for only a year, but the dedication to her music was obvious and it brought improvement on a daily basis. Her songs, as always, brought a wide range of emotions. There was nothing Liam enjoyed more than watching and listening to Molly's lively tunes and her expressive joy playing them. The occasional melancholy ballad, as she was playing now, touched him in other ways. He loved them all as she played, her fingers moving effortlessly along the neck. Liam stretched out in the grass, closed his eyes, and listened as Molly began to sing…

Down in some lone valley in a lonesome place
Where the wild birds do whistle, and their notes do increase
Farewell pretty Saro, I bid you adieu
But I'll dream of pretty Saro wherever I go

She was startled as she heard Liam's voice behind her, joining in on the next verse.

My love she won't have me, so I understand
She wants a free holder who owns house and land

I cannot maintain her with silver and gold
Nor buy all the fine things that a big house can hold

"Liam Clarke, you are going to scare me to death one of these days, sneaking up on me like that!" Molly threw a handful of acorns at him in jest. "But I still love to hear you sing… and to sing with you," she added. Liam wanted desperately to give Molly the pendant in his pocket that he had just purchased for her, but he knew that he needed to wait for the party in a few days. This reminded him that he needed to discuss the details of the party with Molly's mother. She was still working at the tavern, so his conversation with her would have to wait.

Molly was rubbing the fretboard of her fiddle when she interrupted his thoughts. "I need a new set of strings. Where do you suppose there is a shop here in the city where I could find them… and how much would they cost?"

"I know exactly where there is such a shop, and with a selection of fiddles, but you don't have to go there for a set of strings." Then Liam pulled the new set from his pocket and announced, "Happy birthday, Molly!"

Molly was delighted and gave Liam a long hug, thanking him over and over. "Just what I needed," she thought to herself. Then she chided him playfully for not waiting until the party in a few days. "Now I won't have a present from you to look forward to on my birthday!"

"I'm sure there will be some music and dancing at the party, and now you can put the new strings on your fiddle before then," he answered. "The shop is near the State House square… we'll take a stroll down there soon and you can see it for yourself. I feel like the shop keeper would enjoy seeing your fiddle and hearing you play it. He seemed a bit unfriendly towards me when he realized I was one of the many Ulster Scots invading his city. Maybe your instrument and your skills on it will help him see us in a better light!"

"I'd love to take that walk with you as well as out along the Schuylkill. We need to take advantage of everything here... who knows if we'll get back again after settling in Virginia."

"Virginia... or wherever we end up," Liam added. He gazed off in the direction of the Wagon Road and, as each of them had done so many times over the past few months, he dreamed about this new life once they were settled. "I wonder if I'll be like the boy in that song." Molly gave him a questioning look and then he continued. "Lacking the means to be that *'free holder who owns house and land.'*"

"It is far too premature in our journey... too early in our lives to have those thoughts," Molly admonished. "We will take one step at a time and figure it out along the way, Liam. Obviously, there are times for making plans and for having dreams that we pursue, but we can't let the future and its uncertainties keep us from enjoying the present, right?"

"Yes, you're right... I'll depend on you to pull me back into the present when I'm looking too far down the road into my future."

"Or our future, maybe?" Molly questioned. "You deserve better, Liam, better than a lady who just *'wants all the fine things that a big house can hold.'*"

Liam responded with a nod and a smile.

CHAPTER 32

Kate McCourtney stepped out of the Bell Tavern, exhausted from her long day of cooking and serving food. She was thankful that she didn't have to work late into the evening since she had come in long before the breakfast meal. Liam saw her as he passed by the tavern and called out to her.

"A busy day, I suppose?" he asked.

"Yes, very busy," Kate replied wearily. "I don't know where all of those people come from... merchants, businessmen, factory workers... the tables are filled from sunrise to sunset. I'm told that music, dancing, and other entertainment goes on until late into the night!"

"My work on the docks feels much the same way at times," Liam responded. So many people coming in or out of the city... so much merchandise and goods to sell. And we thought the small dock at Letterkenny was busy!" Both of them chuckled at the thought.

"So, what are your plans for the birthday celebration on Sunday?" Liam asked. "And what can I do to help?"

"Pastor Durkin will have a short church service beforehand. The large room in the rear of your family's boarding house can be ours for the afternoon... I've checked with the landlord. Our preference, if the weather cooperates, is to have an outdoor gathering – perhaps at the grove of oak trees since that seems to be one of Molly's favorite places. Your mother is going to help me make a cake, but I think that everyone bringing their own food would work well. There just isn't an adequate place in our boarding houses to cook for a large crowd. If we're outside, it would be a grand picnic, so to speak!"

"It all sounds good to me," Liam responded. "Yes, she likes to find her 'quiet place' for certain, and that seems to be it while we're here. I just left her in the oak grove working on a few fiddle tunes. I had a short day on the docks, so I was able to look in some shops and found a music store where I bought her a new set of strings for her fiddle. I just gave them to her, anticipating some music on Sunday and how she would enjoy having new strings."

"How thoughtful of you Liam!" We don't expect many presents, of course, but anything associated with her fiddle is always a delight to her.

"Actually, the strings were an afterthought. I wanted to get her something special - appropriate, you might say - for her sixteenth birthday." Liam hesitated, not sure that he wanted to show the pendant to anyone before he gave it to Molly, but he needed the approval from an older woman, so he pulled it from his jacket pocket and carefully opened the small box. "What do you think? You know her better than I do!"

"Oh, Liam… it is beautiful! Molly has never had anything similar… and never from anyone as special as you are to her!" Kate reached up and took Liam's face in her hands. "You're wrong… I believe you know my daughter better than I do! I can hardly wait to see her face light up when you give it to her on Sunday. So… does she think the new strings for her fiddle are the only gift?"

"Yes, I believe this will be a surprise," Liam admitted. "Let's keep it that way. Don't tell anyone else about it… although I do plan to show my mother."

"Yes, you do that so I'll have someone else to talk to about it!" Kate laughed.

Liam hurried down the street, pleased to have received such confirmation about his gift for Molly. He was headed for the wainwright's shop where his father was employed. Just as he approached the shop, a newly finished Conestoga was being rolled out of the factory into the street. Liam was amazed at the size and even before he began inspecting the details, his mind wandered toward that day in the future – perhaps in less than a year – when a line of similar wagons, each loaded with supplies and cargo, friends and family from Letterkenny aboard, would be rolling slowly out onto the Great Wagon Road, bound for Virginia.

He ran his hand along the sturdy oak sideboards, examining the joinery and the caulking. Liam understood the need for caulking, since he had heard about the challenges of fording streams along the trip. The iron rims helped support the tons of cargo carried by each wagon. He walked off the dimensions and determined that these wagons were close to twenty feet in length and the top of the sideboards were higher than he was tall. He slid underneath the wagon to look at the supports necessary to handle such a load.

A voice interrupted Liam's examination of the wagon. "What do you think of such a piece of work?" He slid out from under the wagon, hopped to his feet, and extended a hand to the stranger.

"I'm Liam Clarke, just arrived in the city two months ago and hope to be guiding one of these down into Virginia about this time next year. I think they are spectacular!"

"These wagons were designed specifically for travel down the Great Wagon Road. The original ones were built in the next county to the west – Lancaster. I hear the Irish accent, which doesn't surprise me. I have an Irishman named Clarke working for me here. Are you related to Finn Clarke?"

"Yes, he's my father. About a hundred of us from County Donegal in Ulster made the voyage together and hope to settle in Augusta County."

"I'm John Williams, the owner of this shop. Your father and a few others who came with him are fine workers. I'm fortunate to have them. We've more work than we can get done right now with the number of immigrants heading that way."

"I'm working on the docks loading and unloading ships," Liam said. "I would probably rather be working here, a bit closer to the boarding house we're in."

"Perhaps we can work something out." With a twinkle, he added "First, I'll have to find out from your father just what kind of worker you are! Nice to meet you, Liam Clarke!"

"And you as well, Mr. Williams."

Liam took another long look and walked around the Conestoga Wagon. "Could it be possible," he thought to himself, "that I would be driving one of these wagons down into Virginia next year?" As he tried to allow that scene to unfold in his imagination... sitting up high behind a team of horses... the picture in his mind always included Molly at his side.

CHAPTER 33

The Sunday morning of Molly's birthday dawned bright and clear, so the friends and families from Letterkenny, scattered among three boarding houses close to one another, made plans for a wonderful day together in the grove of trees, worshiping, picnicking, and joining in extending birthday wishes. It had been several weeks since they had all assembled together for church, and never in the oak grove, so there was an aura of excitement that seemed to permeate the entire western end of the city.

Kate McCourtney and several of the other ladies were sharing an oven in the kitchen of their boarding house, roasting chicken and vegetables, and baking bread. At Molly's request, Kate had been up early, baking an ample portion of her mother's shortbread which was now warming on the stovetop. Boxty cakes, also from Gracie's recipe, had been cooked earlier as well.

"It will be as fine an Irish picnic as we can put together here!" Kate announced and the other ladies agreed.

Out in the grove of trees, the men were knocking down the high weeds with scythes and setting up a few make-shift benches with borrowed lumber from the wainwrights' shop. Quilts and blankets spread on the ground would have to suffice for most of those in attendance.

Molly was wearing the green and blue dress Gracie had made, a year old, but something she wore only on special occasions, so it still looked much nicer than anything else she wore. Liam watched her walking across the grove with her hair braided as always, but with new varieties of wildflowers rather than her favorite Irish eyebrights and shamrocks. He imagined the pendant, tucked away in his jacket pocket, perfectly hung around her neck. Molly made her way toward him and stood near the back of the crowd next to the Clarke family. One of the elders opened the service with several hymns by Isaac Watts, all of which were common in their congregation in Letterkenny. Whether or not these were known or sung here in America, Molly didn't know. They were among her favorites, nonetheless, and they brought back memories of Ireland. So much had changed in her life over the past two years, but the hymns of the church reminded her of the steadfastness and faithfulness of their sovereign God. The joining of voices today was particularly meaningful on this, her first birthday in America. Molly found herself focused on the words, most of which she had committed to memory, to their promises and their application to whatever the future may hold over the years ahead. Among these choruses, they sang...

O God, our help in ages past, our hope for years to come Our shelter from the stormy blast, and our eternal home...

Love so amazing, so divine, demands my soul, my life, my all...

God is the refuge of His saints when storms of sharp distress invade...

She was still thinking about these words when Thomas Durkin began addressing the group. It was no surprise to any of the congregation that his topic would be clearly applicable to the situation they found themselves in and the necessity of trusting the Lord each step of the way as they moved forward.

He began, as was his custom, with a theme from the Westminster Confession of Faith and the Catechism. "What are God's works of providence?" he asked, and then added "and how do these works apply to us here today and in our future as we move forward to a new home?"

As he paused, Molly wasn't quite sure if Pastor Durkin wanted an answer from someone, or if she was just to meditate and ponder to herself on the answer. She was startled to hear one of the men speak up and come close to the exact answer in the Catechism.

"God's works of providence," he said, "are his wise and powerful governing of all his creatures and their actions, to his own glory."

"Close enough for now," Pastor Durkin chuckled. "You can all study before our next meeting to get the exact words! The idea is clear, however – all that God does in our lives, he does out of His wisdom and power, with the ultimate goal of revealing His own glory."

Several in the group nodded in agreement or gave an "Amen!" in response.

"The second part of the question is the application of this truth to us - this group of people gathered here today - and the unknown challenges that lie before us. Does anyone have a good answer for us?"

There was a long, almost uncomfortable pause before a few people spoke, mostly about praying through the many decisions that would be required. It was Liam Clarke who then stepped forward and spoke.

"The word which brings the clearest application to my mind is "trust." The first time we discussed immigration as a group, I believe I said something similar. I suggested that we send our pastor ahead of us, guided by our trust in God. 'We take risks every day' I said then, and I'm reminded of that today, two years later. The God we serve is both "wise and powerful" as we're reminded in the answer from the catechism. He had those qualities when we decided to take this risk and He still has those qualities today. We have to trust Him."

Molly heard more "Amens" and nodding of heads and was once again so very proud of Liam for his words. She reached down and squeezed his hand, flashed a smile, and listened as Pastor Durkin further elaborated for several minutes on God's providence, goodness, and trustworthiness. Elders' prayers and another hymn concluded their service.

"And now, anyone who wishes is welcomed to stay and picnic, joining in the celebration of Molly McCourtney's birthday!" Pastor Durkin announced.

Food was spread out on quilts, younger children played games and in groups scattered throughout the grove, men had discussions about traveling to Virginia. Someone suggested the possibility of a small contingent of men taking a trip into Augusta County to see the land and community that Pastor Durkin had visited the previous year. That idea would be discussed in more detail later in the evening. For now, the picnic and birthday celebration were the most important.

Molly and Liam had filled their plates and were sitting together on a quilt, enjoying conversation with other young people. As everyone was finishing their meal, Kate came from around the corner of the boarding house with a cake. The group applauded and greeted Molly with hugs.

"Music and dancing," someone called out. Finn Clarke had his fiddle and Molly's as he approached the grove from the boarding house. The two of them played a few dance tunes and then sang a number of ballads. For over an hour, the west end of Philadelphia became saturated with Irish culture, both in stories and song. Other people heard the sounds and gathered with them as well. It was a joyous time for everyone. As Molly finished the last song, friends came up and thanked her for the music and wished her birthday greetings once again.

"How about a walk down by the river?" Liam asked. Molly jumped at the chance, ran to the boarding house to put up her fiddle and was back in an instant. Hand-in-hand the two of them headed down Market Street back toward the heart of the city. At the bridge over the Schuylkill River, Liam turned to Molly and said, "Close your eyes and hold out your hand."

He reached in his pocket and drew out the small, wrapped box containing the pendant. "Happy birthday, Molly."

She was somewhat confused. "You bought the strings and gave them to me. That was sufficient."

"No, it wasn't," Liam began. "I wanted to get you something special, deserving of such a wonderful young lady. Fiddle strings just didn't seem adequate for your sixteenth birthday. Maybe this will be. Open it!"

Molly's hands shook visibly as she pulled at the bow and peeled back the floral paper. She looked with wonder at the garnet stone and delicate chain. With moist eyes, she looked into Liam's face and blurted out every thought that came to her mind. "I've never seen a necklace so beautiful… I've never owned a piece of jewelry… I'll never take it off… and you called me a young lady… a wonderful young lady."

She wrapped her arms around Liam's neck, holding him tighter than she had ever held anyone in her life. Liam responded with a long, firm embrace as well. "I've never been in love, Molly, and I'm not sure what it is supposed to feel like, but it must be something like what I'm feeling now for you."

"O, Liam, I feel exactly the same way. There is no one… there will never be anyone that I could feel this way about. No one that I want to share this life adventure with other than you."

With his own hands shaking as much as Molly's, Liam took the pendant from the box, turned her around and brushed her red braided hair to the side. He hung it around her neck and locked the clasp. She turned around to Liam and he gazed at the beautiful stone centered on her neck. He took her face in his hand and they exchanged a kiss. What lay behind them and their similar Ulster backgrounds would always be important things to share, but they both knew, as they leaned arm in arm on the railing of the Schuylkill River Bridge that their futures on the American frontier would surpass even their fondest memories of Ireland, because in their hearts, they would be "lad and lassie" linked together.

In the evening shadows of Philadelphia, they sang as they had many times before…

> Let every lass link with her lad, blue jacket and white trousers
> Let every lad link with his lass, blue petticoats and white flouncers

CHAPTER 34

Within the next few days, the Letterkenny men had agreed to meet and formally discuss the idea of a small contingent traveling into Augusta County, Virginia to see and examine in more detail the lands that, thus far, only Thomas Durkin had seen for himself. Even as they agreed to make as quick a trip as possible, all the men understood that it would take at least a month of hard travel to accomplish the task.

Pastor Durkin had spent some time trying to understand the larger issues of settlement and ownership of vast tracts of land in the valley to which they were headed. Some of these issues were being decided by the British government, and others by colonial authorities.

"A recent Proclamation by the British has world-wide implications that involve the French and various native American groups. The portion of this proclamation that affects us directly is a line drawn west of the valley where we are headed that will, in theory, keep any new settlement from occurring beyond the mountains. There are many who believe this is an unenforceable line or proclamation. Only time will tell."

"How will it affect our plans?" someone asked.

"The land I have visited and which seems the most likely for our purposes is on the east side of this proclamation line and should not be affected. However, this will make currently available land that we might purchase more desirable to any group of new settlers and perhaps more costly. If we make such a trip to Augusta County, we may find that securing a large tract – to be divided after we arrive – is better done sooner rather than later."

"When would we want to make such an exploratory trip?" asked Finn Clarke. "And how many of us would you suggest going?"

"No more than a few of us should make the trip, in my opinion. I'm thinking primarily of the need for all of us to make enough money in our jobs here to make the trip and purchase land. Leaving your employment for a month of travel could impact all of us in the long run." Pastor Durkin's thoughts seemed agreeable to everyone. "I believe it would be wise to leave as soon as provisions can be secured, and plans made so that the group can be assured of returning before there is any danger of freezing temperatures or early winter weather."

Making certain that there was general agreement among the group with no serious dissent, the men decided to present their thoughts to the entire group. The only remaining question was deciding who would make the trip. It only made sense that Thomas Durkin would be included since he had made the trip previously and had a few connections with landowners, pastors, and community leaders. Most of the men realized that this was a decision they would have to discuss with their families. The meeting with the entire Letterkenny group would take place in a few days.

With almost everyone leaving to head back to their families, Liam walked up to Pastor Thomas. "I want to be part of this first group, Pastor."

"I appreciate your willingness, Liam. Is this something you've been thinking about, or is it a decision based on what you heard tonight? Have you talked it over with your parents? This could be risky or even dangerous… more so, I believe, than when we all go together."

"No," Liam admitted. "I haven't had a conversation with them yet. Of course, I plan to let them know and would hope to have their blessing. I've been thinking about this since I heard the discussion after church on Sunday."

"Well, Liam… You are strong and healthy and seem to be determined. These are all qualities we would probably be looking for. Forgive me, but I am concerned about your youth. We may find it more beneficial to have men with a bit more experience in evaluating farmland or determining the value of property."

"I believe I can do those things," Liam responded.

"Let it be known to the group… we may need to make a decision collectively if there are more volunteers than we want."

"There is a particular reason I feel the need to go," Liam confided.

"And what is that?"

"Pastor, there is a good possibility that Molly and I will want a piece of property of our own. I don't know when, but I believe we will be marrying before much longer. I want to take every opportunity to scout out the countryside of Augusta in order to make the right decision for us."

Thomas Durkin could not contain the smile on his face. "This is good news to hear, Liam, and I'm sure most of our friends and neighbors will be as pleased as I am to hear. Choosing who goes on this first trip will still be a decision made by the whole group, you understand."

"Thank you, and yes, I understand. By the way, we have not told anyone yet about our conversations. I will let you know when you can share these things with others."

"I'll keep quiet until I hear from you," Pastor Durkin agreed.

Liam left and headed back to his family's boarding house rooms finding it hard to believe what he had just shared with his pastor. Hearing himself say the words out loud about plans for a future with Molly seemed almost dreamlike. "I actually said it," he thought to himself. "The frontier of America – with property, a home, and a future together."

Two thoughts came immediately to Liam's mind as he walked toward the boarding house that evening. "First, we must talk to our parents and then… sometime close to Christmas would be an excellent time to ask Molly to be my wife."

CHAPTER 35

Kate was working through the lunch hour at the Bell Tavern, and she planned to visit with Shannon Clarke in the afternoon. Both women had seen the change in their children since Molly's birthday and were anxious to talk to each other about it. Just beyond the row of boarding houses, there was a grassy patch next to a small creek – a place where they could meet and talk at leisure.

"What do you think is going on in the lives of those two children of ours?" Shannon began.

"A lot is going on, that's for certain," Kate responded with a grin. "I just don't know what it is! When she came home that evening of her birthday, Molly was radiant. She could hardly keep her hands off the pendant, but it was more than that. I can't help but think that they are making some sort of plans…"

"Liam was the same. Every day since then, it seems as though his mind has been occupied with something else other than what is going on in front of him, or in our conversation. He has always been very focused and attentive to us, but not these days… he's distracted. So what do we do other than wait for them to approach us?"

Kate pondered out loud, "Surely they will talk to us if they are seriously making plans of some kind… don't you think?"

"I believe we have both brought up our children to be honest with us, confide in us, and to trust us. Let's pray that they will do this now."

It was close to a week before Liam and Molly were able to have a day away from their jobs and spend some time together talking about their future and their conversation at the Schuylkill River. They planned a day in the city where they could be alone and together process the myriad of thoughts swirling through their heads. Liam wanted to take Molly to the music shop he had visited earlier, and both were interested in the public libraries that the city had to offer. Molly was up early, working on some of her school lessons out in the grove of trees as Liam joined her and the two of them headed off for the day.

They were nearing the bridge over the Schuylkill River and took a short detour around the College of Philadelphia and one of the two libraries that the city boasted of. Both Liam and Molly had a love of learning and books, a love instilled in them from their parents, but neither had ever owned more than one or two books and certainly never dreamed of going to school beyond what they had experienced thus far.

"How can a place so young as America have such things as this city has?" Molly pondered out loud, spreading her hands in every direction. "Libraries, colleges, and shops of every kind… It doesn't seem possible!"

"It is quite unbelievable," Liam agreed. "But I'm sure that as we move out into the valley, we will see for ourselves that all of this new world is not like Philadelphia!"

"The 'Back of Beyond' I believe I've heard it referred to," Molly mused. "I remember Gracie telling me that she thought we would find America a land of opportunity and freedom. I suppose that when there is abundant opportunity and people have the freedom to pursue their dreams, this is what happens!"

Inside the library, shelf after shelf of books loomed over them, more topics and titles than they dreamed possible. Molly wandered down the various rows, trying to determine how they were organized and arranged. "This will take more time than we have today, I believe," she spoke to Liam. "Right now, I'm just overwhelmed with the quantity. So many things to learn!"

"And a long life ahead of us to enjoy learning… together," Liam responded.

As they left the library, Liam headed toward the music store and cautioned Molly not to expect a warm reception from the shop keeper. "Something about the way we look and dress, gives us away as Irish. Even if someone only suspects that, all doubt is removed when we begin to speak… just be prepared!"

With a grin and a quick curtsy, Molly replied, "I will be on my best behavior, Mr. Clarke!" They both laughed and picked up their pace, heading down the brick walkway toward the store.

Before entering the store, Liam offered one more piece of advice. "I'm really interested in this gentleman's opinion of your fiddle. Surely, he doesn't see Italian instruments too often in his shop. But… and this is important… keep yours strapped on your back and wait for him to ask about it before bringing it out."

"My, aren't we being scheming and sly… a side of you I've never seen before," Molly teased. "I'll do as you say, and we'll see what happens."

The two of them walked into the shop arm in arm and Liam saw no indication that the proprietor recognized or remembered him from his purchase two weeks earlier. He did, however, fix his eyes on Molly's fiddle case without saying anything beyond giving them a greeting. They walked over to the several instruments displayed on the wall. Molly admired them, but nothing compared, in her mind, to the treasure she had strapped on her back. When the shopkeeper had completed his conversations with two other customers, he walked over.

"You may take them down for a closer look if you'd like. I have quite a few other violins in the back room."

One by one, Molly carefully examined each instrument without asking to play them. Some had no identifying labels, but one did have a name without a location or date. "What do you know about the history of these instruments… where they were made or who crafted them?"

"Very little, I'm afraid," the proprietor admitted. "With an occasional exception, the instruments are brought in, having been passed through a family or simply purchased without anything being known about them. I believe all of those I currently have on hand are made here in America and are not very old."

The shopkeeper retrieved a bow and asked Molly if she would like to try them out. She thanked him, chose the one that most resembled her own, and played a verse and a chorus of *"Barbry' Allen."*

The shopkeeper was impressed, and Molly's music seemed to have melted away any walls of prejudice that had existed. Without any hint of the disrespectful attitude he had displayed on Liam's first visit, he formally introduced himself as Abraham Dickenson. Finally acknowledging the case Molly had on her back, he said, "So, tell me about your own instrument, young lady. I'm always interested in examining what comes into my shop."

Liam grinned at Molly, letting her know that this was exactly how he had wanted the encounter to go. He could sense that the storekeeper was more than anxious to see what was in the case.

Molly slipped the shoulder straps off and laid the case on the counter. Nodding her head to give him permission to open it, Mr. Dickenson slowly raised the lid. Molly saw the look in his eyes and thought that perhaps she even detected a slight gasp as he gazed at her fiddle.

"Oh, my goodness," he exclaimed. "What a glorious piece of work!"

As he picked it up and scrutinized it carefully, Molly imagined that day, as she often did, in a tiny luthier's shop in Italy where Luigi Caruso had first examined his completed work. She also allowed her mind to return to her birthday over a year ago when she first opened the case and the emotions flooded out. In some strange way, Molly always enjoyed watching people see her fiddle for the first time and comparing the reactions.

"Do you play music?" Molly inquired.

"Yes, but perhaps not the style you are most interested in, I'm afraid."

"That makes no difference to me," Molly quickly responded. "As you may have noticed, based on the label, this is an Italian instrument and was not, I'm sure, created to play the balladry and dance tunes of the British Isles. I like to think that the craftsman would revel in the thought that it is still being played… and is still being loved."

"May I?" the Mr. Dickenson requested.

"Of course."

For the first time in perhaps many decades, Luigi Caruso's master-piece was bringing forth the sounds and the style of music that he would recognize. Molly watched and listened intensely, marveling at the idea that although Luigi was probably long gone, the music through his creation still endured. Molly felt small and insignificant at the thought. Once again, she realized how remarkably blessed she was to have it in her possession.

Abraham Dickenson stopped and held Molly's fiddle out at arm's length, turning it over and examining every detail. "So clear, so rich, and mellow… every word I can think of applies. And, of course, beautiful craftsmanship throughout. Without a doubt, this is the finest violin… I'm sorry, it's fiddle to you, correct?… The finest fiddle to come through the doors of my shop."

"She had become the belle of every gathering of musicians in our town of Letterkenny in County Donegal, Ireland," Liam boasted. "Every young man had his eye on Molly McCourtney, 'the red-haired fiddler!'"

"And now it is you with your eye on the red-haired fiddler, I'm guess-ing?" Mr. Dickenson mused.

"Yes, indeed," Liam replied. "And on no one else."

Molly and Liam spent another half hour in conversation with Abraham Dickenson before leaving. They bid goodbye, and their new friend wished them well for their future and in their travels into the frontier. Out on the streets, Molly said to Liam, "It was the music that brought us together with him, don't you think?"

"The music, the fiddle, and most of all, your ability to play… all of those things draw people to each other. They draw people to you, Molly. Let's remember that in the years to come as we settle together in new places and get to know new people."

"Years to come… and settled together." Molly repeated the words slowly, stopping to savor them.

"I'm more certain of that now than when we stood at the bridge on your birthday," Liam recalled. "No regrets at what we shared that afternoon. And you?"

"No regrets, Liam… none at all!"

As they strolled back toward the western end of the city, the two young people discussed when they should have a talk with their families about what was transpiring between them. They stopped at the Schuylkill River to sit on the bank and enjoy the lunch they had carried with them. As they finished, Liam knew that he still had to tell Molly of his desire to take the exploratory visit down the Wagon Road.

"I need to share something with you," Liam began, taking a deep breath. "I've talked to Pastor Durkin about being part of the small group that explores the area of settlement. I want to see it for myself, Molly."

From the look on her face, Liam could immediately tell that he had caught Molly off guard with this idea and that it would take a great deal of convincing to get her backing and support. Rather than lay out his reasoning in any detail, he waited for her response. It came quickly and more strongly than he had ever heard from her.

"Don't you think that is a decision we should make together? And it is something I am uncomfortable with, Liam … very uncomfortable!"

CHAPTER 36

Liam was not about to change his mind on this immediately, but he understood the importance of being in agreement with Molly on the idea. He was willing to listen to her thoughts and, most of all, her feelings on his involvement with the exploration of the site of their new home. She was right… this was something he should have shared with her first of all. Right or wrong in the decision to go on the trip, he owed her an apology for his neglect.

"Molly, let me explain my reasons," he began. "But before that, let me apologize. I'm sorry for not involving you in the beginning. I'm not sure what I was thinking."

"Maybe you weren't thinking at all," she replied curtly. "You're forgiven, Liam but we need to talk through this."

"This is what I'm thinking, Molly. Every decision I'm making since our conversation on your birthday is about our future and what's best for us. I want to see the land, scout it out, and pick the perfect place for you and me. It seems that there is nothing more important than that, and if going on this exploratory trip will help make that happen, then it seems logical to me. I don't want to wait… doesn't that make sense?"

"It makes all the sense in the world," Molly replied firmly, "if we were the only two people involved, Liam… but we aren't. This venture, this step of faith, is about a hundred people and perhaps two dozen families who are our friends… families with as much at stake as we have. I'm as interested and excited as you to have a place of our own, but this exploration of Virginia… the choice of land… it has to be best for everyone involved, not just us.

Molly softened her tone of voice. "I'm certain that this is what you will hear from the others when the trip is planned. They will be happy for us, but not so happy that our wishes or our desires outweigh what is best for the entire community."

Liam stood up, took a deep breath, and walked a couple of steps before turning back around to face Molly. "What you are trying to say is that I'm being selfish, correct?"

Molly hesitated for a moment, but then shook her head in agreement, smiling as she answered. "I love the fact that you are focused on us, Liam. I love that more than you can imagine, but yes, that's what I'm saying. We have to fit our plans into the plans of those we've joined with and whose lives we're pledged ours to. We must practice patience!"

Then Molly jumped up and took Liam's face in her hands. "Stay here with me. Let the men we choose to go ahead of us do the work that needs to be done. Trust them… trust God… as we have thus far." The two of them embraced once again on the banks of the Schuylkill River, packed up their things, and headed out to the west of town.

Two evenings later, crowded into the Clarke's small living quarters around a make-shift table just barely big enough for everyone, the McCourtney and Clarke families enjoyed a meal together, anxious about the reason Liam and Molly had arranged the gathering. Soda bread from Gracie's recipe finished things off and Liam nervously began.

"I'll get right to the heart of the matter. As I think everyone here realizes, Molly and I have continued to grow closer over the past year and we now realize that our relationship is much more than as friends. We believe God has brought us together and we want to make plans for our lives as a couple out on the frontier of Virginia. We hope that we can have the blessings of all of you here as we move in that direction together."

Molly looked around the table, seeing tears from everyone except Patrick who was just trying to make sense of what was being said. Both mothers were smiling through their tears, thinking about past memories and the conversations they had shared about their children. Molly knew that her mother was also crying because she wished that Gracie could be here on this special occasion.

Liam continued, "If all goes according to the tentative plans I've heard discussed, we hope to leave Philadelphia for Virginia next spring, correct?" Heads nodded in agreement.

"Molly will soon be seventeen then and I will turn twenty before the end of the year. We are certain about this decision, and we'd like to leave down the Great Wagon Road together as one of the families from Letterkenny pledging their lives to each other on the frontier. We are willing to wait until just before we leave to get married, which will give us time, we think, to make our plans."

Liam turned his attention to Darren and Kate McCourtney. "I love your daughter and ask your blessing as we pledge our lives to each other."

Molly's parents looked at each other before Darren finally spoke. "We expected this day would come… we secretly hoped that it would come, but perhaps not quite yet." He took Kate's hand and then continued. "I believe I speak for both of us, Liam, when I say that there is no reason at all that we would not welcome this union and ask God's blessing on it. I think we would, however, like some time to process what you have planned and to talk about it with both of you."

"I think this is only fair," Kate added. "Perhaps it is more accurate to say we need some time not so much to process this news, but for us to get used to having our daughter married!" This brought laughter from everyone.

"Fair enough," Liam answered and turned to Molly, hoping she would agree. "Yes, fair enough!" she added with a smile and then turned to Liam's parents. "Finn and Shannon… your thoughts?"

"This makes me so happy," Shannon said. "And it feels so right! Your father and I have stood in the background, so to speak, and watched the two of you for quite some time. Whether we've ever expressed it or not, I think we both dreamed of a day when your friendship would grow into something deeper."

Finn Clarke agreed and then added, "Having my son follow God and demonstrate the wisdom to choose someone like you, Molly is all that any man could ask." He then chuckled, "It is an added bonus that he chose someone who is also a fiddler!"

The conversation in the room lightened up a bit, and Liam kidded with Patrick about his reaction to having a brother-in-law while Kate and Shannon whispered about being grandmothers. Liam took the opportunity to share about how Molly's wise counsel had made him reconsider making the exploratory trip into Virginia. His father then announced that he had been asked to go on the trip himself.

"I promise that I will do my best to make the best decision possible for every family, including the ones newly married."

Molly elbowed Liam playfully. "You, see... having your father there is almost as good as you being there yourself!"

Over the next few weeks, Thomas Durkin, Finn Clarke, and Daniel Walsh, one of the elders from the Letterkenny congregation, prepared for the trip into Augusta County with the vision of buying a track of land to suit the needs of the entire group of new Americans living on the frontier. They would be traveling light, on horseback and with only the essential supplies. Rain or storms were always possible, but the men planned to be back in Philadelphia before any threat of freezing weather.

Everyone that could be there gathered with the men as they departed in early September. Molly joined Liam and his parents as they all hugged before Finn mounted his horse. Already, she felt as though she was part of the family.

"Take care of this beautiful lady while I'm gone, son. We'll be back as soon as we can." With a firm handshake, Liam pledged to do so. Corporate prayers for God's guidance were offered and the three headed out, disappearing down the wagon road that they had all come to see as their avenue toward a new life.

CHAPTER 37

With the small group of explorers searching out adequate land for their settlement, the dreams that had been cast by their pastor in Letterkenny one summer morning just over a year ago had taken a huge step toward reality. Every evening after their departure, a group of their friends and family gathered in the oak grove and corporately offered prayers for their safe return. Kate kept an especially close eye on Shannon Clarke and spent as much time as possible with her friend as she waited for Finn's return with the group.

Molly watched Liam with a new appreciation as he took on the role as caretaker for his mother during Finn's absence. This was the first time she could recall having stood by Liam's side during any kind of difficulty and she cherished the role, knowing that in a life pledged to one another, there would be many periods of struggle. She saw this as a time of preparation and an especially important time to put her trust in God.

Shannon and Liam joined the McCourtney family in dinner most evenings, and Molly and Liam would sit in the oak grove as evening set, sharing dreams, plans, memories of Ireland and, of course, their cherished ballads.

"I'm trying to remind myself," Molly admitted one evening, "that the journey to our future is part of the adventure. I find myself so anxious to get to Virginia that I'm afraid I'll look back some day and not remember all that has taken place along the way."

"That's the benefit of your journaling, Molly," Liam advised. "Writing down the details of our journey makes them more memorable and will help us someday to tell our story more clearly."

"You're right and you need to keep reminding me of that." Then, changing subjects, she asked, "What are your father and the other men looking for when they get to Augusta? How will they know when they have found an adequate place... the right kind of place?"

It took a few minutes for Liam to answer. "We will certainly need a piece of land that can be divided fairly among all the families... with perhaps some common space for larger crop production that everyone would work together. I understand that there are crops that the British government needs from their colonies and will pay handsomely for."

"Such as?" Molly asked.

"Hemp, for example is used for ropes, cords, cloth, all of which are important for maintaining the navy of the British Empire."

"My, you have done some research, haven't you," Molly observed.

"Mostly listening and talking to a variety of people since we began making plans for immigrating. I spent some time with a German merchant in Letterkenny that you may have met. He spoke of building houses out of logs. With Germans migrating into the valley where we're headed, we will probably see those and perhaps learn that method for our first homes."

"I recall Pastor Durkin's letter and conversations with him about the vast number of trees, mostly on hillsides above the valley," Molly recalled.

"Absolutely, and from what I hear, forests are abundant through-out the frontier," Liam answered. "But it is broad, fertile lands that we will mostly require, with adequate water sources... creeks, rivers, and springs. Some of us will surely become wheat farmers, which is a signif-icant crop as I understand it. If there are other settlements close-by with mills available to us, that would be important for the success of our settlement as well."

"As much as I like to think of our Letterkenny group establishing our own settlement with our own church and school, I also look forward to meeting and living with people from other countries and cultures, Liam.

That is one of the most exciting things to me about immigrating here, living among Germans, French, and, of course, those from Scotland and England. We'll always be considered 'Irish' and I'm sure I will always think of myself that way, but the blending together of cultures will make us more similar than different as the years go by, don't you think?"

"Yes, I suppose that's true," Liam agreed.

"And all those people," Molly excitedly thought, "will bring their own music and their own ballads. I can hardly wait!"

Liam chuckled, "Don't get too anxious Molly… remember to enjoy the journey!"

Similar conversations took place every time a group of people from Letterkenny gathered… dreaming, envisioning, and imagining their new lives. The young couple gazed off into the distance, imagining the scenery and the landscape they would encounter in Virginia. Molly finally spoke, "I'll dream tonight of what you have described and what we've talked about. I'm sure at some point, I will be turning what I see and experience in the dreams of our new homeland into words of new songs!"

"I'm sure you will," Liam grinned, giving Molly a hug. "I'm sure you will!"

CHAPTER 38

The first serious spell of autumn weather arrived in Philadelphia in early October and, as Molly stepped outside of the boarding house and headed toward the Bell Tavern, the brisk air somehow reminded her of similar mornings in Letterkenny. She closed her eyes and let her mind wander to the high, grassy meadow, looking out across the fog hanging over the town below her, Dundee at her side. She took a deep breath, trying to imagine the fresh, earthy scent of heather that she loved. She knew that the pink and purple blooms were on display at this time of year and wondered if any of the wildflowers and native plants of her new home in Virginia would ever be as delightful to her as the heather on the Irish hillsides.

Everyone's pace of life and work routine had returned quickly after bidding the exploration group farewell. There was nothing to do now but work and wait for their return. Liam had taken his father's place at Mr. Williams' wainwright shop, so his long walks across the city to and from the docks were no longer necessary. The tavern was not quite as busy as it had been a few months earlier, but Kate and Molly still had an ample amount of work on most days.

Each day that she worked at the tavern, Molly engaged travelers in conversation, learning all she could about what her own travels would be like when that day came to head out to the frontier. A few such encounters came with people who knew some details about the parts of Virginia where the Letterkenny immigrants hoped to settle. Her barrage of questions sometimes bordered on annoyance, and she would find herself apologizing and pulling the reins on her curiosity. Every detail she could discover helped fuel her dreams and increase her excitement.

Molly and Liam seldom had days off from work that coincided, so their occasions to spend time together in the evenings were cherished hours indeed. When they did manage to have whole days alone, they always headed into the city, absorbing everything they could about America from books and conversations with people they met. A number of times since first meeting Mr. Dickenson at the violin shop, Molly had stopped by to speak to him. She had asked his help in finding other musicians in the city, preferably other immigrants, with whom she could share music and ballads.

On one such visit to his shop, Mr. Dickenson excitedly greeted the young couple with good news. "There is another part of the city where some German and Irish immigrants have settled and I understand from some of my customers that they play music regularly, usually on Saturday afternoons. I thought about you when I heard this and hoped you would come by soon."

Molly thanked Mr. Dickenson over and over. "This is so exciting. I'll try my best to join them when I have a Saturday that I'm not working at the tavern," she promised. "I'm sure they won't mind one more fiddler!"

"A beautiful, red-haired fiddler, indeed," he replied, winking at Liam. "The news about your engagement does my heart good and I wish you many blessings in your new life together if I don't see you again."

It was late afternoon when they left the music shop, so Liam and Molly headed west toward the edge of the city, finding a different route that took them near one of Philadelphia's colleges and some areas of the city they had not seen before. They arrived at the boarding house in time to help get dinner on the table. Liam's mother was already at the McCourtney's for dinner, but Liam could tell that there was concern in his mother's mood that was certainly not the way she usually appeared.

Their conversation at the table quickly turned to the welfare of Finn Clarke and the others on the expedition to Virginia. They had promised to return as soon as possible and hoped to be back in three weeks, but everyone realized that venturing out into the frontier, even along the well-traveled Wagon Road, had potential hazards and unavoidable delays built in. One month had passed since their departure and all the Letterkenny group had their faith tested.

"Any number of things could account for delay without jeopardizing their safety," Liam assured his mother. "There are river crossings that could have high waters, for example. They could have had problems with the horses. We knew that the three-week timetable was just an educated guess."

Molly found herself falling into the trap of imagining the worse, but stopped herself and added what she hoped would be words of encouragement, aimed at everyone, including herself, but mostly at Shannon. "Trusting in God and His plan for us… Personally, that's what I have to fix my mind on as we move ahead one step at a time. I suggest we stop talking about bad things we imagine to be or about things out of our control."

"We had only been on *The Allegheny* a few hours," Kate said, turning to Shannon and taking her hand, "when we looked at these two, thinking about how their optimism and enthusiasm would be a valuable asset, keeping us focused on the promises, rather than the perils that may be ahead."

"And here they are, doing just that!" Shannon replied.

Heeding Molly's advice, the friends turned their conversation to more pleasant things and, as always, to memories of their lives before immigration. Molly treasured reliving her memories of Ireland, recalling her words to Liam as the coastline faded from view their first day on *The Allegheny*, that she wanted desperately someday to tell her children about her life before coming to America. Recalling those memories, as they were doing now, ensured that these things would be inscribed firmly in her mind.

Every afternoon when she had time, Shannon Clarke could be found sitting on a large rock near the creek where she and Kate enjoyed gathering and talking. Her eyes were fixed on the Wagon Road where it turned south and left her view. She tried to imagine positive things, but found it difficult to trust, as Molly had encouraged. As Liam would leave his work in the wainwright's shop in the afternoon, he could look to see whether she had taken her place along the creek. Sometimes he joined her, but usually left her alone to work through this in her own way.

Six weeks after the men left on the trip, Kate spotted two men on horseback coming down the road in the distance. As they got closer, she realized it was two horses, but with three riders. The men waved and shouted long before Kate realized it was Pastor Durkin, Finn, and Daniel Walsh. She ran to the boarding house where the Clarke's lived and shouted for joy.

"Shannon," she cried, "They are back! It is Finn coming up the road!"

Shannon hurried outside the boarding house and raced up the road toward the group. Finn Clarke slid down off the horse carrying him and ran toward his wife. As they embraced in the road, friends who had heard the commotion joined in the celebration and called out the news to others.

The workers in the wainwright's shop were leaving for the day, and Liam and Darren walked out of the building just as the men were dismounting and the crowd was gathering. Both of them ran at full speed, Liam hugging both of his parents. Tears flowed freely and Pastor Durkin finally got everyone's attention, announcing that there would be a meeting this evening in the oak grove giving details of the trip, along with a time of thanksgiving and prayer.

"We're so grateful to be back and the news we share tonight will be welcomed by all, I'm sure. We would have been back sooner, but one of our horses took lame and we had to leave him behind. It was a much slower journey with one of us having to walk most of the way."

"Slower, and more tiring," Finn added, bringing laughter from everyone.

That evening in the oak grove, with every person present as far as Molly could tell, Pastor Durkin led the group in prayers of gratitude for the successful and safe exploration to Virginia. Afterwards, Finn Clarke and Daniel Walsh joined Pastor Durkin and gave highlights of their six-week trip to Virginia.

"First of all, thank you all for putting your trust in the three of us. We talked many late nights and early mornings about how difficult it would be trying to settle without a group of us having been there. This was, as you know, my second trip to the general area of Augusta County, but this time we were able to better identify a good place for settlement and to do that with complete agreement among the three of us."

Daniel Walsh unrolled their hand-drawn map of the entire trip, giving some perspective and detail on the exact location of settlement. "Linville Creek in Augusta County, Virginia will be our new home. We have arranged purchase of five hundred acres with plenty of access to water, fertile bottom lands for crops, hillsides with thick standing timber… everything we feel like we need and can afford. That comes to about twenty-five acres for each family. After initially dividing up the land, of course, anyone who wishes to buy or sell some of their tract or other adjacent acreage is responsible for that themselves."

Molly looked around at the group and saw what appeared to be agreement and the nodding of heads. She squeezed Liam's hand, smiled up at him, and whispered "twenty-five acres of our own!"

Finn Clarke spoke next. "We would like to suggest that a small, central parcel be set aside for a church and school and a home for our pastor, unless he wants some acreage of his own. As you can see, there are a lot of details to work out."

"Are there other settlements or homesteads close by, or will we be isolated from any other people?" someone asked.

"Linville Creek lies along the Great Wagon Road, and some parcels of our tract will sit up against the road itself," Finn Clarke explained. "We knew that this path was the primary one for immigration out into the Valley of Virginia, but we really had no idea how much traffic... how many people... we would see along the way. We traveled through a number of established towns, the largest and most significant being Winchester, Virginia. There was rarely a day that we did not see multiple groups headed south and planning to settle somewhere on the frontier, either in Virginia or further south."

Daniel Walsh added, "To answer your question, there will be people moving along the Wagon Road and, we believe, communities such as ours springing up regularly. In the immediate vicinity of Linville Creek, ours will be the only true settlement, but this whole region is called by some 'the Irish tract,' so we will have many people close to us with backgrounds similar to ours."

"I was very pleased to see Presbyterian meeting houses established in communities of immigrants," Thomas Durkin added. "Ours will be one of many in this 'Irish tract!'"

The last question of the evening came from Molly. "I've been told," she began, "that much of this great landscape we're heading for is reminiscent of our Irish homeland... very green and lush, rocky hillsides, and, at least in some places, very mountainous. Did any of you notice that or did that come to mind as you traveled?"

"I certainly thought about this, Molly," Pastor Durkin responded. "I could imagine many scenes from Donegal, minus the coast and shoreline in the distance, of course. I imagine that Ulster Scots traveling the Great Wagon Road without a specific destination in mind, would ultimately choose a place to settle based, somewhat, on how much it reminded them of home."

Molly grinned at Finn Clarke and asked the most pressing question on her mind. "Music… what about music? Any fiddle players, or ballads, or dancing that you encountered along the way?"

Her question surprised no one and brought smiles and even some laughter throughout the crowd. "As we said, this whole region is known as the 'Irish tract,' so I'm certain that you and I will find fiddle players, Molly. There are also German settlers coming into the area and these people bring a great tradition of singing. We'll blend our music with their music, I suppose."

Molly's mind raced at the thoughts that all of these new details brought to her imagination. The land, green hillsides, distant mountains, clear streams, and music. All of this, however, paled in comparison to the thought of she and Liam, with a home of their own. She could hardly sleep that night as she dreamed of the life that was ahead. The words from *Pretty Saro* swirled through her active mind. They weren't ideal, but seemed appropriate…

> *Down in some lone valley in a lonesome place*
> *Where the wild birds do whistle, and their notes do increase*

She drifted off to sleep thanking God for his guidance and mercy that she was seeing more clearly each day. The last thing she remembered before drifting off to sleep… *"O God, our help in ages past, our hope for years to come."*

Six weeks later, with the first snow of the season falling and crunching under their boots, Liam and Molly sat in a tavern near the Schuylkill River in front of a flickering fire. Christmas music from a string quartet was playing. A very plain meal was all they cared to spend money on, but it didn't matter to them… their minds were not on the food, but on each other. They finished their meal and walked back toward the boarding house, hand in hand, strolling slowly as the snow continued to pile up. Crossing the bridge over the river, Liam turned to Molly.

"We stood here a few months ago and pledged our lives to each other, but I want to make it 'official,' if that is the right word. This life ahead of us will mean nothing to me if I'm not sharing it with you, Molly. I'm asking you at this special place and at this time in our lives to be my wife. Whatever the future brings, I want you at my side and I promise to be at yours, always."

Although she expected such a proposal, she didn't know when or where it would be. No place or time could have been more perfect and her exuberant "yes" burst forth almost before Liam had finished his prepared words. They laughed, cried, and hugged for almost an hour as the snow fell and the lamp-lighted streets of Philadelphia glowed dimly.

"Oh, I almost forgot," Liam said as he reached into his coat pocket. He pulled out a tightly folded piece of cloth and opened it to reveal a thin, gold ring.

"Recognize it?" he asked Molly.

"Should I?" was all she could think to say.

"It is Gracie's wedding ring… and before we leave for Linville Creek, it will be yours!"

Molly could not control herself. "Where did it come from? How did you get it?"

"She gave it to your mother before we left Letterkenny… 'just in case' she told your mother."

"Just in case?" Molly asked.

"Yes, just in case this day ever came. And my guess is that Gracie hoped and prayed that it would come. Now, you cannot look at this again until the day of the wedding, agreed?"

"Whatever you say," Molly obliged.

As the two of them headed west on Market Street out toward the boarding houses, they shared with amazement how their lives had come together in such a special way. Christmas was just weeks away and then, the process of buying supplies, tools, wagons, and horses. As soon as winter broke and the warmth of spring arrived, they would head down the Great Wagon Road as thousands before had done… together, as a family.

CHAPTER 39

Christmas could not have been more perfect to Molly. Gift-giving was held to an absolute minimum by everyone… saving funds for the supplies and materials needed for the move was the priority.

A crisp and cold Christmas morning dawned, and the mid-day service in the oak grove was made more bearable by the bright sun beaming down from a clear sky. A few seasonal hymns and a short message from Pastor Durkin and everyone hugged friends, offered Christmas wishes, and scampered back to the warmth of the boarding houses.

In each boarding house, the Letterkenny friends combined their food with one another and gathered in the small rooms to share their Christmas dinner. In addition to what they had managed to prepare, the men had gone hunting the day before, so the holiday meal included ample meat dishes. Laughter rang throughout the building and friends moved freely up and down the halls and in and out of rooms sharing with one another.

When Molly finished her dinner, she met Finn Clarke in the large room at the back of the boarding house on the first floor. Finn had a large fire going and was tuning up his fiddle. For over an hour, the two played Christmas music, choosing to avoid the more festive and favorite dance tunes. All of the left-over food that could not be eaten ended up in the large room and well into the evening, the friends sang and feasted on their Christmas cuisine.

Molly sat in the corner polishing her fiddle and stopped to gaze around the room at the joyous atmosphere. "I can't help but wonder," she thought to herself. "What will Christmas be like for us next year?"

With the excitement of the holiday behind them, everyone's attention was focused on preparations for the spring move. The men were purchasing farming tools, plows, and axes, as well as looking for horses that could be purchased when they were ready to move. Mr. Williams at the wainwright's shop was building their wagons and he had rented them a large warehouse where they could store their supplies. The women's focus was on outfitting kitchens and getting clothing for the whole family. They were also searching for supplies to outfit a school for their new community.

One morning in early March, Molly had a day off from her work at Bell Tavern. She wanted to make one last visit to play music with the friends that Mr. Dickenson at the music shop had told her about. As she left the boarding house, there was a definite feel of spring in the air and that excited her to think about all of the changes that would come with the changing seasons. She spent several hours sharing her own songs and picking up a few from her Irish and German friends. She could not help but wonder if their paths would cross somewhere along the Wagon Road in the future.

Molly said goodbye and scurried out to the western part of the city, knowing that there was always work to be done that she could help with. As she bound into the boarding house, Kate and several friends were packing up trunks with household goods before taking them to the warehouse. Molly also heard the women say that Pastor Durkin would have a meeting this week about setting a more precise date for their departure.

A few days later, word traveled that the meeting would take place so everyone gathered again at the oak grove. Pastor Durkin thanked everyone for coming and began. "I know it is only March, but the word we have received is that it has been a warmer winter with less snow that sometimes comes to the Valley of Virginia. I think it is worth considering an earlier move than perhaps we had thought. We would be running the risk of encountering snow, but the sooner we can arrive in Linville Creek, the better off we will be in terms of getting a start on our homesteads."

"Homesteads," Molly thought. "I haven't heard that word before. It paints a picture in my mind that I can hang on to!"

Pastor Durkin continued. "Just like all of our decisions along this journey, we all need to decide together, and to the best of our ability, we need to be in agreement. So, do we set a departure date sooner rather than later? Your thoughts?"

Molly and Liam were both surprised at the lack of resistance to an earlier move. Then one of the elders suggested preparing to move in two weeks. Pastor Durkin looked around and patiently waited for some opposition. Hearing none, he made the announcement.

"How does this sound? A week from Sunday we'll have a last church service here in the grove and pray once again for the Lord's guidance. We'll spend two days making final preparations and head out that Wednesday."

Liam asked for permission to speak. "Could I suggest one slight variation, Pastor? Could we have a short wedding ceremony after that last church service?" Cheers and roars of laughter rang out, not that anyone was surprised at Liam's suggestion.

"Absolutely!" came the approval from Thomas Durkin.

Molly had been standing with her family but came running through the crowd into Liam's arms.

"Sunday it is!" she cried. "Yes, Sunday it is!" Liam agreed.

CHAPTER 40

Kate McCourtney helped her daughter prepare for this day as best she could. Her mind swirled with memories of every important milestone in Molly's life, but this was the biggest. A friend had loaned Molly a high-necked, white cotton dress and, after searching far and wide for a few early spring blossoms, the flowers were placed in her braided red hair as always. The pendant Liam had given her on her birthday shown beautifully against the white dress.

Kate put her hands on Molly's cheeks and sighed, "My little girl!"

"Always," Molly smiled.

They waited at the back door of the boarding house until the last refrain of the final hymn had ended. Liam was standing in the back of the crowd and had also borrowed a suit that he was wearing handsomely. Molly had never seen him so dressed up.

Pastor Durkin motioned and Molly, arm-in-arm with Darren, strolled confidently toward the gathering. She had never been so sure of any decision of her young life. Patrick and his mother, arms linked as well, followed behind.

Liam had made his way to the front and was standing next to Thomas Durkin. They exchanged smiles and a firm handshake. Molly turned and gave her father a kiss and a hug, then stepped up next to Liam. She couldn't resist whispering, "Nice suit" to which Liam replied, "Nice dress… and pendant." They both stifled their laughter as they turned to Pastor Durkin.

His heart-felt prayer of blessing for the young couple echoed through the trees amid the sounds of birds. Vows were exchanged and Patrick handed Gracie's wedding band to Liam. As he slipped it on Molly's finger, her only thought of the day other than becoming Liam's wife flooded into her mind. "If only Gracie could be here. That is the only thing that keeps this from being a perfect day!"

The ceremony completed, the newlyweds hugged and kissed to the cheers of everyone in attendance. Liam took Molly's face in his hands, "lad and lassie, linked together."

"Always," Molly responded. "Let's go to Virginia," she laughed.

"Let's go!" Liam responded.

CHAPTER 41

Dear Gracie

This is the last letter I will write to you from Philadelphia. As we approach the end of our first year in this magnificent city, it is also the last. We had been told to expect perhaps two years here in preparation for moving out into the Great Valley, but our sovereign God has shown us favor. The wagon train of Letterkenny immigrants will head west the day after tomorrow, out to the frontier or, as some here call it, "the back of beyond." A small group of our men traveled to Virginia last fall and arranged for the purchase of a large parcel of land that will be divided among all the families when we arrive. We have purchased supplies, horses, and wagons for our trip, and we will travel the Great Wagon Road to our destination, a path that many thousands of immigrants like us use to access the various back-country settlements claimed by the British colonies here on the east coast.

Since we arrived in this city, laid out nicely with its orderly squares, handsome brick homes, and more shops, inns, and taverns than you can imagine, so much has happened in our lives. I wish so much that you had been here to experience it with us. So many of the stories and ballads I learned sitting at your knee come to my mind when I'm overwhelmed by the rapid pace of the city and the equally rapid changes in my life. As the coastline of Ireland disappeared at the end of our first day at sea, I exclaimed to Liam, "It's true! I am really a Rambling Irishman… to America, I sailed away and left this Irish nation." Do you remember teaching me that song? I will really feel like I'm 'rambling' when we head out in the huge wagons southwest to Virginia!

During difficult days out on the "Sea of Green Darkness," as you called it, I would often be encouraged thinking about the first time I heard you singing "when we reach the other side, we'll both be stout and healthy." Then you would laugh when you sang the next line about dropping our anchor in the bay "going down to Philadelphy." Please don't think it is these songs that give me hope although I may make it sound that way at times. They just serve to keep me in touch with my heritage and my Irish roots, and, in some way, lighten my spirit. As you and my parents have faithfully taught me throughout my life, my hope lies in our Sovereign God alone and "His eternal purposes are for His own glory... He has ordained whatsoever comes to pass."

Finn Clarke and I brought music to the deck of The Allegheny many times during our voyage and Captain O'Kelly even paid me for keeping the passengers' spirits up through my music. I wish you could hear me play now... not that I don't have a long way to go, but I'm so much better than when we left! I never take out my fiddle without thinking of you, Gracie, and the sacrifice you made to put this beautiful instrument in my hands. I showed it to the proprietor of a music store here in Philadelphia and he said it was the finest instrument that had ever come through the doors of his shop!

I know mother has written to you several times and we do trust that these have reached you. I've not written in a while, and there is a special reason for writing to you now. I've saved the biggest news... and the best... to the end. I'm imagining your reaction as I pen these words telling you that yesterday, I became Liam Clarke's wife! We will travel with our Letterkenny friends to Virginia where we will settle as a family of our own with the others. I find it hard to believe I'm writing this, but it's true! Liam and I decided this last autumn and made it official just before Christmas. We told our parents that we wanted to head down the Wagon Road as a family, pledged to each other, so in just a few days that is what will happen as we leave for Virginia. I'm so happy and trust that this news brings much joy to you as well.

I've been reminded of the many times you teased me about Liam, long before I realized how much he meant to me. So, I'm guessing that our marriage comes as no surprise! I am wearing your wedding ring, Gracie, with love and gratitude.

Our parents are happy and so are our friends. Once again, the lines to a song I learned from you are ones we have teased each other with over these last months… 'Let every lad link with his lass, blue jacket and white trousers, Let every lass link with her lad, blue petticoats and white flouncers.' I believe I can hear your laughter across the ocean as you read this!

By the time you get this, we should be in Virginia, building our community along Linville Creek, south of Winchester. We will be situated along the Great Wagon Road and there is a postal service. I will let you know how frequently letters are delivered and how to make sure they reach us.

I trust that this letter arrives and that you are well. My parents and Patrick are well. We love you and miss you! These are the words I sing to myself more often than any others, although now I've changed it all to past tense! I know you sing them as well, so think of me when you do as I will be thinking of you.

'I've bid farewell to the land of my youth, and the home
that I loved so well.
The mountains grand in m'own native land, I've bid them
all farewell.
With an aching heart, I've bid them adieu, for now I have
sailed far away.

PETER GIVENS

O're the raging foam, here I seek a new home, on the
shores of Amerikay.'
Your loving granddaughter,

Molly McCourtney Clarke

PART 5

In the Great Valley of Virginia c.1765

In 1751, two of the most skilled surveyors in Virginia, Peter Jefferson, father of the President, and his friend Joshua Frye, professor of math at The College of William & Mary, completed their definitive and amazingly detailed map of the Virginia colony. The Frye-Jefferson map provides a good picture of the immigration route taken by hundreds of thousands of Ulster Scots like those from Letterkenny. The Great Wagon Road is prominently highlighted on their map as it heads west from Philadelphia, cuts through mountain passes, spans rivers at major ferry crossings, and makes its way into the wide, fertile valley between the Blue Ridge and The Allegheny mountains.

Many other pathways cut through the extensive forests of the American frontier, but the Great Wagon Road was by far the most well-known and the most significant. As more settlers came to America's shores for a new life opportunity, their presence changed the landscape in notable ways. Wild and inaccessible forests were being transformed into coastal cities such as Philadelphia and into lush, productive land that these new Americans would spend the remainder of their lives working to develop.

As the Valley became more populated, the Great Wagon Road, passing by hundreds of communities like Linville Creek, became the thoroughfare over which goods, services, and cultures moved freely. The road connected not only one Valley town with another, but the entire region to other parts of America, including Philadelphia.

It was in this dynamic atmosphere that Liam and Molly Clarke, along with their families and friends, began carving out a life on the American frontier. In every sense, they watched the world go by their doorstep. Cross-cultural exchanges occurred on a regular basis, and these exchanges brought their own customs, their own heritage, and, as Molly soon began to realize, their own music that would soon blend with her own.

CHAPTER 42

"Are you sure we have everything we need?" Molly asked Liam as he gave her a boost up onto the wagon, preparing to leave. She had walked around it a dozen times or more, looking at trunks, counting boxes, and examining every detail down to the fittings and hinges on the wagon tailgates and the feedboxes for the horses on the sides. Liam let out a deep sigh, turning his attention one last time to the packed bed of the wagon that he and his new wife would guide down the Great Wagon Road into Virginia.

"How many times have you asked me that this morning?" Liam responded playfully. "Yes, we have all of the essentials, the things we're sure we need, but no, I'm not sure we have everything, and we probably won't know until after we've settled in Linville Creek."

"I'm sorry," Molly apologized as she began to lecture herself. "Be patient, Molly. Don't expect everything to work out perfectly. This is an adventure, so enjoy each step. Most of all, trust God."

Liam laughed, "I didn't know you talked out loud to yourself so much!"

"Would you have married me if you did?"

"I believe you know the answer to that, Mrs. Clark," Liam responded.

"I'll never get tired of hearing you call me that," Molly smiled. She whirled around and reached behind their seat, checking once again to make certain her fiddle case was wrapped in its quilt, and in no danger of being jostled about.

"It's still there," Liam laughed. "Right where it was a few minutes ago when you checked."

"Can't be too careful," Molly responded matter-of-factly.

The activity up ahead of them suggested that the wagons were about to head out. A strange feeling swept over Molly, reminding her of the morning they stood on the deck of *The Allegheny* over a year ago as they prepared to leave Letterkenny. Philadelphia was certainly not her home, but here she was again, leaving familiar things behind, and with exciting but unknown - perhaps even dangerous things - ahead of her. "Once again," she thought, "a foot in each of two worlds."

Pulling herself from her daydreams, Molly turned her attention to the remarkable scene surrounding her. Fifteen wagons with teams of horses, twenty families, all of their material possessions packed in trunks and boxes, headed into the frontier. She thought about the many thousands from Ulster who had made the same journey, and no doubt, thousands more to follow. As she had heard people say numerous times before leaving Letterkenny, either "looming peril or exciting possibility" could lay ahead. The thought propelled her once again to whisper a prayer for protection and guidance.

One by one, the wagons in front of them began to move forward. With a crack of Liam's whip, the team of horses strained against the weight and their wagon lurched forward. With the initial jostling, Molly grabbed Liam's arm with one hand and the side of the wagon with the other. Memories of *The Allegheny* came to her mind again as it had left the Lough Swilly and the wind filled its sails, causing everyone to steady themselves until the vessel's velocity stabilized. As their wagon began the slow, but steady rhythm in unison with the others ahead of them, Molly closed her eyes and softly sang the lyrics to *the Irish Lad* the way she had penned them to Gracie earlier in the week...

I've bid farewell to the land of my youth, and the home that I loved
so well.

The mountains grand in m'own native land, I've bid them all farewell.
With an aching heart, I've bid them adieu, for now I have sailed
far away.
O're the raging foam, here I seek a new home, on the shores of Amerikay.'

The pace was slower than either of them had anticipated, but Liam and Molly were thrilled with the landscape, the fields being prepared for spring planting, and the farmhouses situated along the Wagon Road. These scenes fueled both of their imaginations and they dreamed out loud for hours about how their land along Linville Creek would compare with this.

Molly stood up and craned her neck, playfully complaining at the top of her lungs, "But we can't see the mountains yet!" Her mother, in the wagon ahead of them, looked back, laughing.

"Probably another day or two," Liam chuckled. "And at least one river crossing… the Susquehannock. Then we can seriously begin looking for our first mountains." Molly could hardly contain her excitement at the thought.

Their first day of travel was filled with a number of unanticipated delays. Adjusting bridles on the horses, rearranging shifted cargo, small repairs of multiple wagons… all of these should have been expected, but at this point, everyone was anxious to get as many miles as possible behind them. Late in the afternoon, Pastor Durkin, on horseback out in front, called for a halt and he and Finn Clarke walked up to a small cabin along the road. It was obvious that this was a home that they had visited on their previous trip when Finn came out and, in a loud voice, introduced the owners, advising everyone that the wagons could be circled in the adjacent pasture for the night.

Within an hour, there was a fire going inside the circle and food was being prepared. The long day of jostling along in the wagon had obviously taken its toll on most of the group. Although this portion of the Wagon Road was well-marked and in decent condition, there were enough rutted, rocky, and overgrown sections that everyone had plenty of sore muscles and bruises.

A gorgeous sunset glowed in the western sky and a few stars were beginning to show up. Although Molly looked forward to a good night's rest under the open sky, she perked up instantly when someone suggested a bit of music to bring the day to a close. She pulled her fiddle from its storage place behind the driver's seat and worked with Finn Clarke on re-tuning.

"Such bouncing makes it difficult to keep these in tune," Finn moaned.

"I'm just glad that they're not damaged," Molly responded. "Wrapped up in a quilt, they're protected in the storage box which is, I suppose, designed for tools, not fiddles!"

"They're designed for anything of value," Finn chuckled. "Liam's tools or your fiddle!"

No one felt up to dancing and some of the group who had chosen to sleep in the barn were already headed there, in search of soft hay to bed down in. Finn and Molly played a few slow ballads in the glow of the campfire as background to several ongoing conversations about the events of the day.

"Oh, I have a new song," Molly cried. "I caught it from another group of Ulster immigrants I met in Philadelphia. I was going to save it until our first view of the mountains, but I guess it is just as appropriate now as we dream about that day. I'll put in it your heads now and we'll sing it again when we see the first hills beyond the Susquehannock."

Then she hesitated, set her fiddle in her lap and, gathering her thoughts, she began sharing some things that she had been thinking about the past year in Philadelphia. Somewhere out beyond the glare of the fire, she knew that Liam and her parents looked on as she spoke, and these were things she had shared with them.

"Since we made the decision that brought us to where we are today, I've been dreaming about what our new home will look like, and particularly, how much it will look like the place we all called home until a year ago. I am so excited to see Virginia and Linville Creek… those wide and fertile valleys we've heard about. But we don't want to forget Ireland and all the places in Ulster that we loved so much. That is part of why I cherish the songs I learned from my grandmother and from others."

Molly was beginning to tear up as she finished. "So, here is something I've discovered. When I find a ballad that I know is written about Ireland, but can also be about the land or life in our new home, it makes the connection between the two places so much sweeter… does any of this make sense?"

"Perfect sense," Liam called out, smiling.

"Does it make sense to anyone else?" Molly asked. "He only says that because he has to be nice to me now that we're married!" The whole group laughed, including Liam.

"Sing it for us Molly," Pastor Durkin called.

Of all of the songs through the years that Liam Clarke had heard Molly sing, or that he had sung with her, this was now his favorite. The star filled sky, the American frontier before them and, most of all, the opportunity to share it all with Molly at his side… he could not feel more blessed.

Hail to the mountains with summits of blue,
To the glens with their meadows of sunshine and dew.
To the women and men ever constant and true,
Ever ready to welcome one home.
Oh soon shall I see them, Oh see them, Oh see them,
Oh soon shall I see them, the mist covered mountains of home.

Molly had laid a tarp on the ground next to their wagon with quilts for she and Liam. As she dropped to the ground, exhausted from the day, she wrapped herself in a quilt and gazed upward at the night sky. She could hear men still gathered around the fire and discussing the next day's travel. Molly couldn't hear Liam's voice, but she knew he would be involved in the conversation. She fell asleep and didn't wake up until she felt Liam wrapping up in his quilt next to her.

"Good night, Mr. Clarke," Molly chuckled.

"And good night to you... my red-haired fiddler!"

CHAPTER 43

Molly awoke the next morning from a deep sleep. She could feel the sore muscles and stiffness from the previous day's wagon ride as soon as she moved. She was grateful that the design of some of the wagons, including theirs, was altered, allowing for a seat wide enough for several people. She couldn't imagine how sore she would be if she had to walk alongside rather than ride. The sun wasn't quite up yet but she was immediately aware of activity around the wagons and the smell of breakfast. As she stood up and stretched, she said out loud, "How many days will it take to get accustomed to this?"

"No one said this was going to be easy!" Liam chuckled as he stepped around the side of the wagon, giving Molly an embrace.

"No, they didn't. So, I just have to get used to it, right?"

"There won't be anything easy about this life we've chosen. It's hard work out here on the frontier."

"I've never been afraid of hard work," Molly responded with stubborn resolve. "My hair is a tangled mess. Would you help me brush it?"

"Well, this is certainly a skill I've never had to master before," Liam laughed. He managed to get a loose braid that would be adequate for the day's travel. He turned her around, pushed her hair back on the sides and adjusted the pendant on her neck. "Perfect," he smiled.

They put away their quilts and walked to the fire which felt good on this rather cool morning. Kate and Darren were already eating, and eggs and fried pork were sizzling in a skillet along with biscuits in a separate covered pot. Patrick was lying as close to the fire as he could get, wrapped in a quilt. Pointing to the eggs and meat, Kate offered it to Molly and Liam.

"Thanks," they responded together, and Darren poured cups of coffee.

Pastor Durkin yelled loudly from his wagon, "the Susquehannock by sunset! Everybody up… Let's get on the road!"

"Yes," Molly responded. "Let's get on the road… I want to see mountains!"

Within the hour, teams of horses were fed and hooked up to wagons, the fire was extinguished, wagons packed, and the caravan was beginning to form along the Valley Road. Pastor Durkin stood on the porch of the cabin, thanking the owners for their hospitality, and, getting everyone's attention, he offered a prayer for safe travel.

Molly had folded one of their quilts to cushion the seat, and was in place, ready to go. Liam examined the load one more time and climbed up next to her, taking the reins. He heard Molly quietly murmuring over and over, *"Oh soon shall I see them, the mist covered mountains of home."*

"Maybe today, maybe tomorrow," Liam said as he cracked the whip and the team moved forward.

"Today," Molly insisted with a grin.

For most of the morning, they quietly took in the landscape and again marveled at the number of farms, the dry-laid rock fences outlining fields, mills situated along creeks, and rough log cabins. Molly thought that they could hardly go a mile without encountering wagons of travelers or goods being taken to some unknown market.

"This hardly seems like frontier or wilderness," she commented to Liam at one point. "There is so much activity and there are so many people along the road."

"We're still only a day or two out of the city," he surmised. "As we move farther away from Philadelphia, maybe the scene will change… we'll see."

"There is a word I heard from guests at the Bell Tavern and maybe from some of the other Irish immigrants I met in Philadelphia," Molly recalled. It is another name for the Great Valley as we have called it. The word is "Shenando" or "Shenandoah." I like that name better than just "the Great Valley."

"I think my father heard that when he was here earlier. I believe there is a major river with that name… a river that drains much of the valley." Ask him about it when you have a chance.

Molly spent much of the remainder of the morning teaching Liam the tune and words to *"Mist Covered Mountains"* until he had it memorized. Over and over he sang, *'so loving and kind full of music and mirth, in the sweet-sounding language of home.'* "What a sweet lyric for a song… do you have any other new ballads that you've been hiding from me?"

"Perhaps," Molly winked. "Perhaps…"

The men out in the front called for a rest early in the afternoon. A wide creek was nearby and while the horses were taking water, everyone mingled, enjoyed a mid-day lunch and, most of all, stretched sore muscles. Molly decided to ride in the wagon with Kate and Darren for a while, and Patrick climbed up with Liam.

The rhythm of the road and the creaking of wagon wheels into the late afternoon was steady. Molly fought the urge to sleep as the afternoon sun bore down. She hopped down at one point and walked, giving her seat to one of Kate's friends. Occasionally, the condition of the road deteriorated with ruts so deep that the drivers had to detour their wagons through creeks or ditches before returning to the road.

Molly had joined again with Liam in the late afternoon when a noticeable increase in the number of houses and farms began to appear stretching out along the road. "Lancaster," Liam said. "This is said to be the largest inland city in the colonies… several thousand residents, perhaps. I heard Thomas Durkin talk about it this morning around the fire."

Molly looked with intrigue at the number of merchant's shops that lined the streets. "What is the reason for the size and success of a town such as this?" she asked Liam.

"I believe that such places grow up along major transportation routes or at crossroads. Sometimes a group of people with certain skills will like the area, settle there, and bring their combined gifts to the economy. German immigrants are known for such things as working with wood, leather, and metals."

"It's like a small Philadelphia, Liam. I see clothing stores, furniture stores, maybe a clock shop on the corner over there. There are also a few grand houses similar to what we saw in the city. This is so exciting and nothing like what I expected here."

"I believe there are other similar places along the Wagon Road, but most of what we see will be much more rural. At least this is what my father has told me. We'll see for ourselves once we cross the mountains into the…" He paused before adding, "Shenandoah Valley."

"The Shenandoah Valley," Molly whispered. "… and *the mist-covered mountains of home!*"

On the outskirts of Lancaster, the caravan stopped again, and Pastor Durkin held a quick meeting and discussion. "We're a few miles away from the Susquehannock and will not have time to cross before dark. So, do we stay here and cross in the afternoon, or get closer to the river and try to cross early in the morning?" It had been a long day of travel, but most folks seemed to be willing to push on.

They were within sight of the river about nightfall, but the evening's cool air brought mist and fog all along the water. Molly's hopes of catching a glimpse of the first range of mountains would have to wait until morning. Liam joked… "mist-covered mountains… just like the song!"

Dinner was followed by a few ballads around the fire, with some instructions about crossing the river in the morning. Most everyone slept under tarps stretched out from their wagons because of the mist and fog, and what looked like the possibility of rain. Having the largest of the tarps as covering, Molly & Liam called for Kate, Darren and Patrick to bring their own bedding over and join them. Sprinkles of rain began to fall and Finn and Shannon Clarke soon joined them.

"My whole family… except for Gracie," Molly thought to herself. "Sleeping together on the banks of a river in America." She snuggled up closer to Liam who was already asleep, and her mind drifted toward the next day's travel… rivers, mountains, the first views of the Shenandoah Valley… and one day closer to Linville Creek.

CHAPTER 44

Just before daybreak the next morning, with a lantern in hand, Molly walked carefully down the quarter mile of the Great Wagon Road leading to the banks of the Susquehannock River, fiddle strapped to her back. The stars shown brilliantly in the night sky and a faint glow in the east gave her confidence that, as the sun came up, she would see the first ledge of blue mountains defining the boundaries of the Great Valley.

"*Sovereign Lord,*" Molly began to pray as she marveled at the vastness of the stars and constellations laid out before her. "*You have led us to this place, blessed us in this venture, and you have brought me to a wonderful new season of life that I could not have imagined just over a year ago. Thank you for Liam, Father. May I be the life partner he deserves and may we, as a couple, always trust you and your providence in our lives.*"

She pulled her fiddle from its case and began re-tuning it from the night of rain and cool temperatures. As she tuned, she sang...

There shall I gaze on the mountains again,
On the fields and the woods and the burns and the glens,
Away among the corries beyond human kin
In the haunts of the deer I will roam

From up the road behind her came Liam's voice, adding the chorus.

Oh soon shall I see them, Oh see them, Oh see them.
Oh soon shall I see them, the mist covered mountains of home.

Molly quickly turned around. "How did you find me?" she asked.

"Just followed the music," Liam laughed. "There's no one else around here fiddling at the break of dawn! Do you need some company or someone to keep you warm?"

"Sure," Molly smiled. "Come join me!"

As the two of them wrapped up in a quilt on the banks of the Susquehannock River, they listened to the sounds of birds ushering in the morning and watched the sky gradually turn a pale pink. Molly laid her head against Liam's shoulder, the river steadily lapping against the boulders. They lay back in the grass and she nodded off to sleep for a half hour. When she awoke, the sky was light enough that she could see the faint outline of the first of the small ridges in the distance.

"Liam, wake up," she called out. "There they are… our mist covered mountains.

Liam woke up and both of them jumped to their feet. Without a word, the young couple stood mesmerized, gazing at the first of the rising blue mountains they would be crossing into the Shenandoah Valley. There was nothing rugged or breathtaking about them. The line they formed was little more than a soft rise above the surrounding land-scape, but they were mountains, nonetheless.

"It's just like the description we received from Pastor Durkin before we decided to leave… all kinds of landscapes… richness… trees on the hillsides with lush meadows below. It looks like Ireland, Liam… it looks like home!"

"It *is* our home," he reminded her. "Through the gap, across that ridge and perhaps one more, and we'll be turning more southward into Virginia… *"to the fields and the woods and the burns and the glens!"*

"Let's get those horses hitched up and head that way," Molly squealed as she turned and scurried back up the hill to the wagons.

"Remember," Liam cautioned. "Everything takes time… everything is an adventure… enjoy the journey! It may take us most of the day to get everyone and everything safely across the river."

"In other words, slow down, right?" Molly grinned.

"Right!"

As they reached the top of the hill, families were gathered in groups at fires around several wagons, and fresh venison was sizzling in the pan at the McCourtney's wagon. "So, where have you two been so early this chilly morning?" Darren questioned as he poured them cups of coffee.

"I've seen the first mountains," Molly responded gleefully. "A little cool, but I had a quilt and a husband to keep me warm," she chuckled, giving her father a wink.

"Eat well this morning," Kate advised. "It will be a long day as we navigate the river and hopefully, cross the first ridge of mountains that you've been eyeing."

Liam could hear his father talking to a group of men near the center of the wagon circle and he took his plate of food and coffee and wandered that direction. Finn and Thomas Durkin were giving advice on the crossing of the river this morning. Based on their previous trip, they thought they had a plan in mind that would work well.

"The level of the river is quite low right now, something that will not always be the case. In fact, some small creeks will, at times, leave their banks and create quite the issue for us. But, with the conditions as they are now, I believe we can avoid the cost of ferrying our wagons across the Susquehannock by moving upstream to a very shallow spot we saw on our previous trip."

Two of the men mounted their horses to scout out the suggested crossing while everyone else finished breakfast, extinguished fires, and prepared their wagons. Within an hour, the riders had returned and agreed that crossing above the ferry was a good choice.

Gathering everyone together, Finn Clarke addressed the group. "The river is no more than a few feet deep, so we should be able to get all of the wagons across by mid-day. Take even more care than usual to secure everything in your wagon and, in case any water should seep in, I would suggest that you store fragile items that might be damaged by water, up as high as possible. You can hang some things high up on the bows to make sure they stay dry. We'll have at least two men on horseback walking with each wagon and looking out for any holes to avoid."

"We'll take the wagons across in the order you get to the river, so load up and head down to the bank." One by one throughout the morning, the wagons headed down the road to within sight of the river, veered off upstream of the ferry, and eased down into the water. For the most part, it was a slow and steady pace without any major difficulty. Liam and Molly volunteered to bring up the rear of the train and as their team of horses reached the far side of the river, pulling their wagon onto dry land, the whole group cheered, relieved at the successful crossing, knowing, however, that there were other similar crossings ahead, some of which would not be as easy.

It took several hours to reconfigure the loads in each wagon and check and seal any places where water may have leaked in. Molly knew that the hills were farther away than they appeared and the climb through the gap at the top of the ridge would be slower than yesterday's pace, but she was anxious to reach that point where Pastor Durkin had promised they would get their first glimpse of the landscape of the Great Valley. There were still parallel ridges to navigate and another major river crossing over the next few days, but up and over every crest and through every gap they passed, the more clearly Molly would be able to envision her new home and her new life with Liam. It was late afternoon when the teams of horses with their heavy wagons struggled up the final elevation and leveled out.

Stretching out before them was the most beautiful valley Molly had ever seen. The sun was low in the western sky and everything she had heard about this region, what she and Liam were now referring to as the Shenandoah Valley, were laid before her eyes.

"Vast…," Molly said quietly. "A vast landscape… so much land and so much opportunity."

Liam chuckled as he heard her whisper to herself, "so much music!"

Molly perched up on a large bolder outside the circle of wagons after their evening meal. A clearing and the remnants of other fires indicated that many travelers stopped at this point, no doubt with dreams and visions like her own. She gazed out across the expanse, breathing in the cool night air, and watched the stars appear.

Finn Clarke walked up behind her, plucking the strings of his fiddle and trying to recall the tune and the words to the song she had promised them when they spotted the mountains. "Help me out here as you promised, my dear daughter-in-law," Finn chuckled.

"That's the first time you've called me that… don't let it be the last. I love it!"

"I promise, it won't be the last. They are asking to hear the song, so give me a quick lesson."

"The tune is simple, and I'll get Liam to sing it with me… you just follow along." Taking Finn's fiddle, she quickly ran through the tune twice. Around the central campfire, the Letterkenny immigrants gathered and sang, looking out from the hilltop into the Great Valley.

> *Hail to the mountains with summits of blue*
> *To the glens with their meadows of sunshine and dew.*
> *To the women and men ever constant and true,*
> *Ever ready to welcome one home.*

Molly and Liam crawled under the quilts next to their wagon that night. "Another new ballad to teach you," Molly teased as she began humming a tune that Liam had not heard before.

> *And I would love you all the day, every night would kiss and play,*
> *If with me you would fondly stray, Over the hills and far away.*

"Another beautiful ballad," Liam whispered as he wrapped his arms around his wife and the two of them fell asleep under the Shenandoah sky.

CHAPTER 45

Three days later, the Letterkenny wagons rolled through the streets of Winchester, Virginia. Somewhere along the way, they had crossed the line into the Virginia colony, but no one knew where that occurred. They moved through the busy town and to its outskirts, circling in an open field as they had grown accustomed to each night since leaving Philadelphia. Molly noticed that few people on the streets of this town seemed to be paying any attention to them… they were just another group of tired and dusty settlers or immigrants heading along the Great Wagon Road.

Pastor Durkin passed the word around that this stop in Winchester was much more than a rest. They were only a few days' travel from Linville Creek and this was an important supply stop before reaching their new home. Winchester, one of the earliest settlements in the back country, seemed to be prepared for such travelers. It was unquestionably a "tavern-stop" town with many such establishments enhancing the main street, along with a sizable variety of businesses and factories. Just like Lancaster, the city had the occasional brick home that seemed to be patterned after those in Philadelphia.

Tomorrow would be a day spent stocking up on staples of food and tools that weren't purchased or available in Philadelphia. Molly was reminded of her conversation with Liam, questioning whether they had everything they needed. He had told her that they probably would not know if they had everything until they unpacked in Linville Creek. She was able to browse through the stores in town during the late afternoon and, with her mother's guidance, purchase some of their needed supplies. She bought the essentials for a sewing basket, some heavy fabric for farm clothes, enough floral material for a new dress, and two sets of fiddle strings. The Letterkenny families came back to their wagons and compared the purchases they had made.

In spite of her usual enthusiasm, as they got closer to their destination, Molly began thinking more of the difficulties that lay ahead of them in establishing their homesteads. This part of Virginia could hardly be called a wilderness as the first immigrants had seen it a number of decades earlier, there would still be dangers and difficulties ahead.

"We will have to clear land, build our homes, make our clothes, hunt for our own food, perhaps even defend ourselves," Liam reminded her. "We will only be as successful as the tools will allow. Rifle, axe, and plow… these are the most vital to our survival."

"I can handle the axe and the plow… I know how they work," she grinned. "I may need some instruction with the rifle!"

"That day will come soon enough," Liam responded. "Everyone on the frontier needs to be able to handle a rifle."

"And a fiddle?" Molly chuckled.

"Yes… and a fiddle," Liam responded with a laugh.

Kate McCourtney had prepared Irish Stew and boxty cakes as best she could on the open fire. She reveled in watching her family devour the meal. The shortcake from Gracie's recipe was equally enjoyable, despite being cooked on hot rocks.

"Part of surviving out here is figuring out how to do things that once were easy but doing them now in a completely different way," Darren said. "I suppose cooking is the same way… and you've passed the first test!"

Molly found herself in a thoughtful, somewhat reflective mood during the evening. She sat at the fire and gazed around at her friends and family, listening to their Irish voices and stories. She considered all they had been through together over the past year and a half, thinking about what life would bring to them individually and as a group in their future together.

Whenever she had these thoughts, she harkened back to Gracie's reflections. "The Irish have never been the most favored people" she had said, "so our inclination has always been to wander, finding a place of our own to lead our lives and worship God in our own fashion and according to our own convictions." That part, Molly understood. But when Gracie spoke of the "hardness" and "dourness" which Molly understood as being relentlessly severe and stern, she didn't see her people in the same way.

"It is what makes us determined and resilient," she thought to herself. She also recalled Gracie's reflections on the Irish tendency to endure hardships and fight back when threatened. "Maybe all of the things she said are true," Molly then contemplated aloud. Liam interrupted her from behind "I can always tell when you are in deep reflection... some faraway place. Let's go take a walk."

The two of them strolled through the streets of Winchester into the late afternoon, admiring the stone buildings and, once again, marveling at the number of shops catering to the needs of travelers like themselves. As they passed the Stone Quarter Tavern along Cork Street, Molly and Liam listened to the laughter and conversation from inside, and the smell of the evening meal wafting from open doors and windows out into the streets. "It's my night to help with dinner," Molly announced. "We need to head back to camp."

Leftover Irish stew from the previous night was already on the fire and Molly began peeling potatoes, onions, and carrots with the other ladies. Gracie's traditional stew that the family enjoyed so much when they visited with her, always had lamb or mutton as the base for the stew. Beef and some fresh venison, purchased in town that afternoon, provided an adequate substitute, but Molly longed for the day when they were settled and could cook their meals with their own root vegetables and lamb. Kate and Shannon had both experimented successfully with cooking loaves of bread over the open fire, a favorite addition at each meal.

As the sun dropped behind the closest ridge of mountains, Molly found a quiet, grassy patch outside of the circle of wagons to record in her journal her observations and thoughts about the day. Her writing was becoming more focused on the landscape of her new world and the sounds and smells of the Virginia countryside with its lush green fields, wildflower meadows, and seemingly countless varieties of majestic trees. In spite of the newness of everything around her, Molly was beginning to think more and more of Virginia as home. Her practice was to take these thoughts, turn them into lyrical phrases and, hopefully, into her own ballads about this place. Each time she sat with journal and pencil, she remembered her mother's words spoken on *The Allegheny*, "write things to keep and reflect on the rest of your life… something to share with your children…" Molly tried her best to heed those words of advice. Always, in her journaling, there were prayers of gratitude and petitions for protection in their journey and in their new lives.

As she joined Liam and their families around the dying fire, they both noticed the unusually bright smiles on their parents' faces and the few other friends who had gathered in their small circle. "What's going on?" she wondered out loud, looking at each one.

"We've been discussing among us an appropriate wedding gift for the two of you," Darren McCourtney began. "Something obviously affordable but memorable, nonetheless. So, each of us here in this group have arranged for the two of you to spend an evening and a night in the Stone Quarter Tavern tomorrow night before we head out on the last leg of our journey to Linville Creek. You can get some of this trail dust washed off of you, sleep in a real bed, and, as I understand it, enjoy some pretty good food! There is no telling when you may get your next opportunity for such comforts, so we thought this was appropriate." As Darren finished, Molly and Liam were hugging their mothers and friends… then, each other.

"What a special gift," Molly reflected as the two of them wrapped in quilts beneath their wagon for the night.

"And what special parents," Liam added. "We are blessed, Molly, and I trust that we can be the same to our children when that day comes."

"And that day will come, Liam. It will come."

CHAPTER 46

Sometime during the night Molly recalled being awakened as Liam pulled their ground tarp under the wagon to avoid the dampness and light rain that was falling. The mountains were shrouded in a foggy mist the next morning. Regardless of the weather, it was a busy day for the Letterkenny immigrants as they finished purchasing supplies, tools, and making repairs that would carry them safely to their final destination.

Liam spent the morning with the men who had been employed in the wheelwright's shop putting their skills to work on reenforcing and repairing the wagons. It would be disastrous for one of these to break down and, with the added weight of supplies now being purchased, every precaution needed to be taken. Molly helped repack supplies in the wagons, ensuring that the weight was evenly distributed for some rough stretches of road ahead of them.

A group spent the better part of the day in town purchasing the staples and provisions that would be used for the months ahead until, hopefully, a first crop of some essential foods would be ready for a fall harvest. As the wagons rolled back into camp from town loaded with barrels and boxes of flour, oats, corn and corn meal, dried beans, spices, sugar, molasses, rice, salt, and coffee… Molly thought she had never seen such a stockpile. Throughout their time in Philadelphia, each family had been diligently putting up as much dried meat and dried fruit as possible, knowing that this day was coming.

In the afternoon, the skies had mostly cleared, and the temperature dropped considerably, bringing a coolness and freshness to the air, reminding them that it was still spring, and perhaps a late snowfall was still possible. Molly and Liam found their parents, thanked them again for the gift of a night at the tavern, and headed into Winchester. "Bring your fiddle," Liam grinned with a mischievous look that puzzled Molly.

The couple arrived at the Stone Quarter Tavern and already, the aroma of the evening meal filled the building, and the fireplaces were crackling in each dining room downstairs. The proprietor was expecting them and ushered them to a room at the end of the upstairs hallway where they both fell across the straw mattress covered bed, more tired and sore from their travels than they realized.

"I've never been so dirty," Molly laughed as she brushed the road dust from her skirt. "I did bring another dress in my satchel… only appropriate for this special time with my husband, don't you think?"

"I packed another shirt as well," Liam responded. "Let's clean up the best we can with that pail of water I sat by the fire. I'm ready to see what's on the table for dinner!"

Molly cleaned up, brushed the tangles and most of the dust from her hair and slipped into her green and blue floral dress that Gracie had made for her before leaving Letterkenny. "How do I look?" she giggled as she twirled across the room to Liam.

He caught her in his arms and touched the garnet pendant at her neck, then Gracie's gold ring on her finger. "Lovely," he replied, then added, "The dress is nice as well!"

In his fresh shirt, a jacket, and the dust rinsed from his combed hair, Liam stood in front of Molly and joked, *"no blue jacket and white trousers, I'm afraid."*

Molly responded, *"and no blue petticoats and white flounces for me!"*

"That's alright," Liam responded. "We still make a rather dashing couple!"

They left the room arm-in-arm, laughing as they descended the stairs and found a place at a long table next to one of the fireplaces. Other guests were sitting as well and, except for a couple who resided in

Winchester, all of the others were travelers heading farther south along the Wagon Road. The food, as Darren had heard, was exceptional considering the fairly routine fare that they had grown accustomed to during their travels. Smoked ham, along with roasted potatoes and onions were wonderfully prepared. The ham, Molly thought, was particularly tasty and she had a conversation with the innkeeper's wife about its preparation. They were also treated to warm gingerbread for dessert. It was the most satisfying meal Molly could recall since leaving Letterkenny.

"Let's take a stroll," Liam whispered to Molly, mysteriously adding, "and bring your fiddle." The wind was blowing briskly and the temperature dropped as the sun descended behind the closest hills. Molly was glad to have brought the hooded, woolen cloak she had purchased before leaving Philadelphia.

The main street of Winchester, and it's numerous side streets were lined with businesses, but in vacant lots and especially in the fields behind the buildings, there were gatherings and circles of wagons much like their own camp south of town. Each group was illuminated in the growing darkness by a central fire, warding off the evening chill. Liam led the way toward one particular gathering of three wagons ahead of them and, as they got closer, Molly could hear music. As hard as she tried, however, she could not discern anything she recognized as familiar. The cadence, the rhythm, and the melodies themselves… all of it was different, and there was no place in her memory, out of all the music and ballads she had heard or collected in her life, for these tunes. But at its core, Molly could hear the strains of fiddle music! She was confused about it all, but it was exciting at the same time. She stopped in her tracks as they approached, and when she looked up at Liam, she saw a familiar ear-to-ear grin, convincing her that somehow this encounter was planned.

"Come ahead," Liam coaxed. "I want you to meet some special friends."

As he spoke, a young black couple, not much older than Liam and Molly, heard his voice and stepped out from the circle toward them, calling out as they approached. "Is that you, Liam? We'd given up on you coming by this evening as you promised. And this must be your Molly. I'm Kitch Banks and this is my wife, Jewell… the little one is our first born… our son Johnson."

Molly was at a loss for words and that must have shown in her face as both Kitch and Liam began laughing. "Have you never seen people of our color before?" Kitch asked.

"Yes," Molly stammered, "but admittedly, very few in our region of Ireland. I didn't expect to see any out here in this part of Virginia… I'm just surprised, that's all. So, how did you meet?"

"Like every other traveler who has stopped here in Winchester, we were buying supplies in the same place yesterday." Liam explained. "One thing led to another in our conversation, and Kitch told me about his interest in music and invited us to join them this evening."

"Are you here by yourselves?" Molly questioned.

"The three of us and another family of friends. My father, Tom, has turned in already, probably asleep in the wagon."

"No one else with you?"

"I know what you're thinking… You expect that we would have to be enslaved people, right?"

"Honestly? Yes, that is, I guess, my assumption. I'm wrong?"

"Only by the grace of God. The one who enslaved us on a farm along the Chesapeake Bay set us free less than a year ago. But we know the dangers that still exist for us if we should fall in among the wrong people, so we are doing as you are doing… finding new opportunities and, hopefully, lasting freedom. Our goal is to cross the mountains far south of here, through the Cumberland Gap and into the meadow-lands of Kentucke. The land, we hear, is rich, beautiful, and available for settlers."

Tom Banks climbed out of the back of one of the wagons and intro-duced himself. His accent was beautiful to Molly, but unrecognizable and multiple times she had to ask him to repeat what he said. "My father was kidnapped from the Winward Coast of Africa and brought to America," explained Kitch. "He still has the accent that many of those from that area have retained."

"Your music… is it African or something else? I recognize the fiddle, but not in the style you were playing." Then she pointed to another instrument lying nearby, one she didn't recognize. "And this is…?"

"It has many names and is played by various people groups in Africa. It is called an "akonting" in much of Africa… banjar or banjo here in America."

Kitch picked up the stringed instrument with its hide cover and began plucking and strumming in a rhythmic, almost percussive style. Before long, his father was playing melodies on an obviously rough and handcrafted old fiddle that he had pulled out of a cloth bag. Tom handled it well, producing the kind of songs that they had been playing when Liam and Molly arrived earlier.

Jewell handed her baby to Molly who treasured the warm bundle. She held him tightly against her chest, pulling her cloak around him. Jewell then began to dance with Kitch as Tom Banks took up his fiddle. The lively and joyous way in which Tom played and the young couple danced thrilled Molly. After several tunes, she laid out her case and opened it. Tom and Kitch marveled at the beautiful instrument and Tom immediately asked for a sample of the kind of music Molly played.

She spent some time sharing the background of her tunes and her Irish heritage. She told them about Gracie and how the fiddle had come into her possession. This family, with roots running as deep as hers, but from an entirely different part of the world, seemed as interested in her story and her culture as she was in theirs.

Liam and Molly sang *the Irish Lad, the Mist Covered Mountains*, and *On the Shores of Amerikay*. As they finished the last line and more stories were exchanged with their new friends, Molly felt a sadness that she had never before experienced… a sadness that brought tears to her eyes. The idea of her family making a free choice to immigrate to this beautiful land compared with Tom Banks's arrival, shackled against his will, burdened her deeply. She was also overwhelmed at how sharing music with strangers of such diverse backgrounds brought a closeness and broke down barriers as nothing else could. Her short time with the Banks family opened Molly's eyes to another new aspect of this great land that would be her home.

Tom played a few songs on Molly's fiddle and they said farewell to their new friends, encouraging them to stop in Linville Creek when they passed through on their way south. Walking back into town, Molly told Liam, "I don't think I will ever forget this encounter tonight and how it made me feel."

"Neither will I," Liam agreed. "That's why I brought you over here to meet them. Maybe our paths will cross, or our lives will intertwine with them somewhere again in the future."

"That would be wonderful," Molly replied, looking up at Liam. "Thank you for making the arrangements to allow this to happen."

As they cuddled under the quilts in their room at the Stone Quarter Tavern, the coals in the fireplace glowing, and the sounds of music, conversation, and laughter coming from the dining room below, Molly and Liam reflected on how rich and how full their lives had been in the two short years since leaving Ireland.

"So blessed…" were Liam's last words as he fell asleep. Molly's mind and heart, as usual, continued to swirl with the events of the evening and all of the things that had led up to this place and this time in their lives.

"Never," she thought, "would Luigi Caruso, half a century ago, have imagined what we witnessed here tonight. And tomorrow we begin the final leg of our journey… *"O're the raging foam, here I seek a new home, on the shores of Amerikay."*

CHAPTER 47

Aware of the long day of travel ahead of them, Molly and Liam were downstairs in the tavern earlier than any other guests. Fresh-baked biscuits and eggs complemented the ham and re-fried potatoes from their evening meal. After a short conversation with the innkeepers about their travels and thanking them for the hospitality, they headed out onto the streets of Winchester, turning south toward the outskirts of town while the sky was just turning pink and the mountains were beginning to show their outline against the pre-dawn sky. A brisk wind whipped down the main street and Molly pulled up her hood and tightened her cloak around her. They had just reached the edge of town and could see the activity and the fires around the Letterkenny camp. A few flakes of snow were blowing across their path.

They walked into camp and saw their parents around the fire, just finishing up breakfast. "Good morning," Kate smiled, giving Molly a hug. "Sorry, but we don't have anything left except coffee. How was your evening at the tavern?"

"Coffee would be great," Liam responded. "They fed us this morning before we left. I still have some ham and a few biscuits wrapped up in my pocket for lunch. It was a wonderful evening, Kate. The food, accommodations, new friends we met… all of it was wonderful. Thanks again for giving us a time together that we'll always remember."

"Mother, we had an extraordinary encounter with a family traveling the Wagon Road… a family of freed slaves. We played music around their campfire last evening, but nothing like what I've ever heard. Tom Banks had a fiddle and a plucking instrument he called an "akonting." He had roughed his fiddle out of wood himself. It was not even tuned the same as mine! But oh, the rhythms and the cadence and the melodies! Then he played mine…Luigi Caruso would not have recognized his instrument in the hands of Tom Banks. I can't wait to tell you all about it!"

"African music on your Italian fiddle?" The voice came from Liam's father approaching them.

"Yes, and I believe I can repeat a tune or two when we have the opportunity. The other instrument… some call it a banjo… provides great rhythmic background to a fiddle tune. Liam and I shared some of our ballads with them and we all danced."

"It all sounds wonderful," said Darren McCourtney as he walked up. "But we've been told to get ready to move out when the sun comes up over the mountain. Let's get the teams hitched up, fires out, and wagons loaded. As long as we aren't delayed in any significant way, we think we'll be in Linville Creek by tomorrow evening. Rough roads and at least one crossing of the Shenandoah River ahead of us today."

Kate and Molly helped each other pack up the cooking items and other supplies into the wagons, making sure everything was even more secure with the possibility of a rougher stretch of the Wagon Road ahead of them. With a river crossing coming up, they tied as many items as possible to the highest point of the bows supporting the canvas covers of the wagons.

Molly continued to fill in the details of their evening with the Banks. "I got to hold Kitch and Jewell's baby while they played music," she smiled. "His name is Johnson and I believe Jewell said he was born just before Christmas. He was so beautiful… smooth, brown skin, big brown eyes, and dark, curly hair. I could have held him there by the fire all night, I believe."

Kate just grinned and thought to herself, "Motherhood will fit you well, Molly Clark."

The wagons rolled out slowly, a bit later than planned, with occasional bursts of snow and brisk winds. But, as the sun rose higher in the late morning, a beautiful spring day revealed the Shenandoah Valley in all of its richness. Creeks were flowing fast and full. The mountains rising on both sides of the Wagon Road defined the wide, fertile valley as far as the eye could see. The higher elevations of the mountains were dusted with more snow than the valley floor. But to Molly Clark, the most striking thing was how this landscape took her mind back to Letterkenny and, in fact, all of Donegal… the numerous shades of vibrant green, the grasses long and flowing in the breeze, wildflowers that she would someday know the names of. She closed her eyes and remembered the picnic with Liam in the rocky meadow where they sat and imagined what America would be like. She also recalled the letter from Thomas Durkin that was read in their meeting on the day they decided to leave Letterkenny. "The trees on the hillside," he had told them, "stand in contrast to the lush, green valley floor." Molly kept mulling those words over and over in her mind as she now saw it for herself.

"So lush and green," she found herself speaking out loud. Liam's laugh at her words coming out of nowhere jarred her back to the reality of the moment. "Just thinking out loud," she said to him. "Remember, I do that often."

Liam nodded and grinned, "Yes, I remember!"

"The story of immigration to America that we're now a part of makes more and more sense to me all of the time," Molly blurted out excitedly.

"In what way?"

"Arrive in Philadelphia… an established wagon road leads west… turn south where land opens up, abundant and available… and now, look out before us Liam. Each step we've taken is a piece of the story. And this is the result… the prize awaiting those who successfully take the risk. I know that many thousands are doing exactly what we're doing, but I pray it stays like we're seeing it now." She turned to Liam and squeezed his hand, adding, "And experiencing all of this with you as we first dreamed about that day in the rocky meadow… that's the most important thing of all."

Liam responded with a smile and with the lines of a ballad that Molly did not recall ever hearing…

The river never will run dry, nor the rocks melt with the sun;
And I'll never prove false to the girl I love till all these things be done,
my dear,
Till all these things be done.

"Where did that come from?" she questioned.

"You don't think you're the only one who can catch meaningful songs from other people, do you? Or maybe I wrote it myself," he teased.

"I'll add one thing to the immigration story that I was just speaking of… one important thing. What I shared is our own personal story and the story of people like us. But the story of people like Jewel and Kitch and his father is very different." Molly's words trailed off into deep thought.

"What was the best part of meeting the Banks," Liam questioned, trying to lighten the conversation.

Molly looked up at Liam before answering simply, "Holding Johnson."

"I thought you might say that," Liam smiled.

The group stopped for lunch and to rest the horses and check the wagons. The ham biscuits from the tavern were satisfying. It felt good to get down off the wagon and stretch for a while. Molly walked ahead to Darren and Kate's Wagon, inviting Patrick to come ride with them for a while. The farther south they went, the more prominent were the mountain ranges on either side and the more common it became to see other travelers heading both north and south. Soon, the north branch of the Shenandoah River appeared, snuggled up against the base of the ridge they called Massanutens.

Thomas Durkin came riding up beside each wagon. "The water level is high, so we will ferry across the river first thing in the morning. We'll camp on this side in about an hour or so. Plan to be 'home' tomorrow afternoon!" he grinned.

"Home..." Molly said. "Tomorrow afternoon!"

That night was perhaps the coolest of their trip, but clear skies prevailed. The clouds and periodic snow from the morning were gone. Massanuten loomed high above their circle of wagons, and Molly enjoyed the soothing sound of the river's current just below them. Except for their nights at sea on *The Allegheny*, she could not remember such a clear sky with so many stars in view. She and Liam sat up late into the night talking about all manner of things before finally crawling under their extra blankets up against the wagon. They could hardly wait to roll into Linville Creek tomorrow evening.

Their wagons were lined up early the next morning, each waiting its turn to be ferried across the river. Thomas Durkin had already met with the operators the previous day, made the arrangements, and paid the toll. One wagon and horse team at a time crossed, so it took until after noon to maneuver the wagons, people, and supplies to the south side. Safely across the river, the group began heading south at a more rapid pace than they were accustomed to, hoping to arrive in the Linville Creek area before nightfall.

Late in the afternoon, Thomas Durkin and Daniel Walsh rode ahead on horseback to get some guidance from the landowners about where to secure their wagons and horses and finalizing transferring ownership of the land. The hand-drawn map of the five hundred acres that Daniel Walsh had showed them after the exploratory trip the previous fall had now been roughly divided into sections for each family. As discussed, a central church and school building would be central to their community. In typical Ulster Scot fashion, "infields," closer to the houses would be separated from the more distant "outfields," designated as pasture lands for common crops and the grazing lands for livestock. Within two hours, the men were coming back up the road with instructions for their arrival in Linville Creek.

The sun was setting behind the western ridge when they came to the crest of a slight hill and then to a bend in the road. Thomas Durkin's lead wagon stopped and he signaled for everyone to come to the front. "This must be the place," Molly burst out as she hopped down and ran, hand in hand with Liam, toward the lead wagon.

"This is what we've been working toward," Pastor Durkin proclaimed, sweeping his arm across the landscape. "This is where God has safely led us…"

Molly immediately teared up and wrapped her arm around Liam's waist as she took in the scene before her… There was such a variety of pleasing landscapes, more than she had ever before seen in one place. The rich meadow grounds adjacent to the rising forested hillsides added to the beauty, as Pastor Durkin had first described in his letter. Molly could see small streams converging into larger ones and knew that these fed into the nearby river. She pictured in her mind the Irish *clachans*, or clusters of small farms, and the rock walls that would one day designate the various fields and properties of their community.

"With God's help," Pastor Durkin continued, "Our community of Linville Creek will arise from this land that lies before us. Let's circle our wagons, prepare dinner, and build a large fire where we can spend some time this evening in worship and prayer, thanking God for bringing us safely to this place.

The families of Letterkenny gathered that evening with hugs and tears flowing abundantly as they shared their thoughts about such an important moment in their lives. One after one, the testimonies poured out of God's sovereign guidance and rich mercy during their travels and even before they had left home. *"O God, our help in ages past,"* one of the elders began to sing as the gathering came to a close. A hundred voices joined together, echoing out across the Virginia landscape. *"Our hope for years to come. Our shelter from the stormy blast, and our eternal home."* Pastor Durkin brought the worship service to a close with the announcement that in the morning, there would be a formal meeting to lay out plans and priorities for the work that at once needed to be done.

Molly was the first one up in the morning. Fiddle in hand, she took off through the meadow, reveling in the cool wetness of the tall grass and the sweet smell of the spring wildflowers. She headed for a stream where she could see trees growing on the banks along with large boulders, all of which reminded her of Ireland. As she sat on the rocks, basking in the morning sun, she felt obliged to play the ballads she could first remember hearing in Gracie's kitchen. One of the earliest was *Barbry Allen* that Finn Clarke had patiently and carefully helped her work through on her birthday almost three years ago. She played it over and over again before laying the fiddle in her lap and quietly singing another ballad to herself, again changing the words slightly to reflect not just a dream, but what was now a reality…

> *Hail to the mountains with summits of blue,*
> *To the glens with their meadows of sunshine and dew.*
> *Oh now I can see them, Oh see them, Oh see them.*
> *Oh now I can see them, the mist covered mountains of home.*

She looked across the meadow toward the wagons and saw Liam gazing her direction. With her childlike exuberance in full display, Molly headed toward him, running, twirling, and giggling. He couldn't control his laughter as she came closer and closer. He was also reminded of that birthday as well when he watched her come running and squealing toward him with her new fiddle in hand, long red braid trailing behind her and her flowered dress gleaming in the late morning sun.

Later today, they both knew the real work would begin, carving a home out of this place. But for now, Molly Clark simply felt free and alive in a way she had never experienced. And she was certain that the life she was delighting in was not just her own, but a new life within her. Time would tell.

PART 6

From Linville Creek toward the Cumberland Gap

c. 1766

The first spring after arriving in Linville Creek, an outsider would not look at the group of Letterkenny immigrants and think in terms of settlement or community. Only the bare necessities for survival were in place and were put there as soon as possible after they arrived the previous year. Each family had built small log structures or three-sided canvas tents built up against protective grassy banks with a large fireplace in the opening. Crops were planted. The winter had, at times, been harsh with deep and drifting snow, but these conditions were rare, and most of the winter had been at least tolerable.

As they settled and began to carve out this new life in Linville Creek, Molly and Liam's world was changing in ways they could only dream about just a few short years ago in Letterkenny. At the same time, the world around them was changing as well. Before the rumblings of revolution and independence of the American colonies had reached the backcountry, there was immense change in the communities scattered along the Great Wagon Road. European travelers to the region reported stunning growth, with a seemingly endless string of farms, forts, taverns, and villages.

Economic development in the decades prior to the Revolution intensified the commercial significance of the Wagon Road along with its cultural reflections on America as a whole. Travelers followed the road south to the terminus of the Great Valley near present-day Roanoke and continued south through the Blue Ridge into the Carolinas, or headed westwardly into the New River Valley, following the Wilderness Road toward the Cumberland Gap to Kentucky as the Banks family planned to do. These changes were evident to settlers such as those at Linville Creek, and as the demand for goods increased, so did the number of wagons passing by them.

These activities and changes were easy to see and document, but the unknown changes looming ahead in Molly and Liam Clark's lives would test their faith far beyond what they had planned.

CHAPTER 48

James Murphy Clark entered the world in Liam and Molly's cabin in early spring, blue eyed, red headed, and, best of all, robust and healthy. The dangers of childbirth were both real and frightening, especially on the frontier, so Molly was grateful beyond measure for their son's safe arrival. Kate and Shannon were on hand assisting in the birth of their first grandchild. The entire Linville Creek community celebrated the safe arrival of the first of the next generation in their new American congregation.

Liam had built their first home well before winter set in, and a bit larger and sturdier than most of their friends had because of James' impending arrival. Molly reveled in watching her husband in this new role. Every spare minute when he wasn't plowing fields, planting crops for fall harvest, or hunting or trapping, Liam was gathering rocks from the surrounding area to build a chimney and hearth for their cabin. All along their travels on the Wagon Road, he had examined chimneys and the log construction methods. Molly helped in all of these tasks as long as her condition allowed. The finished chimney was the talk of the Linville Creek community, and the others were coming by often to see how it was progressing.

"We may not have much to give to our child this first winter, but we can make what we have warm and secure, that's for sure," he had told Molly.

Building shelter and getting some crops in the ground were everyone's top priority after arriving here the previous year. The total acreage of Linville Creek had been divided into individual tracts and portioned among each family. The size of each section depended on the amount of funds a family could contribute to the total cost, but the tracts for everyone were adequate for beginning life here in Virginia. The parcel of land that Liam and Molly received was somewhat smaller than some other plots. In exchange for less land, however, they chose a partially wooded tract that lay adjacent to the Wagon Road with a creek and a rising hill in one corner that Molly immediately christened her "Virginia rocky meadow." Liam had girdled an adequate number of trees for their small cabin and later, with the help of other men, cut them and brought them to the place they had designated for the initial single room and other later additions.

During the long winter, Molly spent many evenings by the fire sketching out plans for expanding their garden plot just outside of the cabin. This had provided them with potatoes, onions, and other root crops, that, along with salted beef and pork, supplied them until spring. She designated the rough boundaries of the "infields," closer to the house, plots that were worked daily, and the "outfields" of their acreage for larger fields of grain and pastures for livestock. Liam had marked off the borders of the cabin additions that they hoped to have in place before their second winter.

After James' birth in the early spring, Molly's priorities understandably took a different path. Caring for her newborn and balancing that responsibility with the establishment of their new homestead seemed overwhelming at times. When the weather permitted, she would bundle James up in a quilt and head across the fields to Darren and Kate's cottage. Many of the same priorities were going on there, as they were in every household, getting ready for spring planting, improving the living space, and prioritizing the many tasks that needed to be accomplished to insure a successful second year in their new community.

Liam had purchased enough lumber in Winchester to build them a table and a frame for a straw-filled mattress covered with a quilt that Kate had given them. A Dutch oven and a few plates, cups, and utensils were adequate at this point. Much to Molly's delight, he had surprised her with two rocking chairs to round out their furnishings. A thick poplar beam above the hearth served as a mantlepiece where Molly's fiddle sat prominently. "Small and sparse," she thought often as she looked around the cabin, "but it is a fine beginning homestead, and it is ours."

For the first time since her fifteenth birthday and opening the fiddle at her parents' table, Molly was not playing it every day. James took most of her attention and the list of things that needed to be accomplished to help Liam seemed to continually grow no matter how much she thought she had completed on any given day. But the ballads and the sweet music in her head always accompanied her, even if her fiddle remained on the mantle.

One evening when James was particularly irritable, Molly discovered, much to her delight, that playing and singing the slow ballads seemed to have a mesmerizing effect on him and often quieted him. He would focus his blue eyes on her as if he was trying to learn the lyrics or memorize the tune. Rocking him after he had fallen asleep, she turned to Liam, stifling a chuckle. "The songs are not just for my enjoyment any longer… with this effect on James, they have a more important purpose now."

"The music is part of what attracted me to you, so I've always seen it as having an important purpose," he kidded.

Molly's fiddle lay across her lap as she continued to rock her sleeping son and his tiny hand rested on the fingerboard of the instrument. She wondered if he would take to the songs of his Irish heritage as she had. Molly was suddenly saddened to think that the land of her childhood that was so much a part of who she was would never be part of James' life. Telling him of those places and singing those songs to him was more important than ever at that moment.

The flickering light of the fire on her fiddle brought some illumination to the inside of the instrument and on the faded label. As she had often done over the years, she closed her eyes and began to imagine the craftsman whose hands had created her prized instrument. What would Luigi Caruso think of this life she was living and the miles that his fiddle had traveled? What would he think of the kind of sounds she brought from it here in the Great Valley of Virginia, a place that he had never even dreamed of? Thoughts such as these almost haunted her as she tried to fathom them. She took James' hand and gently stroked it along the length of the polished wood.

"I will teach you, James. I will tell you the stories that my grand-mother told me. I promise."

"So will his father," Liam spoke as he stepped up behind them and wrapped his arms around Molly.

They banked the fire, swaddled James in a blanket, and tucked him in a quilt-lined crate that, for now, served as a bed. Liam and Molly talked into the night about the plans and dreams for their land and the tremen-dous blessings they had known in such a short time together.

The following day had been set aside for all the residents to gather at the designated central parcel of land where together they would erect a structure to serve as their new place of worship and as a school. Timbers had been placed there, along with a supply of lumber that was adequate for this first stage of the Linville Creek Presbyterian Meeting House. The work would be a community effort, beginning at sunrise and lasting until evening when a worship service would be held. Thomas Durkin had sketched the plans for a simple open arbor of hewn timbers with a thatch roof. As many pews as could be built out of the lumber would provide seating for at least some portion of the congregation. Later, it would be closed in, but for now, the open plan would have to suffice.

"I like the idea of worshipping in a place where I can look out on the hills and green fields," Molly told Liam as they prepared to head out the next morning.

"It does have a nice appeal to it," Liam agreed. "But a real struc-ture with a steeple and walls is more appropriate in the long run, don't you think?"

"I suppose so," Molly agreed somewhat reluctantly. "But I'll enjoy the open arbor while we have it."

It was a cool morning, and the sun was just rising over the closest mountain top. The fields were saturated and sparkling with the morning dew as they headed for the work site. A pot of Irish stew and ash cakes were their family's contribution to the noon meal. It would be good to get together with all of the Letterkenny friends, something that had happened sparingly through the winter months. Construction of the meeting house, even in its open-sided first stage, would mean more regular church services and other gathering opportunities. Molly watched the sun gradually work its way from the top to the bottom of the distant mountains and she couldn't resist singing to James, who was squinting in the bright morning light.

> *There shall I gaze on the mountains again,*
> *On the fields and the woods and the burns and the glens,*
> *Hail to the mountains with summits of blue,*
> *To the glens with their meadows of sunshine and dew.*

Before they topped the slight hill above the worksite, they could hear the echoes of people at work. Loud voices, laughter, and the sounds of construction… mallets, broad axes, and froes. Molly and Liam both stopped to survey the scene unfolding below. In addition to the group below them, from every corner of their new village families were passing through the meadows and fields heading toward what would soon be their regular place of worship. Molly was overwhelmed at the sight and could hardly wait to join in.

"Let's hurry," she begged Liam as she began bounding down the hill.

"Careful," Liam cried out. "That's a precious bundle in your arms!"

"Yes, he is," Molly spoke to herself. "Irish… American… and Virginian!"

CHAPTER 49

The first winter was behind them and the collaborative efforts of so many people working on the arbor did their hearts much good. The work was hard, but the fellowship along the way was a delight for everyone. Some families had obviously spent more time together over the winter, while others had seen each other only at the occasional church services that were held when weather allowed.

Molly enjoyed listening to the questions and conversation taking place amid the work. "How did you manage the heavy snowfall? Did your fall garden crops last you? When do you plan to plow your infields? Here is something I learned to cook on the hearth." Everyone, of course, was interested in James, a few of the older couples seeing him for the first time. Molly had more than enough offers to watch him during the day while she assisted with the construction.

The men were working on the largest timbers which would be used for the main support of the roof. Each one had to be hewed and squared off with a broad axe before being dropped into the ground. Removing rocks and limbs from the floor of the arbor and smoothing out the ground were tasks that even the children could take part in. Shortly after noon, the food prepared by each family was combined into a wonderful meal.

Darren McCourtney and Finn Clarke had filled themselves with the bountiful spread and were sprawled out, eyes closed, enjoying the midday spring sun. Liam sneaked over and gave each of them a kick on the soles of their boots, calling them back to work. "Let's go, old men," he chided loudly. "There's work to be done!" Startled, the two of them laughed and scrambled to their feet and, along with the other workers, headed over to continue the construction.

By the middle of the afternoon, the upright timbers were secured in the ground, cross timbers mortised in place, and the roof timbers ready for the thatching material to be put in place. Without the communal effort of such a large group, the structure could not have been completed in a day. A large pile of straw, grasses, and saplings had been collected in the previous days and a group of men were layering them and tying them in place late into the afternoon. This was adequate for now, but after each of the next few good rains, patching the thatched roof would be required to identify and repair any leaks.

The roof was completed, and several rows of rough pews built when Pastor Durkin called everyone together thanking them for their hard work. "We will recall this day for many years to come," he began. "And those of you with small children can add this story to the others that you will share with them as they grow up… the stories of how God brought us from Letterkenny to Linville Creek."

Molly took these words to heart, along with Liam, as they both looked down into James' face. Molly renewed her determination to record her life in Ireland and in Virginia through her journals and her music. She remembered her mother's instructions while doing her schoolwork on *The Allegheny*. Her writing, Kate had said, "will be something that you can keep and reflect on the rest of your life… perhaps sharing it with your children someday. Give it your best effort."

"My best effort," Molly whispered to herself and to her son.

Thomas Durkin ushered the congregation into the arbor and took his place on a platform at the front. About half of the congregation crowded onto the benches that had been constructed. Others sat on the ground or stood in the back. With everyone settled, Pastor Durkin drew their attention to the hand painted sign signifying their day's work.

"Linville Creek Presbyterian Meeting House, established 1766 by residents of Letterkenny, County Donegal, Ireland."

"We have been here for about a year," he began, choked with emotion. "But so much of our time thus far has been involved in the tasks of getting settled, getting shelter over our heads, and surviving the winter. I feel as though the work we've completed today building our own meeting house is, in some ways, the real beginning of our community..."

A short dedication of the open arbor followed, once again with prayers and testimonies of God's faithfulness in their lives. They sang with exuberance as they had when they first arrived at Linville Creek the previous spring. *"O God, our help in ages past, our hope for years to come. Our shelter from the stormy blast, and our eternal home."* This was followed by several other hymns before they closed with the traditional Doxology. With joy in her heart, Molly watched the sun disappear behind the distant mountains, the perfect conclusion to their exhausting, but extraordinary day.

CHAPTER 50

Throughout the rest of the spring and into early summer, Molly planted, watered, and tended to the vegetable garden outside their cottage. The land in the Valley, with its rich deposits of limestone, lent itself nicely to fields of wheat and other grains, along with flax. All of these crops, when harvested, would provide for the family and they could be sold or bartered with residents in other communities.

Liam had plowed the field closest to the cottage and sewed it with wheat. By the time of their arrival in Virginia, wheat was becoming one of the largest exports from the colony. A good crop could be ground into flour at a local mill and sold for a significant profit even as far away as Philadelphia.

The couple had made the decision before even arriving in Linville Creek to create a homestead that was as reminiscent of their Irish roots as possible. So, replacing their relatively flat roof with a steep-pitched and heavily thatched one was a change that they hoped to make this season. In addition, a thick, lime whitewash of both the inside and the outside of the cottage did wonders for creating a much brighter living space and a scene that reminded Molly so much of their Letterkenny cottage and farm. The property had no shortage of field stones, so clearing their fields and carefully stacking these into neat fences seemed a never-ending task. It was, however, a necessary part of creating a productive farm, and it helped fulfill their memories of home.

One evening, Liam was on the floor with James, resting from a day of cutting out two small windows, one facing the mountains in the west, and the other looking out toward the Wagon Road. Shutters would be added soon in order to keep out bad weather and the winter winds. The light and the views the windows provided were a delight to Molly.

"I can see the mountains while I'm in the house and in the other direction, I can see travelers coming along the Wagon Road." Her excitement over his work brought deep satisfaction to Liam.

"I heard some interesting news today from a group of travelers along the road," Liam said. "There is some development of a new town going on north of here, maybe halfway to Winchester. It is quite extensive. A mill is already under construction, along with a blacksmith shop. A tavern and a few other shops providing supplies for travelers will be coming along soon."

"Will this be of benefit to us?" Molly questioned.

"I think it will, but only time will tell for sure," Liam replied. "Any services provided that are closer to us than Winchester will be to our advantage in the long run... at least, that is the way I see it. They've named it Woodstock."

"Will there be Irish, do you think... perhaps even from somewhere in Donegal?"

"I've heard this entire region referred to as 'the Irish Tract,'" Liam responded. "Lots of immigrants with stories similar to our own... and many from Ireland. We'll see." He paused, looking intently at Molly. "You would like that, wouldn't you?"

"I'd love it," Molly grinned and then suddenly got excited. "Oh my, what if someone moved here from Gweedore... someone who knew Gracie!"

Liam laughed at her exuberance, but realized quickly from Molly's reaction to his laughter that he should not dismiss the possibility so casually. "I'm sorry," he apologized. "Anything is possible, right?"

The ideas that had entered their conversation that evening... thoughts of home and the grandmother she had left behind, brought dreams of Letterkenny during the night. It was lush and green as she remembered, and Molly found herself up in the rocky meadow with Dundee at her side, singing ballads with Gracie.

All in the merry month of May, when green leaves they were springin
This young man on his death bed lay, for the love of Barbry' Allen

In her dream, Molly, for some reason, saw a younger version of herself but a much older version of her grandmother. She and Gracie sang numerous ballads, but Molly suddenly realized that she did not have her fiddle with her. She was running among the rocks and through the heather searching frantically. She woke up from her dream still mumbling the lines of *Barbry' Allen* to herself. She quickly looked across the room, relieved to see her fiddle in its place on the mantel. Neither James nor Liam were stirring.

As quietly as possible, she crawled out of bed and walked over to the hearth, taking the instrument down from the shelf. Sitting in her rocking chair by the fireplace, she opened the case, imagining, as always, Gracie, Luigi, and scenes from Donegal. As content and grateful as Molly was with the life she had now, stories and dreams such as the one she had just awakened from left her a bit homesick. Cradling her fiddle, she stepped out into the coolness and sat on the stone wall, gazing at the constellations on this clear, moonless night.

"*Thank you, Sovereign God, for the many blessings that have come from your hand,*" she whispered. "*The beauty of this place… for Liam and James… the wonderful families you've given us. Most of all, for calling us into repentance and unto eternal life.*"

Molly began to sing, risking awakening her family, she knew, if she did so too loudly. So, she wandered a short distance from the cottage, across the meadow, enjoying the cool dew around her feet and ankles.

She felt as young as she was in her dream and, for a moment, without a care in the world.

I know dark clouds may gather round me
I know my way may be rough and steep
But golden fields lie out before me
Where all the saints their vigils keep

Sitting on a rock in the field, and as quietly as possible, she played a few of the slow ballads and melodies as they came to her mind. The sweet smell of the meadow, the distant sound of the trickling creek, and the breezes in the trees combined perfectly, and, in Molly's mind, enhanced her fiddle tunes. She felt as if she could stay here until dawn, but knowing that the morning would, as always, bring more responsibilities and tasks than she could possibly accomplish, she headed back. Turning toward the cottage, she saw Liam's tall figure silhouetted against the doorway.

"What in the world are you doing out here in the middle of the night?" he questioned in a half-teasing manner.

"Just getting an early start on the day," she joked as they hugged in the doorway. "Actually, I was enjoying this beautiful night. Did my music wake you?"

"No, I didn't hear you until after I woke up," he replied. "But what brought this about…wandering out in the night like this? I've never known you to do that. Is something bothering you?"

"No, there is nothing wrong," Molly began. "Our conversation last night about Irish settlers coming into the area and thinking about Gracie… caused me to have dreams of home." She told Liam about being back on the farm in Letterkenny, singing with Gracie, and losing her fiddle.

"I woke up in a panic," she admitted sheepishly. "I had to get it off of the mantel and make certain it was still there. It's hard to resist playing it once I open the case… even in the middle of the night!"

Stifling a laugh so as not to wake up James, Liam took the fiddle from Molly's hands. "Let me put that up for you. Get back in bed and warm up your hands and feet before I join you!"

"Gladly," Molly grinned, throwing an extra quilt across her feet. "I need to write Gracie a letter, Liam. I haven't written her since just after James was born although I'm sure mother has done so recently to let her know how things are going here. Remind me to do that soon."

Liam had put up Molly's fiddle and was getting into bed when he responded, "Yes, take the time soon to do that."

She didn't hear Liam's response. Rehearsing in her mind all of the things she needed to share with her grandmother when she wrote, Molly had fallen into a sound sleep as the faintest of morning light began showing in the eastern sky.

CHAPTER 51

Molly made certain that she found the time to write a letter to Gracie over the next few days, giving it to a stagecoach driver she stopped along the Wagon Road who promised to drop it at the postal office in Winchester. She could only trust that this colonial system worked and that, eventually, her letter would reach Gweedore and get into Gracie's hands. She wrote about the building of the meeting house, about Kitch and Jewel Starling, and included a sketch of their cottage and the view she had of the mountains through the windows Liam had cut out. She ended the letter speaking mostly of James…

> *"He is just over a year old and so full of energy… full of himself! There is no doubt, Gracie, of his Irish heritage… His hair is as red as my own and with the brightest blue eyes imaginable! Mother looks at him often and sees you in his face. What I wouldn't give for you to see him and hold him. He has heard many stories of you already and your songs will become a part of his life always! None of my words are an adequate expression of my love for you and I hold the memories of my times with you dearly. Your granddaughter, Molly."*

She walked back up the short trail to the cottage after delivering her letter to the stagecoach driver and, noticing how the brush had encroached onto the trail, she decided to spend some time clearing the path before the sun rose any higher. With a cautious eye on James, who was crawling, attempting to take his first steps, and curious to explore everything, Molly began whacking away at the briars and weeds, finding both the exertion and the results of her effort satisfying. She worked her way down one side of the trail and rested on the bank with James enjoying the view of the eastern mountain range and the road stretching north and south before them. There was not a moment when, looking up and down this great trail, Molly could not see at least one wagon, carriage, or riders on horseback. As she watched, it was all she could do to resist calling out to each one individually to find out where they were going and where they had come from, along with a myriad of other questions. The few travelers who stopped for water where Linville Creek came closest to the road got Molly's full attention as she engaged them in conversation. She met no one on this day from Ireland but encounters with such groups were not unusual here in the "Irish Tract."

She cleaned out some debris around the sign they had set into the bank identifying Linville Creek and began working her way back up the other side of the trail toward the cottage. James was getting irritable, so Molly made haste in clearing only the worst of the brambles and briars. "This will do for now," she thought to herself.

Back at the cottage, the ash cakes wrapped in corn husks had been in the coals long enough to be nicely browned, so Molly and James enjoyed them with some dried apples she took down from the ceiling joists where they had been hanging for a month. She was expecting Liam in the early afternoon since he had left before daylight with some of the other men hoping to bring home some venison from their day in the mountains.

Life on their small Virginia homestead had a rhythm of activity that Molly and Liam were growing accustomed to, although unexpected interruptions were common. They found themselves to be simultaneously herders, ranchers, farmers, and hunters with each task playing an important role in their future success and, perhaps even their survival. In this respect, Linville Creek was quickly becoming similar to other communities along the Great Wagon Road.

Today was Liam's day to be a hunter although everyone knew that autumn was the best season when the weather was cooler, and the wildlife was out foraging and fattening up for winter on chestnuts, beechnuts, and acorns. Fresh game in any season was sustenance, however, and in these days of establishing a farm, that was Liam's priority. Molly saw him coming across the field with the bounty from the morning's trek into the mountains, and she gave thanks for the food that would be on their table, and for her husband's safe return.

"We did well this morning," he beamed as he approached the cottage. "This should last us for a while!"

"How far up on the ridge did you go?" Molly questioned.

"There were some rocky outcrops along the top and we climbed up there to see what the view was like looking west. It is wave after wave of mountain ridges as far as you can see, Molly. It was impossible to tell how wide the valleys are between the ridges, but my speculation is that none of those were as wide or fertile as ours... it is, after all, "the Great Valley of Virginia!"

"I'll expect you to take me up there some day to see it for myself," she pleaded.

"Yes, we will do that," Liam promised. He picked up James and held him high above his head. "You can go with us too when you're older!"

They spent the afternoon cutting up the meat which was mostly venison but included one turkey and a few other game birds. Liam salted it all thoroughly and hung it in their crude smoke house in the edge of the woods. He got the fire started and looked on with satisfaction at his provision for the family.

"In the fall, there will be much more," he said to himself, heading back to the cottage.

"I could smell the smoke from our place, so I had to come over and see the results of your hunt!" Liam turned and saw Molly's father approaching.

"Quite a haul, don't you think? Especially for this time of year," Liam replied proudly. "We're roasting some choice pieces of venison in the fire right now... plenty for you and Kate and Patrick to join us for dinner."

"That sounds good, son. I believe we'll do that. We actually have some things to discuss with you as a family and I came over only partly because I smelled the smoke, but to find time for us all to talk. Your invitation is timed perfectly!"

Liam tried to read the look on Darren Clarke's face. He couldn't recall a more serious or concerning expression in all the years he had known him. Trying to decide whether to ask for some details or to just wait until dinner, Darren interrupted his thoughts...

"Shouldn't you ask your wife before inviting us over?" Darren quipped.

"She'll be fine with it," Liam grinned. "We'll look forward to seeing you. Maybe we'll get James to sleep for a bit before you arrive so he will be good for his grandparents!"

As Darren headed up the grassy lane and across the hill toward his cottage, Liam was trying to decide whether to tell Molly about his concerns. "Maybe I'm making something out of nothing," he thought to himself, but still he could not shake the look on his father-in-law's face... a look that spoke of concern and worry. He took a few moments to examine the rock foundation for the new room of their cottage that he hoped to have closed in before winter. Then, stamping the ashes from the smokehouse off his boots at the door, he walked in, savoring the smell of the roasting venison coming from the fire.

"Did I hear another voice outside?" Molly asked.

"Yes, it was your father. He had smelled the smokehouse and came over to check out my hunting skills from this morning," Liam chuckled.

He turned more serious as he added. "He asked for a time when he and your mother could come over to discuss something with us... from the look on his face, it seemed to be something quite serious."

"Any hint as to what that might be?"

"None at all. I invited them tonight to share the venison with us... I hope that is alright with you."

"Of course," Molly replied. "I have some onions and potatoes from the garden and will pick some greens. We'll make it a real feast. Mother will bring something, I'm certain... maybe Gracie's shortbread recipe."

"Make boxty cakes from our new potatoes. They'll be perfect with the venison!" Liam suggested.

"Oh, yes, they would!" Molly agreed. "I remember a rhyme from Gracie when we were at her house the last time. "Boxty on the griddle, boxty on the pan; if you can't make boxty, you'll never get a man..."

Liam laughed "I've never heard that before. Write it down in your journal so we won't forget it! Turn it into a fiddle tune!"

At the mention of her fiddle, Molly glanced across the room at its resting place on the hearth. "I haven't even had it down to hold it, much less play it for several days. A year ago, I would never have believed that to be the case. Keep after me when I have these spells of not playing," she begged.

"Yes ma'am," Liam answered and then turned his attention to James. "You heard your mother, young man... allow her some fiddling time instead of craving her attention at every moment!"

Liam took James to Molly's rocky meadow where he was able to sing him to sleep for a short time. Molly cut a few fresh greens and began cooking them in a pot hanging over the fire. She began making her boxty cakes and heated up their spider skillet to fry them in. She was overwhelmed with memories of Gracie and being in her Gweedore cottage. Perhaps trying to mimic the environment of those precious days, she began humming and then singing in her best attempt at Gracie's Scottish drawl.

In Scarlet town, where I was born, there was a fair maid dwelling

Whom I had chosen for my own, and her name was Barbry' Allen
All in the merry month of May, when green leaves they were springing
This young man on his death bed lay, for the love of Barbry' Allen

Whether it was because she had the preparations for dinner complete or because of the memories generated by Gracie's song, either way, Molly felt an unsatiable desire to play her fiddle. Taking it off the hearth, she did some fine tuning and began *Barbry' Allen*. Before Liam and James had returned from the meadow, she had played through *Pretty Saro*, *The True Lover's Farewell*, *One Morning in May*, and *The Mist Covered Mountains*. Listening to the sweet sounds, even the feel of the instrument in her hands and resting under her chin fueled Molly's deep longing for connection, not just with her grandmother, but with all of those unknown generations who had gone before her.

As she put her fiddle away and continued dinner preparations, Molly knew that the tunes and lyrics she had just played were now ingrained in her thoughts, she knew, for the rest of the day. When Liam and James came in the door, she swept the toddler up in her arms and danced around the room, singing her loudest as James squealed in delight.

They hadn't been there but an hour or two
Till out of his knapsack a fiddle he drew
The tune that he played caused the valleys to ring.
O harken, says the lady, how the nightingales sing.

The three of them were still waltzing around the cottage when James pointed out the window excitedly. Molly could see her parents and brother coming across the hill, and as she sat him down, James stumbled through the door, picked himself up, and headed toward them. Patrick, loving his new role as uncle, left Darren and Kate and ran down the hill with his arms wide open, encouraging James to run faster.

In the joyous moments of the last hour, cooking, singing, memories of Gracie, and anticipating an evening with her parents, Molly had forgotten that there was a serious nature to the visit. Her father had only mysteriously shared this with Liam earlier that afternoon. As they opened the gate in the fence surrounding their cottage, however, she saw the worry and concern for herself in the faces of both Darren and Kate McCourtney. The tears flowed freely from Kate's face as she reached out to hug her daughter.

"Oh, Molly," she began. "The doctor in Winchester says I have a … serious illness… it could be life threatening. He says we need to go back to Philadelphia for treatment!"

CHAPTER 52

Molly was so consumed with the shock of her mother's words that she could barely get the food preparations finished and dinner served. Liam had suggested that they have their meal before hearing any more or talking through the details of what this all meant. Keeping her thoughts to herself as her husband had advised, Molly could not avoid the feelings within her… the swirling, emotional pain that was racking her.

"How? Why? For what purpose?" These and scores of other questions raced through her mind, and she fought back tears with every morsel of food. Oblivious to the seriousness within the cottage, James laughed and babbled around the table throughout the meal. Kate tried her best to put on a pleasant face and play games with James just as her instincts as a grandmother called for.

When the family had finished dinner, they pulled the rocking chairs and a bench outside where the early evening sun would soon drop below the western mountains. They enjoyed the shortbread that Kate had brought, and with Patrick wrestling with James out in the meadow grass, Molly's parents began to fill in the details of the news that had brought them here tonight.

"I began having headaches about six months ago," Kate began. "I thought very little about them at the time, but as the weeks and months went by, they got worse and more frequent."

"You should have told us earlier," Molly insisted. "When did you see a doctor?"

"The trip we made to Winchester a few weeks ago was for supplies, as we told you, but also to visit a doctor there." Kate took Darren by the hand, and, from her look, he knew she wanted him to pick up the story.

"The doctor in Winchester called it a canker or a cancer in her brain. Only by operating can they tell how deep the growth is and whether it can be removed." Darren paused and let out a deep sigh. Before he could continue, Molly fired off a string of questions in her attempt to grasp every bit of information that might assist her in facing the future.

"How dangerous is the operation? What is the likelihood of its success? Are there other options? When do you plan to go?"

"Philadelphia is really our only option for finding the doctors that can answer all those questions," her father responded. "Obviously, an operation is dangerous, the possibilities of success… we just don't know."

"When will you need to leave?" Molly questioned. "How soon?"

"We're making arrangements, but there are many things that need to happen," Darren explained. "I've sent word to John Williams to see about getting my job back at the wainwright's shop. I've also asked him to see if there is availability at the boarding house where we lived before… I can only hope that the letter gets to him."

Almost in unison, Molly and Liam asked, "What can we do to help?"

Kate turned her face out toward the meadow and tears again began to run down her cheeks as she looked toward Patrick and James still wrestling in the grass, now damp with the evening dew. She dropped her face into her hands without responding to Molly's question.

"How much have you told Patrick about this," Molly asked her father.

"Only that your mother is sick, and we will need to go to Philadelphia," Darren answered. "We feel like that is enough for now… unless he presses us for more."

There were times in Molly's life when childhood was still a fresh memory, and when, if for only a moment, she was carried back to an uncomplicated and joyous time filled with youthful wonder. But now, in the glow of the sunset, she gazed toward the meadow as well, listening to the squeals and laughter, and the full weight of her role as daughter, mother, and older sister crashed down and consumed her as never before.

Expanding on their earlier question, Liam asked again. "I know there are things you need, perhaps things you have yet to even think about. How can we help?"

"It would be so hard to leave Patrick behind," Kate began. "But in some ways, it would be much less complicated."

This was obviously something that had occupied much of their conversation over the past weeks as Darren picked up the same thought. "If Kate is hospitalized for a long period of time or if she simply needs rest at home, it would be so much simpler with just the two of us there."

With a reassuring and hopeful glance toward his wife, he added, "We could get her well again and back home to Linville Creek much more quickly!"

Liam gave Molly a smile and replied, "The least we can do is keep him here with us until you return. I know he would miss you, but I believe he and James would find it enjoyable! I hope to have the extra room under roof by the time winter sets in. It won't be completely finished, but an extra room, nonetheless."

"Our first regular school classes at the meeting house will probably begin in the fall. It would be best for Patrick and help keep his mind off of worrying about you." Molly added.

"Thank you so much," Darren responded. "Let us explore the idea with Patrick and see what his reaction is, then we will let you know. Our most immediate need is financial. We will do whatever is necessary, but we may find that selling our portion of land to someone else is the only resolution."

"That would mean everything we have sacrificed for since leaving Letterkenny," Kate added sadly.

"I would consider that a last resort," Liam quickly added. "I think we would all agree that God brought us here safely and directed us to this place. There must be another way. How widely have you shared this among the community and the congregation?"

"We have let Pastor Durkin know about it, and he took the trip to Winchester with us to see the doctor there. We asked him to share it only among the elders until we had talked to you."

"It's important that everyone knows of your need and has the opportunity to help," Liam said. "We made our journey here with friends. We are building our community and our church congregation together. That didn't stop the day we arrived. It still continues… we're in this together."

"We will do everything possible," Molly added, "to ensure that you have a farm to come back to. At church on Sunday, we will have Pastor Durkin advise the congregation of what is going on and the financial need."

The four of them spent some time in prayer, interceding for Kate and for the wisdom and the resources needed to make the trip to Philadelphia. Molly watched her parents and brother walk up the path across the meadow, silhouetted by lantern light until they disappeared over the top of the hill. Liam took James back inside and began rocking him to sleep while Molly continued to sit outside, pondering the events of the evening.

"I'm going up the hill for a bit," she called to Liam. "I need some time alone, if that's alright."

She took a lantern, headed up to her special place at the top, and gazed at the heavens. She imagined for a moment that she was back in Letterkenny in her rocky meadow, a place and a time in her youth when such problems as she now faced didn't seem possible. Molly let her mind wander to such thoughts for only a few minutes before bringing herself back to reality. Alternately praying and sobbing, words from her study of the catechism brought comfort, even without bringing full understanding. *"Your works of providence, O Lord, are your most holy, wise, and powerful preserving and governing of all of your creatures."*

Gracie had once taught her a musical arrangement of a few lines from a Scottish psalter of the mid 1600s that came now to her mind. *"I am in the house of God, like to an olive green. My confidence forever hath upon God's mercies been."* Taking great comfort in these words, Molly determined that her confidence in God's mercies, so evident in her life, would be at the forefront of any trials that lay ahead. "As they should always be," she chided herself.

She thanked God for these reminders of both His providence and His mercies. Then she headed back to the cottage where Liam had James sound asleep and tucked into the cradle he had recently fabricated from some pieces of lumber salvaged from their day of work on the meeting house. He looked up as Molly walked in the door. By the faint smile on her face, he guessed that she had come to some point of resolution at her rocky hideaway on the hill.

"You look like you feel better," he said. "What did you and the Lord discuss up on the hill?"

"He did most of the talking," she chuckled. "I did most of the listening and will now try to obey!"

She sang the lines from the Scottish psalter and repeated to Liam her determination to use these lines and the catechism that she had meditated on as her guiding beacon in the difficulties they faced with her mother's illness.

"Tomorrow, we need to go visit Pastor Durkin and talk about having a time of sharing with the whole congregation and corporate petition on mother's behalf."

"Absolutely," Liam agreed. "I expect he has already given some thought to this and will be ready to do so as soon as we ask."

The next morning was cloudless and sunny as Molly walked across the meadows and grassy lane to the meeting house and Thomas Durkin's small cottage nearby. He was tending his garden, but Molly saw the books and papers on a small table, evidence of her pastor's work on the sermon for the upcoming Sabbath. He beamed and gave a wave as he looked up and saw Molly approaching.

"Well, good morning, Molly," he began. "I've been expecting you and Liam since talking with your parents earlier this week. I'm so sorry about the news and have been in prayer for your whole family."

"Thank you... Liam was planning to come with me but had some chores that he needed to take care of."

The two of them sat together on the stone wall around the garden as Molly shared her feelings with her pastor and friend. He knew all of the details from his conversations with Darren and Kate, but his concern now was for this young mother in front of him whom he had known and watched grow up since childhood.

"How are you and Liam handling this, Molly? It's not the kind of thing any of us expected when we came here, but that is how life comes at us at times, isn't it?"

"Yes, it is, but I'm coming to terms with it. God was kind in giving me guidance last night... thoughts that will bring comfort throughout this ordeal." After a deep sigh, she added, "If I remember to hold onto them!"

"I will help you and remind you of that," Pastor Durkin offered.

"Liam and I would like to ask that the congregation be given the opportunity to assist them in their trip back to Philadelphia and with the medical bills. Anything our friends can offer will be greatly appreciated and helpful, although obviously not covering nearly the entire cost."

Molly then added, "It could help them avoid having to sell their land... at least for now."

"We will make the need known this Sunday. We will get the word out and people will have a little time to contemplate and pray about how to help."

"Thank you so much," Molly said, wiping away the tears. "You're a good friend as well as a good pastor."

The two hugged goodbye and Pastor Durkin picked up James, giving him a playful twirl. "You've got a great mother and father, young man. Don't ever forget that!"

Molly headed back toward the cottage and let James crawl through the meadow grass along the way. She stopped twice to speak to neighbors and was freshly reminded of how quickly Linville Creek had become their close community and the center of their world. As she topped the hill and their cottage came into view, Molly was surprised to see a wagon near the smokehouse and a man standing in the yard with Liam. At this distance, she could not recognize him as anyone she knew, but she picked up her pace and carried James down the hill.

As she got closer to the cottage, a woman came out of the back of the wagon, looked in Molly's direction, and began running toward her with wide open arms, a toddler behind her. Suddenly, Molly squealed with delight as she recognized their friends from Winchester. It was Kitch and Jewel Banks!

CHAPTER 53

No visit from friends was ever as well timed or welcomed as the Banks family's arrival in Linville Creek. Despite having spent only one evening with them the previous year in Winchester on their way through the Great Valley, it was an encounter that Molly and Liam reminisced about often and they longed for another opportunity to spend time with Kitch and Jewel.

"Your father?" Molly questioned Kitch.

"He died of pneumonia last winter while we were camped in Winchester. His illness and the aftermath of his death led us to staying longer than we had expected."

Kitch's happy countenance saddened as he shared the death of his father. For a few moments of rejoicing over the unexpected arrival of their friends, Molly had forgotten about her own concerns. Now, she was facing someone who had gone through similar circumstances, and she was abruptly reminded that losing her mother was indeed a possibility… one that she should prepare for. She whispered to herself, "*My confidence forever hath upon God's mercies been.*"

"I'm so sorry, Kitch."

"Thank you. So… here we are in your new settlement, behind in our scheduled travels but delighted to be here with you."

"And we hope that you will stay for a while," Liam interjected. "You can set up your camp close by the cottage and eat meals with us. I'm sure Johnson and James will have fun with each other."

"We would like to get farther south before winter arrives," Kitch said. "We've heard that there is a group of freed slaves ahead of us going to

Kentucke. They will set up a winter camp and we'd like to catch up with them if possible. We've no idea if, when, or where we might find them, so maybe we can spend some time here with you before continuing that way."

Even though they had spent only a single evening together in Winchester, the connection was immediate, and Molly had thought of Jewel as a close friend. She was overjoyed with the thought of having her close by. The two of them headed into the cottage while Liam took Kitch to show him their land and perhaps introduce him to some of the other Linville Creek neighbors. Seeing him ride through the community accompanied by a black man may surprise some of the residents, but he did not expect any other reaction. Liam was convinced that anyone who spent even a few moments with the Banks family would accept them wholeheartedly.

The two families had one of the most enjoyable evenings together of any Molly could recall since settling here. Jewel insisted on doing most of the cooking, preparing a stew utilizing spices, herbs, and techniques new to Molly, but resulting in wonderfully new flavors. Molly and Liam shared the news of Kate's illness and the plans for the church service on Sunday. Likewise, Kitch told them the details of his father's death and their adjustments since then.

After dinner, the cottage was filled with stories, laughter, and, most of all, music and dancing. Molly discovered that Kitch Banks' fiddling skills matched those of his father, and she marveled at how such new tunes and rhythms could have been bound up, hidden inside her instrument, in a sense, waiting for the hands of someone from another place and time to unlock them. But that was exactly what she had done, taking Luigi Carusso's instrument and adapting it to her own Irish heritage.

"Music is adaptable to any culture," she remembered hearing Tom Banks say during their night of music in the fields outside of Winchester. "How true that is," Molly thought to herself as she watched Kitch. "And I'm witnessing that at this very moment."

For the next few days, Kitch helped Liam complete the rock walls for the additional room to their cottage and the two of them worked to set up camp for the Banks. Being late summer, it did not take nearly so much planning for protection from the weather. Molly and Jewel, when not tending to the children, worked in the garden, shared cooking techniques and recipes, and visited throughout the community. Shannon Clarke invited them for lunch and, along with Molly's mother, the four women shared an afternoon of life experiences.

Molly realized soon after Kitch and Jewel's arrival that her friend had a wealth of knowledge about the useful wild plants and herbs that were available and she wanted to take advantage of her knowledge. The two of them rode and then walked up on the higher mountains and scoured the hillside as Jewel picked bittercress, beebalm, thyme, and a variety of mints, explaining to Molly on the wagon ride back to the cottage how to dry them and transplant them in her garden.

On Saturday, Liam and Molly's parents came over along with a number of other neighbors for an evening of music and a community meal. After everyone had eaten and the evening sun was going down, the men built a fire just beyond their rock wall to illuminate a large area for dancing. The scene reminded Molly of the evenings of music aboard *The Allegheny*, but at the same time, all of the things that had transpired since then made it seem like a lifetime ago. She was overjoyed and grateful for those blessings, but her mother's illness still hung over her.

"Confidence, Molly. Have confidence in God's mercies," she reminded herself once again.

"Lead us, Molly," some from the group called out, interrupting her thoughts. "Just like we were out at sea!"

Molly chuckled and stepped into the circle, inviting Finn Clarke to join her. They played *The Irish Lad* through multiple times in spite of James wanting her full attention as he hung onto her dress. Liam joined them in singing a rendition of *The True Lover's Farewell*. She could see lanterns coming over the hill, illuminating the path for late arrivals, some coming on foot, others in wagons. As she looked around at the faces of these friends, most of whom had known her since birth, she was struck by the thought that even though these were individuals she had known for years, the community they were building here in the Valley was still new. Each one had a role to play in the success of the community... perhaps this was hers.

"Fiddling sustains and helps build the culture of Irish community," an old gentleman in Letterkenny had once told her. "That's exactly what I'm doing here," Molly thought.

The instruments dropped out near the ballad's end, but the voices continued as everyone joined in the last chorus. Molly closed her eyes and listened as the tune seemed to echo off the surrounding hills and melt away into the darkness. She then locked eyes with her mother and, in the firelight, could see the tears as they sang...

> *O fare you well, I must be gone and leave you for a while*
> *But wherever I go, I will return, if I go ten thousand miles*
> *My dear, if I go ten thousand miles*

Both Molly and Liam were anxious to get Kitch and Jewel involved in the festivities, so she invited them to stand. "Bring your banjo up here, Kitch... you've got to be part of the music!"

"Most of you have met our friends Kitch and Jewel Banks... and their son Johnson. We met in Winchester last year as we headed here to Linville Creek. Liam and I thought our paths would never cross again, but this past week, much to our surprise and pleasure, here they are! Kitch's father passed away over the winter and that has delayed their travels south of here and eventually to Kentucke."

Molly looked at Kitch with a questioning expression. She did not know whether to share their former enslavement and now, their freedom. She simply had not asked them about this uncomfortable subject and how to address it. After an awkward pause, Liam stepped up to speak.

"This is not an easy thing for any of us to speak to, but it is important, nonetheless. The colonies here have been importing enslaved people from the west coast of Africa for over a century. Kitch's father was one of those... ripped from his family and brought here in chains. We left Ireland and came to this land on our own free will, but people like Tom Banks did not. Kitch and Jewel were not born in Africa but were born into the horrible institution of slavery."

"Could I finish the story, Liam?" Kitch interjected.

"We were set free not quite two years ago from a farm in Maryland. This only happened when Mr. Banks, our owner, felt the conviction of God regarding the system of slavery. We are so grateful that, in more ways than one, God has given us freedom. Whatever you may have heard about the continent my father was brought here from, our family's understanding of the sovereignty of a kind and benevolent God is not very different from yours..."

"With a few cultural African differences," Jewel spoke as she gave her husband a gentle elbow in the ribs.

"Yes... There were some things that my father could not quite let go of from his cultural past... things that he incorporated into his Christian belief system. We understand, however, that even with documents that say we are free, there are dangers for us. We have been led to believe that in Kentucke, the situation may be safer for us. Thank you for the welcome to Linville Creek over these past few days. We look forward to the rest of our time here... and seeing you in church tomorrow!"

"Amen!" shouted Thomas Durkin to the enjoyment of the whole group.

"Yes, Amen!" echoed Molly. "It should be of no surprise to any of you that part of our connection with the Banks is through music. I have never heard any music to my knowledge that has African influences and this instrument that Kitch is holding was also unknown to me until we met them last year. In his hands, my fiddle sounds completely different. So, everyone get ready!

For the rest of the evening, what Molly Clarke had begun to think of as a kind of musical conversation between fiddle and banjo carried across the meadows and hills of Linville Creek. The driving, percussive ringing of Kitch Banks' banjo kept the beat for the melodies that she and her father-in-law produced on their fiddles. The friends gathered there were fascinated. Jewel led others in dancing for over an hour before she retired to their camp to get Johnson to sleep. Kate soon took James into the cottage and began rocking him as well.

As the singing and laughter soon began to quiet down, and, as they had become accustomed to from their days at sea, Molly led the group in a final closing song, this time, a verse and chorus of *The Mist Covered Mountains*.

As families were gathering their belongings and beginning to make their way back home, both Molly and Darren found themselves in conversations about Kate's health. As much as she appreciated the kind words and sympathy, Molly quickly became weary of the barrage of questions and hearing her own repetitive responses. There was so little to add to what everyone seemed to already know... her mother was seriously ill, the headaches were getting more frequent and excruciating, and the only possible solution seemed to be an expensive and extended trip back to Philadelphia. Anything else was speculation on Molly's part. *"Confidence in God's mercies"* she repeated dozens of times to neighbors before the last of the group had departed.

With the excitement of the evening and the anticipation of Sunday's church service, Molly and Liam were pleasantly surprised at a restful night of sleep. Often times they walked to services at the meeting house, but today they took the wagon and the Banks rode with them. As they approached, it was obvious that there would be a crowd in church which didn't surprise Molly with the wide-ranging concern and love for her parents in the community.

As long as she could remember, Molly had sat under the teaching of Thomas Durkin, so she was familiar with his habits and mannerisms, as well as his patterns in conducting services. So, it did not surprise her that he announced ahead of time that today's sermon would be shorter than usual in order to give adequate time and attention to the special needs facing her parents. Each of the hymns that morning contained truths that seemed especially relevant to their situation at hand. Even short phrases touched Molly as she sang under the open arbor of the meeting house.

"He is *'Our shelter from the stormy blast'*… the *'refuge of His saints,'* our *'protection when storms of sharp distress invade.'"* All of these promises and more swirled through her head and penetrated her heart.

As the voices faded on the final hymn, Pastor Durkin called Darren and Kate to the front and the three of them exchanged a long embrace. Already, Molly could hear the weeping around her. She took a deep breath and steadied herself for more. Fortunately, James was content, playing in the straw covering the floor and she tried hard to focus on what was being said.

"This has been a difficult week for all of us, and especially for Darren and Kate and their family. But even as I speak those words, I'm reminded that we're all family and that we all took this adventure and this new life upon ourselves together, pledging to help and support each other as families do. It has never been more important for us to remember this and, of course, to remember the good and faithful God who guided us here… as part of His family."

"Confidence in God's mercies," Molly reminded herself once again as Pastor Durkin continued.

"I can't imagine that there is anyone here who has not heard the news that we're talking about, but Kate has a cancerous growth in her brain causing more and more serious and debilitating headaches. Doctors in Winchester have strongly advised Darren and Kate to go to Philadelphia for treatment and they plan to do that as soon as possible."

Looking in Patrick's direction and giving him a wink, he continued. "Patrick will remain here with us in the care of his sister's family so that Darren and Kate can focus on getting her well and back here with us!"

"And to keep up with his school lessons," Kate interjected vigorously to everyone's laughter.

"With a few exceptions, they have made arrangements, sending word ahead to some of the people we all knew in Philadelphia. Hopefully, a job and adequate housing will be waiting. The greatest need, which should come as no surprise to any of us, is the finances. Having a job will, of course, be helpful, but just the cost of the trip, unknown medical bills, and leaving their piece of land fallow and unproductive… all of this will add up to quite the burden."

Pastor Durkin took a deep breath and looked slowly and thoughtfully across the congregation before continuing. "None of us are wealthy, I know. For the most part, our stories are the same. We sold everything to get here and then invested it all in land, homes, and supplies. We haven't been here long enough to reap much in the way of profits. But there is a need among us and an opportunity, once again, to see God's faithfulness as we show generosity where it is possible."

Tears were flowing freely by this time and Thomas Durkin turned to Darren and Kate, asking if they wanted to add anything before having a time of prayer.

"It is not in our nature to ask for help," Darren began. "Many of you perhaps feel the same way. We tend to be proud and independent folks. The last thing Kate and I want is to have to sell our land, but we will if we must. We're trusting God to provide and trying, as my daughter reminds me, to have *"confidence in God's mercies."*

Hearing her father quote her own words from the Scottish psalter back to her caused the tears to flow even more freely. Pastor Durkin explained to the congregation that any contributions would be collected by the church leadership over the weeks before Darren and Kate headed north. The service ended with prayers by the elders, centered on having confidence in God's provision, mercy, and healing in Kate's life.

Liam turned to Molly and embraced her lovingly. "We will survive this," he promised. "This is our first big test as a family… let's pay close attention to how God works."

"Yes, I will be paying attention," Molly agreed hopefully. "I need to find a way to help them, Liam. I need to do something tangible… perhaps even sacrificial. That's what my parents have always done for me and that's what I will to do for them!"

Those thoughts dominated Molly's mind as the wagon rambled over the meadows back to their cottage. Kitch and Jewel were moved by all they had witnessed during the morning. They talked nonstop about the community that had been planted here, the families' devotion to each other, and their love and confident trust in God's sovereignty. All of this touched them deeply.

But Molly heard almost none of the conversation between their friends and her husband, nor the babbling and laughing of their two little ones. She was absorbed in thought with the promise she had spoken to Liam. What sacrifice would God have her make for her parents in this time of need? The answer would come soon, and in a way that she never expected.

CHAPTER 54

Over the next several weeks, Darren and Kate prepared for their upcoming trip to Philadelphia with a great deal of help from Finn and Shannon Clarke. The two couples had always been close, worshipping together, owning adjacent farms, and seeing their children grow from childhood friends to a married couple with their own family. But the situation now with Kate's illness and the frightening future they faced brought a completely new level of connection and honesty between them.

One morning as the two women sorted through the cooking utensils, clothing, and other sundry items that needed to be packed or left behind, Kate tearfully blurted out to Shannon, "Forgive me for the jealousy I'm feeling for you,"

Even though she was gradually growing accustomed to her friend's mood swings during these difficult days, Shannon was surprised by the admission. "Jealousy?" she questioned.

"I know it's wrong, but I can't seem to help myself. You get to stay here and enjoy the family and this beautiful place we've sacrificed so long and hard to get to. I've loved sharing it all with you and now…" Kate fell across the bed, unable to continue. Shannon gave her friend time to cry before speaking what she hoped would be words of comfort.

"Do you remember those early days on *The Allegheny* when we watched our children grow closer together and we talked of what I believe we called their 'optimism and energetic enthusiasm?' You said that their attitudes would keep us focused on the promises, rather than the perils ahead."

Kate nodded, "Yes, I remember that. One of us also noted how God's plans for our lives often surprise us. I suppose that happens in good ways and in ways we would not necessarily choose ourselves."

"I was more frightened in those days than I let be known, but I leaned on your strength then, Kate," Shannon confessed. "I also leaned on your strength during those long weeks when we waited for Finn and the others to come back from the early expedition here. Now, I promise that I will be as strong as I can, so that you can lean on me."

"While we both lean on God... '*Confidence in God's mercies*' as Molly is constantly reminding me," Kate replied tearfully as they continued their work.

Molly and Liam were assisting her parents as much as the labor around their own farm would allow. With Kitch's help, Liam was determined to get the stone foundation and lower walls of the addition to their cottage completed before the cool temperatures of autumn arrived. This was his priority around their cottage. Finishing the walls to their full height and completing the roof would have to wait until spring, but an adequate, although crude covering would make the cottage much more comfortable with Patrick moving in for an extended time.

"One more load of field stone, delivered as requested," Kitch announced as he guided the horse and cart up to the large pile they had already gathered over the past few days. "Every size and shape imaginable... I'm just glad I'm not the one having to piece them together into a structure."

"You keep bringing them to me and I'll figure out where they fit," Liam laughed. "Actually, this is probably all we can handle right now. I could not have done this without you, my friend. I will repay you in some fashion before you leave."

"No payment required," Kitch quickly replied. "Welcoming us here, allowing us to camp in your fields, sharing meals with you... that is more than adequate compensation."

"Are you two at a stopping place?" Molly called from the cottage doorway. "Jewel has fixed us some mid-day nourishment. She is teaching me so much about ways to prepare foods and they're all delicious!"

"You'll be the only woman in this part of Virginia serving food with African influences," Liam chuckled.

"And playing music with African influences as well," she answered quickly.

The stewed okra, black-eyed peas, and roasted yams were staples for the Banks, preserved for their travels, but new to the foods Molly and Liam were accustomed to. All of these, along with a legume they called peanuts, had African origins and were foods Jewel had learned about from the older slaves, including her father-in-law, Tom Banks.

"Yams kept the chained slaves alive in the hull of the ships, according to my father," Kitch shared. "They are good... I love the taste and the many ways he taught us to prepare them, but I've never eaten one or never will again without thinking about the awful conditions he told us about on those ships."

Changing the subject, Kitch said, "Enough of this talk for now. I wonder if Molly would allow me to get my hands on that fiddle for a few minutes before Liam begins working me again."

"Absolutely," Molly responded, springing up from the chair and pulling her instrument from the mantle.

For the next half hour, both Molly and Liam watched and listened, mesmerized by Jewel Banks' beautiful singing of spirituals and field work songs, accompanying her husband's fiddle playing. Molly found herself once again pondering her family's own free choices to migrate here and pursue their dreams while others, like the friends in front of her, had no such choices. She also thought, as she often had, how her instrument was not only created for a completely different kind of music, but Luigi probably did not even know about the cultures, the people groups, and the music across the world that could bring life to his creation, allowing its "voice" to continue and endure.

"I love my father's fiddle simply because it was his," Kitch spoke thoughtfully. "But some day, I will own a better instrument, maybe not as nice as yours, Molly, but perhaps… we will see."

"Music is adaptable," Molly pondered aloud. "Your father said it is adaptable to any culture." She paused and thought about her next words carefully as they expressed things she had thought about before but had never seemed as relevant as they did here in their cottage with Kitch and Jewel Banks.

"Music also breaks down barriers that may exist among people whose lives could not be any more dissimilar," she offered. "Just look at us. Without the connection of music, we would have never discovered this friendship and then the deeper connections we have with one another."

"I'm glad you reminded me of those words from my father, Molly. We miss him and will continue to miss him the rest of our lives. There is so much to learn about who we are and where we've come from when we listen to those who have traveled before us." Molly shared her memories of Gracie, how much she treasured that time with her, and how she had sacrificed to get Luigi's fiddle into her granddaughter's hands.

"Kitch's father was sacrificial and generous to us as well," Jewel commented. Then, looking at her husband, she hesitated. "Should we tell them?" Kitch dropped his head as if trying to decide what to say next… then he continued the story.

"Our owner's plantation on the Chesapeake Bay was quite large… and quite valuable. Mr. Banks' convictions about his slaveholding were such that he sold all of his assets, including his land, and divided most of the money among those he had held in captivity. He only kept a modest amount necessary to relocate his family to an area north of Philadelphia. That compensation from our former owner will allow us to buy a farm and establish a home in Kentucke, hopefully with a group of other freed slaves."

"You are the first people we have told this to since we began traveling," Jewel interjected. "Somehow, it seemed appropriate to share considering the friendship we've developed with you."

"Surely God has been watching over you and providing for you in a way that you would never have expected," Liam responded.

"Yes, He has," Kitch and Jewel responded almost simultaneously.

James and Johnson had been enjoying their time together as the conversation took place among their parents, but they were both getting restless and requiring more attention. "I wish they were old enough to remember their short time together for the rest of their lives," she sighed.

"Don't we all," Liam agreed. Then, jumping up from his chair, he gave Kitch a slap on the shoulder. "Let's get back to that rockwork, my friend!"

The September sun shone brightly through the rest of the workday, and the two young men were pleased with their progress on the cottage addition. There was a touch of autumn coolness in the late afternoon as they ended their work. Before the sun dipped behind the western ridge, Liam helped Kitch reconfigure his tarps and wagon up in the field in a way that provided a bit more space and protection from the elements. Molly and Jewel had taken the little ones over to help Kate and they were returning across the hill just as the men finished.

"How are your folks doing today?" Liam inquired as they pulled up and climbed out of the wagon.

"Alright, I guess," Molly replied. "They would like to head out within the next two weeks and probably miss any winter weather. Each day closer to their departure, it seems that they are a bit more anxious."

"And you?" Liam asked as he gave Molly a hug.

"Yes, I'm anxious as well. You do plan to go over to their place to help out tomorrow, don't you?"

"First thing in the morning! Your father is trying to pack as little as possible but wants to be prepared with some basic tools and such... so much unknown lies ahead of them."

"I'll go along if another opinion would be of value," Kitch offered.

The two of them headed across the hill on foot early the next morning since Molly and Jewel were taking the boys up on the mountains to look for roots and herbs. Deeper into the fall, perhaps a month or more, they would all be out gathering the nuts from the massive chestnut trees that they were growing to depend on in a number of ways since arriving in Virginia.

Darren was out in his tool shed when they reached the farm. Liam could see another wagon coming from the opposite direction, still too far away to recognize the driver. It did not take long as they approached to see that the other arrival was Thomas Durkin.

He threw up his hand to welcome them. "Well, I did not suppose that anyone else would be visiting here so early in the morning. How are you two?"

"We're fine. We came over to help Darren pack for their trip. It's hard to say what things they might need and what things are unnecessary and would just 'get in the way,' so to speak... or weigh them down."

"We thought that another couple of suggestions on the matter couldn't hurt," Kitch interjected.

"Good thoughts, both of you," Pastor Durkin commented. "Darren and Kate are both feeling some anxiety and perhaps not thinking as clearly or practically as they need to. Your opinions will be valued and, hopefully, welcomed."

"My purpose for being here is to give Darren the funds that people have handed over to me. Although I'm confident that our congregation is being as generous as possible, no one has much in the way of 'excess' considering the sacrifices we've all made just to get here and establish the beginning of our life in Linville Creek."

"Every little bit helps!" The new voice came from Darren as he exited the shed. "Yes, I'll be the first one to admit that some anxiety is growing, I'm afraid."

"*'Confidence in God's mercies'*, your daughter says," Pastor Durkin reminded Darren as he handed him an envelope with the collected funds. "But some anxiety is certainly understandable... by me, at least, and I believe our Lord understands that as well."

"Thank you for that reminder, Thomas," Darren responded as he excused himself and headed back into the shed, followed by Kitch.

Liam continued his conversation with Pastor Durkin. "Molly is confident that God is guiding her to some great and tangible gesture... something 'sacrificial' she calls it... that will assist Kate and Darren. I don't know what that might be as we're in the same situation as almost everyone else... not much excess to spare right now."

"As long as I have known Molly," Pastor Durkin offered. "She has had an exuberance and confidence that sometimes defies the rational and subdued ideas the rest of us come up with. Sometimes we chuckle at her, but let her follow whatever He is guiding her to do in this instance, Liam."

Liam was struck by his pastor's frankness and the conviction that perhaps he had not paid enough attention to his wife's vision of a sacrificial way to help her parents.

"I will pay more attention to what she is discerning from Him. Thanks for giving me that good word, Pastor."

The two men parted ways and Liam entered the tool shed where Kitch and Darren were busy separating tools into manageable piles and discussing how one single tool could have multiple uses. Liam stood in the doorway as the morning sun rose higher and began to stream into the shed. He looked at his father-in-law as memories flooded him of this man he had known his whole life, first as a neighbor, then as a church leader, but now as a member of his family.

"So, have you selected the good ones and culled out the bad?" Liam questioned, half serious and half in jest.

"Getting closer, with Kitch's expert advice. He has a way to look at a single tool and see many uses in it... very helpful!"

Kitch chuckled, "My father knew that skill well, having grown up on the west coast of Africa in a culture where material possessions were limited. He never stopped doing that and passed it along to me, I suppose."

It was early afternoon before Liam and Kitch headed back across the hill where their wives were working in the garden and arranging their harvest of roots and herbs they had collected up on the mountain during the morning. They would let these dry in the sun on the rock wall and then hang them up to completely dry and be used in the many new recipes Molly now had gathered from her friend. Through the remainder of the afternoon, Liam and Kitch worked on the roof for the addition to the cottage and made some much-needed repairs to the Banks' wagon in anticipation for their continued travels down the Wagon Road sometime in the next few weeks.

They enjoyed dinner and music together before parting company for the evening. Molly had enjoyed the time with Jewel and the diversion from constant thoughts about her mother's health. But as delightful as it was to have their friends around, she was grateful for an evening just with her family. James went to sleep early, so she and Liam built up the fire as the coolness of the evening settled in and pulled their rocking chairs up to the hearth. Molly filled Liam in on the morning she and Jewel had spent with the boys on the mountain and Liam shared the events of their time with Darren and the disappointment with the fairly limited collection that had been received.

"Pastor Durkin says I should pay more attention to your thoughts about how you might help your mother and father at this time. Perhaps I haven't been as attentive as I should be… Forgive me."

"Forgiven," Molly responded, smiling. "'Sacrificially' is the key word, Liam. There is nothing I wouldn't do to help them out, but we're like almost all of our neighbors with so little in terms of material things or funds that would help."

"I know and they understand that as well," Liam responded.

"With one exception," Molly said, continuing her thought.

She slowly rose from the rocking chair and reached for her fiddle from the mantle. Her hands shook visibly, and tears began flowing freely as she turned toward Liam, holding her treasured instrument.

"Since the day I received this on my fifteenth birthday in Letterkenny, I have never given a single moment of thought to the material value of my fiddle. Of course, it is valuable to me, but only because Gracie and my parents sacrificed to put it in my hands. I've treasured it for the years I've been entrusted with it… you know that better than anyone."

It took Molly a few minutes to collect herself and continue as she reached out for Liam's hand. He could see what was coming and had begun to tear up himself as he listened to his wife open her heart in a way he had never seen.

"If selling my fiddle, as valuable as it has been to me, will help my parents in any way, it is worth doing."

Liam let out a long sigh. "I'm not going to question your judgment on this, Molly, especially after my conversation with Pastor Durkin this morning. But make sure this is what you want to do. You can't just give it up to anyone… it has to be in the right hands, someone who will treasure it as you have. Agree?"

"Agree," Molly responded. "And I believe I know who that someone is!"

CHAPTER 55

Molly could not recall the last time she had climbed out of bed as early as she did the following morning without having to focus her attention on James who was still sleeping soundly. Her early rise was not out of excitement or joy, but sheer conviction that what she was about to do was absolutely the right thing and an answer to her prayer. She could not see or hear any activity around the Banks' wagon or campsite, but she did not want to miss the earliest opportunity to talk to them.

"In fact," she thought, "I'll have breakfast for all of us and invite them down as soon as I see them stirring."

She gathered some eggs, put venison in the skillet to begin cooking, and quickly prepared tattie scones, covering the bottom of the Dutch oven. Molly quietly pulled one of the rocking chairs out into the cool morning air and was wrapped up in a quilt as the first rays of sunlight touched the distant mountaintops. She loved watching the daybreak across the meadows and the gradual top to bottom illumination of the western ridges.

She rehearsed in her mind how to approach Kitch Banks with the idea of buying her fiddle. As she had told Liam the evening before, she did not know how to put a price on it and hated the thought of asking too much. She certainly did not want to put any undue pressure on their friends. These questions raced through her mind and caused her to begin questioning her idea.

"Maybe I should give up this whole crazy notion," she muttered to herself. "But if this is God's answer to my prayer… finding a way to sacrifice for my parents… I certainly don't want to ignore that."

"*Merciful and kind Father,*" she prayed, "*May I be obedient to your ways and to your direction at this critical time.*" She leaned back in the rocking chair and looked up at the few remaining visible stars fade away into the brightening sky.

Jewell was the first to emerge out of their shelter, holding Johnson as she began stirring the coals in their fire pit and adding a few pieces of wood. She looked up and saw Molly, giving a wave in her direction. With the quilt still around her shoulders, Molly waded through the meadow to invite their friends to breakfast.

"Good morning," she called out as she approached. "I was fortunate this morning… my family is still asleep! I have breakfast cooking and would love for you to come down and join us."

"That sounds wonderful," Jewell responded. "It looks as though your family is up now."

Molly turned toward the cottage and saw Liam holding James in the doorway. As his father sat him down, James began crawling and stumbling through the wet grass up the hill toward her. Molly hurried back toward the cottage, calling over her shoulder to Jewel, "We'll look for you in a half hour or so."

Liam greeted her at the door. "It looks like we're having company for breakfast… are you sure about what you're getting ready to do? It won't be easy, Molly."

"Easy, no…," Molly hesitated. "But the right thing to do? Yes, without a doubt."

The two families enjoyed the hearty meal and, as they finished, Molly began. "I have a proposal to make, and you need to listen and consider carefully what I'm about to say, understanding that there is no pressure on your part."

Kitch and Jewel Banks looked at each other and at Molly and Liam with questioning expressions, having no idea what was about to follow. Molly took a deep breath and continued…

"Since my mother shared the news of her illness with me, I have had a deep conviction from the Lord that I should make some sacrifice contributing to their medical expenses and travels back to Philadelphia. This has been even stronger knowing that the contributions from the congregation, although generous, are simply inadequate to meet their needs."

Molly got up from the table, removed her fiddle from the hearth, and turned back to their friends. "This is the only thing I own of any value and, as precious as it is to me, it is worth the sacrifice if it helps them in any way."

Jewel interrupted, "Molly, you can't part with…"

"Yes, I can," Molly insisted forcefully, cutting off Jewel's objection.

"Not only can I do this… I must. The thing I can't do is put it in the hands of someone who will not treasure it, appreciate it, and play it with the proper kind of loving care it deserves. I know you would do that, Kitch."

Molly paused at this point but had one more thing to say before listening for the response. "You have told us the generosity of the man who set you free. I will not put a price on my instrument, but, if you are agreeable to what I'm proposing, I will leave it to your own conscience to determine what is fair and all of the money will go to help my parents. Don't even tell me how much and I will never ask."

"I don't know what to say," Kitch stammered and looked at his wife across the table. "We will have to think about and pray about this before deciding. I would want our contribution to be an anonymous one if this is what we decide to do. Give us a day or so… is that acceptable?"

"Absolutely," Molly smiled.

Two mornings later, Thomas Durkin found an envelope of money inside the door of his cottage and a note simply reading "for the McCourtney's expenses. Given with love." At church the following Sunday, he gave the envelope to Darren and Kate and announced to the congregation that this anonymous gift had almost doubled the total contributions. The elation within the congregation was overwhelming. Long hugs, tears of joy, and praises to God for his provision lasted long after the service had ended.

"I've never been prouder of you, Molly," Liam spoke as they climbed into bed that evening. "Whether you ever play the fiddle again or not, I will love you... but I will surely miss your music."

"Oh, there will be more music... you can count on that," she chuckled. The mysterious nature of her comments aroused Liam's curiosity, but the hour was late, and he decided to wait and let that mystery be unveiled in its own time.

A week later, Darren and Kate had boarded up their cottage and loaded the wagon for the journey to Philadelphia. They spent the last night with Liam and Molly and, despite the crowded conditions and the separation that was about to occur, they made the best of the evening. Liam and Patrick had spent more time together than usual in these final weeks and Kate was comforted by the brotherly bond they had developed. She was confident that this would make the separation much easier.

Almost the entire community of Linville Creek had gathered in a clearing as Kate and Darren's wagon rambled down the grassy lane and pulled onto the Great Wagon Road, pointing north. Between the hugs, goodbyes, and a prayer of blessing by Pastor Durkin, it was close to an hour before they were ready to head out. Darren and Kate were both in tears as they hugged Molly, Patrick, and James.

"Your job," Kate sobbed, holding Molly's face in her hands, "is to take care of your precious little one... and to take care of your brother, as well."

"And your job," Molly cried, wrapping her arms around both her mother and father, "is to take care of yourselves and do whatever you can do to get well. Remember..."*Confidence in God's mercies.*"

"Always," Darren agreed. "We will be back…"

The crowd had begun to disperse as the wagon carrying her parents disappeared over the first hill. Both Liam and Thomas Durkin offered to stay with her, but Molly insisted that she needed this time alone to "process and pray," as she liked to think of it. After a while, she walked up the grassy lane, meandering through fields surrounding their land, eventually climbing up to her rocky meadow, gazing across the various parcels that comprised Linville Creek. Approaching her favorite rock, she stopped suddenly, confused, then laughing out loud at the sight of her fiddle case.

"I thought you would end up here," Liam chuckled as he walked out from behind the rocks with James. "I felt the need to be up here as well. By the way, Kitch says the fiddle is still yours until they leave."

The young family stood arm in arm taking in the sights, both of them thinking of all that had happened in the past few years. "When I came up here the night they shared the bad news with us, I was overwhelmed with problems," Molly shared. "Now, it is the responsibility of caring for Patrick that seems overwhelming and knowing that they aren't here to lean on as before."

"You've still got me," Liam smiled. "Lad and lassie linked together."

"Of course," Molly agreed. "Lad and lassie, indeed… with confidence in God's mercies." As always, appropriate lyrics swelled up from within her memory, and together they sat on the rocks and sang.

O fare you well, I must be gone and leave you for a while
But wherever I go, I will return, If I go ten thousand miles, my dear,
If I go ten thousand miles.

"They will return," Molly and Liam spoke together.

EPILOGUE

"There is naught but care on every hand, in every hour that passes…" the Scottish poet Robert Burns had written. Gracie spoke these lines more than once to her granddaughter and they were the only words Molly Clark could bring to mind as she stood in the Great Wagon Road on a blustery fall morning in 1766.

Just two weeks earlier, she and Patrick had stood arm in arm as they watched their parents head north along this path back toward Philadelphia with an unknown and frightening future before them. That day was unusually warm for this time of year, but the pleasant weather and bright sunshine had made their departure slightly easier for Molly. It was as if, in her optimistic nature, she thought the weather itself was perhaps forecasting a good diagnosis for her mother from the doctors in Philadelphia. She prayed fervently that this was the case. Her thoughts about the sovereignty of God, taught to her from childhood and so easy to believe in good times, were not so easy on that difficult day.

Since then, when she watched Darren and Kate's wagon climb the hill and curve out of sight, Molly had reflected thoughtfully and often about the difference in their trip down the road a year and a half ago when everyone in their community was excited and anticipating their new life in Linville Creek. The Great Wagon Road was the primary conduit of the colonial backcountry, bringing people and goods into and out of the Great Valley. It had served this purpose for many decades and the Letterkenny immigrants had observed firsthand the growing number of travelers. The road itself had not changed in any noticeable way since their arrival here. The mood now, however, was so different… and so very frightening. Molly now looked upon the road not simply as the avenue she and Liam and their friends had traveled to establish a home, but now as a place of heartache. She refused to allow her thoughts and emotions to linger over the real possibility that she would never see her mother and father again, although they had assured each other and trusted God that this was not the case.

Today brought heartache once again as she stood in the same road with Liam and Patrick, a blustery October wind in her face and even an occasional shower of snow coming off the higher elevations of mountains that still held on to their array of brilliant fall colors. James was wrapped in Molly's thickest quilt to ward off the wind and cold although in his eagerness, he struggled to get down and explore. This day, she faced the opposite direction from the previous week and prepared herself to watch another wagon, carrying the best friends she and Liam had made in Virginia toward a different, but similarly unknown future.

Molly finally set James down to play with Johnson. They scurried around after each other, oblivious to the emotional departure that was taking place with their parents. Molly and Liam hugged their friends, trying to grasp the impact of this double adversity that had come their way...her parents heading north, and now, Kitch and Jewel heading south.

Molly felt conflicted, wanting to go with them and wanting to be with her parents, but knowing that Linville Creek was home. This was where God had led her and where she belonged. "A foot in two worlds," she recalled thinking on the deck of *The Allegheny*, leaving Ireland and also when leaving Philadelphia. And now, once again, on this day, she could feel her heart being tugged in multiple directions.

For the past month, she had spent every spare minute she could find playing her fiddle, but the time had come now to hand it over to its new owner. She could not have imagined that she would one day give up something so precious, but the sacrifice and the opportunity to help her parents in this difficult time was worth it... and she knew it was the right thing to do. Luigi's instrument could not be in better hands than those of Kitch Banks.

With one last hug and a tearful goodbye, they watched the Banks wagon creaking south down the Great Wagon Road... the road that had brought them here among the mountains and lush fields, a place that had become even more significant to Molly than Ireland had been when they set sail from Letterkenny a year and a half ago.

Patrick ran ahead toward the cottage, but Molly and Liam wandered hand in hand, up the grassy lane slowly and silently. Before long, Molly began, half humming and half singing, *The Irish Lad, the Mist Covered Mountains, and Barbry Allen.* Liam laughed quietly as he listened to an almost cheerful lilt in Molly's voice.

"Thomas Durkin was right about you," he smiled.

"In what way?" Molly questioned.

Waving his arms and mimicking their pastor's booming voice, Liam said "Her exuberance and confidence sometimes defies the rational and subdued ideas the rest of us have."

"He said that about me?" Molly chuckled. "And is that a quality you find pleasing?"

"Absolutely," Liam replied, pulling her close as they approached the cottage. "You promised me recently that your music would never stop. As I hear you singing, I'm thinking this is what you meant… what I'm hearing from you now?"

"The singing is only part of it," Molly replied as she dug down into the pocket of her wool overcoat. Pulling out her hand, she held the leather pouch Captain Kelly had given her as they departed *The Allegheny* in Philadelphia. Jingling the pouch, she smiled, "Most of it went to the collection for my parents, but there is enough still here to allow me to at least start looking for another fiddle! Nothing will ever compare with Luigi's instrument, but that's alright." She paused and cast a glance south down the road. "It is in good hands and being played lovingly even as we speak."

Molly spent some of the afternoon up in the rocky meadow, alone with her thoughts and praying for understanding and acceptance of the new set of circumstances that had come their way. With the passing clouds came showers of snow, but then the sun would suddenly appear, helping to warm things up. The gusty winds and dropping temperatures in the late afternoon, however, drove her back down the hill to the safe haven of their cottage where Liam had built a crackling fire and was heating up Irish stew. "Delicious," Molly remarked at the dinner table, smiling at both Liam and Patrick.

The atmosphere in the cottage that evening was subdued, and the conversations seemed somewhat forced as both Molly and Liam focused on helping Patrick settle into the partially completed new room in the cottage. They prayed together each night for their parents' safe travel and for Kate's health.

"No accompaniment," Molly said, trying to lighten the mood. "But what is to keep us from singing?"

"Nothing at all," Liam quipped, and the four of them, including James, waltzed around the cottage and sang to their hearts' content.

After her brother had headed to his makeshift pallet on the floor of the extra room, Liam and Molly, with James in her arms, rocked in front of the fire. As she did every night, in her mind she calculated the number of days her parents had been on the road, their presumed average miles each day, and with her daily journal and crude map she had kept of their own trip from Philadelphia, she tried to imagine where they were along their journey. She also had made it a habit to cast her thoughts across the Sea of Green Darkness back to Gracie's cottage in Gwedore, imagining the smells from the oven and her grandmother's voice, singing the ballads that Molly cherished.

As she tucked James in his cradle and climbed into bed that evening, Molly looked across the room at the empty spot on the mantle where her fiddle had always been. Sometime soon, she promised herself, another fiddle case would occupy the same spot. She drifted off to sleep in Liam's arms that night reminding herself that, although she had given up Luigi's beautiful instrument, she had not lost the most important and valuable things in her life. Her faith, her heritage, and her family and friends were so deeply ingrained, they couldn't be taken away. Her deep and longing connections through music for those who had gone before her had not been lost… and never would be. These songs and traditions were still in her head and in her heart… just as she had learned them from Gracie.

BIBLIOGRAPHICAL
ESSAY

Much of the material in this book seems to have been swirling around in my head and heart for more than half of my life. Trying to acknowledge where all of the information came from is, for me, practically impossible. A number of books and resources were helpful, however, in developing the historical and cultural background of the narrative.

A number of general works have been on and off my bookshelves on an almost daily basis since the beginning of this project: *The Scotch Irish: A Social History* (Leyburn); *Scots and Scotch Irish Frontier Life in North Carolina, Virginia, and Kentucky* (Hoefling); *From Ulster to America: The Scotch-Irish Heritage of American English* (Montgomery); *The Scotch-Irish in America* (Ford); *A History of Appalachia* (Drake); *The Appalachians: America's First and Last Frontier* (Evans, Santelli, and Warren); *and Appalachia, A History* (Williams). *The Encyclopedia of Appalachia* (Abramson and Haskell, editors) has been a constant companion for many years and continued to be during this project.

I could not begin to think or write about the natural history of the region without constantly referencing *Where There Are Mountains: An Environmental History of the Southern Appalachians* (Davis) and *The Height of Our Mountains: Nature Writing from Virginia's Blue Ridge Mountains and Shenandoah Valley* (Branch and Philippon, editors).

The Great Wagon Road from Philadelphia to the South: How Scotch-Irish and Germanics Settled the Uplands (Rouse) has been a standard reference work for over fifty years. A newer and highly academic treatment of the Great Wagon Road story is *The Great Valley Road of Virginia: Shenandoah Landscapes from Pre-History to the Present* (Hofstra and Raitz, editors). Both works have been invaluable.

High Mountains Rising: Appalachia in Time and Place (Straw and Blethen, editors) continues to be my favorite single volume on the history and culture of our region. It was my textbook for teaching Appalachian History for twelve years at Virginia Western Community College. I treasure that work and reference it often.

No work on the musical heritage of our region could be completed without the beautiful book (and accompanying CD) *Wayfaring Strangers: The Musical Voyage from Scotland and Ulster to Appalachia* (Ritchie and Orr).

A large part of any story of the Ulster Scotts' migration is about geography. There are several historical maps that help, but none as valuable as *A Map of the Most Inhabited Parts of Virginia*, published in 1751 by Peter Jefferson, father of the president, and his friend Joshua Fry. The Great Wagon Road is clearly drawn and identified on this extraordinary piece of work. As someone who still loves maps, it is little wonder that a framed copy of the "Fry-Jefferson Map" occupies a prominent place in my home, a Christmas gift from my children. Many of the geographical features, towns, and even spellings in the book come from this helpful source.

Identifying lyrics to 18th century songs is a constant moving target, not because they don't exist, but because of the multiple variations with lines from one song often "borrowed" and added to another song. Particular phrases can sometimes be found in each variation and back to 16th century broadsides. In the book, Molly did what people still do, they hear a version of a song that is slightly different and make it their own. As I researched the lyrics for ballads such as *the Nightengale, the True Lover's Farewell, On the Shores of Amerikay, Lord Gregory, Pretty Saro, Barbry Allen, the Irish Lad, the Mist-Covered Mountains of Home* (and others), if I found a single source that identified it as having roots from centuries-old traditional ballads, I assumed that to be the case. My sincere apologies if I've erred in any way.

Finally, Blue Ridge music and the settlement of the region are topics I've enjoyed and discussed with friends, colleagues, and family for longer than I can remember. You know who you are, and I hope you remember those discussions that have certainly had an influence in the course of this work. Thanks to each of you.